...easing Mr. Darcy, no.... ....
....al Movie. Teri is also a contributing
writer ....w.HelloGiggles.com, a lifestyle and entertainment website founded by Zooey Deschanel that is
....t of the *People* magazine, *TIME* magazine
...nd *Entertainment Weekly* family. Teri loves books,
travel, animals and dancing every day. Visit Teri at
www.teriwilson.net or on Twitter, @teriwilsonauthr.

# SUMMER ROMANCE WITH THE ITALIAN TYCOON

JESSICA GILMORE

# HOW TO ROMANCE A RUNAWAY BRIDE

TERI WILSON

MILLS & BOON

First Published in Great Britain 2018
by Mills & Boon, an imprint of HarperCollinsPublishers,
1 London Bridge Street, London, SE1 9GF

*Summer Romance with the Italian Tycoon* © 2018 Jessica Gilmore
*How to Romance a Runaway Bride* © 2018 Teri Wilson

ISBN: 978-0-263-26508-8

38-0718

**MIX**
Paper from
responsible sources
FSC
www.fsc.org   **FSC® C007454**

This book is produced from independently certified FSC™ paper to ensure responsible forest management.

For more information visit: www.harpercollins.co.uk/green

Printed and bound in Spain
by CPI, Barcelona

# SUMMER ROMANCE
# WITH THE
# ITALIAN TYCOON

## JESSICA GILMORE

Thanks to everyone at Yorkshire Wildlife Trust for a lovely eight years—especially all the fabulous past and present members of the Development Team. Miss you all! xxx

# CHAPTER ONE

MADELEINE PERCHED ON the edge of the small wooden jetty and slipped her bare feet into the cold lake, shivering at the first shock of icy water on her bare flesh. Cold as the glacier-fed lake remained despite the summer sun, the refreshing lap of waves against her hot feet usually soothed her, aided and abetted by the view. Even after nearly a year living in the Dolomites, the magnificent mountains soaring into the sky filled her with utter awe. The only thing marring her enjoyment of the landscape was the graceful castle on the other side of the lake, its delicate spires mirroring the mountain peaks. Madeleine was completely over admiring ancient, imposing seats of power; she much preferred the traditional chalets which populated San Tomo, the small village at the head of the lake.

But today she barely felt the water, hardly noticed the view. Pulling a crumpled envelope out of her pocket, she slipped the heavy cream card out of it and flipped it over, reading the engraved gold words yet again. Not that she actually needed to read it. By now she knew the brief contents off by heart.

*Lady Navenby*
*requests the pleasure of the presence of*

*the Honourable Madeleine Fitzroy*
*at the wedding of her son,*
*Lord Theo Willoughby, Earl of Navenby,*
*and*
*Miss Elisaveta Marlowe*
*at Villa Rosa, L'Isola dei Fiori*
*31st August*
*RSVP to Flintock Hall*

Madeleine turned the piece of card over and over, aware that she was frowning, her mother's voice echoing in her head warning her that she would get frown lines. What, she wondered, was the point of an expensive Swiss finishing school if she didn't know the correct etiquette when one was invited to one's ex-fiancé's wedding? Especially if one had made it all the way up the aisle and to the actual altar before said fiancé became an ex?

Not that she had any intention of actually *attending* this wedding. The last thing anyone really wanted was the groom's last bride-to-be hanging around like a modern-day Miss Havisham, the ghost of weddings past. But should she send a gift? If so, of what value? Theo and Elisaveta had her blessing, of course. After all, she was the one who had actually halted the wedding, right at the iconic 'Any persons here present' part.

No, it wasn't the happy couple that worried her. They belonged together in a way she and Theo never had. Madeleine stared down at her morose reflection in the water. She just hoped that this new wedding of Theo's, just a year after their own failed nuptials, wouldn't resurrect the intense and intrusive press interest in Madeleine herself.

Taking a deep breath, she tried to push the panic back down to where it usually lurked, never quite quelled but never acknowledged. She was safe here, far away from the British press and a scandal which surely most people had forgotten about. It had just been so unexpected. She'd never been a tabloid headline before—and fervently hoped she never would be again.

All she wanted was the whole mess to be forgotten. To move on. To be simply Maddie, no longer the Honourable Madeleine with all that entailed.

*Speaking of which*—she glanced at the watch on her wrist—'simply Maddie's' lunch break was nearly up. It took twenty minutes to walk around the small lake to the castle, where emails, to-do lists and myriad duties awaited her. Maddie shoved the envelope back into her pocket and scrambled to her feet, mentally calculating what she had to do that afternoon. Confirm numbers with the McKellans, finalise menu choices with the Wilsons and chat to the florist about the Shepherds' desire to only have buttercups and daisies in all their floral arrangements. The florist considered herself an artist and Maddie wasn't looking forward to conveying the bride's wishes and the ensuing conversation about the barbaric taste of the English.

Maddie was fully aware that it was more than a little ironic that a woman who had officially Had Enough of weddings *and* ancestral stately homes had secured a job combining both these elements. Yet here she was, wedding and event planner at Castello Falcone, ensuring the mainly British brides—and their grooms—had the perfect Italian wedding experience. At least she was getting a salary for her labour. The first money she had actually earned in her twenty-six years, as opposed to working all hours for love, board and an allowance. It was liberating, literally and metaphorically.

And by the end of the year, she would have enough money saved to head off somewhere where nobody had ever heard of the Honourable Runaway Bride.

*Just one more moment.* Maddie turned back to the mountains, raising her arms in a silent commune with the sun, with the landscape, with the heady fresh air. Closing her eyes, she basked in the sensual warmth of the sun on her face, the scent of pine. She stayed still for several seconds, arms still raised high, head tilted back until the sound of the church bell, dolefully ringing out the quarter-hour, reminded her that she really needed to be getting back. She lowered her arms and opened her eyes, only to freeze in place.

A man was getting undressed on the other side of the lake.

It wasn't a big lake, but long and skinny, the distance from one shore to the other widthways less than three hundred metres, perfectly swimmable if you didn't mind the cold. Which meant Maddie had a clear view of the small cove on the opposite shore and of the man purposefully and neatly divesting himself of trousers, of shirt, of socks and shoes until he stood there in just a pair of swim-shorts.

*Look away*, her conscience bade her. He was perfectly entitled to his swim, whoever he was. And she had places to be and many, many things to do. She certainly shouldn't be here ogling—because that, she guiltily admitted, was exactly what she was doing. Only she couldn't tear her gaze away.

He was tall and perfectly sculpted. Long, muscular legs led to a slim, defined torso which broadened out into a strong set of shoulders. Maddie could make out tousled dark hair, although his features were blurred. Unexpectedly desire hit her, hot and heavy, swirling low in her stomach, weakening her knees. Nostalgia followed, equally potent. It had been so long since she had experienced anything this intense. If ever.

'So you're reduced to gawping at half-naked strangers,' she muttered, half in self-disgust, half in self-deprecation as she made herself turn away. 'Face it, Maddie, this journey of discovery of yours is going to have to include getting back in the dating game. You want someone to really, passionately love you? They're going to have to get to know you first.'

Not that she *had* ever really dated. A series—a very short series—of monogamous, semi-serious relationships with suitable young men that she had eventually ended when she considered herself to be in real danger of dying from actual boredom, until she had allowed herself to get engaged to Theo Willoughby. Engaged even though he had never, not once, made her tremble with desire. Nor, she admitted, had she him. No wonder they'd both been content to drift through the two years of their engagement barely seeing each other—and barely touching when they did.

She took one last look back and stilled. The man was looking across at her, and even over the lake she could sense his predatory intenseness. Heat flickered through her veins as she stood there, trapped under the weight of his gaze, über-conscious of his semi-nudity, all that flesh so splendidly displayed, feeling, under the weight of his gaze, as if she were equally unclad. Her mouth dried, her limbs heavy, under his spell, as if he were some male Medusa, turning her into a statue with a look alone.

Somehow Maddie summoned up the resolve to turn away, to walk nonchalantly as if she didn't know that he was still staring at her, as if his gaze wasn't burning holes in her back. And then, just like that, the pressure lessened, and when she plucked up the courage to glance back he was in the water, cutting through the lake with single-minded, bold strokes.

She paused to watch him swim. She had no idea who he was, but the unsettling encounter combined with the wedding invitation had to be a sign. Theo had moved on—to be fair, he had moved on the second she had halted the wedding if not before—and it was time she shook off all those labels that had held her back for so long: dutiful daughter, the runaway bride, the Honourable Madeleine. It was time simply Maddie discovered the joys of falling in love as well as the joys of working for a living. She'd promised herself the chance to live, to have fun in this time of exploration. It was time she stopped hiding behind her work, behind her fear, and seized every opportunity.

Of course, there weren't that many opportunities for spontaneous romance in Castello Falcone or San Tomo, the tiny village which traditionally served the Falcone family. The pleasure spots of Lake Garda were twenty kilometres away, Verona and Milan further still. It was the peace and solitude which had drawn her here in the first place.

Lost in thought, Maddie barely noticed as she walked through the small, cobbled village square, with the church at one end and the magnificent wooden town hall at the other, passing through the narrow streets on autopilot. It wasn't until she found herself back on the lake path that Maddie realised that she'd missed the turning, which took her around the back of the castle and in through the discreet staff exit, and instead she was heading towards the much grander—and private—gated driveway. She stopped, irresolute. It would take longer for her to turn around and go the right way and it wasn't as if staff were actually forbidden from using the main entrance.

The fact this path would take her past the small cove where the mystery man was bathing had nothing to do with her decision to carry on. She focused on the path ahead, determined not to look to the right at any point, yet unable to stop her gaze sliding lakewards, just a little, as she approached the cove.

Nothing. No one. No piles of clothes. No bathers. Just a small curve of sand and the water.

That couldn't be disappointment tightening in her chest, could it? Because that would be ridiculous. If things had come to such a pass that voyeurism was how she was getting her admittedly very few kicks then maybe she should just admit defeat and start creating memes of kittens.

Putting her head down, Maddie trudged determinedly on, only to stop with a shocked gasp as she ran straight into something hard. Something that emitted an audible *'oof'* as her head rebounded off it. Maddie stepped back, embarrassed heat flooding her as she looked up, an apology spilling from her lips, only for the words to dry up as she looked into a pair of steely blue eyes. Eyes fixed directly on her.

*'Trovi bella la veduta?'* the owner of the eyes enquired sharply.

Maddie spoke fluent Italian, but every word she had

ever known deserted her. 'I... I'm sorry?' She cringed as her words emerged, brisk and clear and so utterly English she sounded like Lady Bracknell opining on handbags.

'I asked,' and she cringed further as the man switched to perfect English, 'if you were enjoying the view?'

Oh, no—oh, absolutely no way was this happening. Maddie stepped back and took in the man properly. Tall, dark-haired, looked as if he was sporting a decent pair of shoulders under the white linen shirt, hair ruffled and still wet. Still wet...

The swimmer.

Dante raised an eyebrow, but the slim, blonde woman didn't say anything further, fixing her gaze firmly on the second button of his shirt. He raked her up and down assessingly—tall, with a willowy grace when she wasn't running into people—her long, silky blonde hair twisted into a smooth ponytail. She didn't look like one of the wedding guests who trooped through the castle gates with clockwork regularity to swill Prosecco and party into the early hours, rarely taking the time to notice the exquisite setting, but who else could she be? So few tourists found their way to the small San Tomo lake, most preferring the well-trodden loveliness of the more famous Garda and Como or to head deeper into the mountains.

The woman's pale cheeks flushed a deep rose-pink as she finally lifted her head and met his gaze full-on. Her own gaze was steady, strengthened by a pair of cool grey eyes which reminded Dante of the lake on a winter's day; almost silver, tinged with a darkness that spoke of hidden depths.

'I wasn't looking where I was going—please forgive me,' she said, her voice clear and bell-like.

'Distracted, maybe? The views can quite take one's breath away.' He allowed a knowing intonation to creep into his voice but, although her colour heightened, her expression stayed cool.

'The mountains are magnificent, aren't they? I can't imagine ever taking them for granted, ever not being overawed.'

'Glad to hear they've made an impression, *signorina*...' He paused and waited, watching her torn between good manners and reluctance to prolong the conversation.

'Fitzroy, Madeleine Fitzroy.' She smiled then, the kind of polite smile which was clearly a dismissal. 'I am so sorry again. It was nice to meet you.' And with that she turned and walked away, back along the path. A calm, collected walk as if she was not at all flustered. Dante stayed still for a moment, enjoying the sway of her hips, the curve of her waist, set off by her neat linen shift dress.

The ping of his phone reminded him of his duties. He couldn't stand here for ever, no matter how pretty the view. Tomorrow he would go for a long hike, up into the mountains, just as he had when he was a boy. But today he needed to catch up with paperwork, get to know any new staff who had started in the last few months, settle back into the castle after far too many months since his last fleeting visit.

The woman had disappeared around the curve of the lake path and Dante set off in the same direction. The path was as familiar as his own reflection, memories around every turn. Even now, after all these years, after all these regrets, he had to stop the moment Castello Falcone came fully into view. Had to admire the way the natural stream had been diverted to create a continuous cascade through fountains and ponds to fall down the terraced slopes. Appreciate how the natural and formal so seamlessly blended together in the landscaped gardens— and, rising above it all, the many spires of Castello Falcone. The setting was more fairy-tale than any movie-set designer could imagine, centuries of scandal and secrets locked up inside those walls. His own included.

His phone pinged again, this time telling him he had a call, and he pulled it from his pocket, frowning. He'd promised Arianna he'd try and take a break this summer, but he could never truly switch off. Too much rested on him. He flipped the phone over, his mood lightening when he saw his sister's name on the screen, mentally calculating the time difference. It must be midnight in New Zealand.

'*Ciao, Luciana. E tutto okay?*'

'Why wouldn't it be?'

Dante suppressed a smile at the familiar voice. After a decade on the other side of the world his sister had an accent that was a unique mixture of her native Italian and a New Zealand twang, and she usually spoke English, even to him, liberally strewn with Italian endearments and curses. His chest tightened. How he wished she were closer, were here to help him raise Arianna.

'It's late,' he pointed out mildly. 'I'm surprised to hear from you, that's all.'

'I just want to make sure that you're okay, *mio fratello*. Are you at the *castello*?'

'Arrived this morning,' Dante confirmed as he resumed his walk up the sweeping driveway, reaching one of the sets of stone steps flanking the terraces. 'Arianna's au pair will bring her along in a couple of days when I've made sure everything is ready.'

'Good; it's time she returned there. It's not healthy to keep away. For either of you.'

Dante did his best to bite back his curt reply, but the words escaped regardless. 'Her mother died thanks to the treacherous mountain roads. I was on the other side of the world. Arianna was left all alone…'

'The roads didn't kill Violetta,' his sister cut in. She knew her cue; after all, they'd had this conversation more times than Dante could remember. 'The mountains didn't kill her…not even the ice on the road was responsible. It was the driver of the car she was in. It was the drink and drugs. Arianna was safe enough with her nanny, with all the rest of the staff. Stop torturing yourself, Dante. It's been over five years.'

Over five years? What did years matter when the end result was the same? His daughter left motherless, his wife's death a dark stain on his soul.

'I know how long it's been, Ciana.' How long to the day, to the hour. Just as he knew how unhappy his wife had been. How, once she'd got over the initial excitement at living in a castle, she'd felt caged in by the mountains, isolated by San Tomo's remote location, how much she resented him for travelling so much, working so much— although that work paid for her extravagant lifestyle. That unhappiness, that resentment, that isolation had killed her—and Dante knew exactly who was to blame.

It wasn't the ice, or the car, or her lover, or the drink or the cocaine that had killed his wife. He had. And no matter how hard he worked he would never be able to atone, never make it up to his daughter. 'I'm fine, Luciana. Looking forward to spending the summer here. To getting away from Roma for a couple of months.' He glanced back towards the lake. 'I've already been for a swim.'

'The first swim of summer? How I miss it. I always knew it was the holidays as soon as I was in the lake. No study, no etiquette, no expectations for two whole months.' Luciana's voice was filled with melancholic nostalgia. Dante rolled his eyes, glad she couldn't see him. He knew full well his sister's house had stunning mountain views on every side, that she could walk down to a lake ten times the size of San Tomo in less than five minutes and her three sons spent most of their time on the water.

'There's plenty of room if you want to come for a visit any time.' The offer was genuinely meant, but Dante knew she was unlikely to make the two-day flight back to her native country any time soon, not with three boys aged between five and eight and the extensive vineyard she owned with her husband to manage.

'*Grazie*—it's been too long since I saw my niece. Now, Dante, I wanted to ask you a favour.'

Here it was, the reason for the call. 'Mmm?' he said noncommittally.

'My *amico*, Giovanna, you remember her? She recently got divorced—her husband was *not* a nice man— and she's moved to Milan. She could really do with a friend. Will you take her out? Maybe for dinner?' Luciana's voice was sly and Dante didn't try and hide his sigh.

'I'm not planning to spend any time in Milan this summer,' he said as repressively as possible. He should have known this conversation was coming; after all, it was at least three months since his sister had last tried to set him up.

'She has a villa on Lake Garda and spends all her weekends there. That's not far away. You could do with some time out as well, Dante. Just a few dinners, no expectations.'

'*Perdonami*, Luciana, but I'm not looking to make any new friends, to date anyone. I know you mean well, but please, stop trying to set me up with your friends.'

'I just hate to think of you all alone, brooding away.' Luciana sounded throaty, a hitch in her voice. Dante knew those signs all too well; his sister was going to cry.

It would be different if she was close by, if she could just see that he and Arianna were both well, both happy. But he knew how much she fretted about being on the other side of the world, how much she blamed herself for promoting Dante's marriage to Violetta. She just wanted him to be happy. How could he be upset with her for that? If only he could stop her worrying…

'I'm not alone…' The words spilled out before he had a chance to think what he was saying. 'I met someone, but it's really early days, so don't get excited.'

A little, teeny white lie. What harm could it do? If it made Luciana happy—and stopped her trying to set him up with any newly single friend then surely it was allowable? Maybe even the right thing to do.

'You met someone? Who? Oh, you *man*, you, why didn't you say something before?'

'It's not serious. I didn't want to get your hopes up.' Plus, the tiny point that he'd only just thought up his imaginary girlfriend.

'So? Details?' Luciana demanded and Dante stopped dead. Details? Of course his sister would want details.

He swivelled, looking out over the lake for inspiration. His gaze fell on the jetty almost directly opposite, on the woman he had seen standing there, on the intense way she had watched him, as if he represented something she needed, something she yearned for.

Despite himself the blood began to heat in his veins, his heart thumping a little louder. He'd been annoyed, sure. His coming-home ritual interrupted, the sheer intentness of her stare intrusive. And yet... There had been something almost sensual about the moment. The two of them separated by hundreds of metres of water and yet connected by something primal. He'd felt a little like a stag in the prime of his life, preening for attention. She the doe, unable to look away, waiting to be claimed.

'She's English,' Dante said slowly. 'Tall, blonde.'

'English? Okay. And? What does she do? Where did you meet? What does Arianna think?'

Dante seized on the last question gratefully, his inventiveness already giving out. 'Arianna doesn't know yet, so don't say anything when you video-call her. Like I said, it's early days. Luciana, I'll call you later this week; I have only been here a couple of hours and I need to meet the new staff and look over the new event planner's business plan.' Hopefully by then he would have thought up a story that would pass muster. Planned out a summer-long romance, followed by a regretful breakup in the autumn and his sister off his back for a good few months.

'Okay, but I want to know all about her,' Luciana threatened. *'Ciao, Dante.'*

*'Ciao.* And, Luciana? Thank you for calling. For always calling.'

*'Stupido,'* she murmured and hung up.

Dante slipped his phone back into his pocket, for once

the smile playing on his lips unforced. He did appreciate every phone call; he just wanted Luciana to stop worrying about him. Now, thanks to the stroke of genius that was his imaginary girlfriend, he'd achieved that.

For now.

# CHAPTER TWO

'THAT'S GREAT. I look forward to meeting you in two weeks' time.' Madeleine replaced the phone handset and leaned back in her chair. There was no need for her to speak to Sally Capper again, but—she made a private bet with herself—there would be at least another four conversations before the bride arrived in San Tomo.

Of course, *every* bride put a lot of trust in Maddie's hands. She organised their pick-ups at the airport, she allocated rooms to their guests, sometimes ensuring that larger parties were also accommodated in the village. She arranged ceremonies at the church, at the town hall and in the small chapel in the *castello*—always reminding the couples to have a legal ceremony at home first to cut through the extensive Italian red tape. She advised on menus, she organised the decoration of the hall or the courtyard. She booked hairdressers and make-up artists. She received wedding dresses and made sure they were pressed and stored properly. In fact she had four hanging in the cedar closet behind her right now.

She soothed tears and tantrums, listened to diatribes about selfish relatives; she was counsellor and advisor. Some brides fell on her as if she were their best friend when they finally met. Others treated her as if she were there to do their every bidding, with no thought of pleases and thank-yous. Maddie didn't much care either way. She was here to do a job, that was all.

The truth was, most of the weddings left her cold, their very perfection unsettling. The only times she felt a glimmer of any emotion was when the bride and groom didn't care if the playlist was disrupted for a song or two, laughed if it rained, smiled benevolently when a great-uncle rose to his feet to make a long, rambling speech— because in the end all they cared about was each other. Maddie would watch those couples swaying later in the evening, eyes locked, and her heart would ache. Would anyone ever look at her that way—or would she always be practical, helpful Madeleine with the right name, the right upbringing and the right can-do attitude?

All she wanted was someone, some day to look at her as if she was their whole world.

Maybe she should get a dog.

She turned at the sound of voices in the courtyard behind her office. She'd waved off the last party yesterday and the rooms had all been cleaned and made up ready for the next, so no one should be out there. Maddie stood up to see better, but couldn't see anybody.

Stretching, she snapped her laptop shut, deciding she wasn't going to get much more done today; another wedding party would be arriving tomorrow and the exhausting cycle would begin again. Technically she was supposed to take the two days between bookings off, but she rarely did. There would be plenty of time for leisure and adventure when she finally had enough saved to begin travelling properly.

Picking up her bag, she stepped over to the little oval door which took her onto the covered balcony walkway with stone steps leading down into the courtyard. Her office was at the very back of the castle, overlooking the beautiful, cobbled courtyard with its gracious arches, flower-filled pots and imposing marble fountain which marked the centre.

Madeleine had been offered a room in the castle, but she had taken a small apartment in a chalet on the outskirts of the village. She had grown up surrounded by the old and grand at Stilling Abbey. She knew all about graceful arches and medieval halls and battlements. About draughty corridors and smoking chimneys, about slippery, steep stone steps and tiny windows which let in hardly any light. About furniture older than most people could trace back their family trees and dirty oil paintings featuring disapproving-looking ancestors.

No. Let the brides and grooms exclaim over the romance of it all from their four-poster bed while she went home to her little one-bedroom apartment with its glorious view of the lakes and its humble furnishings chosen for comfort alone. There wasn't a single antique, nothing worth more than a handful of euros in the apartment, and Maddie liked it that way, although she knew her mother would wince at the clashing bright colours of the throws and cushions with which Maddie had personalised her little home.

She started down the old stone steps, mentally totting up all the things she needed to do the next day, not registering the small group in the corner of the courtyard until she reached the ground. The sound of her heels on the cobbles must have advertised her presence because the three men all stopped talking and turned as one. Maddie paused, smiling automatically, registering her boss, the castle general manager, Guido, and an older man she recognised as one of the accountants from the Falcone headquarters in Rome.

Her heart stuttered to a stop as her gaze moved on to the third man. What was the bather from the lake doing here? By the flare in his blue eyes he was as surprised to see her as she him—but then, it was a tiny valley, one small village, where everyone knew each other. The chances of the mystery man not being connected with the castle were far less than running into him.

After the first flare of surprise his expression smoothed into neutrality as he stepped forward. 'Nice to meet you again, *signorina*.'

Guido looked from one to another. 'You know one another?'

'We ran into each other at the lake, but we haven't been formally introduced,' he said.

Maddie clenched her fists at the mocking tone in his voice, but managed to twist her mouth into a smile. 'Literally ran into each other. My fault.'

'I believe the *signorina* was transfixed by the view.'

Maddie's fists tightened as her smile widened. 'My mind was elsewhere,' she agreed, trying her best not to let him see how easily he riled her.

'Maddie is one of our hardest workers. We are very lucky to have her.' Guido stepped in, to Maddie's profound relief. 'Dante, this is Madeleine Fitzroy; she looks after all the weddings here at the *castello*. Maddie, let me introduce you to Conte Falcone.'

Maddie had already started to extend her hand and continued the motion automatically, even as her mind raced with the new information. It wasn't the dark-haired man's title that threw her—most of Maddie's family had titles—it was the realisation that he was her employer.

The first employer she had ever had and he'd seen her ogling him down at the lake. Was that an automatic disciplinary?

'You're the events planner?' He sounded as surprised as Maddie felt as he took her hand. It was just a brief touch, but a jolt shocked up and down her arm, her nerves tingling from the encounter.

'I…yes. I…'

*Nicely done, Maddie; pull yourself together.*

After all, she'd had tea with the Queen three times and managed to make polite conversation over the finger sandwiches just fine. There was no way this tall man with the sardonic smile was more intimidating than meeting the Queen of England. 'I've been here nearly a year now; I started last September.' A couple of months after her non-wedding, desperate to get away from the limelight she had found herself in, away from the camera lenses and the headlines, from her mother's disapproving and palpable disappointment. A friend of a friend had mentioned that she knew of a job somewhere remote in the Italian Dolomites for someone with good organisational skills and fluent Italian, and Maddie had jumped at the opportunity.

'You approved her appointment before you went back to Roma at the end of last summer,' Guido said. 'Maddie managed events at two similar venues in England.'

So her CV had carefully omitted that one of those venues was her own ancestral home and the other belonged to her ex-fiancé? The blatant nepotism and lack of a salary didn't change the fact that Maddie had managed them both expertly, and she had had no qualms about using that experience to get herself a real paying job.

'*Si*, I remember. I was expecting someone a little

older, that is all. I seem to remember at least eight years' experience at the highest level...'

'I started working young,' Maddie said, lifting her bag higher onto her shoulder, signalling clearly that, lovely as this encounter was, she had somewhere else to be.

'Obviously.' His smile didn't reach his eyes and Maddie shifted, uncomfortable with the scrutiny.

'Are you in a hurry?' Guido asked her. 'I was planning to show the Conte some of the changes you have made to the accommodation. But you can explain your thinking much better than I can, if you have time to accompany us.'

Maddie shifted again. Usually she would jump at the opportunity to showcase some of her work; she was proud of what she had achieved over the last few months. But she felt uneasy spending any more time under Dante Falcone's all too penetrating glance.

'I'm sure the *signorina* has more inspiring things to do with her evening; a walk around the lake perhaps?' the Conte drawled, his eyes gleaming at her.

Maddie tilted her chin defiantly. 'Of course I'd be glad to show you around. If you'd like to follow me?'

Maddie's job revolved in and around the courtyard. The top two storeys of the old stables which made up two sides of the rectangle had been converted into guest accommodation, comfortably housing around sixty guests in comfortable en-suite bedrooms. The ground floor of one block was fitted out with a sitting room, a library and a games room, whilst the other block was home to the large dining room serving breakfasts and dinners throughout the week, as well as a drying room for walking boots or skis for the more adventurous wedding guests.

The oldest part of the castle made up the third side of the quad. The medieval hall was often used for the wedding ceremony and reception, although in summer some guests preferred to hold the wedding al fresco. That was just one of the innovations Maddie had brought in when she had been appointed.

Now she had to impress the Conte with the rest. Let him mock. Bookings were up and referrals at an all-time high. Her record spoke for itself.

Maddie led the way into the grey flagstone entrance hall which linked the two stable blocks and paused by the comfortable leather sofas, cushions plumped up perfectly to welcome weary revellers. A coffee table between them was heaped with crisp new magazines and literature detailing walks and day trips. The sideboard held jugs of fresh mountain flowers and a chalkboard was propped against the wall opposite, the names *'Tom and Nicky'* written in a swirly script, ready to welcome the next happy couple.

'Although the *castello* is very beautiful, and architecturally sound, bookings were a little more intermittent than I would have expected,' she explained, proud of how firm her voice was. But why shouldn't it be? She had this.

'This is why I wanted a dedicated wedding planner,' Guido said. 'We got many enquiries, but only a few converted into bookings. We are so remote here, and the winters can be harsh, so our summers were busy but the rest of the year not so much.'

'It's just a case of turning those perceived negatives into positives,' Maddie said. 'Positioning the castle as a winter wonderland through the colder months, making the isolation a strength by ensuring everything they could possibly need is right here, although we can organise trips to Garda or Verona or Milan. We organise airport pick-ups, help brides and their guests with travel itineraries either side of their stay with us.'

She opened the door that led into the dining room. The wooden tables were set out café-style, each with small jugs of fresh flowers in the centre. 'There is always coffee on the go in here, along with iced water, but guests can order any other drinks they need from the kitchens. Depending on the arrangements we have with the bride and groom, this might be free, or the guests might have individual tabs. We usually have some kind of cake or biscuits and bowls of fresh fruit available all day as well. Breakfast is always served as a buffet, dinner too unless the couple pay more for a more formal serving.'

Maddie was aware of the Conte's gaze, fixed firmly on her as she talked, but she blocked it out, determined that by the time her tour was concluded that sardonic gleam would turn to interest and the only expression on his admittedly handsome face would be approval.

Dante had to admit that the English girl had done wonders. The last time he had seen these rooms they had been furnished formally, antiques from the castle forming the bulk of the furniture, ancient mountain views and various ancestors framed in thick gilt decorating the walls. It had all been stripped away, plain white walls now livened with colourful abstract prints, and rooms filled with comfortable-looking brown leather sofas and chairs, heaped with bright throws and cushions. Shelving had been erected in both rooms, filled with books and board games. It looked clean, comfortable and homely, despite the size of the rooms.

The same magic had been wrought upstairs. The bedrooms were also freshly painted in white, the wooden beds made up with white linen and cheerful silk cushions and throws, with matching rugs on the polished floorboards. 'Sometimes a bride and groom like to decorate to a theme, so we've kept the accommodation neutral in case we need to dress the rooms up to match,' Maddie explained. 'There are still some of the castle antiques around—that huge vase, for example, but they're accents now, not overshadowing the whole. What we haven't stinted on is quality. All the toiletries, the linens, the chocolates are locally sourced. We want the stables to feel more like a high-end hotel, not like a hostel. All the rooms are Austrian twins so we can make them up as twins or doubles, depending on what we're asked to do.'

'It's very impressive,' Dante admitted as they reached the final room on that corridor, a sunlit room with cheerful yellow and orange hints. It was, and he especially liked how Maddie had managed to ensure that no two rooms felt the same, her judicious use of pictures and ornaments giving each one its own identity. 'But new sofas, new beds, new linen—it can't have been cheap.'

Not that he couldn't afford it, but the wedding lets were just a tiny part of his business concerns. The Falcone fortune came from agriculture, from shipping, from olives and wine. He was glad the castle was more than a glorified summer residence, glad to provide legitimate employment for those villagers who needed it, but he wasn't running a charity and the Castello Falcone needed to pay its way.

'It wasn't. But I believe the results speak for themselves. We're already fully booked for next year and a third of the year after, and we managed to fill every spare week this year from April onwards.' Maddie met his eyes with a cool gaze of her own, but Dante could see a swirl of uncertainty behind the grey depths.

'Impressive,' he said softly and watched, fascinated, as the uncertainty dissolved, her eyes lightening to silver, her diffidence disappearing until she was glowing with achievement and pride—deservedly so.

The air stilled, thickened as their gazes locked. Guido and Toni, his accountant, had returned downstairs to look at something that needed replacing, leaving Dante alone with his new event planner. And suddenly that felt like a dangerous place to be.

This was his home, his workplace—and more importantly his daughter was arriving in two days. There was no time for a discreet affair, even if Maddie was interested.

No, better not to think about an interested Maddie, not with the two of them alone, with her eyes still fixed on his, her lips parted. Not with the memory of how she had watched him across the lake still crystal-clear in his mind.

'I think that's everything,' she said a little huskily, colour mounting in her cheeks as she practically marched out of the bedroom and headed towards the stairs. 'I'm sure Guido has already talked you through the strategy we put together.'

'Have you also made changes to the master bedroom suite?' Dante stayed as still a predator as Maddie stopped, one hand on the top of the stair rail.

'A few.'

'Show me.'

Her eyes flashed at the order, but she didn't speak, just nodded her head slightly before descending the narrow staircase. Dante followed, trying not to watch the sway of her hips, the way her hair moved as she walked. If he had any sense he would allow Madeleine Fitzroy to get on with her evening and check out the honeymoon suite by himself. After another dip in the freezing lake.

Not that he had any interest in spending more time with Maddie. This was business, plain and simple. If she had made changes it made sense that she was the one to explain her rationale to him. His decision was completely unconnected to the knowledge that ever since he had seen her across the lake staring at him with such unabashed curiosity something dormant had woken inside him, running insistently through his blood. Not because describing his fake relationship to his sister had made him aware of just how cold his life really was.

Intentionally cold, but when loneliness bit it did so with sharp intent.

It only took a few moments to cross the courtyard to the big, arched wooden door studded with iron which led into the oldest part of the castle. The wing where the staff quarters and offices were sat at a right angle to the ancient hall, with the more modern parts of the castle—a mere five hundred years old—complete with the famed turrets and terraces, faced the lake beyond that.

'I changed nothing in here,' Maddie said quietly as she preceded Dante into the vast room. 'It's perfect as it is.'

It was, with its arched ceiling criss-crossed with beams, the stone floor and the leaded stained-glass windows shadowing the floor in colour. A dais stood at one end filled with flowers. Chairs were already laid out in neat rows, each one dressed in white linen, more flowers punctuating the end of each row on tall plinths.

'Tomorrow's couple are getting married the day after they arrive, so we're all set up and ready,' she said.

Dante watched her as she stopped and surveyed the room, her sharp gaze sweeping every corner, making sure nothing was missed, pulling a notebook out of her bag and scribbling a few words. It was like watching a dance, or listening to finely read poetry, she was so in tune with her surroundings, oblivious to her companion as she wrote, paced a few steps, frowned and wrote again. Dante wasn't used to being forgotten, especially by women. It was a novel sensation—and it brought out a deeply buried, animal wish to make her notice him, the way a bird must feel as he preened to attract a mate.

He pulled out his phone and began to scroll through his messages, ruthlessly clamping down on any animal instincts.

'Sorry, I just noticed a couple of things.' Maddie put the notebook back in her bag and gestured towards the spiral staircase at the end of the hall. 'Shall we?'

'Of course.'

The staircase led directly into the honeymoon suite. Last time Dante had set foot in it, it had been a dark, richly decorated suite of rooms, little light able to penetrate the stone walls through the window slits. Ancient tapestries had hung on the walls, the flagstones covered with antique rugs, and dark, heavy furniture had dominated the space. It had felt baronial, grand and imposing—more like the lair of a medieval seducer than a romantic getaway.

He stopped as he reached the top of the room and swivelled, unable to believe his eyes. How could this be the same space? 'Where have the walls gone?' he managed to say eventually.

'They weren't original, don't worry. In fact they weren't even Renaissance like the rest of the castle, but a nineteenth-century addition, according to the architect I consulted,' Maddie said hurriedly, her gaze fixed anxiously on him. 'What do you think?'

The apartment was now one huge room, much lighter thanks to the clever use of mirrors picking up the faint light and reflecting it back into the room. The same imposing four-poster—a bed that legend had it Dante's great-grandfather times several greats had used to seduce women away from their husbands, until he had foolishly turned his wandering eye on a Borgia wife—was still in situ, but, placed at one end of the room and heaped with cushions, it looked inviting rather than intimidating. The matching wardrobe and chest of drawers also looked more fitting, now they no longer dominated the space.

The fireplace had been opened out and was, despite the summer's day, filled with logs ready to be lit. A comfortable chaise, loveseat and sofa were grouped around it. A small dining table, already laid for two, sat on one side of the room, low bookshelves lay opposite it and thick rugs covered the cold stone floor.

Dante stood stock still, taking it all in. How could such a dark, stately space feel so welcoming just because a couple of walls had been removed?

It wasn't just the walls though. It was the mirrors, it was the choice of painting, the cream rugs with the hint of gold, the dainty china on the table, the…hang on, the *what*?

'Why is the bathtub in the middle of the room?' Dante blinked again, but sure enough it was still there. Mounted on a tiled dais, the antique cast-iron bath that had used to reside in the bathroom now sat slap bang in the middle of the room. A freestanding wooden towel rail stood on one side; a slender console table on the other held candles and bath oils.

'We turned the bathroom into a wet room.' Maddie glanced at him, long eyelashes shielding her expression. 'Guido offered to email you the plans, but you said you trusted us to do the details.'

'*Si.*' Dante was still transfixed by the bathtub. Noting how it was in every possible eye line. How a man could lie in bed and watch his bride bathe, the candlelight casting a warm glow over her skin. 'And this is the kind of detail you like? The idea of watching someone bathe?'

'I...' She stopped.

Dante waited, lounging against the wall, eyes fixed on her as intently as hers had been fixed on him.

'Many luxury rooms have the bath in the main space.' Maddie turned away, but Dante had already spotted the red on her cheeks, on her neck. 'It's nothing new.'

'I'm quite aware of that,' Dante said silkily. 'It can definitely add a certain intimacy to an evening.' He deliberately took his time over the word 'intimacy', drawing out every letter as he spoke. 'That's not what I asked, Madeleine. I asked if you like to watch people bathe.'

'I...' she began again, then paused, before turning and determinedly fixing her gaze on his, head high, as proud as a young goddess. 'I owe you an apology. I intruded on a private moment earlier today and I...' She paused again, her eyes darkening. Dante watched, fascinated.

'No, actually I don't apologise,' she said, head even higher. 'You were bathing on a public beach—anyone could have seen you. If anyone should apologise, you should for trying to embarrass me.'

Dante stayed stock still, torn between amusement at her indignation—and shame. She was right; he *was* trying to embarrass her. Why? Because of the thrill that had shot through him when he noticed her watching him, had realised how enthralled she was, how safe it had been to retaliate, to look back with a lake between them?

He was her employer, had power over her. It was beneath him to indulge in these kinds of games.

'*Mi scusa*, you are right. It was wrong of me. It won't happen again. Thank you for your tour, *signorina*; enjoy your evening.' With a nod of his head Dante turned and left, vowing as he did so to keep every interaction with Madeleine Fitzroy professional and brief. They might be sharing the *castello* for the rest of the summer, but it was a big space. There was really no need for them to interact at all.

# CHAPTER THREE

DANTE LOOKED OUT of the window. The lake was calm, the sun reflecting off it in myriad dancing sparkles, the mountains rising behind in a majestic semicircle. His chest tightened with the all too familiar mixture of longing and loathing. Once the *castello* had been his home, the place he loved more than any other. Now it was a constant reminder of his marriage. His greatest failure.

He resolutely turned back to his computer screen, but as he did so his gaze fell on the framed photo on his desk; a black and white portrait of a young woman cradling a baby. Violetta with a newly born Arianna.

If Dante had had his way all pictures of Violetta would have been destroyed the day after her funeral, but he knew that their daughter needed to grow up seeing her mother around her house, to know her face, to hear her name spoken. So he had gritted his teeth and kept Violetta's photos and portraits on walls and desks in Rome and here in the *castello*—and if he felt the bitterness of guilt and self-loathing each time he saw her face then wasn't it simply what he deserved?

He couldn't regret a marriage which had brought him his daughter, but he could excoriate himself for being the kind of fool to fall for a beautiful face and to project his own hopes and dreams into the woman who wore it. If he'd been older, wiser, had actually bothered to look behind the mask, then he would have seen that all Violetta wanted was the title and the *castello*—and the second of those had palled soon enough. She was bored, he worked too hard, was away too much. He thought motherhood might soothe and focus her. He'd been tragically wrong.

Wrong and blind. Too caught up in his own narrative. He'd never make that mistake again. How could he trust himself when love had proved nothing but a lie? Violetta had loved the title. He had loved a façade.

The tragedy was he had really fallen hard for that façade. Loved it truly and sincerely. Part of him mourned it still.

'*Al diavolo,*' he muttered. It was a beautiful summer's day; somewhere in the *castello* grounds his daughter was playing. Work could wait, especially on a weekend. He'd learned that lesson at last. But as he pushed his chair back his computer flashed up a video-call alert. Dante hovered, uncertainly, before lowering himself reluctantly into his seat and pressing 'accept'. Only a few people had his details. It must be important.

'*Ciao!*'

Dante leaned back as the screen filled with his sister's beaming face. Luciana was ageless, five years older than him, mother of three, but no wrinkles marred her olive skin, her hair as dark and lustrous as it had ever been. Only her eyes, he noted, seemed dull with fatigue, her smile maybe a little more forced than usual. 'Twice in one week. To what do I owe the pleasure?'

'Is that any way to greet your only sister?' Luciana asked, not giving him time to answer. 'Where's my niece? Did she arrive safely?'

'She's out playing and yes, she's already familiarised herself with every corner, just like we used to do.' Luciana and Dante had been heartbroken when their parents moved from the castle to the austere townhouse in Milan when Luciana hit her teens. Dante had sworn then that when *he* was the Conte he would never live anywhere else.

For four years he hadn't. He'd thought they were happy years. Had he been wilfully blind or simply ignorant?

'And? How are things with your mystery girlfriend?' Luciana's gaze sharpened. 'Did you tell me her name?'

Of course he hadn't—and Dante knew his sister was fully aware of that fact. 'I don't believe so.' He sat back even further, legs outstretched, grinning as his sister narrowed her eyes at him.

'Dante, don't be tiresome.'

'Early days, remember?'

'*Si*, I know. But I've been so worried about you, *mio fratello*, I just want to share in your happiness that's all. Tell me a little about her, about how you met.'

*Damn.* Now what was he supposed to do? He'd never been very good at this kind of thing even when the object of his supposed affections wasn't made up. Dante glanced towards the lake, hoping for inspiration. A group of young people, armed with kayaks and paddleboards, were on the beach just outside the castle gates—probably wedding guests. Guido mentioned that Maddie had introduced water sports for the summer months.

Maddie. Of course. He had already based his fictional girlfriend on her physically. What harm in borrowing a little bit more?

Crossing his fingers, he attempted a casual tone. 'She

works here at the Castello Falcone. I met her when we had a planning meeting last month.'

'*And?*'

'And what?'

'Did you like her immediately? Was there chemistry?'

Dante thought back to the moment when he had glimpsed Maddie across the lake, gazes holding, blood thundering. To the way he had been aware of every inch of Madeleine while she showed him around the stable block, the way he had tried to get under her skin, repayment for the way she seemed to get under his. The way he had assiduously avoided every place she might be in the three days since they'd met, working from the office in his suite of rooms in the main part of the castle instead of setting up in the main offices at the back as he usually would. 'I don't know about like,' he said slowly. 'But there was definitely chemistry.'

'And now you'll be working together all summer! Just promise me, Dante, don't try and sabotage this out of some ridiculous sense of loyalty to Violetta. It's been five years. It's time to move on.'

Dante didn't answer. He *had* moved on, but he had learned his lesson; his heart couldn't be trusted. If he was ever to consider marriage again it would be to someone practical, someone who could help him run his business empire and wouldn't be overawed by the social demands his title still commanded even in republican modern-day Italy.

'So you met, there was chemistry and now you and… what's her name, did you say?'

Dante knew when he was beat. 'Madeleine. Maddie.'

'Now you and Madeleine get to spend the summer together. It couldn't be more perfect. I can't wait to meet her.'

Hang on, *what*? 'Meet her?'

'*Si*; oh, silly me, that's the whole reason for the call. I've been so tired, Dante, not at all like myself—Phil even made me go and see the doctor, ridiculous, over-bearing man.' Luciana's voice softened as she said her husband's name, just as it always did.

Dread stole over Dante's heart. He hadn't been imagining the dullness in Luciana's eyes, the shadows darkening them. 'Is everything okay?'

'Apart from having a dozen tests and goodness knows how many needles stuck in me? *Si*. At least, the doctor wants me to slow down for a while, but nothing worse than that. But how can I, with the boys and the vineyard and my fundraising and everything else I have to do? The truth is I'm just run-down. So Phil is insisting I take a good, long vacation. That I come home for a few weeks and let the Italian air revive me.'

'You're coming here? To San Tomo?'

'Isn't it wonderful?'

'Yes.' And it was. Of course it was. If only he hadn't just lied to her.

'I thought I'd spend a few days with you and then head to Lucerne to see Mama. I can get to know Arianna properly all over again and meet your Madeleine, plus get away from this dreary winter. My flight leaves in three days, via a stopover in Singapore. I'll be with you on Thursday!'

'Thursday?' Dante mechanically took down his sister's flight details, promising someone would be there at the airport to pick her up; all the while his brain was whirling, trying to work out a plan. Luciana would land in Rome in less than a week. She may choose to spend a few days in the apartment she had inherited from their father there, but knowing his sister she would be straight onto the high-speed train which would whisk her up to the north of the country in a matter of hours.

He had four days to work out a plan.

Maybe he could say his girlfriend had had to return to England?

Only he had not only named her and described her, but he had also given the name and description of someone here in the *castello*.

Maybe he could send Maddie back to the UK for a few weeks—or to his Rome office or Milan?

Only she had a summer's worth of weddings lined up and ready to go.

He could admit the truth. Break his sister's heart in the process—and find himself dating half of her friends in order to make it up to her.

He was in trouble whatever he did.

Unless…

Maybe, just maybe, he could salvage this situation after all.

Maddie hadn't felt like taking her usual lunchtime walks around the lake over the last few days. Her whole body still flushed when she thought about the moment she realised that her mystery bather and the Conte Falcone were one and the same—and when she remembered the peculiarly charged feeling permeating the air when he'd turned his whole focus onto her.

Instead Maddie had been exploring the vast gardens at the back of the castle. The formal walled gardens and flower gardens gave way to woodland and there were plenty of paths to wander through, plenty of interesting sights to discover, from little stone summer houses to statues, all relics of a nineteenth-century Falcone with a taste for whimsy. She had a similar ancestor; he had installed a gothic folly by the Capability Brown designed lake. It was a popular wedding spot now, which probably made her Byron-idolising ancestor turn in his equally gothic grave.

Maddie stopped when she reached the carved stone bench she'd discovered yesterday, sitting down in the pretty flower-strewn glade to eat the small picnic lunch she carried with her. She'd soon learned that if she didn't leave her desk she wouldn't get a chance to eat. There was always some crisis. At least this current crop of wedding guests seemed sensible; they were, in the main, a cheerful outdoorsy lot and today most of the party had headed into the mountains for a trek, some of the younger contingent taking kayaks onto the lake instead.

Unwrapping her sandwich, Maddie stretched her legs out, tilting her head to the sun. Bliss.

Only…she had the sense that someone was watching her. She gave the glade a quick glance around. Nothing. But Maddie couldn't shake off the feeling that she was definitely not alone. Had one of the castle dogs followed her out, looking for a bite of her sandwich? *'Ciao,'* she called out and waited, feeling a little foolish as she was answered with nothing but silence, until a branch rustled and a small, slim girl stepped into the clearing.

Maddie had had very little to do with children, and to her eyes the child could have been any age between five and ten. Her long, dark hair was in two messy braids, wisps escaping at every turn, and there were smears of dirt across her face, but Maddie noticed the cut of her torn shorts and the quality of her T-shirt. This urchin was expensively dressed—and didn't care about keeping her clothes neat.

'You look like you've been through the wars,' Maddie said in Italian.

The girl gave her a tentative smile. 'I've escaped.'

'Where from?'

'From the *castello*. My au pair wanted me to take a siesta. Sleep! On a day like this.' The girl looked scornfully up at the sky and Maddie had a moment's sneaking sympathy for the hapless au pair tasked with taming this wild child.

'It does seem a shame,' she agreed, breaking her sandwich in two and holding half out to the fugitive. 'Here, you must be hungry. I know adventuring always gave me an appetite when I was your age. I'm Maddie.'

'Arianna Falcone.'

Of course she was. Now Maddie could see the Conte in the proud tilt of the girl's chin, in the blue of her eyes. 'Nice to meet you, Arianna.'

'So this is where you're hiding?'

They both jumped guiltily as a stern voice echoed through the glade and Maddie felt her treacherous body jump to attention as the Conte strode into view. He looked cool despite the heat of the day, in well-cut linen trousers and a short-sleeved white shirt.

He took in the situation with one cool glance. 'Aiding and abetting my daughter, *signorina*?'

'Only with half a sandwich.' Maddie smiled at the unrepentant child.

'That's half a sandwich more than she deserves. *Piccola*, poor Isabella is looking everywhere for you. Go, find her and make your apologies.'

'But it's too lovely a day, Papa. I don't want a siesta.'

'Then, my child, you shouldn't have got caught. But, as you were, go and take your chastisement like a Falcone. Then, if you're good, we can go sailing this afternoon.'

The mutinous expression lightened and Arianna threw her arms around her father before taking off and running back in the direction of the castle, her half of Maddie's sandwich still clasped in her hand. To Maddie's surprise, and no little apprehension, the Conte made no move to follow his daughter, remaining in the glade and fixing Maddie with an inscrutable look.

With an inward sigh she put her own half-sandwich back in its bag. The cook had stuffed it full of mozzarella, rocket and sun-dried tomatoes; there was no way of eating it in any kind of dignified way, and Maddie needed all the dignity she could muster in front of this man.

'It's a lovely day.'

Small talk? Seriously. 'Yes.' Not the most articulate of responses, but all that expensive education teaching Maddie etiquette hadn't prepared her for how to answer when a man said one thing, but his body language said something quite different. Dante Falcone was ramrod-straight, gaze fixed firmly on her, looking more as if he was about to deliver a lecture rather than discuss the weather.

Deliver a lecture or devour her whole. Maddie curled her hands into fists, refusing to give in to the urge to smooth her red skirt down, but she couldn't help recalling what happened to girls in red who talked to wolf-eyed strangers in the woods.

*Oh, what big eyes you have...*

'Would you be kind enough to accompany me on a

short walk? There is something I would like to discuss with you.'

Maddie tried not to give her half-sandwich a longing look. She wanted to sit, eat and just be, not go for what was bound to be an excruciatingly uncomfortable walk. She had spent less than two hours in Dante Falcone's company and in those two hours he had deliberately embarrassed her, she had embarrassed herself, she'd been borderline rude several times. Why would she put herself through a second dose of that?

'Please,' he added. And then he smiled. And that changed everything.

The smile transformed Dante Falcone's face, softening the sharp, lean edges, transforming the saturnine look into something warmer, something Maddie wanted to get close to, his good looks no longer remote, statue-like, but flesh and blood and all the more attractive for that. Desire, new, hot and heavy, flooded through her, drying her throat and taking all capacity to think and reason away.

She reached for words, any words, but found none. Instead she nodded as he turned away towards a path she hadn't yet explored, supremely confident that she'd follow him. And she did, her feet powerless to disobey.

'You speak Italian very well.'

That was ironic; right now she could barely manage English. 'I went to a finishing school near Geneva. We spoke mostly French and Italian there.'

Maddie sensed rather than saw the rise of his elegant brows. 'And what brought you into event management?'

'I kind of fell into it,' she said carefully, but the Conte didn't react, merely waited for her to carry on and reluctantly she did. 'I grew up in a house a little like the Castello Falcone.'

'I see.'

There was no condemnation in the words, but Maddie couldn't help bristling. People often assumed that she'd spent her time floating around like some Jane Austen heroine, arranging flowers and making calls and considering it work. She straightened her shoulders, matching her pace with his. She was proud of what she had achieved. It would be nice if someone else was too.

'When I was growing up my family made a half-hearted effort to make Stilling Abbey pay its way; there was always a part of the roof to be repaired or a chronic case of damp or a huge heating bill. My parents thought allowing the public onto the premises once a month for two hours would be enough to raise some money—and they resented the mild intrusion of that. But when I was fifteen, I realised the reason why the much less architecturally and historically interesting manor house further along the valley was always busy—why they were actually making money—was that they made visitors feel welcome. That more opening hours, a café, a playground for the kids and space for weddings and parties were the key. All I had to do was convince my parents and find the money to get everything ready.'

It sounded so easy, summarised like that. But the reality was it had taken months to persuade her parents to open up the sacred ground of generations of Fitzroys to the general public five days a week, months to apply for the loans and grants to get the basic infrastructure in place. In return she had agreed to go abroad to finishing school for her A-level years. There might not have been money for the roof, but there was always money to ensure the children received the right kind of education. In Maddie's case an education which would enable her to marry well.

Her great-great-great-aunt might have been a famous suffragette, but feminism had yet to penetrate the thick medieval walls of Stilling Abbey.

'Impressive. Why did you leave?'

The old feelings of anger and unfairness hit her squarely in the chest and Maddie blew out a deep breath, almost welcoming the familiar bitterness as it washed away the last remnants of desire. 'The abbey is entailed along with the title.' Again she sensed Dante raising his eyebrows in surprise. 'And in England the title goes along to the eldest son, not the eldest child.'

'Same here, but titles are merely an historical anomaly and estates must be divided fairly amongst the children. My sister received half of my father's estate.'

'Not the *castello* though?' Maddie couldn't stop a sharp bitterness coating her voice.

'She lives in New Zealand so she had little use for it. But she also thought the Falcone ancestral home should stay with the title.'

'At least she had a choice.' Maddie speeded up her pace, furious with herself for giving so much away. She had loved every stone of the old abbey, known every inch of the grounds, thrown herself into making it a profitable concern—but it had been made very clear to her that she had no long-term future at her home. Her brother might care more for geology than history but the abbey was his. Maddie had even joined forces with other people in her position, eldest daughters, adopted children and children born outside of marriage, all disinherited by an old patriarchal system. But for all her justifiable anger she had been keenly aware just what a privileged problem being cut out of the succession to a title really was. In the end she had done her best to let go of the resentment and decided to do what she had been raised to do; marry into another ancient estate instead.

That hadn't turned out that well either.

Dante didn't say anything for a few long minutes and Maddie was relieved as she stomped along. That was all her past. No more aristocratic titles for her. The only time she would step inside a stately home would be in gainful employment or as a paying visitor—apart from the times she went back to Stilling Abbey as a visiting relative with a life of her own elsewhere.

No. She had a plan. Over the next few years she intended to find out who she was when she wasn't an Honourable, wasn't the daughter, sister or wife of someone deemed more worthy because of his Y chromosome.

See what she was worth apart from her value as a blue-blooded brood mare. If anyone would ever look at her the way her ex-fiancé looked at his soon-to-be wife.

'Is that why you came here? For a fresh start?'

Maddie sucked in a breath, surprised at the insight in the casual question. 'Partly. I wanted to get away from the UK, to travel, to stand on my own two feet—but that takes money and I don't have any of my own.' She glanced at him with a self-mocking smile. 'One doesn't need anything as common as wages when one lives at home and waits for a suitable Duke or Earl to come along. I'm here for the cold, hard cash.' And to get away from England and her old life, but there was no need for Dante to know about that. She'd exposed enough already.

'And then?'

'Travelling,' she said promptly. 'I am going to see the world.'

'All of it?'

'As much as I can. I'm going to work my way around. One thing every girl who has grown up in a huge, falling-apart house knows how to do is use their hands. I can waitress, clean, muck out horses, pick fruit. I'm not afraid to get my hands dirty.'

'What *are* you afraid of?' His voice was soft, reflective, almost as if he was asking himself the question.

How could she answer that when the choice was so wide? Afraid she would never have a perfect kiss? That no one would ever look at her as if she was the most desirable being in the world? That she would never know who she really was? She'd never admit that to the tall, dark man next to her.

'I'm a Fitzroy. We don't admit to fear.'

Their walk had taken them deeper into the pine forests which populated the mountain shelf on which San Tomo and the lake resided, the path beginning to wind up into the slopes. Dante stopped and turned and Maddie followed suit, surprised to see they had already begun to make their way uphill along the meandering path. The valley spread out before them, the lake reflecting the brilliant blue of the sky. In the centre of their eye line the graceful spires of the Castello Falcone soared, mirroring the mountains behind.

'My sister is coming to stay next week,' Dante said abruptly and Maddie glanced at him, sensing that the reason for this unexpected walk might become clear.

'That's nice.' Sometimes banalities were the best thing to fall back on. That she *had* learned at finishing school; Small Talk for Beginners.

His mouth quirked into a half-smile and Maddie's heart gave a skip. '*Si*. We are close, Luciana and I. She...' He paused. 'She worries about me. About Arianna.'

'Oh?' Maddie's mind raced. She knew little about her employer, but she had heard that he was a widower, that his young, beautiful actress wife had died tragically in a car crash on the sometimes treacherous road down to Milan. There was some kind of mystery, a hint of scandal, but she had never enquired further. She knew all too well how easily rumours could start, how things could be misrepresented.

'She thinks I need a partner, that Arianna needs a mother. She has many friends who she considers suitable.'

'She would get on very well with my mother. She is always sending me details of potential husbands.' It had taken less than a month since Maddie had walked away from the altar unwed for her mother to suggest a new groom.

'Luciana is under the impression that I am in a relationship. A romantic relationship,' he clarified, his brows drawing across his forehead as he spoke.

'Under the impression?' Maddie couldn't stop the grin spreading across her face. 'How did that happen?'

Dante drew himself up, the very epitome of dignity— if it wasn't for the guilty expression in his eyes, rather like that of a small boy caught out in mischief. 'I may have told her a small falsehood,' he admitted and Maddie's grin widened. 'For the best of reasons. It made her happy to think I was dating and it stopped her trying to set me up with her friends. It seemed like a good idea at the time to invent a short-term relationship that would end amicably in a few months' time.'

Why on earth was he telling her this? 'But now she's coming to visit? That's awkward. Could you pretend that your mystery girlfriend has had to go away on business? Or maybe she just dumped you?'

'She dumped me?' Dante couldn't have sounded more outraged if they had been discussing a real relationship.

'Of course, otherwise there's no reason for your sister not to keep setting you up. Pretend you're nursing a broken heart and you need some time to regroup.' Judging by the confusion in Dante's eyes he didn't often get teased. It was nice to turn the tables on him.

'The problem is…' He took a deep breath and apprehension curled Maddie's stomach as he turned to her, pride, embarrassment and an indefinable heat that Maddie could feel in every nerve ending in his gaze. 'The problem is, she's under the impression that I am in a relationship with you. So, Maddie Fitzroy. I was hoping that you might do me a favour and pretend to be my girlfriend for the next few weeks. A young lady with your birth and education should be able to carry it off perfectly. What do you say?'

Her birth? Her education? Not Maddie herself, but her genes. Again. Would she ever get to be just Maddie? She tilted her head, every inch the Honourable once again. 'I'm sorry, *signor*, but I am afraid what you're asking is impossible.'

'Why?'

'Why? You must see that it's out of the question!'

'Not at all. I've told her that the relationship is in its early stages, so she won't be expecting an established couple. She's only spending a week here before going to see our mother in Lucerne. We will say that you're very busy with your work. That way you have a perfect excuse not to spend too much time with us—and when it's unavoidable I'm sure you will manage admirably. You have the necessary qualities to cope.'

The necessary qualities? No matter where she ran, was she always going to be seen as nothing more than a convenient consort? No, worse; here she was nothing more than an *imaginary* convenient consort.

'How kind of you to say so,' she said, every word bitten off as coldly as she could manage. 'But I'm afraid I must still decline your offer. I have to get back to work now. It's been...' She paused, searching for the right word. 'It's been interesting talking to you. Goodbye.'

As Maddie turned and stalked away, she was conscious of another emotion trying to dig its way through her indignation. Disappointment.

The Conte discombobulated her; she wasn't sure she liked him at all. But she was drawn to him on some primal level, in a way she had never experienced before. Maddie hadn't known what to expect from their walk, but a small part of her had thrilled to the heat she had sensed between them, had wanted to discover more.

But it looked as if she had imagined the heat. That the only attraction she had for the Conte was through her name and her convenient background. It was an all too familiar story. But this time she was saying no.

# CHAPTER FOUR

HE HAD ONE day to come up with a plan—and so far he had nothing.

Dante swivelled and looked at his great-great-grandfather's portrait for inspiration. None was forthcoming. Maybe it was for the best. Maybe it was time for Dante to have a long overdue discussion with his sister. To tell her the truth.

His chest tightened. It wasn't just that he didn't want to upset her, for her to know he had deceived her. It wasn't even that it was easier to bury every feeling apart from his love and protectiveness for Arianna, rather than face the mess he had made of his life and marriage. It was knowing how vulnerable confiding the truth to his sister would make him.

She knew some of it. Knew Violetta had been unhappy. Knew she had cheated on him. Knew he blamed himself for throwing his energies into work rather than repairing his tattered marriage. But she didn't know how he had been duped. Didn't know that Violetta had never loved him. Didn't know that he had loved a phantom.

A marriage gone wrong was a tragedy. A marriage based on deceit was nothing but a sick joke and he the fool at the centre. Five years later it still haunted him, the knowledge of how easily—how willingly—he had been duped.

He stilled as he heard footsteps approaching the door. Nobody visited the old picture gallery; it wasn't part of the publicly accessible part of the castle. That was why he came here to think—he could always count on being alone.

The handle turned, the door opened—and Maddie stood in the entrance, her face mirroring the shock he was sure was on his, before she concealed it with a polite smile.

Dante was getting very used to that particularly polite expression. It wasn't blank, more a carefully smooth look, the kind which could take the user from a hospital visit to a diplomatic lunch without causing offence to anyone. It served her well; he'd seen it employed to calm a drunkenly belligerent wedding guest, to soothe a chef when she'd informed him of three unexpected food intolerances which threatened to destroy a planned menu.

And she used it with him, every time they inadvertently met. It was different from the open, sunny smile she greeted her co-workers with, different from the affectionate, almost conspiratorial grin she shared with Arianna, who seemed to have latched on to her.

'I'm sorry,' Maddie said, every bit the professional. Her dress was spotless and cool-looking despite the advancing hour and the heat of the day, not a hair in her neat chignon out of place, her make-up discreet and fresh. 'I didn't realise anyone would be in here. I'll come back later…'

She took a step backwards, her hand on the door. It would be easier to let her walk away, to continue to brood alone, but Dante halted her. 'Don't leave on my account. What do you need in here?'

'Oh, well, one of my brides wants to dress in a historically accurate way, but doesn't know where to start. I offered to send her some pictures of the past Contessas to give her inspiration. I did warn her that there are a lot of different styles, but she doesn't know if she wants renaissance or reunification so I'll need to photo a selection.' She raised the small camera she held as if proving her words.

'Come in. Take your photographs.'

After a quick glance at him, Maddie stepped warily into the room. 'Thank you. I won't be long.'

Dante nodded and resumed his study of his great-great-grandfather but all his concentration had disappeared; instead he was keenly aware of every step Maddie took. Aware of the way she sized up the pictures, the focus on her face as she photographed the suitable ones, the swiftly hidden amusement at some of the more outlandish dresses. And he knew the exact moment she stopped in front of the portrait of Violetta he had commissioned for their wedding.

'She was beautiful, yes?' he said, not looking at either Maddie or the portrait.

'Very.' She paused. 'I'm sorry I couldn't help with your sister. Have you come up with a solution?'

'Not yet.' Dante took a deep breath as he turned and looked at Maddie—and at the portrait. The two women couldn't have been more different, Violetta dark, her lush curves poured into a designer ball gown, her eyes proud, smile mocking, a stark contrast to Maddie's blonde slenderness and neat, efficient look. 'I'm sure I'll think of something.'

'Of course. I'm sure you will.' Maddie turned away, heading back to the door before stopping and swivelling to look back at him. 'It's just… I can't help wondering why you lied to her in the first place. I get that you're close, that you don't want her to worry, but why does she care so much? I want my brother to be happy, of course I do, but I wouldn't fuss him to the stage where he started propositioning random employees to lie to me and pretend they were in a relationship.'

Put like that, the whole scheme did sound a little insane—if you didn't know Luciana, that was.

'I'm sorry,' Maddie said quickly. 'As I said, really it's none of my business.'

But it was. Dante had made it her business when he had tried to involve her. And no matter what he told Luciana tomorrow, when she arrived at the *castello* and met Maddie her curiosity would be piqued. The name and description were a perfect match after all. Luciana would be bound to wonder why Dante had chosen this particular woman as the model for his pretend girlfriend, would be bound to come up with all kinds of crazy theories.

And they would be crazy. Wouldn't they?

Dante looked over at Maddie, cool and poised, her calm gaze fixed on him as she waited for an answer. Maddie was very attractive, of course. They had only just met. That was why she had been the first person to come to mind; there was no more to his choice than that.

He could see Luciana's mocking look as she took apart that explanation all too clearly. He was going to have to come up with a better reason than that.

'My sister introduced me to Violetta.' Dante saw the moment Maddie's glance flew to the portrait, watched her eyes soften, and he winced.

'I see.'

But of course she didn't. She probably believed, as so many others did, that his heart had died with his wife. That the reason he hadn't dated again, was still single five years later, was that no one could replace the beautiful young Contessa.

For some reason he didn't want Maddie to believe that. The truth might be uglier but it was real. 'I was only twenty-two.' It was like talking about someone else; Dante didn't even remember that carefree boy with the world at his feet. 'My father had recently died and I had inherited the title and half the family business. It was a lot to take on—and Luciana was about to move to New Zealand with her husband to help run his winery. My mother had already left for Switzerland and so all the family fortune was in my inexperienced hands. Luciana was worried about leaving me, insisted on spending all the time she had left in Italy with me—and that's when I met Violetta.'

He stepped closer to the portrait and gazed up at his wife, memories flooding him as he tried to sort out the truth from the fictions—the fictions she had woven, fictions he'd willingly believed. 'She was several years older than me—our paths would probably never have crossed if it weren't for Luciana. But when they did...' He closed his eyes briefly. 'Violetta got pregnant very quickly. It wasn't planned, but of course I offered to marry her.' It wasn't just an offer; he'd jumped at the opportunity. It wasn't until much later that he'd begun to wonder just how much of an accident the pregnancy had been.

'We didn't know each other very well, not in all the ways a husband and wife should know each other before they make their vows. The truth is it wasn't a very successful marriage.' Dante winced at the understatement of the century. 'Apart from Arianna, of course. I can't—I *don't*—regret anything that resulted in my daughter; Luciana knows this. She feels responsible and nothing I say changes that.'

Maddie took another step forward, until she was almost close enough to touch, close enough so that Dante could see the concern in her grey eyes. 'But I still don't understand why you need to pretend to be in a relationship—with me or anyone. I mean, you're tall, dark and not too horrendous to look at. You seem to have all your own teeth—and what have I forgotten? Oh, yes, you're rich, titled and own a castle; you're a great dad. Surely nice, compatible women must be queuing up around the block. If you're not still in love with your wife then what is stopping you from dating any of those women? You'd get your sister off your back and have some fun while you're at it. Why go to all this subterfuge?'

'I drove my wife away. That's why she died. Arianna is without a mother because of me and she has to come first. I have no time and no inclination to pursue any kind of relationship.' Dante snapped his mouth closed. He'd said too much. He swallowed, moderating his tone with some effort. 'My sister has been unwell. I didn't want her upsetting herself further about me or Arianna. But it was wrong of me to lie, wrong of me to drag you into it. Please accept my apologies.'

Maddie looked up at the portrait again. Violetta Falcone had been a stunning woman, all fire and passion and pride. No wonder the Conte had fallen so hard for her. And how could she fault him for lying to make his sister happy? Maddie understood all about family pressure; after all, she had spent so much of her life trying to make her parents happy, to get their approval.

She'd finally realised that nothing that fulfilled her would satisfy them, that they couldn't see past their own small, narrow world and wanted her contained within it. Dante's lies came from love. How could she fault him for that? All she had ever wanted was unconditional love. It had taken almost marrying a man who *didn't* love her for her to realise that.

Dante wasn't asking for a lifetime. He wanted a mere week.

And would a week with him be such a terrible thing?

She slid a glance his way. His lips were pressed together, expression shuttered, as if he hadn't just confided in her in a way she suspected the proud Conte seldom confided in anyone. Her stomach tumbled as she took him in. The expanse of olive skin exposed at his throat, the sharp cheekbones, the sensuous curve of his mouth. Maddie swallowed, desire pulsing through her. No. Spending more time with Dante Falcone wouldn't be that terrible at all.

She had told herself that she would never be anyone's convenient relationship again. But the Conte needed her. Maybe not physically or emotionally, but he still needed her. And she needed to step out of her hiding place sooner rather than later. Out of her comfort zone. To confront her fears—and her desire.

Maddie took a deep breath. 'A plane ticket.' To her surprise her voice was strong, even though she quivered at the thought of the deal she was about to propose.

Dante's brows shot up.

'And overtime. Double time for any time I spend with you and your sister. But no one here must know what we are doing. I don't want any gossip or speculation and it wouldn't be fair for your daughter to think we were dating. So you need to tell your sister that we are keeping things quiet for now because we are seeing where things are going. Those are my terms.' Maddie's heart hammered as she spoke. What on earth was she doing? Could she really handle a week in Dante Falcone's company?

'Why have you changed your mind?' His glance was sharp, penetrating, as if he could see straight through her, to that pathetic need to be wanted, to be needed.

Maddie straightened her shoulders. This was different. He *did* need her—which meant she held all the cards. 'Because I realised that this could be a mutually beneficial deal. And because, although I don't think you should have lied to your sister, I understand why you did. Your motives were good.'

'She arrives tomorrow.'

'Then we'd better get our stories straight—if my terms are acceptable.'

'Very acceptable.' He held out his hand and, after an infinitesimal pause, Maddie took it. His fingers closed around hers, strong and sure, his touch scalding through her body.

Did she really believe she held all the cards? Suddenly she wasn't so sure. 'Good. That's decided.' She stepped back, her hand cold, empty as she loosened it from his. 'What next?'

'Next we need to get our stories straight, to decide on how we met, what we were wearing, what we spoke about—believe me, we must have every detail agreed; there is nothing so small my sister won't want to know.'

The enormity of what she had agreed to shivered through her. This wasn't just about having a few friendly chats with Dante's sister. This was about pretending to be falling in love. Something she knew nothing about. 'Then we had better schedule a meeting.' The business-like term was reassuring. She could do business.

'A meeting sounds delightful.' Maddie's eyes narrowed at the amusement in the Conte's voice. 'But maybe a little formal in light of the situation? Let me take you out for dinner somewhere away from here and we can talk properly there. Where do you prefer? Riva? Milan? We could even make it to Verona for the evening if we leave soon. Or do you prefer the mountain restaurants? The trattoria in the next valley is very good, but we are more likely to be recognised there. We could go a few valleys over; have you been to the Russo Leone? It used to be very good and it's a little more discreet.'

'I haven't been to any of those places. I actually haven't left San Tomo yet...' Maddie's voice trailed off as Dante fixed her with an incredulous expression.

'Scuzi?'

'The food at the *castello* is so good, I usually eat here, or cook for myself. Occasionally I go out to the *ristorante* in the village. I just haven't had a chance to explore further afield.'

'But you've been here for, what, nine months?'

'Ten.'

'But what do you do on your days off?'

She cringed a little inside at the shock in his voice. 'I don't really have days off.'

Dante stared at Maddie, but she couldn't meet his eyes. 'We overwork you so much?'

'No, no, I just like to make sure everything is okay. I may have a slight tendency to control-freakery.'

'A *slight* tendency?'

She scowled. 'Okay. I am a complete control freak, but that's what these brides need. Someone here all the time so every niggle is smoothed out straight away. They expect me to be on call twenty-four hours a day while they are here…'

'And on the two days in between?'

'The next bride usually needs a lot of reassurance in the forty-eight hours leading up to her wedding,' she said defensively. 'I'm not in the office *all* the time. I go for walks. Read a book…'

'Madeleine, why are you here?'

'I told you. To save up, to get away…'

'You came to Italy for that, but surely you could have saved more and quicker if you'd stayed at home.'

Of course she could have. Dante paid her well—but she had elected not to live in the castle and even with her frugal, hard-working lifestyle that made it harder to save enough to start her travels. The overtime and plane ticket she had agreed with Dante would be a welcome addition to her savings. Maddie lifted her chin and finally met his keen gaze. 'I needed to get away, to be somewhere new, to be someone different.'

His expression was all too understanding. 'You want to be somewhere different. You want to start your adventures and yet, *signorina*, you hide behind your work, not exploring anything this place has to offer. I wonder if it's the lack of a plane ticket holding you back from starting a new life, or whether it's you?' He inclined his head in a brief gesture of farewell. 'I'll pick you up in three hours. Dress smartly.'

Maddie didn't say a word as Dante smoothly negotiated the car around the mountain curves; she was still hearing the echoes of his earlier parting shot.

How *dared* he accuse her of holding back? He knew nothing about her.

But the truth of his words stung. She *was* scared. Scared that if she stripped away the purpose that had always fuelled her then there would be nothing left. That no one would notice her at all.

So maybe she should treat this week like an opportunity. At the end of it she would have her plane ticket and enough saved up to start her new life. Let this next week be a practice for her new life. Forget the old, dignified, playing by the rules Maddie and become the kind of person who saw every turn in the road as an opportunity.

Starting with the man sitting next to her, lean hands carelessly on the wheel, the flex in his muscles effortless as he manoeuvred the car through hairpin bends. Because, painfully insightful as he may have been about her, he had also revealed an equal amount about himself.

So his marriage had been no fairy tale? At least he had tried, had staked everything on love. The gamble might have failed, but as someone who had been about to walk, eyes wide open, into a marriage based on trust, friendship and convenience, how could Maddie blame anyone else for wanting more from their life? Better to risk it all and lose than never to risk at all.

But when Dante Falcone lost he just walked away, closing himself off from love and hope like some mythical beast, hiding behind his castle walls. So afraid that his sister or that anyone would see his vulnerabilities that he preferred to pay for a temporary girlfriend than admit his fallibility.

But Maddie had seen a crack in his walls that day by the lake. Not just in the way he had responded, the way he had looked at her, but in the way he had needled her, provoked her afterwards.

She had got under his skin.

A smile curved her mouth. *She had got under his skin*. Of course she had. Why else would he have used her face, her name, for his imaginary girlfriend?

And, she admitted, he had got under hers. Otherwise why would she have agreed to this insanity? The plane ticket and overtime would ensure she could leave at the end of the summer, sure. But was it really the money— or was it the game that had tempted her?

She'd never had the opportunity to play before.

Here was her chance and she had nothing to lose.

Lost in her thoughts, Maddie barely noticed her surroundings until Dante manoeuvred the car around the last hairpin bend and the glory of Lake Garda was spread out below: impossibly blue, ringed with mountains, ancient villages perched high above or clinging to the water's edge. Maddie was incredibly fond of their own lake, but, biased as she was, she had to admit that San Tomo paled into insignificance beside this awe-inspiring expanse of water. She sat forward, eagerly taking in every detail as they drove the last few miles towards the lake and the buzzing town of Riva, with its cobbled streets and cosmopolitan air. Why had she kept herself hidden away in her valley like some kind of lesser-tressed Rapunzel when all this was on her doorstep?

To Maddie's surprise, Dante bypassed the road to Riva, sweeping past the turn-off, heading instead towards a small harbour right at the very head of the lake. He pulled into a small car park and, before Maddie had a chance to even gather her thoughts, her car door was opened for her and a young man in a smart white nauti-

cal uniform inclined his head as he helped her step out
of the low-slung sports car.

She looked around, glad to be standing on her own
two feet, her stomach a little uneasy after the fast, curving drive despite Dante's expert handling of the vehi-
cle. They were standing in a small glade. A short path
cut through the trees leading to a wooden jetty where a
beautiful small yacht was moored. Another young man
in the same white uniform stood on the deck, busily coil-
ing ropes in a way that looked competently nautical to
her inexperienced eyes. She looked questioningly up at
Dante as he joined her.

'I didn't want our conversation to be overheard,' he
said by way of curt explanation, and then he smiled, that
same sudden smile which had so comprehensively dis-
armed her before. 'Besides, you said you hadn't explored
the area. What better way to see the lake than to be *on*
the lake? We have several hours before it gets dark yet.
The sunset is incredible viewed from the water.'

There was nothing she could say to this apart from
'thank you' and within ten minutes Maddie found herself seated on a comfortable padded bench on one side
of a table set for two as the yacht cast off, edging out
onto the still evening lake. Small flotillas were making
their way into shore, pleasure cruisers processing in a
stately fashion up and down the lake and other yachts
and boats could be seen dotting the lake as far as Maddie could see.

'This is lovely,' she said, accepting a Bellini with a
smile at the waiter and took the handwritten menu he
was proffering her. And it was. Even with the artificial-
ity and awkwardness of the situation, some of the cares
Maddie carried with her twenty-four hours a day seemed

suddenly not to be quite so important. So the Hathaway dress hadn't arrived yet? So the chef was threatening to take his leave during the Johnson nuptials, offended by the amount of dietary requirements emailed in? So the Lastinghams needed four-hour extra staff to ensure the bride's warring parents were never left alone at any time during their five-day stay? It would work out. It always did. And after all, they were only weddings—it was the marriage that counted and only the couple at the heart of all the frivolity and flounce had any sway over that.

For the first few moments they talked sparingly, comments confined to their menu choices, the beauty of the landscape and the elegance of the yacht, but once they had both ordered and the waiters had refilled their glasses and set olives and tiny bruschetta topped with fresh tomato, peppers and anchovies in front of them, Maddie knew it was time to step up a gear or two.

'Okay,' she said after she'd popped a bruschetta into her mouth, almost swooning at the perfect balance of garlic, salt, olive and tangy tomato. 'Let's do this.'

Dante leaned back in his seat, one hand curved elegantly around his glass, eyes gleaming with amusement—and an interest that Maddie could feel zapping right through her body all the way down to her toes. '*Bene*. Why don't you start? Tell me about yourself.'

Maddie took a long sip of her drink before setting her glass down and regarding Dante. 'A one-woman monologue on the origins of Madeleine Fitzroy? That doesn't sound like much fun for either of us. Let's make this a little more interesting. How about we play twenty questions? I ask you five questions, anything I want. And you can ask me five in turn. But we have to be prepared to answer our own questions…'

'Any questions?' The gleam in his eyes had intensified and Maddie reached for her glass, needing the support of a task, any task, to give her a reason to break eye contact, which seemed suddenly more intense than she could handle.

'As long as you're prepared to answer the same question honestly,' she said as coolly as possible.

For an impossibly long moment the Conte simply looked at her, his blue eyes unreadable, and then, just as the tension had risen to an almost unbearable pitch, he nodded. '*Si*. I agree. So, my first question. Have you ever been in love?'

# CHAPTER FIVE

MADDIE STARED. HAD she *what*?

First off, this was an unfair question because hadn't Dante Falcone already told her that he'd been besotted with his wife, so he was one up on her already? Secondly, she'd expected that they would start off with where they were born and favourite colours—innocuous warm-up questions; not go straight in for the million-dollar round.

And, thirdly, she wasn't sure of the answer.

'I…' She stopped and took another sip of the Bellini, her mind racing. She was twenty-six years old; she had been engaged to be married. But had she ever been in love? Infatuated? Besotted?

But she knew she was prevaricating. There was only one honest answer.

Maddie put the drink down and looked over at Dante. 'No. I've never been in love. The nearest I came was a crush on my ski instructor when I was at finishing school—but we all had crushes on our ski instructors; it was a rite of passage. Actually Daisy Anstruther-Jones married hers. It was a fearful scandal, but they're still married, she had twins last year and they run a ski school just outside Geneva, so really it all worked out for the best for her.'

She tried not to sigh. Lucky Daisy. Maddie had envied her even then, despite the gossip and thinking eighteen was very young for such a commitment. Daisy hadn't cared that Matt didn't have a trust fund or a title or connections— she had ignored all her family's pleas and threats and followed her heart. If only Maddie's heart had ever felt so sure about anything or anyone.

'And did your ski instructor return your feelings?'

Maddie raised her eyebrows. 'Is that one of your questions? Either way I don't reply to another question until you answer yours. Have *you* ever been in love?'

She thought she knew the answer, but Dante didn't reply and the silence went on and on until he said just one, bleak word. 'No.'

'Oh.'

'I thought I was. But the woman I loved didn't exist. I had no idea who Violetta was, not truly. I fell for a face and a façade. So, no. Never. And yet…' He took a sip of his drink. 'It felt real. A reminder that romantic love can't be trusted. I won't make that mistake again.'

Maddie was beginning to regret her impulsive suggestion of a game; it was all getting too dark far too soon. Too real. With a relief she looked up and saw the waiter approaching, their first courses on a gleaming silver tray, and she waited until her *risotto al funghi* had been placed before her before speaking.

'I'm sorry. I know what's it like to be engaged to someone you're not in love with—but I can't imagine how much more difficult it is to be married and in the same situation. It must have been very lonely.'

Dante's eyes met hers, surprise and relief mingling in their depths. 'That's exactly what it was. Very lonely—

loneliness compounded with the knowledge that I was a fool.'

'You were twenty-two, weren't you? If you can't make mistakes in your early twenties, when can you? And at least you have the excuse of *thinking* you were in love. You were brave enough to make the leap. That has to count for something.'

'And you? How did you manage to get engaged without love? And yes, this is my second question.'

Maddie picked up a fork and prodded her risotto, the rich aroma a little less enticing than it had been a few moments ago. 'If I was ever in love with anything it wasn't a person—it was a place. My home. It's like nowhere else, hidden in the middle of the rolling Downs, surrounded by forests and gardens and fields—most of the abbey was torn down by Henry VIII, but the old refectory is part of the house and the ruins can be seen all about the gardens. I spent my childhood playing on them the way other children play on swings and climbing frames. But, as I told you, my brother is to inherit even though he was never interested in running a big estate, and when I turned twenty-three my mother made it clear that I needed to find a home of my own, even after I'd turned the estate around, started to make a profit for the first time in decades.'

She fell silent as she scooped up a portion of the risotto, the rich, aromatic flavours going a little way to unravel the knot in her stomach. 'Anyway, to cut a long, dull story short, I went to stay with my godparents— my godfather had just been diagnosed with severe heart problems and his wife was finding it hard to cope—and so I just took over there. Flintock Hall is set on a large estate just like the abbey and even though they didn't open to the public there were still tenants and staff and estate managers to deal with. And I did. It meant Lady Navenby could concentrate on her husband and their son, Theo, could stay in London and work. He came back at weekends though and we spent a lot of time together.' Her voice trailed off and she summoned up her best social smile as she glanced over at the silent Dante.

'I'm not sure who thought of marriage first, although I know Theo's mother was very keen on the match. And as Lord Navenby's health weakened he began to worry about the succession. He wanted to know Theo was safe and happy before he died, that there would be an heir to the Earldom, that his name would continue. Somehow it just became common knowledge, became assumed that I would marry Theo, provide the heir, and in return I would get the home I needed. That's how it's done, right? We trade our fortunes, our lineage for a title and a home. Tale older than time. Then, one night, when Lord Navenby was in hospital and fading fast, we were told he only had days, not weeks. We were in shock. He'd seemed to rally a little, so we weren't expecting... Anyway, emotions were running high and when Theo drove me back to the hall he kissed me for the first time. For comfort, I think. If there were no fireworks, well, it wasn't horrid either. And then he asked me to marry him. I wasn't coerced into it. It made so much sense; the fact we didn't love each other seemed irrelevant. We liked each other well enough.'

'So what happened?'

'We got right to the wedding day. I was in a white dress, the marquees were set up, guests had arrived— we got all the way to the altar. And it hit me. Just what I was doing. That my whole life would be one long, even plane. No passion. No huge unhappiness either, possibly, but no huge joy. Every day the same. That I was selling myself short. I just couldn't do it. No house, no security was worth a lifetime of polite existence with someone who merely liked me. I'd spent my childhood living like that. I knew I wanted more. And,' she added, forking up another scoop of risotto, 'it turned out he was in love with someone else anyway; he was just too much of a gentleman to jilt me so close to the wedding.'

'You got all the way to the altar and called it off?' Dante's expression was full of admiration and it warmed Maddie through to see it. She was so used to being an object of pity or amusement. No one had ever admired her impulsive action before. 'That took some courage.'

The hard shell with which Maddie had encased herself ever since her wedding cracked a little and she blinked back sudden, hot tears. 'I just couldn't say vows I didn't mean, pledge myself to a man who wanted *what* I was, not who I was. Even though I think it was the only time my mother had ever really been proud of me...' She stopped, embarrassed at having revealed so much. 'Anyway. There was quite a lot of publicity—Theo is an Earl and successful in his own right, and my dad is a Baron; the family has links going back to the Norman Conquest. It doesn't mean anything, not really, but the gossip papers and blogs loved the whole blue-blooded nonsense. They called me the Runaway Bride and followed me everywhere until I came here.'

'So *that's* why you came here? Why you've barely left the valley?'

'I know it seems silly. I wasn't that famous. The publicity was more of an inconvenience, an embarrassment, than anything really serious. But I liked the anonymity I found here. Liked being out of sight and out of mind. The only thing is, Theo is getting married in a few weeks—and this wedding will definitely go ahead. It might stir things up again. That's why I want to get on with the next stage in my plans and leave Europe altogether sooner rather than later. Just disappear for a while.'

Maddie waited until the waiter had taken away her risotto, replacing it with the chicken she had ordered, served with fresh sautéed vegetables and a delicious-looking sauce before she spoke again, glad of the opportunity to turn the conversation to lighter topics. 'My question, I think. If you could have any superpower, what would it be and why?'

Dante blinked, his fork, half-filled with his own meal, arrested halfway to his mouth. 'My what?'

'Superpower. That's my first question.'

'To read minds. To know what people are really thinking beyond the words and the smiles.' His own smile was grim and Maddie knew he was thinking of Violetta. So much for lighter conversation.

'I don't think I would want to know what's in people's heads. Too much information in every way. I would want to fly. Then I wouldn't need to wait for a plane ticket, I could just take off and land anywhere.'

'The flyaway bride, not the runaway bride?'

The joke was so unexpected that Maddie could only stare in disbelief before breaking into a grin as she imagined the scenario. 'My veil billowing out behind me? My mother would have been even more furious than she already was—that veil was antique lace! Okay, another one. What animal would you be if you could turn into any animal at all?'

Dante leaned back, his eyes narrowed in amusement,

*that* smile back on his face. Maddie tried not to let her gaze linger on his mouth, glad that he couldn't actually read her mind as she followed every curve of his lips, the finely sculpted lines of his austerely handsome face. 'A falcon, *naturalmente*. According to family legend, my ancestor could indeed turn into a bird of prey, to spy on his enemies.'

'Handy party trick.'

'And you?'

'Right now a sloth sounds pretty appealing. I've never known how to just stop and relax; maybe it would be good to have some enforced downtime in the sun.'

'Interesting choice. Are sloths on your list of things to see?'

'Pretty much at the top,' Maddie admitted. 'I'm planning to go west, not east, head to the US, work my way right through Central America—via the sloths—into South America.'

'Intrepid.'

'I haven't done it yet.' There was a world's difference in planning and doing. Maddie knew that all too well. There were so many things she had never done: slept in a tent or a hostel—although she had survived boarding school—carried her belongings on her back, cooked over a campfire, worked in a bar, travelled by bus. She could plan to her heart's content, download itineraries and timetables, but taking that first step—that had still to be proven. She still had to summon up the courage to put a lifetime of wanting to be needed, to be occupied, of proving herself through service behind her and just live for the moment.

Maddie eyed the man opposite. She doubted Dante Falcone ever allowed himself to live for the moment either. Never allowed himself a single impulsive decision since the day he had fallen for a woman he never really knew at all. Not until he lied to his sister and pretended that he was in a relationship with Maddie herself. She had to learn to be free—it was a lesson he could do with as well.

Over the rest of the excellent dinner Dante found out that Maddie's favourite colour was cobalt-blue and, after some thought, decided his was the exact shade of brown of his daughter's eyes. He admitted a teenage dream to become an artist, while Maddie explained she had agreed to attend the Swiss finishing school because her parents allowed her to sign up for an online business and marketing course at the same time. 'Girls like me have two choices,' she'd said as they waited for their tiramisu to be served. 'The brainy ones go to Oxford and Cambridge or somewhere with a decent helping of People Like Us: Bristol, Edinburgh, St Andrew's, of course, and make connections to help them in their high-powered careers, whilst the really forward-thinking ones bag a husband at the same time. The less brainy go to finishing schools and learn to make a decent *cordon bleu* meal and put on a dinner party; or they take a secretarial course and get a PA job in the City *or* look superior in a Chelsea art gallery until *they* bag a husband. It's all still very 1950s. My parents had no idea what to do with a daughter who just wanted to learn about return on investment and profit margins, so we compromised. Not for the first time.'

Over the excellent tiramisu they had each chosen their desert island books—the *Aeneid* for Dante, *Pride and Prejudice* for Maddie—and their desert island music. His a live recording of *La Bohème* from La Scala and

Maddie, after much agonising, had decided, to his equal
agony, on her own personal Taylor Swift playlist.

'So,' Maddie said when they had established their favourite places and chosen their final meals, 'I call that
a success—I think we know a reasonable amount about
each other now. Enough for people who have only known
each other for a few weeks anyway.'

Dante couldn't help but agree. Disconcerting as Maddie's game had been at the beginning, it had actually
been fun to try and decide whether he would want a
classic steak or a really good plate of pasta for a last
meal and to listen to why Maddie thought Costa Rica
was her perfect place, even though she hadn't been there
yet. In fact he didn't remember being as relaxed or entertained since…well, since his father had died, his sister had moved away and he had assumed the mantle of
the Falcone empire.

Even when it was just he and Arianna together he
found it hard to relax. He had to be father and mother
both, confidant and tutor, indulgent parent and strict
teacher. Good cop and bad cop. And this was the easy
stage—her teen years were getting ever closer, with all
the worry they were bound to bring.

'Agreed. I still don't know how any civilised person
could want baked beans for their last meal…'

'On white buttered toast!'

'Nor do I see the attraction of a creature that sleeps
the whole time, but I will try and read *Pride and Prejudice*. Or,' he amended, 'I will watch the film.'

'No, the television series. You need to be completely
absorbed in it.'

'Maybe,' he said cautiously, not wanting to commit
himself to too many hours watching English people

drink tea and dance at balls. 'Shall we take our coffees
and go and sit at the prow of the boat? The sun will set
soon and the view should be quite spectacular.'

Maddie nodded assent and got up from the table.
Dante took a minute to admire her long, coltish legs,
displayed to advantage in the short full skirt of her silver dress, her arms bared by the thin straps, hair loose
and flowing down her back. She was, he had to admit,
looking magnificent, all tanned limbs and tousled hair.
He followed her to the front of the yacht and stood beside her as she leaned on the ship rail, looking out over
the water to the mountains and the reddening sun. The
deckhands had cleared their plates and melted silently
away, the captain out of sight in the cabin above. It was
as if they were all alone on the wide lake under the pink-
streaked sky and suddenly, despite the freshness of the
evening air all around them, Dante's lungs constricted,
his chest tightening. It was a setting made for romance—
but he was done with romance. This evening was all
about business and all the jokes and dreams they'd shared
didn't change that.

'How long does your sister think we've been dating?'

There, Maddie felt it too. That need to keep the conversation businesslike in such seductive surroundings.

'Less than a month. We are at a very early stage in
our relationship. I haven't been to the *castello* since last
summer, Luciana knows that, but there is no reason we
couldn't have met for meetings in Milan.'

'Hmm.' She wrinkled her nose as she turned to him,
and Dante couldn't look away from its perfect pertness.
'I've already told you I have never been in love. Before
Theo I dated several very nice, very acceptable men but
quite frankly would much rather have been planning a

new pathway through the wood or organising an event than spend too much time exchanging sweet nothings with them. And they felt the same—I was more of a useful trophy, someone to stand at the side of a rugby match and cheer or a decorative escort to social events they couldn't avoid rather than someone they couldn't stop thinking about. But I've seen people falling in love...'

'And?'

'And they're nauseating. Always touching, always looking for each other or at each other or deeply into one another's eyes.' For all her humour there was a wistfulness in Maddie's voice that spoke to Dante, a yearning he understood all too well. A yearning to be understood, to be wanted, to be loved.

A yearning he never intended to fill again. That want was all too seductive—and couldn't be trusted.

'Not everyone.'

'No, and of course we are trying to be discreet.' Maddie turned and took a step closer to him. She was a tall woman and the heels she wore added another two inches to her height, but Dante could still look down onto the top of her golden head—until, that was, she looked up at him and he was lost in the grey depths of her eyes. Were those silver flecks he could see?

'Discreet,' Dante agreed, not capable of doing much more than parroting the word. How could one step make such a difference—one step and a glance? One moment they had been standing side by side in a perfectly calm way, having a perfectly rational conversation—and yes, he had noticed how attractive she was; he was still in the prime of life after all. And yes, he had discovered that he liked Madeleine Fitzroy, admired her sense of humour and obvious intelligence, despite her taste in music and food, and *that*, considering the week they had ahead of them, was all to the good. But now he couldn't tear his eyes away from her upturned face, his gaze moving with difficulty from hers, only to stutter to a stop as he reached the pink lushness of her mouth. Now the attraction had cranked up a gear or ten and Dante suddenly found it hard to catch his breath.

'But your sister is going to be looking for those signs that even discreet people can't help displaying. The looks, the odd touches here and there. The kisses.' Her mouth parted on the last word and Dante swayed forward, just a little, like a bee scenting nectar.

Maddie's scent enveloped him, floral with hints of citrus adding a refreshing bite. He was almost dizzy with the intoxicating scent, with the pink of her mouth, with her nearness.

'That complicates things a little.' Now it was his turn to take a step closer, so close they were almost—almost—touching. So close he knew another millimetre would bring their bodies into alignment. 'I think we need to be prepared.'

'Prepared?' Now she was the one repeating his words to him and when Dante dragged his gaze back to meet hers he couldn't help but feel a primal satisfaction at the glazed look in her eyes, at the way her tongue darted over her plump lips, the way she swayed ever nearer...

'We should practise. Looking like we're falling in love. Maybe with a little touching...' and he ran one finger lightly down her cheek and along the silken line of her mouth. Maddie's eyes fluttered shut and it took all Dante's resolve not to pull her to him, crush her against him and taste her.

But this was a business contract and, for all the pheromones clouding the air, for all his blood was thundering around his body, it had to be a meeting in the middle. One step by him, one step by her, mutually agreeable terms.

'That makes sense,' Maddie breathed, leaning her cheek against his touch like a cat seeking adulation. 'Practice makes perfect after all.' She slipped her arm around his waist, her hand splaying on his back, and Dante could feel the imprint of every finger clearly through the thin cotton of his shirt. Slowly, so slowly it took everything he had not to groan, she raised herself on tiptoe and pressed one light, teasing kiss on his mouth.

Dante froze at the warm contact, as electricity zapped straight through him. What was he doing? He'd known this girl had fire the second they had connected across the lake and yet here he was, allowing himself to be burned, allowing her heat to melt the ice that encased him and kept him safe.

He should step back; their point was well and truly made. They needed to remember to act like lovers.

But was there any real difference between acting like lovers and *being* lovers? When they both knew the score?

'Maybe we should practise a little more.' Was that his voice? So ragged? So hoarse? Dante didn't want to think, to dwell, to analyse a moment longer. Instead he stepped back, away from her touch and slowly, deliberately, walked behind Maddie, sweeping her long length of hair aside. He took his time, kissing his way down the column of her throat, savouring the tang of her skin, exultation running through him as she leaned against him, a sigh escaping her parted lips. His hands moved to her bare shoulders, his fingertips running up and down her upper arms, enjoying the feel of her skin under his.

'You taste so good,' he whispered in her ear and felt her shiver at his words.

'Dante, I…' She captured his hands with hers and turned, eyes luminous in the approaching twilight. 'I can't. Not here. Not on the deck. Anyone could walk up at any time.'

She was right. He should signal to the captain to turn the boat around, to make their way back to shore, drive her back to her apartment, drop her off and then do his best to sleep this intoxication off. He should—and he would. If that was what she wanted. '*Si*. Of course…' He swallowed, knowing he was too close to making himself vulnerable. 'There's a suite. On the boat. We don't have to return to shore until I say. Until you say. If you want…'

'A suite?'

'Just a few steps away.'

Maddie smiled then, soft and seductive and yet a little shy. 'Then what are we waiting for? I believe we have a lot more practising to do yet, *signor*.'

# CHAPTER SIX

MADDIE COULD HARDLY believe her own daring as she allowed Dante to take her hand and lead her down the short staircase into the boat's interior. She, Madeleine Fitzroy, had never, ever engaged in this kind of impulsive, wild behaviour before. There had been nothing urgent or desperate about her past relationships—they hadn't been unpleasant, but the best word to describe her past experiences was 'nice'. At twenty-six she was more than ready to graduate from nice to amazing.

And somehow she sensed tonight was the night.

Maybe it was the way every touch made her shiver. Maybe it was the gleam of intent in Dante's cool blue gaze. Maybe it was the curve of his mouth and the promise inherent in his smile. Maybe it was the deep yearning low in her stomach, a sweet ache in her breasts, a need to touch and be touched that was so strong it overpowered any other thought.

Or maybe it was because Dante was right when he had accused her of hiding. Maddie had left her home, her country, everything she knew in order to reinvent herself. But getting on the flight had been the limit of her impulsiveness. Once she had reached Italy she had hidden behind a laptop for ten months, living vicariously through other people's dreams and hopes and desires. No more.

She needed to reach for what she wanted. No more sleeping through her own life like the sloths she was so desperate to see. No more allowing other people to make decisions for her, going along with the status quo because it was safe and easy and she knew her role was to keep things smooth. No more pouring all her desire and passion into ancient buildings that didn't even belong to her and would still be standing long after she was gone. No. She wanted an adventure, right? Well, she was starting right here. Right now.

Being adventurous—*being* an adventuress.

She barely noticed the short corridor, all her focus on the feel of Dante's hand in hers, the breadth of his shoulders, the promise in his stride. They reached a polished wood door and Dante opened it, gesturing her inside. 'I am just going to call the captain and ask him to sail and dock in Desenzano—if that's all right with you. The staff all live near there. They can return in the morning and sail us back to Riva.'

Maddie turned at that. 'They won't mind if we stay on board?'

'Why would they?' Dante raised an eyebrow. 'The boat belongs to me. Paolo, the captain, and his nephew work for me full-time.'

He kept a fully staffed boat on Lake Garda even though he stayed in the region for just a couple of months every year? Just how rich was Dante Falcone? Money didn't impress Maddie—after all, one of her cousins owned a good third of Scotland and another had married an oil tycoon and lived in the kind of lavish luxury last seen in an eighties soap opera. Maddie herself had been brought up in the kind of aristocratic gentility that found an excess of money a little vulgar. But despite herself she couldn't help being a little impressed by the extravagance.

Dante strode over to an intercom panel on the wall and after pressing a button began to speak in low, rapid Italian. Maddie took a deep breath, taking advantage of his momentary distraction to look around at her surroundings—and to clear her head a little.

Maddie hadn't been on many boats before; those she had been on had certainly been comfortable, bordering on luxurious—but they didn't compare to this. Dante had brought her into a suite to rival any five-star hotel. She stood in a sumptuously outfitted sitting room, the dark wood of the polished floor echoed by the panelling on the walls. The outside wall was all glass, offering breathtaking views out onto the sunset-lit lake beyond. A vast white sofa curved around, facing a cinema-style screen on the wall, the screen flanked by recessed bookshelves. A glossy desk took up the corner, the laptop already set up, showing this was a place where Dante came to work as well as play.

The door behind the sofa was half-open and Maddie could see an equally big room, this one dominated by a huge bed. She swallowed at the sight of it. She wasn't in this room for a tour of the boat's interior. She was down here because of that bed. Her legs were suddenly a little wobbly, her palms dampening at the realisation. Could she really be about to spend the night with a man she barely knew?

'Second thoughts?'

She jumped as Dante's low voice reverberated through her. She hadn't heard him walk up behind her.

'No... I...' But of *course* she was having second thoughts. Maddie so desperately wanted to be someone else, someone new, but making the jump was so much harder than she had anticipated.

And yet...the one time she had been really impulsive, the one time she had listened to the screaming of her heart, not the sensible drum in her head, she had called off her wedding. She hadn't cared about the scandal, or the 'spectacle' she had made of herself—according to her mother. She had just gone with everything her body and her soul were telling her. And it had been absolutely the right thing to do.

'Maddie. It's fine. We can...'

Reaching up, Maddie laid one finger on Dante's lips and watched with satisfaction as he swallowed, his pupils dilating at her touch. 'We can what? You're not backing out on me, are you, Conte Falcone?'

'No.' The low word was almost a growl, igniting a fire in Maddie's belly as Dante stepped close, one hand slipping around to caress the nape of her neck. Maddie shivered as his skilled fingers brushed her skin, the memory of his kisses in that very spot still reverberating through her body. He brushed his other hand down her cheek and she closed her eyes to better lose herself in the gentle caress, swaying closer, her whole body aching in anticipation until finally—finally—his mouth descended on hers and she fell willingly and wholly into his embrace.

His kiss was soft—at first—tantalising Maddie with the promise of heat. Emboldened, she finally allowed her hands to explore the muscles and planes of his back and torso, skimming over his shirt, searching for a way through the cloth frustrating her need for skin on skin. His own touch remained provokingly light, one hand caressing her neck, the other at her waist, his fingers stroking from the curve of her hip to the bottom of her ribcage but no further. Maddie's breasts ached with the need for that touch to reach them and with a low moan she pressed herself closer, grabbing Dante's shirt to pull it out of his waistband, purring with satisfaction as she finally felt hot skin under her fingertips. With a primal satisfaction she felt him quiver at her touch, heard his breathing speed up as his kiss intensified. Maddie held on as tight as she could, losing herself in heat, in sensation, in want and need. She had never felt like this before. This wild, this uninhibited. She wanted to touch, to taste him everywhere; she didn't want him to stop touching her.

She was barely conscious of their movement as Dante, still kissing her as if she was the most desirable woman in the world, slowly walked her through the door into the bedroom. The large bed was no longer intimidating; it was exactly what she wanted, what she needed. Dante was who she wanted, who she needed. They had one night. She intended to make the most of every single moment.

'Morning, sleepyhead.'

Maddie stirred, opening one eye to see sunlight streaming in through the window. With a shock she realised she hadn't been aware when they had docked, when the crew had left. All she had known was sensation and moans and desire.

She automatically reached up and smoothed her hair, desperately trying to think of the right expression to say *'Well, thank you for a lovely evening and a rather sensational night; now let's never speak about it again*

*because if I have to work with you and remember the
things you did to me—and the way I responded—I may
never be able to look you in the eye again'.*

'Morning,' she said instead.

'I've been out and got you a coffee and some pastries.
Your phone has been buzzing away as well.' Dante put
a cup of coffee and a bag filled with tiny, flaky pastries
onto the bedside table and dropped Maddie's phone onto
the bed.

'Thank you.' She sat up slowly, one hand gripping the
sheet, making sure it covered as much of her as possible.
The problem with being adventurous was that she hadn't
bought any night things, any spare underwear—all she
had was a strappy silver dress. If Dante drove her back
to the castle, make-up smeared under her eyes, hair tan-
gled and in that dress, she might as well hang a banner
from her window that said 'Yes. I slept with my boss'.

The coffee smelt amazing but Maddie reached for her
phone first, her stomach churning as she saw the furiously flashing light which denoted messages. Her fingers were clumsy as she tried several times to unlock
her screen with her fingerprint, giving up and punching
her code in instead, smothering a curse as she mistyped
the numbers, eventually managing to bring up her messages. Ten missed calls, as many emails, all flagged important. Wiggling the sheet a little further up her body,
she pressed 'voicemail', all too aware of Dante leaning
against the wall, watching her.

The tension ratcheted up as she heard Guido's excited
tone, only to dissipate as his words sank in. Easing back
on her pillows, she listened to the rest of her messages
then quickly checked her emails.

'Everything okay?'

'Kind of. Tomorrow's guests aren't coming. They've called the wedding off.' Her voice wavered a little on the last word, memories of the manically unreal days after her own curtailed wedding resurfacing. 'Better now than later, I suppose. Don't worry. They've paid in full and there are no refunds at this stage.'

'So what does this mean for you?'

'I need to make sure everything they ordered has been cancelled. We don't need the ornate flower sculptures or the band or any of the excursions now. That's just a couple of hours' work though. It doesn't have much effect on me or the castle staff, apart from making this week a little easier, I suppose. I'll be answering queries from booked-in and prospective brides as usual, but we're all ready for the rest of the summer. All the food and decorations for the next couple of months have been agreed on and ordered, excursions booked in…' Her voice trailed off. Maddie was so used to juggling the dual demands of catering to the wedding party currently in situ with the organising for future brides that she wasn't sure how she would fill her time without half her workload.

'So you'll have some spare time?'

'Possibly,' Maddie agreed cautiously. 'Why?'

Dante's grin was pure wolf. 'Looks like you'll be earning that bonus and plane ticket after all. You can use those hostessing skills of yours to help me persuade my sister that I am more than capable of looking after myself so that, even when you've left and I have to admit to her that I am single once again, she won't worry about me or try and set me up with her friends.'

'I…'

But of course she had agreed to this proposition already and without work as a buffer there was no reason for her not to spend more time with Luciana—and by extension with Dante. 'Of course,' she agreed with as much dignity as was possible when she was wearing nothing but a sheet.

It was one thing to wear a sheet when they were both in similar stages of undress, but quite another when Dante was fully dressed—not in the formal shirt and trousers he had worn last night but the most casual clothes she had seen him in to date. Black jeans skimmed his hips before hugging powerful thighs in a way that made her muscles clench in physical memory of just how strong his legs were. He'd teamed the jeans with a soft grey T-shirt, the stubble on his chin combining with the relaxed clothes to give him a sexy morning vibe almost as intoxicating as the smartly dressed intensity of the evening before.

'Excellent. I'm picking Luciana up from Verona later today. Why don't we head there this morning and spend the day sightseeing before we meet her train?'

Why don't we *what*?

'I don't really have the right clothes for sightseeing. I wasn't expecting this.'

*This* was the best euphemism she could think of for the night they had shared, and her current state of undress. Dante's suggestion of a day together went well beyond their agreed parameters. But it was a suggestion Maddie was surprisingly keen to agree to, despite at least a hundred reasons why it was a bad idea. She fumbled for those reasons, not sure if she was trying to get out of the day or if she wanted Dante to talk her around. 'And I really need to get those cancellations done this morning. Besides, doesn't Arianna want to meet her aunt?'

Never over-egg with three excuses when you only need one. Dante's grin just grew a little more wolfish as Maddie talked on and he folded his arms as she finished, the picture of relaxed ease.

'The laptop on the desk is configured to the Falcone network, so after you have eaten your breakfast you can send all your emails easily. Meanwhile, I can go and purchase anything you need for the day. As for Arianna, she has made friends with a girl her age in San Tomo and has been invited to spend the day swimming with her and begged me to excuse her. Anything else?'

*Yes! My agreement is to pretend to your sister that we are in a relationship, not to spend the day in Verona— Verona, for goodness' sake, city of romance and doomed love—sightseeing after the best night of my life!*

Maddie hitched the sheet a little higher. Any higher and it would be a veil. She felt a little like the grandma peering out at the big bad wolf, unsure whether he was going to eat her up or not. And half wanting him to…
'We could go back to Riva and then head to Verona later to pick up your sister if that's easier.'

'We could, but you have never been to Verona. It's just a forty-minute drive from here, so why not take advantage of the opportunity to see it?'

'I agree it makes sense, but won't it complicate things?'

The look Dante shot her was bland. 'Complicate?'

'After last night.'

'It wasn't just last night,' he said softly and Maddie's body heated so quickly she was sure a neon glow could be seen shining through the sheet. 'I seem to remember this morning too…'

Dante watched Maddie with amusement. Last night's confident siren had faded away, the cool, poised, professional woman gone, replaced with an adorably confused and even more adorably tousled girl hiding behind a sheet, cheeks aflame.

'Maddie,' he said, low and coaxingly. All he wanted to do was stride over to the bed, take the phone from her hand and kiss her until all the doubts melted from her eyes. But that kind of persuasion wasn't in their agreement. Nor was he going to give in to that kind of instinct, that kind of lust and need and want.

But it still took everything he had to stay leaning against the wall, to keep his body relaxed, his face neutral. 'We can, of course, return to the *castello* if that's what you prefer. But the fates have gifted you with a week off. Why not take advantage of their kindness?'

'I'm just not sure spending any more time alone together is a good idea.'

'I see. You think we've had enough practice? Last night was enough?'

'Yes; no, I… Last night was amazing, but today I… Oh! See?' She sat up and glared indignantly at him. 'This is what I mean about complicating things.'

'Madeleine. It's only complicated if we let it be.' *Liar*, his body whispered.

'I know. The problem is…' She paused. 'Look. I wanted to—you know—last night. I've wanted to since that first day—and you have as well,' she added defiantly.

Dante didn't deny it—couldn't deny it. *'Si.'*

'So what now? What do we do all week? Pretend it didn't happen? Admit it did and chalk it up to a learning experience and be more careful next time? Or…?'

Dante was voting for *or*, whatever 'or' might turn out to be. 'I think you might be overthinking things, *cara*.'

The endearment slipped out before he could curb it. But luckily Maddie didn't seem to have noticed it. 'Maybe. I just want to know where we stand.'

'Maddie. You are a beautiful woman. We spent a very nice evening together, enjoying each other's company. We will be spending a great deal of time together this week, pretending that we are falling in love. Why not just enjoy the ride?'

She bit her lip and Dante couldn't tear his eyes away from the plump flesh, the neat indentation of her lip. 'You make it sound so easy.'

'That's because it is. By the end of the summer I will be back in Roma, you will be cuddling small bears covered in mould and these days will be just a memory. Why not make them a nice memory? And so here we are. With a beautiful day ahead of us. Where shall we spend it? Back in the *castello*, or shall we set our scene in fair Verona?'

'Don't misquote Shakespeare; it's not as if Romeo and Juliet ended that well.' But Maddie smiled as she spoke, her grip on the sheet loosening, allowing it to slip down, unveiling her graceful neck, her slim shoulders.

'Ah, but we're just playing at lovers. That makes us completely safe. And just to make sure, I promise that, no matter how annoying your cousin, I won't murder him in the street.'

'That's a load off my mind. I don't actually like my cousins all that much, but I'd rather they weren't slaughtered in a duel. So we just see where things take us? I can do that.' Maddie reached for her coffee and the bag of pastries, her eyes brightening as she peeked inside at the selection he had chosen. She selected a simple *cornetto* before holding the bag out to him. 'Okay, *signor*. You're right. It would be lovely to see Verona. Thank you.'

Dante managed not to react as the tension left his body. He didn't want to think too much about just why it had mattered that Maddie had agreed that this brief affair could continue. Better to settle on the reason that the week ahead would be much easier if they were physically comfortable with each other. Or remember that it had been nearly a year since his last discreet affair and surely he was due another.

'Why don't you shower and sort out your emails and I will go and purchase whatever you need for the day ahead?' he suggested.

'Really? You don't mind buying me underwear?' Maddie asked through a mouthful of crumbs.

'Why would I? I have a daughter, after all. I am an expert in how to braid her hair in at least five different ways, I have talked to her about growing up and adolescence, am ready to sit and rub her back and feed her ice cream when she gets her first period—buying you some mascara and tights really doesn't come close to the panic I felt when Arianna first asked me about how babies are made.'

'I bet you're a wonderful father.'

'I do the best I can.' He could never make up for the fact his daughter was motherless. Never forgive himself for his blindness, for dismissing Violetta's unhappiness, for allowing himself to live in a daydream rather than reality. But he had sworn on the day he'd buried his wife that his daughter wouldn't suffer for his folly. That he would be father and mother both, that she would always come first. And she did. Even though she had an au pair, Dante still did as many school drop-offs as possible, picked her up whenever he could. He sat in ballet school waiting rooms and cheered on the side of football fields, he watched films about princesses and films about spaceships and films about talking dogs, read to her every night he was home and, yes, his braiding skills were now legendary amongst Arianna's friends. 'Write me a list of what you need and I'll be as quick as I can.'

'Thank you, Dante.' Maddie had barely called him by his given name and an unexpected thrill ran through him at the precise syllables. 'For everything, for making this so easy. For last night. I never... It was never like that before.'

Dante froze. The truth was it had never been like that for him either, not even in those first heady days of infatuation with Violetta. Never been so sweet, so all-consuming. But he didn't want to dwell on why that might be—or make himself vulnerable in any way. 'No need to thank me.' His smile was purposefully intimate. 'I enjoyed myself too.'

Her answering smile matched his, elegant brows arching in a question. 'Oh? That's good to hear. I was thinking...' Maddie's voice trailed off suggestively.

'Yes?'

'Well, if you don't have to rush off then maybe we could practise a little more. Just to make sure we haven't forgotten anything.'

'You are a very conscientious woman, Signorina Fitzroy,' Dante told her as he walked purposefully towards her, unbuttoning his shirt, aware of Maddie's gaze fixed on his every move. 'Amazing attention to detail.'

'I try,' she whispered, her chest rising and falling with her shallow breaths.

'I agree it's wise to make sure we didn't forget anything. After all, didn't we agree that practice makes perfect?' And as he sank onto the bed, enveloped by her scent, her arms, her need, Dante couldn't help but think he was willing to practise for as long as it took.

# CHAPTER SEVEN

'I CAN'T BELIEVE it's taken me nearly a year to come here,' Maddie said wistfully as she slowly turned a full three hundred and sixty degrees. They were standing in the Teatro Romano looking out over the ancient city of Verona. 'It's so beautiful—and so different from San Tomo. It seems incredible that it's so close.' Instead of lakes and mountains, here were rivers and hills, Roman ruins interspersed with medieval houses and newer builds, the ages merging into one beautiful whole.

'I never thought that I would need to scold one of my employees for working too hard,' Dante teased her. 'But in your case, *signorina*, I make an exception.'

'I send my wedding parties here all the time, suggest places for them to go, book tickets for the opera, but have never thought that maybe I should come along as well.'

'You like the opera?'

'I'm not sure,' she admitted. 'I've been to Glyndebourne of course, but it was always more of a social occasion than a musical one.' She held her hands up, laughing at the look of horror on Dante's face. 'I know, I'm a philistine.'

'I will get us tickets for the festival here,' he said firmly.

'You don't have to…'

'Luciana will want to go. Consider it part of your duties as well as your education.'

'Education and work in one outing? Fabulous.'

But despite her words she couldn't help the tingle of anticipation at the idea. Not just because she would get the opportunity to view one of the most famous cultural events in the world, but because Dante wanted her to experience something he loved.

And from someone so private that was a heady thought indeed.

Not that the cool and proper Conte had been much in evidence today. After they finally resurfaced from the bed, Dante had headed back out into the town to purchase Maddie a suitable outfit for the day. Even after the night they had shared she'd felt a little embarrassed scribbling her demands—and her sizes—down, but he had brushed her concerns and her offer of payment aside, returning with something really pretty and expensive, judging by the cut, blue-silk maxi-dress covered in a gorgeous flowery pattern. He'd teamed the dress with dull gold sandals and a matching scarf, also supplying her with exquisitely beautiful lace underwear that Maddie thought ruefully must have cost more than all her sensible sets of bras and pants put together. Luckily she carried a few essential travel cosmetics in her bag, so she'd managed to powder her nose and tame her hair before he returned. After reassuring both Guido and the distraught bride that everything was in hand, she had spent a busy hour ensuring everything that could be cancelled was.

At least by waiting until she'd got to the altar to call off her own wedding she hadn't had to do anything except cancel the honeymoon. The bemused guests had been invited to stay and enjoy the food and music and, in the end, most of them had. Maddie herself had danced until midnight—hence the photo which had appeared in most of the papers of a bride alone on a dance floor in full white dress and tiara. The first time she had ever just *been*, without caring what anyone thought. The first and last time—until last night.

Dante had driven them to Verona in the same car he had transported her down the mountainside in last night. Maddie hadn't asked how the car had miraculously appeared at the other end of the lake. She was beginning to realise that the *castello* was just a very small part of the Falcone empire and fortune. Which made Dante's determination to make his sister happy just that little bit more endearing.

Endearing—not a word she'd expected to use about the Conte. And not, considering both the tenor of their agreement and the way she'd thrown caution overboard last night, a word she needed to be using. Endearing was too friendly, too sweet a word.

A little like the day they were spending together. It was both sweet and friendly—but with an edge. An awareness of each other that stayed with them every step, every touch. Every time Dante spoke, Maddie remembered the way his mouth felt on hers, on her body, remembered the endearments he had whispered in the dark of the night. Every time their hands briefly touched she had flashbacks to the way he had touched her last night. A reminder that this was no normal day. It was a prologue to the real business, the real reason they were spending any time together at all.

'And so,' Dante said as they finally reached the top of the theatre and gazed down at Verona spread before them, unreal in its beauty and antiquity, 'there she is. Verona in all her glory.'

'Glorious,' Maddie murmured, every nerve ablaze with awareness of Dante's proximity. Her body swayed towards him, yearning for his touch. Part of her gloried in this new sensation, in the abandonment he had induced in her—but part of her shrank from it. Maddie was no prude, she wasn't naïve, but she had assumed— she had hoped—that if she ever felt this kind of passion then it would be accompanied by love, not something as prosaic as a business contract. She knew Dante found her attractive. But he'd said very clearly that he didn't want a relationship with anyone. That he didn't believe in love.

Whereas Maddie believed wholeheartedly in love. She just wasn't sure she'd ever find anyone who loved her. After all, she never had. Oh, she knew her parents would tell her not to be so silly, so sentimental, that of course they loved her. But it was a love balanced by approval, by doing the right thing, by conforming. Every time she broke out of the established mould—even when it was for their benefit—she felt them pull away.

She wanted to be loved no matter what.

Dante's voice broke into her thoughts and she pulled herself back into the present. How spoiled she was! She was having a perfectly lovely day—after a perfectly lovely night. What else did a young, free woman need? 'What would you like to do next?'

There was only one possible answer. They'd walked along the river, crossed the gorgeously crenulated Ponte di Castel Vecchio and admired the castle itself. They'd wandered through the various piazzas, stopping off for coffees and a long lunch along the way, before spending a restful hour in the Giardino Gusti, glad of the shade in the heat of the summer's afternoon. Now they had nearly two hours before meeting Luciana's train and there was one key destination they had yet to visit.

'I know it isn't authentic…' she began and Dante interrupted.

'Of course,' he said resignedly. 'Bring a girl to Verona and she has to stand in an overcrowded courtyard to stare at a balcony which was added long after the date the supposed occupant of the house used it, to pay homage to a pair of teenagers with chronic communication issues.'

'It wasn't their fault. They didn't exactly have smartphones in the fourteenth century.' Maddie didn't know why she was defending a pair of fictional characters so vehemently. But standing here in Verona, where the fourteenth century didn't just seem relevant but practically modern while she was surrounded by Roman ruins, Romeo and Juliet seemed less like people in a play and more like the embodiment of hope and dreams. Even if it had all gone famously wrong.

'One moment Romeo is sighing over Rosaline and the next he's falling for Juliet. If Juliet hadn't been a Capulet and they hadn't rushed into marriage, who knows who he would have fallen for next? As for Juliet… She should have listened to her mother and married Paris. These mad passions don't last,' he finished, a hint of bitterness penetrating the irony.

'That would have made a fascinating play. And of course,' Maddie answered sweetly, 'I forgot how sensibly everyone always behaves in opera. Lots of sitting around discussing things rationally over tea and cake.'

'It's the music that makes the opera, not the story.'

'Not true—it's passionate music inspired by passionate characters. And it's the same in Shakespeare; the language is what moves us, what makes the story. After all, Shakespeare recycled most of the stories.'

Dante sighed in the long-suffering way of one who already knew the answer to a question about to be asked. 'So, knowing that neither Romeo nor Juliet have ever been proved to actually exist and also that the balcony is a later addition, would you still like to go?'

'Absolutely. Consider it an advance payment for the opera.'

Dante muttered something that sounded more than a little like 'philistine' but didn't demur any more; instead he took Maddie's arm in a surprisingly pleasant proprietorial gesture and guided her down the steps. Maddie was more than capable of walking down a set of stone steps, even if they were two thousand years old and a little unsteady in places, but it was nice to find herself being taken care of rather than the person doing the caring.

Nice and novel.

It was about half a mile's stroll to the famous balcony, crossing back across the river and making their way through the cobbled streets until they finally reached the small courtyard thronged with people. Greenery covered the high walls on one side and it was easy to imagine a youthful lover climbing up it to reach his lady-love. Maddie shivered despite the heat, despite the crowds chattering in at least a dozen languages. To be loved so desperately, to be wanted so intensely that you would rather die than be separated. Melodramatic? Sure. But also so intoxicatingly sweet. A sweetness every fibre in her body yearned for. Last night had been incredible, mind-blowingly, fantastically incredible, but instead of fulfilling a need it had just opened up the chasm inside her heart a little wider. Maddie didn't just want good sex, lovely as that was—really lovely; she wanted love. Not because of how she made someone's life easier but because of who she was. She wanted someone to see inside her and love and desire all of her.

Who would have thought the sensible Honourable Madeleine Fitzroy would turn out to be such a romantic? It certainly wasn't from her upbringing. None of her ancestors had a romantic bone in their body, the Bryon-worshipping, gothic-folly-building nineteenth-century would-be rake aside, and he wasn't so much romantic as a *romantic*. He had yearned for adventure and daring deeds of valour rather than love.

Her mother would probably prescribe a long dog walk and a cup of cocoa. Her father would pat her on the head and tell her—remind her—that she was a good girl. If Juliet had been a Fitzroy she would have married Paris, just as Dante had said, knowing her duty and doing it obediently. But if she had wavered, had allowed herself to follow her heart and woken up in that tomb with her dead swain lying across her, poison bottle clasped in his still warm hand, then would she have died for love or would she have allowed herself one solitary tear and then got on with her dutiful life, only occasionally allowing herself to remember her entombed lover?

Maddie suspected the latter.

But at least Juliet would have lived out her life knowing that she had once been loved to the point of madness. Would Maddie ever know the same? She'd take a week of wild passion over a lifetime of duty any day. Otherwise she might as well have married Theo.

'Would you like to go inside the house? There's a museum, I believe.' Dante's voice broke into her reverie and Maddie pulled herself back into reality.

'No, thank you. This is great. Look at all these people. I wonder what they're thinking?'

Tour parties, young couples kissing under the balcony, lone sightseers, families with fractious toddlers or sulky teens, older couples holding hands… All of humanity seemed to be represented in the square.

'That it's too busy in here and they want a coffee—or better still a glass of wine?'

'They're not thinking about coffee,' Maddie said wistfully, her gaze drawn to a couple around her age who were staring into each other's eyes as if nobody else existed. At that moment the young man dropped to his knee and presented a box to his blushing girlfriend. 'Oh, my goodness—look, Dante. How romantic. A proposal. Oh, thank goodness she said yes. Can you imagine how embarrassing it would have been if she hadn't? Oh, what a romantic place to choose.'

'A busy square full of tourists?' His voice was full of cynicism and Maddie's heart ached for him. He'd told her he'd been besotted with his wife—how had that young man full of love and hope turned so bitter?

'It might not be the most private place, but it shows some imagination.' Maddie sighed. 'When Theo asked me to marry him we had just got out of the car and were walking towards the back door at Flintock Hall. It was slippery underfoot, thanks to the frost, and I was so busy trying to make sure I didn't fall I didn't hear what he said. It was part of a longer speech about how grateful he was for all I did, and how we had known each other all our lives and how much he respected me. No wonder I didn't hear the "wouldn't it make a lot of sense if we got married?" part.' She smiled as she watched the couple enthusiastically embrace in the midst of a circle of well-wishers. 'I'm not one for public displays of affection or for overly complicated proposals, but if anyone ever proposes to me again I want romance and heart. Not that it seems likely right now. You're the first man I've kissed in over a year—and we're all about business.'

'Not *all* about business,' Dante said softly and Maddie felt the increasingly familiar heat flush through her at his words.

'Okay, maybe not *all* about business. But not all about romance either. Don't worry,' she added hurriedly. 'I'm not asking you to suddenly start buying me roses and to serenade me under a balcony. I would just like to know that one day I will fall in love with someone who loves me. Just the basics really.'

'People used to write love notes and stick them on the walls, but that is now strictly forbidden. But they say that if you touch the statue of Juliet,' Dante grinned, slow and dangerous, 'specifically her right breast, then that will bring good fortune in love.'

'Really?' Maddie looked over at the bronze statue doubtfully. 'That seems a little over-familiar. Poor Juliet. I don't think she signed up to be groped by a bunch of strangers.'

'Maddie. It's a statue.'

'You think I should do it?'

'I think it's nonsense. The statue, the superstition and romance. All of it. But you don't, so here you are. What harm can it do?'

Maddie chewed on her lip. On the one hand the very idea seemed embarrassing. To touch a statue—and so intimately—and signal to the world that she was lonely and looking for love. On the other hand she had promised herself she would be open to new experiences. To stop worrying about how people perceived her. To relax and enjoy life. Dante was right; she was already here. Why not join all the other tourists, none of whom seemed to give touching the statue a second thought?

Besides. She *did* want love. She wasn't in a position to turn down any chance to increase her luck, no matter how unlikely it seemed.

'Okay, then.' She lifted her chin and gave Dante as jaunty a grin as she could manage. 'Wish me luck.'

Dante leaned against the wall and watched Maddie as she approached the statue, head back and shoulders as taut as if she was heading into battle—which in some ways she was. Not just because she had to get past the other people vying to caress the statue, but because she was setting out her stall and asking the universe for love.

His body tensed. Part of him wanted to pull her away and warn her that she was heading for nowhere but heart-break and loneliness. Tell her that she should have gone through with her wedding because respect and similar goals were the best foundations he could think of to build a marriage and a family on.

But part of him wanted to applaud her courage. Wished he had her ability to hope and believe.

Though he had to ask the question—what the hell were British men thinking? How on earth had someone as sexy and intelligent and interesting as Maddie ended up thinking she needed a statue's help to find love? She should have been snapped up years ago, not allowed to measure her worth through her name and her ability to run a large estate.

She gave him a quick, almost flirtatious glance over her shoulder and Dante gave her a thumbs-up as she reached out and almost reverentially placed her palm on the statue, her hand flat on the side of Juliet's breast. Maddie closed her eyes and murmured something Dante couldn't make out before stepping back and relinquishing her place to the next eager tourist who, Dante noted disapprovingly, didn't treat the Shakespearian heroine with the respect she deserved.

'So?' He straightened as she neared him. 'Feel any different?'

'Oh, yes, the world is full of opportunities. Any second now one of these men is going to fall to his knees before me and profess his undying love.'

'I hope they won't mind waiting a week,' Dante said drily. 'You are otherwise engaged, after all.' It wasn't jealousy or ownership that prompted him to take her hand. He really had no need to be jealous and he had no desire to have any claim on her. He just wanted to ensure he didn't lose her in the crowd as they exited the bustling square. But he had to admit, the softness of her hand in his felt—well, it felt nice. Right.

'Thank you.'

He looked at her enquiringly.

'For suggesting today. I've had a really good time.'

'Me too.' And he had. 'It's been too long since I've been here. Violetta preferred La Scala to the festival; she liked going to the opera to see and be seen, not for the music. She preferred the shopping in Milan. The couple of times we came here she got bored quickly. She would want to shop and to lunch and that was that.'

'In that case, maybe I shouldn't mention that I was hoping we'd have time to browse in a couple of the book-shops we passed?' Maddie shot him a quick, apologetic glance. 'Don't worry about it. Now I've ventured here I'm pretty sure it won't be my last visit. It's just so beautiful. So much history in one place.'

She wanted to go to a bookstore? Not to a designer dress shop, or one of the many luxury bag or shoe shops, or the expensive make-up stores? She didn't want to browse the jewellery counters? That was the only type of sightseeing Violetta had enjoyed, and she would always return laden with bags, despite wardrobes full of unworn clothes at home. It wasn't that Dante had begrudged spending a penny on his wife—the opposite. He had adored lavishing gifts on her. It was just that, no matter what he had bought her, it was never enough. It never made her happy—*he* never made her happy. And, in truth, she hadn't made him happy either. She had never tried to enjoy his interests or wanted to spend time on the things he liked doing and by the time he had realised how little they had in common it was too late. In the end he had come to the opera alone, come to explore the ruins alone, peruse the bookstores alone. He'd been alone long before he was bereaved. He just had never admitted it.

Luckily he knew better now. Knew that loneliness wasn't something to fear; rather it was a safety to embrace. A timely reminder on a day when the personal and business were melding together in a way he hadn't expected, on a day when he found himself relaxing his guard. A day when, for one moment, watching Maddie touch the statue, he had hoped all her dreams came true and wished he could be the man to do that for her. A foolish wish—better he wish that she was never disillusioned. That if love came it was kinder to her than it had been to him.

'A bookstore? Of course, Verona is famed for its book-shops,' he said and Maddie beamed.

'Good! I've read all the English books at the *castello* several times over—and my written Italian is by no means as fluent as my spoken.' She was still chattering as they reached the first shop, only stopping when she took in the shelves of books, her mouth falling open in awe.

'Go, browse,' Dante told her. 'We still have time.'

'I never want to leave this place,' she said solemnly, heading towards the English section as if she were drawn there by the Pied Piper.

Dante stood and watched her, noting the reverential way she selected a book, the way she was instantly absorbed as she read it, and was conscious of a nostalgic longing for the young man who would once have lost himself in dreams as she did. He turned hurriedly, wanting, needing to break the connection and his gaze fell on a table of journals. Diaries, recipe books, travel writings. He picked up a gorgeously embellished travel journal, remembering the light in Maddie's eyes as she had talked him through her plans. A light he had wanted to bathe in, even as his heart twisted at the knowledge that her plans involved being a long way from him.

No. He should be glad for her—and relieved for himself. She was leaving at the end of the summer—and that made her safe. As long as he remembered that she was leaving, as long as he remembered that ultimately she wanted what he could no longer give, then he was safe.

And safety was all that mattered.

# CHAPTER EIGHT

'WHERE DO I PRESS?'

'Right there. That's it.' Maddie shifted slightly. For a small, skinny child, Arianna seemed to weigh an awful lot, especially when all her weight was on just one knee. 'And then press there and there... That's it! You've just finalised a booking.'

'All by myself?'

'All by yourself,' Maddie confirmed, smiling at the child's evident glee. 'You're a natural. I'll have to be careful or I'll find myself out of a job.'

'What's this? You're not annoying Maddie, are you, *piccola*?'

They both jumped at the sound of Dante's voice and Maddie swung the chair round, noting with a slight feeling of guilt the flare of surprise in his eyes as he noted Arianna on her knee. They had agreed to be extra careful with each other around Arianna and ensure that Luciana said nothing either, but when Arianna had shown up in Maddie's office that morning, she hadn't been able to bring herself to send the small girl away; something in her eagerness to learn—and the wistful loneliness in her eyes—struck a nostalgic chord. Besides, Maddie reasoned, as far as Arianna knew, Maddie was nothing but an employee, so what harm could letting her hang around do?

To her surprise she was enjoying Arianna's company. Maddie had never spent much time with children before, had always found herself unsure what to say, but with Arianna conversation was easy, whether they spoke in Italian or whether Arianna practised her sometimes excellent, sometimes idiosyncratic English.

'Not annoying, working.' Arianna tilted her chin. 'This will all be mine one day; I need to learn how to look after it.'

She reminded Maddie so much of herself at a young age that her chest hurt with bittersweet nostalgia, old, weary scars flaring back to life. Once she had had the same pride in her name, in her surroundings, in her family. The difference being that Dante laughed at his daughter's arrogant words, swinging Arianna up in the air as he did so, whereas Maddie would have been hushed, reminded that the abbey would belong to her brother, not her. It seemed so harsh, to tell a child she was only a temporary resident, to ensure she never could feel fully at home. Harsh and useless, because Maddie had loved Stilling Abbey fiercely anyway. Part of her always would.

'Oh, well, in that case, I'm sure there are many jobs you can do, *cara*; I know the gardeners can do with someone to help them weed and the kitchen can always use another washer-upper. I did every job in this house at some point,' Dante added and Arianna stared at him solemnly.

'Then so will I.'

'Good girl, that's the best way to learn.' Maddie looked up at Dante, her heart squeezing at the sight of the tall man holding his daughter close. 'How's Luciana? Has her jet lag kicked in?'

'She's still in bed and if she doesn't get up soon it is going to take her whole stay before she adjusts. Ari, go and see if your aunt will wake up. I thought she might want to walk up to her favourite *ristorante* for lunch. The view's glorious,' Dante said to Maddie. 'You will love it.'

Maddie waited until Arianna had skipped out of the room before she replied. 'Do you think that's a good idea? If I accompany you on a family day out?'

'Of course.' He was completely the haughty aristocrat. 'Luciana was so weary yesterday she barely registered you. A family day out is exactly the kind of scenario she needs to see to stop her worrying.' He paused, the haughtiness slipping off his face. 'She looked so tired, even allowing for the jet lag and travel. I hope she isn't keeping anything from me.'

Maddie studied him, the worry in his eyes, etched into his face. On the drive back from Verona yesterday evening she had been struck by the easy, companionable bond between the siblings, evident despite the age gap, the distance that usually separated them. And she had been struck by the way they assessed each other when thought unseen. The concern shadowing Luciana as she glanced at her brother, mirrored by Dante whenever he looked back. For the first time she understood why Dante had lied, had wanted to stop the sister he evidently adored from fretting.

'It's a long journey; she's bound to be tired. The mountain air will do her the world of good.'

'So you'll join us?' It was more of a command than a request and, although Maddie still wasn't sure spending too much time in close proximity with Luciana was wise, she nodded her agreement.

'I realised yesterday that now you have agreed to pay for my ticket I can afford to leave at the end of the summer like I'd originally hoped. I'd like to be out of the country before Theo gets married, not because I think the press will chase me down or because I'll be broken-hearted, but because it feels right. Like the perfect time for a fresh start. It seems a shame not to see a little of the countryside before I leave and I still haven't explored the mountains at all.'

'Don't get carried away. This isn't a day out. You'll be working the whole time.'

'I know. Convincing Luciana we are in love whilst making sure Arianna suspects nothing.' Maddie slid out of her chair and stepped over to where Dante stood. 'Are you up to it, Conte?'

She didn't want to think about what she was doing, why her whole body was throbbing with desire as soon as she looked into his cool blue gaze, why her nerves were skittering in hope, in anticipation of his touch. They were planning a family walk, not an afternoon liaison. But all Maddie knew was that the moment Dante had dropped her off yesterday evening, she had been aware of just how alone she was for the first time since she had arrived in Italy. Her apartment no longer felt like a haven of independence, but small and cramped, her bed uncomfortable as she had tossed and turned, barely sleeping, reliving memories of the night before.

She wanted, needed more than memories. She needed touch. To touch and be touched. To be reminded that she lived. Existed.

What harm could a kiss do? Another night? Two or

three or four? She was leaving. So as long as she reminded herself that this was just an interlude before her real adventures began then she was quite safe.

'You doubt my acting skills?' Dante's voice was hoarse, his gaze no longer cool but full of heat, and Maddie's whole body flamed at the sight, at the knowledge that she had elicited that reaction.

'No, I'm sure you'll be fine. But if you wanted a quick rehearsal...' She allowed her voice to trail off suggestively.

Disappointment swept through her as he stepped away, only to retreat as he slowly and deliberately, his gaze holding hers, closed and locked the door to her office. 'A rehearsal sounds like an excellent idea, Signorina Fitzroy. However, I can't promise it will be quick...' And then, at last, his hands were on her as his mouth found hers and Maddie kissed him back fiercely, slipping her arms around him, luxuriating in the feel of his skin under her fingertips. Surely she wasn't foolish enough to mistake this for anything more than lust and pleasure? No, Maddie knew exactly what Dante was offering her, so she might as well enjoy it while she could.

'Where have Arianna and Luciana gone?'

Dante looked up as Maddie rounded the corner, the blood rushing to his veins at the sight of her. No cool, professional Madeleine today. Instead her long, tanned limbs were showcased by tiny denim shorts and her close-fitting vest top, her silky hair pulled back into a loose knot, tendrils curling in the heat. He liked seeing the cool, organised Madeleine Fitzroy rumpled and casual. She looked very much as she had when he had left her office earlier, rosy with exertion, damp with sweat.

He cast a quick glance around the mountain-top restaurant, cursing the other diners, the waiters, everyone whose presence stopped him pushing her up against the terrace balustrade and taking her right there, under the mountain's gaze.

Dante swallowed, glad his voice remained steady. 'One of the other diners was driving back to San Tomo and offered to give them a lift. It's a long walk back down and they both seemed tired.'

'A lift sounds nice,' Maddie said. 'But I think I prefer walking down; it's all the extra pasta and bread and tiramisu I have to carry with me I'm not sure about. Why was I such a glutton? I must be at least a whole other person heavier. In fact I don't need to walk; you can probably just roll me down the mountainside.' She joined him at the balustrade, leaning on it with a deep sigh, one that seemed to come right from her toes. 'It is so beautiful here. I know mountains, of course, but this kind of Alpine lushness never seemed Italian to me before. Now it always will.'

Dante followed her gaze. The *ristorante* was high on the mountain, right on a peak, with stunning views across green valleys framed by white stone peaks. This was his home, the landscape of his heart. And yet he had exiled himself for five years, would spend most of the year far to the south in the bustle of a city. Better not to think about why, better to just enjoy every day as it came and let the mountains and lakes restore his soul, a little at a time. 'You ready to walk back?'

'I think so.' She patted her stomach. 'Let's take the first part slowly though. I'm not joking about the rolling part.'

The paths were all clearly signposted, a vast network

of walks and hikes throughout the whole district. It was possible to take cable cars up to the next shelf, or down to the lower slopes, roads criss-crossed the mountains and valleys, but as they turned the corner and the *ristorante* was hidden from sight the modern world fell away. It was just the two of them in the majestic landscape. The path cut through a flower-strewn meadow populated only by mild, incurious cows, each adorned with a bell around its neck, the faint jingling adding to the birdsong piping up at intermittent intervals. Maddie didn't speak for the first few minutes, her eyes bright as she looked around her, her full mouth curved into a smile of pure joy.

'I could stay here for ever,' she said finally, so low he could hardly hear the words. 'Right here, right now. If there's a heaven then surely it must look like this. Oh, Dante. You are so lucky to belong here.'

But he didn't. Not any more. 'It's been too long since I've walked like this. Once I roamed these mountains more like a goatherd than a future *conte*, spent my winters skiing, the rest of the year climbing and walking. They were in my blood. Are in my blood. But Violetta didn't like to hike or to ski. She didn't like the mountains at all, said they were threatening, bleak. She saw beauty in restaurants and yachts, not in nature.'

'What a shame, to live surrounded by this and not to appreciate it.'

'The last two years of my marriage I would hike alone. Looking for answers, for peace, for happiness. But no matter how far I walked I could never leave my problems, my loneliness behind.'

The words just spilled out. Whether it was the way Maddie just listened quietly, no condemnation or surprise in her clear grey eyes, just acceptance, or whether it was the way they seemed alone in the world as they walked through the meadow, he didn't know.

'I'm sorry. There's nothing worse than a bad marriage. As someone who narrowly escaped one, I think I know what I'm talking about. Not that Theo isn't lovely—he really is. In a very driven, overactive way. But he isn't for me. And I'm not for him. We would have bored each other senseless within months.'

'By the end I would have settled for bored,' Dante said bleakly. 'Violetta liked to be the centre of attention. And for the first two years she was. But as time went by, as I recovered from my infatuation, the less time I had to spare to pander to her vanity. If I wasn't going to fawn over her, well, she would settle for an argument instead. It made no difference to her if I wanted to fight or not, or even if I joined in—she was quite capable of escalating up to full hysteria, complete with smashed ornaments and screaming, without my input.'

He stopped, shocked by how much he had revealed. He had never told anyone, not even Luciana, about the last eighteen months of his doomed marriage.

'Oh, Dante.'

'The more scenes she created the more excuses I found to stay away, to travel.' Dante rubbed his chin wearily, the rasp of his stubble grazing his palm. 'It was wrong of me. It just inflamed Violetta more and of course it meant I didn't see Arianna for days, sometimes weeks at a time. Violetta would accuse me of not caring about our daughter, she would say I resented her for being born, that I blamed her for our marriage. She would say it in front of her—I don't know how much Arianna remembers. She was only three when Violetta died.'

'I can see why it was easier to stay away. For Arianna's sake as well as yours.'

'I knew she was safe.' Dante couldn't stop now. The words lancing his wounds. Painful as it was to excavate the ruins of his marriage like this, excruciating as it was to see with the clearness of hindsight just where he had gone wrong, it was still somehow cleansing, letting someone else hear the evidence and pronounce judgement. 'Violetta lost interest in her very early and left her to her nanny much of the time while she visited Milan and Rome. She hated San Tomo, complained that she was lonely, and I expect she was. None of her friends were there and she was a woman who needed the adulation, the stimulation of others to keep her happy. I should have agreed to her demands that we move to Milan, but I wanted my daughter raised in the *castello* as Luciana and I had been. And I didn't trust Violetta. Left to her own devices in a city for much of the time, I feared she would embarrass me. I was young. It's not an excuse, but I hadn't learned the art of compromise.'

'Some people never learn it. And you *were* young.'

They reached the pine forest and Dante led the way in, glad of the gloom, the trees towering overhead. 'At times I almost hated her.' He'd never said the truth aloud, barely even admitted it to himself. 'And I despised myself for being so weak because when she decided to turn on the charm in the beginning I fell, even knowing how temporary the reconciliation would be. Knowing she had as little respect for me as I had for myself, as I had for her. By the time I became immune to her charm we were locked in a self-destructive spiral, but I didn't want to admit to myself, to the world that I had made such a monumental mistake. Nor did I want to lose Arianna, and Violetta made it clear they came as a package. She might not want to be troubled with a child most of the time, but she didn't want me to have her either.'

'What happened?'

He exhaled, the memories toxic. 'Violetta had been away partying a lot and I put my foot down. Young and arrogant and embarrassed is a bad combination and I handled the situation—handled her—badly. I see now I should have let her go. Given her the house in Milan she demanded and let the marriage slowly disintegrate. The shine of the title had worn off by then; I don't think it would have taken much persuasion by a suitable lover for her to walk out. Instead I threatened to cut off her allowance if she didn't calm down, insisted she spend the winter at the *castello*. That she act like the Contessa Falcone, like a mother. And then I went away again, on a three-week business trip to the other side of the world, feeling as if I had acted like a man, solved the situation.'

'No one likes a tyrant,' Maddie said, but there was no condemnation in her voice. That was fine. Dante had enough for both of them.

'No. I didn't try and understand how Violetta felt. Didn't appreciate that she was highly strung and spoiled and bored. That she wanted the besotted boy who had danced attendance on her and told her that she was the most beautiful, desirable woman in the world, not a tired businessman who spent half of his life on planes and the other half in his study. Who didn't ever want to party unless there was a deal to be done, had no interest in her life, in her friends. Who treated her like a frivolous, naughty child, who reserved all his spare time for their daughter. You see…' he managed a smile but he knew it was bleak '…we were equally at fault. And so…she decided she had had enough. That she would leave me. In typical Violetta fashion she decided to do it as dramatically as possible. I know now she had several lovers during our marriage. She contacted the most recent and begged him to rescue her and he set off straight away.'

'Only they never made it. How sad.'

'They were both drunk and there was evidence of cocaine use. I had no idea she used, missed all the signs, although looking back it was clear she'd been using from the start. He drove too fast, skidded on some ice and the next moment Arianna was motherless and I a single parent.'

'I am so sorry.' Maddie slipped her hand into his, clasping him tightly. Her hand felt so comfortable, so right. He clung on with no idea how to let go.

The fact he didn't want to let go was the most terrifying thing of all.

'I made a vow that day that Arianna would never suffer for my mistakes. That I would always put her first, be father and mother to her. And I also vowed that I would never be so foolish again, never let lust blind me. You want romance, Maddie? You're not alone. Oh, those people looking at that balcony yesterday, like you, they believe in love, in fate and destiny. But love blinds you, makes you act like a fool. It's not beautiful or perfect, it's cruel and demanding. It's capricious, temporary. Be careful it doesn't hurt you. You might decide your Earl wasn't such a bad bet after all.'

Maddie halted and turned to him, her eyes full of compassion. 'She really did a number on you, didn't she?' she said, her mouth quivering. 'It's absolutely fine to learn from our mistakes, Dante, but we shouldn't dwell on them. And learning means we do better next time.

Don't shut yourself off because of one bad experience. You have a lot to offer the right woman. A lot beyond the castle and the title and the rest.' She stood on her tiptoes and pressed one light, sweet kiss onto his mouth. He wanted to grab her, consume her, but stood motionless as she pulled away.

Because she was wrong. He had nothing to offer beyond the castle and the title. The rest had been buried with his wife—and it was no more than he deserved.

# CHAPTER NINE

'DANTE SEEMS VERY taken with you.' Luciana slid a sly smile Maddie's way. 'A sister can tell these things.'

'Oh, no,' Maddie protested. 'It's still just...'

'Still just early days. I know. He keeps telling me the same—as if that will change anything. Just like he thinks he's doing his best not to look at you when other people can see. But he can't help it. He thinks I don't notice but I do.'

Maddie hid a wince. Luciana was noticing things that definitely weren't there. Things had been decidedly cool between Dante and Maddie over the last week. It was as if he had shown her too much on the walk through the mountains and it had spooked him—which was probably for the best. Maddie could manage the haughty Conte, could just about handle the passionate man who made her body tremble—but Dante opening his heart, showing her his vulnerabilities was too much for her. She wanted to make things better, to heal him, to show him that love didn't have to hurt.

Which was ironic, because seriously, what did she know about love? Besides, Dante was exactly the kind of man she had sworn to steer clear of: rich, titled, owner of the kind of ancient house she could manage in her sleep.

She was bred to wed a man like Dante and the whole reason she had left England was to forge her own destiny, not revert to type.

'What a beautiful day.' Luciana stretched luxuriously. 'I could lie here for ever.' It was a perfect day, with the sun delivering exactly the right degree of heat, the light illuminating the mountains and the water so they almost hurt with their intensity and vibrant colour. Maddie and Luciana had brought Arianna down to the small lakeside beach and were lying on sunbeds, toasting themselves, while she splashed around in the shallows with the insouciant resistance of youth to the chill of the water.

'Me too. I can't believe my next bride arrives tomorrow and my vacation is over.'

It had been an action-packed few days. They had explored more of Lake Garda, visiting several of the villages and towns along its banks, and spent another day trekking high into the mountains, before taking Arianna to a thrillingly long summer toboggan run. The night before, Dante had carried out his promise—or threat—to take them to the opera and, to her surprise, Maddie had found herself absorbed in the tale of passion and tragedy unfolding on the stage in front of her, swept away by the music and performance.

Luciana was sharp and funny, Arianna delightful. And Dante the consummate host. Everything would have been perfect if it weren't for the undercurrent of uncertainty that ran between Maddie and the Conte. That knowledge of something hot and powerful. If only she didn't know how his muscles felt under her questing fingertips, didn't know how his skin tasted. Didn't know the precise shade of blue his eyes darkened to when passion consumed him. She was on edge around him, every nerve attuned to his touch, jumping in response to a casual hand on her arm, her body reacting to the most polite smiles.

And Luciana watched it all. Of course, she thought they were hiding a real relationship from Arianna. She had no idea they were covering up a real temporary relationship from each other.

Luciana turned to look at Maddie, her expression hidden behind her oversized sunglasses. She was a formidably beautiful woman, tall and voluptuous with an air of complete certainty that everyone wanted to be near her, would indulge her. And they did. She was a universal favourite with all the castle staff, could coax Dante into anything. Maddie envied her poise, her appetite for life. 'Do you get much time off when there are weddings here?'

'Not much.' Maddie closed her eyes as she felt the sun soak straight into her bones. 'There are always other people on duty, of course, but I like to know what's going on at all times.'

'But your guests don't stay for the full week? The *castello* is back to normal two days a week?'

'They usually arrive on Friday afternoon and are gone by lunchtime on Wednesday,' Maddie confirmed. 'It gives us plenty of time to set up for the next family.'

'Hmm. That gives me an idea, but I need to speak to Dante. Talk of the devil. Dante, *cara*, over here.'

She waved and Maddie's heart jumped at the sight of the tall figure walking towards them. She suddenly felt exposed in nothing but her bikini, even though the sensible black design covered far more of her body than Luciana's flamboyant leopard-print confection.

'*Ciao.*' He stood in front of them so Maddie would

have to crane to look up at him. Instead she focused her gaze firmly out on the lake, watching Arianna practising her dives off the jetty. 'Luciana, I meant to ask. Do you want me to drive you to the train station tomorrow or are you hiring a car and driving to Lucerne? I'd lend you one of the *castello* four-wheel drives but you're flying back from Switzerland, aren't you?'

'In a hurry to be rid of me, *mi hermano*?'

'Not at all,' he said. Maddie could feel his gaze on her and could almost read his mind. When Luciana went they would no longer have any need to pretend, no reason to spend any time together. Relief mingled with regret. Maddie would ready herself to leave and Dante would sink back into the same solitary life he'd been determinedly not enjoying for the last five years. She brushed away the twinge of regret. That was his choice.

'But,' he continued, his gaze still burning into Maddie, 'I know you only have a week left and Mama is missing you too. It would be selfish of me to keep you from her.'

Luciana didn't answer for a few moments and when she did she didn't answer her brother directly. 'It's Mama's birthday in two weeks' time.'

'*Si*. I am planning for Arianna and myself to spend a couple of days in Lucerne and to take her out for lunch.'

'Lunch? For her sixtieth birthday? For shame, Dante.'

'As she won't admit to a day over fifty-four, I'm not sure it matters,' he said drily. 'What do you suggest instead?'

'A ball. Here, like the ones we used to have. Oh, Dante. It would be gorgeous and Mama would be so happy. What do you say?'

Maddie stopped pretending not to listen, turning to

Luciana in surprise as Dante exclaimed, 'A *what*? Impossible!'

'Why? Maddie has told me that there are no wedding guests staying here on a Wednesday or Thursday night. We could hold the ball on a Wednesday. Set up as soon as your wedding guests have gone. Oh, Dante, remember the balls Mama and Papa used to hold? The music and the dresses—flowers everywhere. So elegant. I couldn't wait for the day I could stop peeping through the gallery and actually attend myself...' Luciana stopped, lost in a nostalgic reverie and, despite herself, Maddie caught Dante's grimly amused eye. He grimaced at her before returning his attention to his sister.

'And when do you propose to hold this ball? Next week?'

'Don't be ridiculous. That doesn't give us nearly enough time. No, the week after.'

'The week after!' Maddie exclaimed as Dante said, 'You're serious?'

'Of course I'm serious.' Luciana sat up and removed her sunglasses, all the better to fix her brother with a hard stare. 'It's our mother's sixtieth birthday, Dante. She was still in mourning for her fiftieth. Remember? I persuaded her to come over to New Zealand, but her heart wasn't in it. Let's give her the kind of party Papa would have wanted her to have. I know it's short notice and I know it'll be a lot of work, but if we all work together I'm sure we can do it.'

'You won't even be here in two weeks!'

Luciana smiled up at her brother. 'I can change my flight. In fact, I spoke to Phil yesterday and he's going to see if he can get the school to let the boys have a couple of weeks off. It would be lovely to show them the place I grew up in.'

Maddie couldn't help but admire Luciana's almost arrogant confidence that events would pan out just the way she'd decided. 'So you'd stay here and not go to Lucerne?' Maddie held her breath as she waited for the answer. She had promised Dante a week—and that week was almost up. She didn't know if she could manage another fortnight. Especially while he was so cold and shuttered whenever they weren't with Luciana.

'How could I leave with so much to do? Mama will get the train across to us—or Dante could collect her.'

'You have got it all planned out.' But to Maddie's surprise, Dante didn't sound so horrified by the idea.

'I know it sounds impossible. But whatever strings you can't pull, Dante, Maddie can. She knows everyone. I knew this was possible yesterday morning when I waited with her in her office. She was charming florists and suppliers until they were promising far more than she asked for. Besides, we have a whole castle's worth of staff to help; the chefs will be delighted to have the opportunity to impress Mama's society friends and your business contacts. How long since the terraces have been used to entertain, huh?'

Maddie had always thought it a shame that the dramatic terraces with their views of the lake and gorgeous fountains and colourful flowerbeds weren't open to the wedding guests, not even for photos. Guido had told her that the insurance was too prohibitive but she suspected it was more that Dante wanted to keep part of the *castello* private. She turned and stared over at the Castello Falcone with narrowed eyes, imagining lanterns lighting the steps, little tables and chairs set out on the lawns, a marquee down here by the lakeside… String quartets on the terraces, something more bluesy here and a proper dance band in the Medieval Hall. 'But who would come on such short notice?' she asked, reality reasserting its prosaic head.

To her surprise the brother and sister looked at her with identically amused—and slightly smug—expressions.

'The first party at the Castello Falcone in over a decade?'

'The problem will be stopping gatecrashers, not getting people to come.'

'Many of Mama's friends spend the summer in the lakes and mountains anyway. No one is an impossible distance away. And those who are further away or abroad? I'm sure there will be some quickly cancelled plans,' Luciana said. 'There are plenty of unused bedrooms; we can easily put up the aunts, uncles and godparents in the *castello* itself. Run coaches down to Riva for everyone else.'

Dante stared across the lake, brow furrowed in thought. 'I agree it's a lovely thought, Ciana, and Mama would love it, but…'

'Then it's decided!' Luciana jumped to her feet with the litheness of a girl of sixteen rather than a thirty-something mother of three. 'Thank you, Dante! I'll call Mama right now and get the guest list settled and find out when she wants to come and then I'll call Phil and tell him to get booking flights. I can't wait for Arianna to meet her cousins. Ari,' she called over to the still-swimming child. 'Come back with me? I'm going to call your *nonna* and then you and I need to plan a shopping trip to Milan!'

Arianna shouted back her agreement, emerging from

the water like an enthusiastic Labrador, shaking water everywhere without a care as she grabbed her flip-flops, bestowed a quick soggy hug on Maddie and her father and ran after her aunt. Dante stood stock-still, staring after his sister, before shaking his head and barking out a short, humourless laugh. 'I should have known she didn't need me to actually consent. As soon as she thought of it, the ball was a done deal.'

'At least Arianna will be happy her aunt's staying longer,' Maddie said cautiously, horribly conscious that this was the first time she and Dante had been alone in the week since they'd returned from their mountain walk. She didn't want to look at him but her gaze was inexorably drawn to his. He looked tired, stubble on his usually clean-shaven jaw. Had the last week been as much of a burden for him as it had been for her?

'She's had a wonderful week. She adores Luciana—and she's really taken to you. It's going to be hard on her when her aunt returns home and you leave. I think we'll return to Roma then; it'll be easier for her to adjust back in the city. Look, this plan of Luciana's; she's obviously expecting you to help. It's not part of your duties. I'll talk to her.'

'No, honestly, Dante, it's fine. I don't mind.'

His brows rose. 'You don't mind suddenly having to organise a ball for what, I will warn you, will probably be two hundred people in just over ten days?'

'Not at all. It's not like I'll be doing it all alone and Luciana's right—we have a lot of expertise here in the castle. Besides, she's counting on my help. I don't want to let her down.'

'Did she ask you to help?'

'Not exactly. I've only just heard about it as well. But I would have said yes anyway. I like to be useful.'

'Tell me, Madeleine Fitzroy. Do you ever say no or are you so desperate to be needed that you'll say yes to anything that comes your way? Seven-day weeks? Impromptu balls? Marriage to a man you don't love? A fake relationship? Did I even need to agree to financial inducement or would you have agreed anyway? Always accommodating everyone but yourself.'

Maddie froze at the mockery in Dante's voice. She'd thought—what? That maybe he liked her just a little too much; that was why he'd kept his distance from her. Stupid girl. He thought her a doormat, nothing more. And he was right.

She clambered to her feet with a tenth of the lithe grace Luciana had displayed, hurt making her limbs clumsy as she grabbed her sundress, wrapping it around her body as if it were armour, securing the belt with unnecessary vigour. 'I'm saying no to this conversation.' Proud of how strong her voice sounded, she stuffed her feet into her sandals and took off, away from the *castello* and duty and a family she was once again on the outside of. She didn't much care where she walked. She just needed to get away.

'Damn.' Dante cursed as he watched Maddie march away, tall and elegant—and hurt. Hurt he had caused with hateful words. Words designed to provoke a reaction. Any reaction. Which made him no better than Violetta...

Maddie had been so hard to read all week. Friendly with Luciana. Sweet with Arianna. Courteous and polite to him, no less, no more. She'd fulfilled their brief perfectly. Luciana was sure they were mad for each other, was urging him to make it public. 'Only people hot for each other are so very cool,' she had told him gleefully.

But Maddie had been very careful not to catch his eye, not to be alone with him. Her hand hadn't sought his, her smiles were for others. There had been no intimacy, verbal or otherwise, since they had walked back from the mountain. Since he had opened his heart to her.

But, he hadn't reached out either. Hadn't wanted to overstep, take her generosity for granted. Had he—maybe—come over as a little stand-offish? Violetta's angry words rang in his head, as clear and potent now as they were five years ago: *'You are a statue, Dante. Carved out of nothing but marble. No emotion, no fire. I need a real man.'*

Was that what Maddie had seen this last week? A statue? Had he used up all his openness as they walked down the mountain before retreating behind his mask? Dante suspected the answer might be yes. Even last night, at the opera, he had confined himself to commonplace remarks about the music and plot, been assiduous in providing refreshments and making sure Maddie and Luciana were comfortable, but he had barely even told Maddie how beautiful she was—and she had looked spectacular in a dark blue jumpsuit, her hair twisted into a loose braid. Nor had the music swept him away as it usually did. He'd been too on edge, distracted.

*'Accidenti,'* he cursed again and then, before he could remind himself why keeping his distance was a good thing, he took off after Maddie, jogging along the river path.

It didn't take long to catch her up; she was standing by

the lake just a few hundred metres along the path, staring into its blue depths, her expression as inscrutable as ever.

'*Mi perdoni*. I was very rude. It was inexcusable.'

Maddie didn't answer for a long moment. When she did her voice was bleak. 'Yes. You were. But it doesn't mean you weren't right.'

'I have no right to judge you; I barely know you.'

She flinched at his words. 'No. I don't suppose you do. I don't suppose anyone does. Not even me. That is what this time away from England is supposed to be— trying to find out who I am when I strip away family and strip away obligation. But all I did was get caught up in your family dramas.'

'I asked you to.'

'And I jumped at the chance. You're right, Dante. I need to be needed. I want to be wanted. If I'm not useful, then who am I?'

'Maddie, you are a warm, compassionate woman. A warm, compassionate, hardworking and intelligent woman. You don't need other people's approval to validate you.'

She looked up at him, her eyes so dark a grey they were almost black. 'I shouldn't but I do. Pathetic, I know. That's the worst part—I do know and yet I make the same mistakes over and over.'

'Maddie.' Dante stepped forward and laid a hand on her shoulder, her skin impossibly smooth, impossibly silky, and his hands ached with the memory of how soft she had been under his hands. How warm, how welcoming, how comforting. How intoxicating. 'I need to apologise for this last week. I put you in a very difficult position and I want you to know how much I appreciate

it. It was always going to be hard lying to Luciana without adding in other complications…'

'By complications you mean sleeping together? That
was my decision, Dante, and I own it. Let me have that
at least.'

'But I allowed our intimacy to scare me away and
that was wrong.'

'You've been avoiding me.'

'I have,' he confirmed. A wry smile escaped him.
'Which, considering I was simultaneously paying you to
pretend to be my girlfriend, was foolish as well as rude.'

A brittle laugh escaped her. 'All you've done is convince Luciana that we are mad for each other. She's noticed how we never touch or look at each other and she's
decided it's because we'd spontaneously combust if we
did.'

'She might be right,' he said hoarsely. Satisfaction ran
through him as Maddie quivered under his hand. 'Every
time I look at you I remember what you feel like, what
you taste like…'

'Please. Don't. It's hard enough.'

He stepped back, his hand dropping to his side, his
whole body chilled despite the heat of the summer's
day. 'I should never have asked you to lie for me. I just
wanted…' He closed his eyes briefly, trying to find the
right words. 'Sometimes, Maddie, it seems that all I do is
hurt people—Violetta, Luciana, you—and yet all I want
is to do what's right. I know that anything grounded in
deceit is wrong and yet I blundered on and here we are.
I should have been honest with Luciana in the beginning. Maybe it's time she and I have that conversation.'

Maddie frowned. 'I can't disagree; I think a lot of
heartbreak could have been saved if you had been honest

earlier. And maybe it is time to have a real, proper talk with your sister. But I also think you should wait until after the ball. Enjoy the next few weeks; save the serious discussion for afterwards. She looks so much better than when she arrived; wait till she's even more rested.'

'I can't ask you to keep pretending...'

'Yes. You can. You can ask—and then it's up to me to decide whether I am happy to carry on or not. But, Dante, if I do say yes there will be some rules. I may be your employee but that doesn't mean I don't deserve to be treated with respect.'

'Understood. I should never have made you feel that was in doubt.'

'No. And I shouldn't have allowed you to. Deal?' She held out her hand and Dante took it.

The feeling of coming home as he clasped her cool hand, felt her fingers enclose his, was so profound it almost hurt. Hurriedly he let go. 'Deal.'

'Okay. I'd better go. I have a feeling Luciana will have already stirred the entire staff up into a frenzy and we do have two weddings to host before the ball.' But although she shifted as she spoke she didn't actually move, her storm-coloured eyes fixed on his.

'This might be your last moment of calm for two weeks. If I were you I would enjoy it. I have a feeling everyone is going to be turning to you a lot over the next few days.' He hesitated. 'Maddie. You can tell me to go to hell but I have to ask. Why do you need other people's validation? You're clever and organised and brilliant with people. You're creative, clear-thinking—Guido has been singing your praises for months. The *castello* is actually beginning to pay its way and a lot of the credit for that goes to you. And, not that it should matter, but I have to be honest and point out that you are also incredibly beautiful and sexy as hell. The world should be at your feet. I see that, we all see that. Why don't you?'

Maddie just stood and stared at him, her mouth half-open in surprise. 'I… No one has ever said that to me before. Thank you.'

'Then you are surrounding yourself with the wrong people.'

'That is probably true. The problem is, I'm related to half of them.' She smiled but it was a half-hearted attempt.

'Didn't you single-handedly turn around your family fortunes?'

'Pretty much.'

'I'll love Arianna no matter what she chooses to do, but if she shows a tenth of the initiative and drive you did when she's sixteen I'll be unbearably proud. How can they not be?'

Maddie's smile didn't reach her eyes. 'The problem was, I was born first. That meant my parents had a couple of years of worry until my brother came along and made sure the title and estate were safely secured. You understand that; you have the Castello Falcone. It's bred into you. Part of you. Everything the whole family does is about preserving it, readying it for future generations. That's implicit. But if, like me, you're not destined to inherit, then you spend your whole childhood knowing you have to leave it. That you're only ever a visitor, a footnote in the family history, not the main character.'

She sighed and then began to walk along the path again away from the *castello*, Dante falling into step beside her as they rounded a bend and began to climb away from the lake and through the pine forest. After a long pause she began to speak again, almost as if she were speaking to herself. He just a bystander. 'It didn't make sense when I was little. I was the oldest—not that being the oldest necessarily makes anyone the perfect heir, but still—so why was Teddy going to inherit? I just couldn't understand it. But every time I pointed out how unfair it was for women to be excluded from the succession it was as if I was committing family treason—it was even worse when I got briefly involved with a pressure group of other women pushing for change in the archaic laws.'

'Did your family feel as if you were criticising them?'

'Maybe. I didn't mean any of it personally, but of course my father had an older sister; his father too. I can see why they were—are—so resistant.' She sighed. 'They weren't even that comfortable with all the work I did to make Stilling Abbey profitable—because the money goes with the title. It wasn't really my place to get involved. I just didn't *know* my place, that was the problem—is the problem. Now I don't know where I belong at all. That's what I need to figure out.'

'You must have been lonely.' Dante couldn't imagine it. He too had been brought up in a grand old house owned by generations of his forebears, although he knew, unlike Maddie, that one day it would pass to him to look after. But, although he and Luciana had been brought up in a house that was larger than the norm, older than the norm, it was still filled with love and affection.

'I was. You know, Teddy's school reports were exclaimed over, mine ignored, even though my marks were better. My mother wanted to know why I wasn't making the right friends, going to the right parties—fitting in and making social contacts were more important to her than any grade. My dad praised me when I looked nice, or if I was in some stupid catwalk show, or won a gymkhana, but he didn't ever praise my maths grades. I just wanted them to be proud of me. Is that so wrong?'

'It's not wrong at all.'

'They gave me my head for a time, but when Teddy finished university it was made clear that I had got too close. That I needed to step back, step away. Oh, they never said anything outright, but they froze me out.' Her voice broke and instinctively Dante reached for her hand and she grasped it as if he were a lifeline. 'That's when I went on a visit to Theo's parents' and I just never left. They needed me and they were so grateful for the smallest thing. It was intoxicating. I just wanted to be part of them, their family, their home. To be wanted and needed and appreciated. Marrying Theo would give me all that—a family. Only he didn't want or need me at all.'

'Then he's a fool.'

'No. He's not, although it's very kind of you to say so.'

'Maddie.' Dante halted, pulling her to a stop, and she looked up at him, her eyes still darkened to stormy grey. All he wanted was to wipe away the doubt and sadness he saw there. 'I can tell you honestly that everyone at the *castello* will miss you when you leave. And not just because you are hardworking, but also because you're you. When Guido heard you were leaving at the end of August he threatened to walk out unless I paid you enough to make you stay.'

Maddie's smile was tremulous. 'That's very kind of him.'

'Nonsense. No one cares about your name or family here. They care about you.'

Her smile was tremulous. Dante couldn't tear his gaze away from her full mouth, wanting to kiss the doubt and unhappiness away.

'I don't mind helping with the ball because I think it will be fun to see the *castello* in its full glory. And personally I would feel uncomfortable if Luciana knew we'd deceived her. I like her and I don't want things to be awkward. So I'd rather keep pretending until the ball is over if that's okay with you—I leave a few days later anyway.'

'Your ticket's booked?' Dante didn't want to think about why that thought disturbed him.

'I did it yesterday. Thank you. And for the bonus. It was more than I was expecting.'

'Enough for the sloths?'

'Oh, yes. I'm planning a whole week hanging out near the sloth sanctuary before I head down to Peru for trekking and culture. With the bonus and my savings I've enough to travel through Central America; I won't need to look for work until I get to Australia. So, do you agree? That it's best we keep pretending?'

Dante swallowed. 'I think that will work. I do have a suggestion though.'

'What's that?'

'Back on the boat, in Verona, we said we'd see how things went. Remember? I think we—I—have made a mess of this week. I'd like to do better.'

'Oh?' Maddie's mouth trembled. 'And how are you proposing to do that?'

'I was hoping…' He stepped forward, deliberately backing her up until she was leaning against a tree, her eyes shadowed by long lashes as he looked down at her. 'I was hoping we could seal our new start with a kiss.'

He waited, unsure whether he had overstepped, whether it was too late, whether reigniting the passion that had flamed so brightly it had almost burned him was a mistake. But all he knew was that he couldn't spend two more weeks with Maddie and not kiss her. Not touch her. Not consume her as she consumed him.

'A kiss? Is that wise?'

'Are kisses meant to be wise?'

'Maybe not,' she said and looked up at him at last, her eyes vulnerable in their trust, with their need. 'Maybe that's the point. Maybe that's what we both need, some carefree kisses.'

'Maybe.' But there was nothing carefree about kissing Maddie as his hand travelled down her arm to her waist, as his other hand tilted her chin, as his skin thrilled to her touch and his heart beat in unison with hers. As their eyes locked, as his mouth slanted towards her, as he heard her sigh in anticipation and his whole body thrilled in response he knew that every kiss would have its price. But there was no way he was going to stop. Could stop. Not while her touch urged him on, her body melding into his. Whatever the price, he was willing to pay.

# CHAPTER TEN

'OH, MADDIE! THIS is wonderful. You are a genius.'

'I'm not sure about that,' Maddie said, laughing at Luciana's exuberance. 'Although the *castello* does look rather magical. But I had a lot of help. Everyone has worked so hard.'

They had. Not only the *castello* staff, who had pulled double shifts and forgone days off, but most of the village had turned out as well, offering their services as waiters, cleaners, pot-washers—anything that needed doing to ensure the ball was a success. Apparently it was a tradition for the villagers to help out at *castello* events, not just because they were well-paid for doing so, but also because the staff party that followed on was legendary and no one wanted to miss out. It was a little odd to see the schoolteacher mixing cocktails and the woman who cut Maddie's hair serving canapés, but it also made the whole ball feel even more like a family affair with everyone pitching in.

Luciana had insisted that Maddie should attend, despite her protestations that it was much easier to deal with any last-minute hiccups if she wasn't in a long dress and heels. But she'd been overruled. Maddie suspected that her friend just wanted to watch Dante and Maddie dance together. It looked as if Luciana would get her wish. Maddie had promised him one dance.

Just the one. Because tomorrow Luciana and her family would be departing back to New Zealand and there would be no reason for Maddie and Dante to pretend they were anything other than two lonely people who had made a temporary connection any more. This Cinderella would be jumping on a plane in just a few days and the Conte would return to Rome and his life there. It was time for their summer idyll to come to an end.

Which was all for the best because the last two weeks had been terrifying—a pretend girlfriend by day and a secret lover by night. The days had been easy. As predicted, she'd been far too busy to spend much time with Luciana and her family. The few moments she had been able to snatch away from her work she'd been busy booking accommodation in the US and Central America, making sure as much of her first month was organised as possible.

But at night…that was Dante's time and he made the most of it. Maddie was existing on barely any sleep and yet she'd never felt more energised. She finally understood why her friends had glowed at the beginning of a relationship, the potent, heady mixture of hormones and sex and desire making every nerve end come alive.

If only it were just sex. *That* she could handle. After all, she was well overdue an indulgent affair. But it was so much more—and that she was finding a lot more difficult to manage.

It wasn't that Maddie didn't appreciate the late-night lakeside picnics—and the late-night skinny-dipping. Or the evening trips back to Lake Garda for dinner on board the boat as it sailed out across the lake. Or the dinner in the tiny mountaintop restaurant. Or even the night he had brought pizza to her apartment and they'd eaten it in bed whilst he'd helped her plan out her first month's travels. No, she appreciated every moment of it. Only, in a way, she had preferred the morose man who couldn't even look at her.

Because that man would have been easy to leave.

Unlike the man whose smile still hit her with its sweetness, the man with the knowing touch, the sweet kisses and who seemed to know exactly what she wanted before she did.

She knew the rules. No strings, no ties, for a few weeks only. She'd helped write them after all.

She just hadn't appreciated how easy they would be to break.

'You look beautiful.' Arianna appeared at her side and was gazing up at Maddie with a worshipful expression that caught at Maddie's heart.

'So do you,' she said honestly. The usually grubby urchin who lived her life in shorts and a T-shirt was wearing a red dress, her dark hair shining as it fell down her back confined with a large bow.

Arianna pulled a face. 'Zia Luciana insisted. I would have refused, but she's made the boys wear suits.' She pointed over to the other side of the medieval hall where three small boys were standing scowling mutinously, each of them spic and span in neat blue suits. 'That's far worse, isn't it?'

'My sons look very handsome,' Luciana said indignantly. 'Come on, Arianna. Let's make sure your *nonna* is ready for her grand entrance. She wants all her grandchildren to escort her.'

'And then we can play!' Arianna twirled round, her

skirts swirling around her knees. 'Maddie, will you dance with me later? The boys don't dance. They think they are too cool.'

'No one is too cool to dance, don't worry, Arianna. I bet we can get those boys on the dance floor and having fun.'

'Run over to your cousins, Ari.' Luciana ran a hand through her small niece's hair. 'And take them up to Nonna's room. I'll be there in a minute. I just need to check everything is in place.'

'Luciana,' Maddie said, laughing as she watched Arianna strut over to her cousins, every step proclaiming that she was in charge. 'Everything is in place. We've been through it ten times.'

'The band know the signal?'

'Yes.'

'The guests all know to be in the hall?'

'I have people rounding up any strays.'

'Dante has his speech ready?'

'He was pacing up and down and muttering it to himself, so, yes, I believe so. Go, get your mother and we can get this party started.'

'You are an absolute treasure. There is no way I could have done this without you.'

'Nonsense!'

'I am serious. And my brother looks happier that I have seen him in a long time. Forgive me for saying this, but it's a different happiness to before. More measured, less feverish. He was a boy then. This is a man's happiness.'

'Luciana…' Maddie shifted, uncomfortable with the topic.

'And Ari adores you. My heart used to break for her,

but I can go back to New Zealand happy, knowing that you are here.' Luciana leaned forward and embraced Maddie with a kiss on both cheeks, before turning and heading out of the hall. Maddie stood and watched her go, her chest tight.

Everything had escalated so far beyond her control. She had never intended to get so close to Luciana—to like her, to enjoy her company. Now what had seemed like a harmless deception done for the best of intentions seemed cruel, manipulative. And as for Arianna... Maddie's chest tightened even more, the pain almost making her gasp. The one consolation was that the small girl didn't know about either the fake or the real relationship between her father and Maddie. But Maddie had allowed herself to get too close to the child. Had allowed herself to care for her—and, worse, she knew Arianna was getting far too attached, searching her out, confiding secrets, seeking reassurance.

At that moment she saw Dante. He looked good in formal evening wear, the severe, clean lines suiting his austere handsomeness. He stood, unsmiling, listening courteously to the elderly couple who had greeted him. Maddie watched him, drinking in every fibre of him. The dark hair she loved to muss out of its usual order, dark blue eyes capable of freezing—or heating—with one glance, sharp cheekbones, wide shoulders tapering down to a narrow waist. It may have been the way Dante looked that had pulled her in that first day by the lake; it was partly the way he looked that had enticed her to throw caution to the wind and stay with him on the boat that first time. But the pulse beating insistently at her neck, her wrists, the tops of her thighs had nothing to do with mere looks.

No. She was attracted to his quiet, un-showy thoughtfulness. The way he wanted his sister to stop worrying, his dedication to his daughter, his commitment to the village and the people who worked at the *castello*. She was attracted to those rare flashes of humour. To the way his smile transformed his usual serious demeanour, giving him a warmth and sweetness most people never suspected that the Conte Falcone possessed.

And in just four days she would get on a plane and would travel to the other side of the world. It was unlikely she would ever see him again. Maybe that was for the best. Because whatever Dante wanted from the rest of his life it didn't include her.

As if he could hear her thoughts across the crowded room Dante looked over at her and their gazes caught for one long moment. Humour and heat mingled in his gaze and Maddie wished that she could walk over to him, slip her arm through his and claim him as hers, publicly and irrevocably.

Hang on. She *what*?

Taking a step back, Maddie was relieved to feel the cold security of the wall propping her up as her legs trembled, her stomach swooping like a starling in full murmuration. This wasn't the deal—not the deal she had made with Dante, or the one she had made with herself. The last few weeks had been the first step in a new adventure, in claiming her identity as a new Maddie. They hadn't been about putting down roots in any way, especially not romantically.

And yet that was exactly what she had done.

Somehow she had allowed Dante Falcone to claim a place in her heart—only, ironically, he had as little interest in being there as she had in having him there.

'Fool,' Maddie muttered. 'Utter fool.' Only she could get herself into this kind of mess. At least her departure date was fixed. If she could just make sure Dante suspected nothing, left with her head high and a smile on her lips, then at least her dignity would be intact. Just not her heart.

Dante took a breath, relieved to have a moment to himself for the first time that evening. It seemed that no time at all had passed since the Dowager Contessa had, as planned, descended into the medieval hall from the gallery above, flanked by her four grandchildren. She had been greeted by a room full of her friends and relatives, a large contingent of Luciana's friends and some of Dante's business associates, as well as family associates and neighbours. The band had immediately struck up a medley of her favourite songs, starting with the Beatles, before Dante had welcomed everyone to the first Falcone ball in over a decade and toasted his mother's health.

After the formalities the crowd dispersed. Some stayed in the hall to dance to a selection of sixties tunes, others mingled on the terraces or made their way to the marquee by the lakeside. Waiting staff circulated with trays of drinks and canapés, buffet tables were set up in the formal dining room and in the courtyard, and entertainers amused the partygoers with magic tricks, acrobatics and spectacular professional dancing. All the fountains had been switched on, water cascading down the series of terraces like a waterfall, illuminated by the lamps which had been threaded through all the trees and hedges. The Castello Falcone looked stunning, like a scene from a modern-day fairy tale. The last time it had been so vibrant, so alive had been for Dante's wedding.

Dante's mouth tightened. Violetta had been so excited she was getting married in a real castle—and he had been so proud that he could give her that opportunity. He had so willingly and happily bestowed his home, his title, his love on her. But all she wanted was the first two of the trio and even they had palled after a while. His love had never been enough.

It was funny that Maddie had almost married for the same reasons. That she too had chosen a title and a grand old house over love. Only in the end she had walked away.

He glanced at his watch. Half-past eleven. Half an hour until their dance. He had barely seen Maddie all night. She was supposed to be enjoying the ball as a guest, but she was probably running around behind the scenes, making sure everything was going smoothly. The only way to get her to stop would be to make her—he'd have to insist on a glass of Prosecco, maybe a walk down to the lake. Not that they would get any privacy with over two hundred guests plus staff milling around—and his mother, whose sharp, blue-eyed gaze missed nothing.

Maddie and he had managed to keep their liaison a secret from her so far; there was no point being outed now when his family were departing tomorrow and Maddie herself had booked her flight to leave in just four days' time.

Dante's hands tightened on his glass stem. He'd only known her for a few weeks and yet somehow she had become an integral part of his family, his life. Somehow Dante knew that the way she relaxed with him was unusual, a privilege. Not just in bed, but also the way she teased him, allowed him to tease her. The way she confided her hopes and dreams, her fears. Inspired him to confide his. Not many people saw that side of Maddie.

Maybe it was a good thing she was leaving before he got too used to having her around.

'Dante, there you are.'

He turned as Luciana called his name and smiled affectionately at his sister, magnificent in tight red silk. 'I have to admit I thought you were crazy when you suggested holding a ball in such a short period of time, but you have done a wonderful job. Mama looks radiant. She has barely left the dance floor all night.'

'Last I heard she was dropping all kinds of heavy hints about the years she spent in London before she married Papa. If we believe her then she was serially dating a number of rock 'n' roll stars! If I have to hear one more story about what she got up to in her "garret on the King's Road" then I am sailing off to the other side of the lake, just me, a bottle of Prosecco and no more mental images of my mother in a teeny miniskirt flirting with half of London.'

'She was really beautiful though. She still is,' he added hurriedly, just in case his mother was behind him. 'But I would still rather not hear about the time she posed nude for a certain celebrity photographer.'

'No. Really no,' Luciana agreed, snagging two glasses of Prosecco from a passing waiter and handing one to him. 'Here, to us. The Falcones. Who really know how to throw a party.' She frowned, glass still held up to his. 'Maddie should be here. I wouldn't have been able to organise half of this without her. I only had responsibility for the guest list—which, let me tell you, was no mean feat; the great-aunts were a week's work alone—and she did the rest.'

'She's very capable.'

'She's more than that. I love her, Dante. She's exactly what you and Arianna need. No nonsense, organised, she understands our world, but has a lot of heart. Mind you don't let her slip away.'

Deceiving his sister for one week had been hard enough. But deceiving her for two more weeks, watching her get close to Maddie, seeing the happiness in her eyes whenever she caught sight of the two of them together…that was a whole other level of deceit and he had struggled to reconcile it with his own code of honour and responsibility.

'Ciana…' he began impulsively, but was interrupted by Arianna, flying over to him, her hair its usual tangle, her sandals long since discarded and smears of something that looked very much like a good half of the chocolate fountain down her dress.

'Papa. Papa.'

'*Si, cucciola mia.*'

'Did you know Maddie is leaving?'

'What?' Luciana turned to him, eyes wide in surprise.

'This was only always a temporary job for her, *cara.*' Dante took Arianna's hand. 'She has been saving up to travel the world. Doesn't that sound exciting?'

'But I like her! I don't want her to leave.'

'Ari, we're leaving too. In just a couple of days. Your aunt and cousins will go back to New Zealand and Nonna will go home to Lucerne and you and I have to go back to Roma for school and work. It's been a lovely summer, but even the best summers turn into autumn eventually.'

He did his best to keep his voice light and unconcerned despite the tears gathering in Arianna's eyes, the suspicion and disbelief in Luciana's gaze and the heaviness in his heart. He didn't really want Maddie to fly off to the other side of the world. He would have been quite happy to keep their relationship going for a little longer, to allow it to peter out naturally. But this was what Maddie wanted, what she had been saving for, planning for, what she needed. Not a lonely widower whose heart was so locked away the chains were probably rusty with disuse.

'Ari,' he said again, coaxingly. 'This separation isn't for ever. You and I and Nonna are going to spend Christmas in New Zealand with Zia Luciana and the cousins. They live on a huge vineyard in the mountains. Best of all it will be summer there. We can spend our Christmas boating and swimming—won't that be fun?'

'But Maddie won't be coming with us?'

'No, she won't. Maddie has her own life to live, *bambina*. Her own adventures to have.' Adventures far from here. Far from him.

'Can't you tell her not to go?'

'No. And I wouldn't if I could. She's looking forward to it very much. So, even though it's hard, you need to remember you're a Falcone and say *adieu* with a smile.'

Arianna's lip wobbled and she turned and fled into the crowd without replying. With a sigh Dante straightened and turned to meet his sister's accusatory glance.

'She's leaving?'

'Ciana…'

'Don't you *Ciana* me! Why didn't you say anything?'

'Because I didn't want you to worry. Look, I like Maddie. But I did tell you that our friendship is still in very early days. Maddie has plans. Plans that don't, can't include me, and I have a life incompatible with those plans. We both knew that when we got closer and nothing has changed.'

'Dante Falcone, you are a fool.'

Dante blinked at the vehemence in his sister's voice.

'That girl might be the best thing to happen to you, to Arianna. And you're going to just let her walk away?'

'I'm not going to just let her do anything. Maddie is a grown woman.' And he knew all too well what happened when plans, needs didn't align—chaos and heartbreak.

'Have you said anything, asked her to stay?'

'No. No, I haven't. Because it wouldn't be fair.'

'Why not?'

This was why he had lied in the first place: Luciana was relentless. Dante's control snapped. 'Because I am not the kind of man Maddie needs.'

'No? You keep telling yourself that, *mio fratello*. But I think she is exactly what *you* need. And if you don't at least ask her to stay then you're an even bigger fool than I thought.' And with those closing remarks Luciana grabbed another glass of Prosecco and stalked away, leaving Dante staring after her.

This—this was why he couldn't be honest with his sister. She didn't understand. How could she? He was the Falcone heir. Responsible for hundreds—thousands—of jobs. He had to look after the family empire, the livelihoods of dependents, investors and staff. Custodian of the family name, title, holdings for the next generation. Failure wasn't an option. And yet he had failed spectacularly. Failed at marriage. At parenting. At love. It wasn't pride or fear or heartbreak that stopped him trying again. It was pragmatism. He couldn't be trusted to give his heart to someone who wanted it, who would value it. It made sense to keep it guarded.

Only, Arianna had so enjoyed the company of her aunt and Maddie. She needed a mother figure in her life, someone close by, not half the world away. He had always promised himself that he would put his daughter first. Maybe he should reconsider his decision to never remarry. He could look for someone safe. Someone who knew the rules, played the way he did. Someone he could trust. A partner, not a lover. The idea had been unthinkable just a few weeks ago, but Maddie had thawed him. Given him some of his self-respect back. He would always be grateful to her for that.

Lost in thought, he made his way back to the ballroom for the midnight dance, which would be followed by the presentation of the birthday cake. The ball wasn't due to end until the early hours for those with the stamina to keep going. The first coach would head back to Riva at one; the last wasn't due to depart until five, after coffee and pastries had been served to the final guests. Dante had no doubt that his mother would be the last one on the dance floor.

As he reached the double doors he sensed someone watching him and, looking up, he saw Maddie. She stood just inside the doors, a little paler than normal, but otherwise her usual composed self. He knew she had spent the whole evening flitting between the kitchen, the ballroom and the dining room, anticipating problems and solving them before they occurred, making sure every guest was comfortable and happy. But there was no sign of the hard work on her face. Her blonde, silky hair fell in a shining sheet. She wore silver, just as she had that first night on Lake Garda, this dress floor-length and full-skirted, the strapless bodice revealing a tantalising hint of cleavage. She wasn't wearing any jewellery, her make-up subtle, letting the dress take centre stage. But no dress, no matter how expensive, could outshine Maddie. Dante swallowed as he surveyed her from head to toe. The dip of her waist, the swell of her breasts, the long-lashed eyes. She was so beautiful, so elegant. Like a young queen surveying her kingdom.

*And she was his.*

The possessive thought came from nowhere. Shocking in its certainty. Dante's hand tightened compulsively on his wine glass. Pushing the thought, any thought away, he strode towards her, watching every tell-tale sign that his presence affected her. The way her eyes widened, the hitch in her breath. The pulse beating wildly in her exposed throat. The primal side of him roared its approval, pheromones flooding the air so thick and fast it was as if he could see them rising in a cloud to envelope them, separate them from the rest of the room.

She was his. Tonight at least. And then he had to let her go.

As he reached Maddie the band quietened and the band leader took to the microphone to announce the midnight dance. His mother, escorted by one of her many admirers, took to the centre of the dance floor and, watched by the hushed, appreciative crowd, waited for the first strains of her favourite song. Finally they came, the unmistakable sounds of the Beatles' 'Something', and slowly the pair began to waltz and Dante held his hand out to Maddie.

'My dance, I believe.'

Without a word she came to him, her arms slipping around his neck as he held her close. Bodies melding together as if they belonged, the music taking over as he guided her around the floor.

'Had a good night?' she asked after a while as the song blended into 'And I Love Her'. Dante tightened his grip.

'I didn't see you all evening. I thought you were supposed to be a guest, not running around working.'

Her eyes fell, but not before he saw the shadow in them. 'I had a lot to do. That reminds me, Dante. Ari heard me discussing my plans with Guido and I'm afraid she was upset.'

'I know, she came to see me.'

'I'm sorry. I meant to talk to her and tell her in person. But how could I explain it was a secret and her aunt couldn't know? I just didn't realise she would be so upset.'

'She cares about you. We all do,' he added and her cheeks flushed a delicate pink. 'Luciana was there when Arianna came to me. She knows you're leaving too.'

'I'm sorry.'

'No, don't be. They had to find out sometime.'

'Is Luciana very cross with me?'

'No. She's cross with me. She thinks I should persuade you to stay.'

'I see.'

The music slowed again and he pulled her in tight. She fitted him so perfectly, as if she was made for him and he for her. But life wasn't that neat. Lust faded, love wasn't infinite and hearts weren't wise. Maddie had dreams, and he couldn't, wouldn't stand in her way. He didn't want to ever see the same disappointment in her clear grey gaze that he had seen every day in Violetta's during the last two years of their marriage. Maddie may have changed his life, given him hope—but she didn't belong with him, whatever other people said, whatever he might want in the secret places in his heart.

He came to a decision. 'Maddie, I need to speak to you. Alone. There's something important I want to give you.'

Maddie came to an abrupt stop. They stood there, looking at each other as the rest of the dancers swirled around them.

'Tonight?'

'Now.' Something had to change, Dante knew that now and there was no point delaying any more. He couldn't follow his heart—but he could listen to his head. Before she could reply the band struck up the familiar strains of 'Happy Birthday' as the chef wheeled in an enormous and elaborate cake. Dante swore under his breath and Maddie stepped back.

'You need to be here for this.'

'*Si*. Meet me by the lake. In fifteen minutes?'

Her laugh was nervous. 'You're being very mysterious.'

'By the lake. I'll see you there.'

She opened her mouth as if to speak and then nodded. 'Okay. Fifteen minutes.'

Dante stood still and stared at her, drinking her in. Unable to stop himself, he reached out and ran one finger down her cheek, feeling the shiver that ran through her at his touch in his very core. Was he about to make the biggest mistake of his life? Setting his jaw, he stepped back, finding the right smile as he turned and greeted his mother, leading her towards the cake, and by the time he managed to look back Maddie had disappeared.

# CHAPTER ELEVEN

IT WAS A good ten-minute walk through the vast old *castello* and down the gardens to the lake, but Maddie was barely aware of her route, or who she spoke to on the way down. The terraces were almost deserted, most of the guests back in the ballroom for the toasts and cake, and she could slip down the steps unaccosted. All she could see was the curious expression in Dante's eyes, a mixture of longing and regret.

The marquee by the lake was similarly empty, the jazz band taking a well-earned rest, the staff back up at the *castello* for the next half-hour. Maddie made her way to the bar and poured herself a glass of wine before curling up on one of the cushion-strewn benches which looked out over the lake, her heart hammering. What was so urgent Dante had to tell her tonight?

And why did she have the very clear feeling she wasn't going to like what she heard?

'Here.' She jumped at the rough voice as Dante passed her a glass of wine and with a start she realised hers was empty. It was the first thing she had drunk all night. She had wanted to stay alert and in control in case anything went wrong. 'The hall is emptying. I think quite a few people are headed here.'

'Then let's go.' Maddie allowed Dante to pull her to her feet and lead her out of the marquee and along the same path they had trodden just a couple of weeks ago, when she had unburdened her soul for the first and only time. 'Did your mother like her cake?'

'*Si*, she's loved the whole evening. Thank you for all that you've done.'

'There's no need to thank me. I'm just happy it all worked out.'

'It all worked out because of you.' Her treacherous heart warmed at the praise, reaching for it greedily. 'You are part of the *castello*. Everywhere I go people sing your praises; they love you. No one wants you to leave.'

Maddie swallowed, her throat burning with suppressed tears. She loved Castello Falcone and all who lived and worked within it too. Walking away was going to be the hardest thing she had ever done, even harder than calling off her wedding. But just like her wedding she had no choice but to leave. She'd got too close, too involved, and for all it felt like home she knew she didn't really belong here either. 'It's a very special place,' she managed somehow, proud of how steady her voice sounded.

'My family adore you, especially Arianna.'

What on earth was going on? Why had he pulled her away from the ball to tell her this? 'Your family are amazing—and Arianna is a real credit to you. You've done a fabulous job with her, Dante. I hope you know that.'

He didn't answer for a while, waiting until they reached a small cove. Maddie had arranged for seats to be put there in case any guests strayed this far down the path and Dante guided her towards them. Any faint hopes he'd simply lured her away to kiss her faded as he sat on the seat opposite, leaning back so that they weren't even within touching distance. Maddie sipped her wine and waited, the blood rushing in her ears.

'She is lonely,' he said eventually, his voice emotionless. 'She is too much alone and her cousins are so far away. Arianna needs a mother. I need a partner. Someone who can help me run the Falcone business interests. Someone who understands diplomacy, society, business.'

Maddie stilled as hope unfurled a tentative tendril. 'That makes sense.'

'I chose badly last time. Let my heart lead my head. I can't afford to do that again. Can't put my family, my daughter through that again. I always hoped that if I met someone I could trust, someone who understood my world then maybe I could contemplate marriage again, but I never thought it really possible. And then I met you.'

She watched him, the austere lines of his face softened by the moonlight and the lanterns strung around, and the realisation that had hit her in the ballroom returned in all its painful intensity. She loved him. Loved him in a defy-her-family-and-perish-in-a-tomb kind of way. Completely and utterly.

Earlier this evening she had vowed not to act on it, not to let him know. Was it possible she had got it all wrong? That there was a happy ending to the ball for her? *Say it, Dante*, she begged him silently. *Tell me you love me.*

But he didn't look like a man on the verge of a declaration, more statue than flesh and blood, a muscle beating in his jaw the only sign that he felt anything at all. 'These last few weeks I've realised I can't let the past hold me back, can't let the past spoil my daughter's future. Maddie, you have shown me that companionship needn't be a war zone. That marrying again is probably the best thing I can do for my family, for my home.'

'Oh.' How was her voice so calm when inside she was more turbulent than a storm-tossed sea? Hope and joy and anger and disappointment and dull, dreary grief all jostling for prominence. Was this a proposal? A warning? A bid for her blessing? She couldn't tell. And she didn't know which of the answers was worse. What she did know was that a treacherous part of her was hoping that it *was* a proposal, blunt and prosaic as the words were. Not because of his title, not because of the *castello* or the fortune or any of the trappings that she had allowed to sway her before. But because she loved him.

*Fool*, she told herself fiercely. Someone threw her a few scraps, praised her and she was so grateful she just fell at their feet? Whatever Dante had just said to her, surely it couldn't be a proposal? Because if it was that then it would break her. Surely Dante knew that. He knew what she yearned for. Had made her feel that maybe it was possible. That one day someone would see through the cool, poised, organised façade and love the girl within. She'd known Theo a lifetime but he had never seen that need in her and she hadn't understood him in return. She'd only known Dante a month but already understood him all too well. Knew he was afraid. Afraid to feel. To love. The words he had just uttered a final proof, if one were needed.

Could she stay with him on that basis? Be part of this beautiful place? Help raise Arianna to become the exceptional young woman Maddie knew she could be? Marry the man she loved, knowing he would never be able to give her his heart, his soul? The part of Maddie who still felt she wasn't worthy of a heart and soul, who just needed to be needed, who just wanted a home, was shouting loudly that of course she could.

It was so tempting.

But not tempting enough.

Besides…he hadn't actually asked her.

The silence stretched out, long and uncomfortable, as Dante visibly searched for words. 'I'm not looking for love, Maddie. Love is an illusion. A drug. It passes and when it's gone it leaves nothing but hollowness and regret. Esteem, compatibility, respect? These are much better foundations to build a life together on.'

'Are they? I've been there, Dante, and I don't agree.'

'I know you walked away from such a marriage before, but this is different. I'm different.'

Yes. It was different. It was worse. Theo wasn't capable of breaking her heart, but the man next to her had infinite capacity to do so. And he was.

'You deserve better, more. Arianna deserves more.'

But it was as if he hadn't heard her. Instead he reached into his pocket. 'I have something for you.'

Time froze, the air still, the faint sounds from the ball receding away to little but echoes. What was he doing? Was this a ring? If there was a ring and a bended knee, would she be able to walk away? What if he said those three words she'd waited her whole life to hear? But the package he pulled out was too big to be a ring, a rectangular package. He held it out to her wordlessly and she took it in trembling hands, folding back the silk it was wrapped in.

A book.

'It's a travel journal. For you to capture your memories.' His eyes were on her, hunger and regret mingling in their blue depths. She turned the book over and over. It was handmade, illustrated, exquisite. It was almost the perfect present.

Almost…only it meant goodbye. This book was Dante's way of sending her away. He was going to marry someone else, some perfect stranger he would never love. 'It's beautiful.' Tears gathered in her eyes, hot and thick, spilling down her cheeks faster than she could wipe them. 'Thoughtful and…' She couldn't finish. 'Dante. Please. Don't marry someone you don't love.'

Carefully she wrapped the book back up and got to her feet, walking over to him and pulling him to his feet in turn. He didn't resist, but nor did he touch her in return. The book was a goodbye and he had already retreated from her.

'Don't marry someone you don't love,' she repeated. 'Not when we have this. It's rare and wonderful. Don't throw it away.'

She reached up and ran a hand along his jaw, searching his gaze as she did so. There was desire, yes. Heat. Resignation. And hope. Maddie knew, even if he hadn't admitted it to himself, that part of him was begging her to take a chance on him, to thaw him out, to hang on in there and hope that one day he would be capable of loving her.

But that wasn't enough. Maddie wanted someone who was capable of loving her now. Of needing her, not because of what she could do for them, but because of who she was.

'Don't give up on love,' she begged him and, standing on her tiptoes, she pressed her mouth to his.

He didn't stop her, didn't step away; instead he kissed her back, fiercely and hard. This was no sweet farewell

or romantic goodbye; it was hard and unyielding and raw
and Maddie took every moment of it, digging her hands
into his hair, sliding them down his back, remembering
every muscle and sinew in his glorious body, allowing
him to explore her with the same fervency and need. It
would be so easy to base a marriage on this. So very
easy, and if she suggested she stay, she suggested he
marry her, she thought he would probably agree.

Instead she stepped away, instantly cold as she stood
alone. 'I'd rather be alone my whole life than settle,
Dante.'

'You won't need to. One day someone will come along
who deserves you.'

'Maybe. But I need you to know,' she summoned up
all the courage she had, 'I need you to know that if you
had been able to tell me that you loved me tonight and
asked me to stay then I would have said yes. That if you
allowed yourself to love me I would stay. I'm not Violetta. And you're not the boy you were back then. We're
two adults who could have made each other very happy,
I think.'

She stepped closer again, allowing her body to thrill
to the sensation of his nearness one last time as she
pressed a final kiss to his cold cheek. 'Goodbye, Dante.'

And she turned and walked away.

The next few days passed in a merciful blur. Somehow
Dante had managed to get back to the party, thrown
himself into being the consummate host, the dutiful son,
convincing everyone that he was having a fantastic time.
But as he laughed and danced and entertained the remaining guests he was numb inside. It was as if his body

had been taken over by someone who knew what to say, what to do, while Dante had shut down.

Maddie loved him.

And he had stood there and allowed her to walk away. What had he thought would happen? That she would listen to his plans for a sedate, sensible life and offer to be part of it? That wasn't what he wanted anyway. There was nothing sedate about Madeleine Fitzroy.

Besides, he knew who she was, what she wanted, and he would only have been able to offer her a pale facsimile of that. What had she said in Verona? 'If anyone ever proposes to me again I want romance and heart.' He had no romance and his heart was closed.

But if his heart was closed, then why were her words, her absence haunting him like this? If a business deal fell through then sure, it stung, but he didn't dwell on it. Learned any lessons needed and moved on. Didn't wallow in failure.

Dante sat back in his chair and allowed his glance to focus on the picture of Arianna framed above his desk. She looked so like her mother in that picture. The same mischievous expression, the same glossy hair and pointed chin. Only her eyes, a dark, long-lashed blue, came from him. And for once the resemblance to her mother didn't invoke the same old sickening guilt.

The truth was he had really, truly thought he was in love with Violetta. He'd been captivated by her. Infatuation, maybe, but it had felt more real at the time than anything he had ever experienced. He knew, then, just why Romeo had come hotfoot back to Verona, poison in hand, to die by the side of his love, because, then, the thought of life without Violetta had been unbearable. She had consumed him, subsumed him and he had fallen gratefully at her feet. Looking back, he could see why. It wasn't just her opulent beauty, her sensuality, her capricious sweetness—he had been lost, searching for a sense of who he was. His father's death had been so sudden, so unexpected, leaving Dante with responsibilities he hadn't expected to shoulder for another twenty years. Luciana was leaving Italy for good, and his mother, heartbroken, had retired to Lucerne, so she could build a life free of constant reminders of her beloved husband.

There Dante had been, just twenty-two, unsure of who he was, how he would cope, and Violetta had given him a path. He'd seen himself through her eyes—or so he thought—and a powerful, attractive man had stared back at him. He'd wanted to be that man so badly and, rather than grow into him, learn to be him, he'd taken a shortcut and allowed his relationship with Violetta to define him. Ironically, in the end, it had been the birth of Arianna which had both made him into the man he had wanted to be and signalled the end of his marriage. The moment he'd held his daughter everything made sense. She came first. For her he threw himself into work, building on his father's legacy, safeguarding and growing the Falcone business and investments. But as his life had fallen into place, as his way became clear, Violetta's had begun to fall apart. Without his besotted admiration she didn't know who *she* was, motherhood bored her and she had no interest in working beside him.

He saw it all so clearly now. But back then he had been at the mercy of his emotions, and they had led him badly astray, not just at the beginning, but also all the way through his marriage. He hadn't had the maturity or the common sense to handle his wife.

He wasn't responsible for her death. Only Violetta

had made the choice to get into that car, to take those drugs. But he carried responsibility for the death of his marriage. His love hadn't grown as he matured; rather it had withered away and he had blamed Violetta for that. To be fair to Violetta, she had always been true to herself; she hadn't changed. He had.

But what if Arianna had been in that car?

The thought still kept him awake at night, haunted him. He could have lost his daughter that day. She had to come first. And that meant ensuring he didn't allow his emotions to influence his decision-making. Not even— especially—where his relationships were concerned.

Arianna was hurting now. But she would understand one day that everything he did, he did for her. Wouldn't she?

He sure as hell hoped so. Because right now he was struggling to understand himself. That insistent feeling that maybe he was making the biggest mistake of his life. That he was holding himself back through fear. Through stubbornness.

Dante turned back to his computer, staring at the spreadsheet awaiting his comment as if it might have the answers, his mind unable to focus on the numbers.

He and Arianna had returned to Rome two days before and were installed back in the luxurious villa he had bought five years ago. It had been decorated and furnished by one of the city's top interior designers to fit his brief of a comfortable family home and yet somehow it never really *felt* like home. He'd always liked the Eternal City, but living there full-time, even with the benefit of extensive private gardens, was just too much. So much traffic, so much noise, so much hustling and busyness. A world away from the tranquillity of San Tomo and

Castello Falcone. He'd wanted that contrast then. Now every car horn, every shout, just reminded him of everything he didn't have.

He glanced at his watch. Noon. Maddie would be on her way to the airport, if she hadn't arrived there already. Her flight to New York left at three. She was spending three nights in the city before taking the train down the East Coast all the way to Florida, stopping at several destinations along the way, before flying down to Costa Rica and beginning her travels proper. He could see her, her travel bag on her back, hair scooped back into a no-nonsense ponytail, her eyes determined.

He knew every step of those first two weeks of her travels. From the moment she booked into the five-star hotel in New York he had insisted on treating her to, to the day she set foot in the nature reserve in Costa Rica. Had planned it with her, advised and commented. The truth was, it hadn't felt real. More like they were planning an imaginary journey than a real one, one which would carry Maddie irrevocably away from him, probably for ever. The summer in San Tomo had been a moment out of time, an idyll. Not real life.

Which it was. Wasn't it?

What would have happened if he had dared to look further into his heart on the night of the ball? What if he hadn't made a sudden decision to tell Maddie that thanks to her he was ready to move on, but had taken her on that same walk along the river and told her he loved her and wanted to be with her for ever? What if she had said yes, as she'd indicated she would have? Would he and Arianna have stayed in San Tomo and they all lived happily ever after?

He'd never know.

And knowing he didn't actually believe in happily-ever-after brought him no satisfaction, just an all-consuming suspicion that maybe he was missing out on really living.

The door opened and Arianna mooched in. Dante's heart squeezed at the sight of her. She hadn't been her usual exuberant self since the night of the ball. She wasn't usually one for tears, but she had wept whilst waving her aunt and cousins off, whilst saying goodbye to her *nonna*. The only time she hadn't cried was when they left the *castello* and she had said her *adieu* to Maddie. She had heeded his words, chin up, a proud smile on her lips even as her eyes burned.

Dante wasn't sure exactly what he had said to Maddie or she to him. Commonplace platitudes, no more. She had been back to professional, smooth Madeleine Fitzroy. Gracious and polite to the last, no sign that two days before she had been begging him to tell her that he loved her.

'I'm bored,' Arianna announced.

'Why don't you call one of your friends?'

'They're all still away. No one comes to Rome in August except tourists. If I was in San Tomo I could swim or climb a mountain or play with Flavia or have a sailing lesson or—'

'I get the picture.' Dante cut his daughter off before she listed every single activity in the mountain village.

'Why did we have to come back anyway? You could work there just as easily. Why can't we live there all year round? There's a *scuola primeria* in San Tomo.'

There was. Dante and Luciana had both attended it before moving to the International School in Milan. 'Don't you like living in Rome?'

'Yes, but I'd rather live in San Tomo and ski in winter

and be on the lake all summer. I was happy there—and so were you,' Arianna said with the keen perceptiveness that sometimes surprised him.

'We were on holiday…'

'You were more relaxed. Not as tired.'

'I…' It didn't seem right that his eight-year-old daughter thought him tired and overworked.

'When does Maddie get to New York?'

'Tonight.'

'I wish she wasn't going,' Arianna said in a small voice and Dante pulled her onto his knee.

'You and me both, *bambina*,' he said under his breath.

Arianna turned and snuggled into him, her hair tickling his chin. Dante held her close, protectiveness and love consuming him. 'Papa. Can I tell you something?'

'Anything. Always.'

'I made a wish. In the wishing well at the *castello*.'

'Hmm?'

'I wished for you and Maddie to fall in love. I wanted her to stay and marry you and for you not to be sad any more and for me to have a *mamma*,' Arianna said in a rush.

Dante couldn't speak, holding Arianna tighter as her words sank in. He wasn't just hurting himself, he was hurting Arianna. 'Ari…'

'I really liked Maddie, Papa. Didn't you?'

'*Si*. I did.'

'Does she know?'

'No,' Dante admitted.

'Why not?'

'It's not always easy to tell someone. You'll learn that one day.'

'That's silly,' Arianna said scornfully. 'If I like some-one I'll always tell them, otherwise how will they know?'

'How indeed?'

'You should tell her.'

'I…' Dante stopped. Arianna was right. He should tell her. Tell her everything he couldn't articulate even to himself. Find the romance and heart she deserved. 'You're right, Ari. I should tell her. How do you feel about getting away from Rome for a few days?'

'Sure. Where are we going?'

'New York. Let's go and find Maddie and tell her we miss her, shall we?'

# CHAPTER TWELVE

MADDIE PRACTICALLY LIMPED into the opulent hotel foyer. She wasn't sure she had ever walked so much in her entire life. Sightseeing in Manhattan was, it turned out, excellent practice for walking the Inca Trail. According to her phone, she had been averaging twenty kilometres a day.

She looked at the lifts, just twenty feet away, trying to work out if she had the energy to get to her room. Maybe she needed a little fortifier first. She sank into one of many comfortable loveseats on one side of the foyer, every muscle in her body sighing in relief as the cushions cradled her tired body. If she ever got a place of her own she was going to call this hotel and find out their furniture supplier and order this exact loveseat. And then she would never leave it.

It would be handy if she could also take the service home with her. She had no sooner sat down than one of the neat, friendly waitresses was by her side, smile perfectly in place.

'Good evening, Miss Fitzroy. Did you have a good day?'

'Yes, thank you. I walked down to Brooklyn.'

The waitress's eyes widened. 'Walked?'

'It doesn't look quite so far on a map,' Maddie explained. 'I wanted to explore the Lower East Side and it seemed to make sense to do so on the way down and then walk back up the West Side. I leave tomorrow morning. There's just not enough time to do everything.'

She'd arrived in New York late afternoon two days ago, reasonably alert and refreshed thanks to a First Class upgrade she suspected Dante had paid for. A sweet gesture, but one she couldn't help wishing he hadn't made. She wanted to forget about him, forget about what a fool she had been, forget about the moment she had begged him to love her. Instead every comfortable, pampered moment of her flight she couldn't help thinking how easy it had been for him to treat her. Had it been done as a surprise when he'd paid her bonus, or was it a guilty way of apologising for the way their friendship had come to an abrupt end?

Not that it mattered either way. The only option she had was to carry on with her plans and hope that in time her new experiences would relegate the summer—and Dante—to the back of her mind.

But right now she was still raw; she just refused to allow it to ruin her longed-for trip. She'd spent the first evening wandering around the genteel Upper East Side where her hotel was based before an early dinner in her room. Yesterday she had explored Central Park and the famed Metropolitan Museum before facing the hurly-burly of Times Square and the Theatre District. She'd intended to go and see a show and grab dinner out, but at the last minute she'd retreated to her room and another room service meal in front of the TV. She knew that the next few months would involve many meals alone in strange towns and cities, but she just didn't have the heart to begin yet. There seemed to be happy couples and families everywhere she looked, rubbing in her own lonely state.

Tomorrow she would be more adventurous. She was spending one night in Philadelphia and then a night in Washington and another in Richmond, Virginia, before two nights in Charleston and a further two in Savannah. Her last stop was Florida, where she had a four-night stay before flying down to San Jose. This first two weeks was a way of breaking herself in gently, scheduled trains in a country where she spoke the language. More of a holiday than real travelling.

Once she hit Costa Rica it would all get real. A new language, a different culture. She'd really be on her own. No more five-star hotels like this; she would be bedding down in hostels instead. She might as well make the most of this while she could.

The waitress's soft voice recalled her to her surroundings. 'Can I get you anything, ma'am? A coffee—or maybe a cocktail?'

'A coffee would be lovely. Thank you.'

Maddie sat back in her chair and looked around her. Everyone seemed so put together and confident, as if being surrounded by marble pillars and high, gilt-edged ceilings was commonplace. But they probably thought that about her as well. She always had had the ability to blend in.

She smiled her thanks as the waitress put her coffee in front of her and, for the hundredth time that day, resisted the urge to look at her phone. She was only allowed to do so every two hours. But she could check it every minute and it wouldn't change a thing. Dante wasn't going to get in touch. He had said goodbye to her as coolly and casually as if she were nothing more than the employee she was meant to be. As if his body didn't know every inch of hers. As if they had never confided their deepest fears to each other.

No, she scolded herself. No more. Her time with Dante was done; it was dust. She was moving on into a whole other phase of her life. No longer the obedient Honourable Madeleine, no longer the Runaway Bride, no longer the amenable and helpful Maddie. She wasn't sure who she would be when she finished this experience, but hopefully, like Great-Great-Great-Aunt Ophelia, she would be transformed.

Suffragette, VAD nurse, challenger of primogeniture and all-round badass, Maddie's aunt had lost her lover in World War One, had her bid to inherit Stilling Abbey and the title thrown out of court and, as a result, been ostracised from her outraged family. Undaunted, she had jumped on a boat and explored South America, returning home five years later to become an actress and writer. She was simultaneously the family black sheep and their biggest source of pride. Maddie had been raised on stories of her exploits. It was a photo of Ophelia holding a sloth which had first ignited Maddie's desire to follow in her great-aunt's footsteps. What would she think of her great-niece sitting around and feeling sorry for herself? Not very much. She'd be far more likely to poke her with her parasol and tell her to pull herself together than to offer sympathy.

Tonight, Maddie decided, she wouldn't hide herself away. She would go to a restaurant…she would go to a bar. She might even, feet allowing, go dancing. And she wouldn't think about Dante Falcone once.

Okay. Once, maybe. But no more.

Decision made, she finished her coffee and, wincing at a particularly tender blister, got to her feet. As she did so the waitress came back over, an envelope in her hand. 'Ma'am? This came for you earlier.'

Maddie accepted the envelope in some surprise. Her name was typed on the front. No address. It must have been handed in personally. But she didn't know anyone here, did she? And nobody apart from Dante knew she was here. Her family were aware of her plans to travel, but she hadn't sent them the itinerary yet, meaning to do so from Florida. She knew her mother would consider her whole trip self-indulgent nonsense. She'd been against her leaving England in the first place.

Maddie walked slowly to the lift and, once inside, opened the envelope, pulling out the card within, staring in some puzzlement at the contents. A VIP pass to the Empire State Building for that evening.

'Odd.' No name, no explanation. She had mentioned to the receptionist that morning that she was hoping to go up the iconic tower before her train left in the morning. Maybe they had purchased the ticket for her?

She turned the ticket over. It was date stamped for eight p.m., two hours from now. And hadn't she been intending to go out tonight, tempting as room service and another night curled up in her suite was? This was a sign. She was in the city that allegedly never slept; she really should experience it after dark.

The lift doors opened and Maddie stepped onto the plushly decorated landing. Dante had booked and paid for the hotel, before the ball and the ending of their relationship. It was a far fancier hotel than Maddie, who when in London always stayed at her mother's club with its single beds and boarding-school air, had ever experienced. Her stay was made even more luxurious when she discovered that she had been upgraded to a suite with a gorgeous sitting room with views over Central Park, a bathroom larger than her bedroom at home, complete with a bath big enough for two and a walk-in shower that would probably manage an entire rugby team.

It was incredible, but a little big for one. She felt lost in the huge bed, lonely.

Maddie opened the door and stepped into the suite. Fresh flowers had replaced the still blooming bouquet on the dining table. Fresh wine and chocolates sat on the sideboard and a jug of iced water was ready for her, as if they had timed her return exactly. She really should text Dante and thank him for both the suite and the flight upgrade but she couldn't bring herself to make contact. If he'd booked them after the ball then it was almost as if he was buying her off. He probably wouldn't see it that way, but she couldn't help but think of it as a way to easily assuage his conscience.

She would text him from Costa Rica, she decided. A breezy picture of a sloth with thanks thrown in. And that would be that.

Maddie spent a good hour soaking in the bathtub, watching a TV show as she did so, letting her tired feet recover from their exertions. It didn't take her very long to decide what to wear—carrying her clothes with her for the next four months meant she was travelling light. A couple of pairs of shorts, one pair of lightweight walking trousers, several vest tops and two light hoodies, her bikini, one cotton sundress and one silky dress in case of a more formal occasion. Everything crease-resistant and quick-dry. She wasn't sure her Aunt Ophelia would have approved. She was always incredibly elegant, even when halfway down the Amazon.

Maddie opted for her silky dress and a wrap in case of over-enthusiastic air-conditioning and slipped her feet into her flip-flops. Tonight was good practice for the rest of her trip. No fear, no regrets.

To Maddie's surprise a car was waiting for her. Not a yellow cab, but a sleek, black luxury affair with leather seats and darkened windows. She felt a little like a film star as the driver handed her into the back seat and the car purred quietly through the manic Manhattan traffic. When she got to the famous Art Deco building the driver handed her out and another uniformed man took over, ushering her through the security checks, past the queues of waiting people straight into a lift, then another and then, to her surprise, a third smaller lift.

'Welcome to the one-hundred-and-second floor, ma'am,' the man said as the doors opened and he gestured to her to step out.

The lift opened out, not onto the iconic wraparound balcony she was expecting, but into a room with windows all around, each with a dizzying view of the city. The room was almost empty, just one figure standing at the far end, looking out at the view.

Maddie turned. 'I think there's been…' but the lift doors had already closed. How awkward! She was alone in the room with a stranger.

Only he wasn't a stranger.

He didn't need to turn round for her to recognise him. She knew that stance anywhere. It was Dante.

The lift doors had closed and Dante knew he had just ten minutes. It was highly irregular. The Empire State

Building didn't offer private viewings. However, Dante had contacts who had contacts and somehow a miracle had occurred. He had ten minutes.

Which meant he really had to turn and speak.

He just hoped he found the right words. Remembered the right words.

Slowly he turned round. Maddie stood by the doors, staring at him as if he was the ghost of mistakes past. His heart stuttered as he drank in the sight of her, tall and elegant as ever in a long blue dress, her hair pinned up. Only the vulnerability and uncertainty in her eyes was new.

'*Ciao.*'

Not a great start, but not too terrible either. You couldn't go too wrong with a simple greeting.

'Dante? What on earth are you doing here?'

'We missed you,' he said simply.

'But why the elaborate set-up? You knew where I was staying. Or you could have called...'

'Heart and romance. You wanted heart and romance.'

Understanding flared in her eyes, followed by hope before she wiped all expression off her face. 'Yes. I did.'

Dante took a deep breath. Either he was about to make a colossal fool of himself or... '"Arise, fair sun, and kill the envious moon, Who is already sick and pale with grief That thou, her maid, art far more fair than she."'

Maddie just stared. At least she hadn't laughed. Emboldened, he took a step forward and then another until he was close enough to touch. '"Did my heart love till now?"' Was that his voice, so husky? '"Forswear it, sight! For I ne'er saw true beauty till this night."'

'Dante...'

'Maddie.' With relief he abandoned the carefully rehearsed lines from *Romeo and Juliet*. 'I am a fool. I refused to listen to what my heart was saying. It was so wrong in the past I didn't dare trust that this time it could be right. I told myself the best thing I could do was to let you go. To plan a life without you in it.'

'Dante…' she said again, but he ploughed on. If he didn't speak now he never would. 'When you left, I told myself that it was for the best. That you deserved more, that I didn't deserve anything. But the truth is I was too afraid to try. Too afraid to get it wrong again. Too afraid that I might let you down.'

Her mouth wobbled. 'You could only let me down by not trying.'

*'Ti amo,'* he said huskily. 'I love you and I want the whole world to know it. I know I might be too late. I know I probably have lost your respect. That evening by the lake you asked me to love you. You shouldn't have needed to ask—I should have proclaimed it to the whole ball. I hadn't dared admit my feelings to myself—although it seems that my sister and daughter both knew more about how I felt about you than I did. I would have been lying to you if I had spoken then. But I can tell you tonight, in absolute truth, that I love you and if one day you would consider marrying me then I will spend my life proving to you that you did the right thing.'

Was she hallucinating? Was she really standing in a glass room one hundred floors up listening to Dante Falcone proclaim his love for her? Maddie reached out and ran her hand down the dear remembered planes of his face, the warmth of his skin proof that he was really here, not a figment of her overtired imagination. 'I can't believe you're here.'

'Arianna and I arrived yesterday. She's back at the hotel with a sitter,' he added. 'She's part of me. The best part of me. We come as a team, so it felt right she came too.'

'She's here? But I leave tomorrow!'

'I know.' His smile was tender and Maddie curled her hand around his cheek, unable to let go, convinced that if she stopped touching him he would disappear. 'I helped plan this trip, remember? I know every place, every stop. So,' now he looked unsure, as unsure as she had ever seen him, 'if you would allow two gatecrashers then Ari and I would love to accompany you to Florida, where she is planning to go on every roller coaster in the state. If you would rather travel alone then we understand. In that case we will fly to Florida and Ari's plans still stand. And I...' His voice trailed off. 'I will wish you all the love and luck in the world.'

Maddie's heart was so full of joy and hope it ached with a sweetness entirely new to her. Her lonely trip would no longer be lonely. Dante wanted to be with her; Ari was here. No tables for one and long nights trying to convince herself she was having fun. 'I'm sure there's room for two extra passengers,' she said, wondering why he wasn't touching her yet. Couldn't he see that she was trembling with need? 'Just to Florida?'

'After Ari has made herself suitably scared we need to go home. I am planning to sell the Rome house and move back to the *castello*. But I think you should carry on with your plans. I don't want to step in your way.'

Maddie could feel tears burning in her eyes. 'Plans can change,' she said. 'If a better offer comes along.'

'I'm not sure it's better, but it's all I have, Maddie.' Finally, finally he had taken her hands in his, his touch igniting a fire within her she never wanted to burn out. Maddie stared up at Dante, drinking in the austere lines of his face, quivering at the heat and passion burning in his eyes. How could she ever have thought this man a cold statue?

'Madeleine Fitzroy. *Ti amo. Vuoi sposarmi?* I love you. Will you do me the greatest honour and become my Contessa, my wife?'

*Yes!* her heart shouted, but she stilled it. 'On one condition.'

'Anything,' he promised, his heart in his eyes, and Maddie held tightly on to his hands, unable to believe that all that love, that desire was for her.

'I still want to see sloths…' she said, her mouth curving into a provocative smile. 'What do you think about honeymooning in Costa Rica?'

'If you marry me I will happily spend my honeymoon with mould-covered bears, anywhere you desire. Maddie, I know how much time you have spent planning and looking forward to this trip. Are you sure you want to cancel?'

'Postpone,' she said. 'I still intend to go to every single country on my list, but I don't have to do it all at once. I'd rather go with someone by my side, share my adventures with someone. If you'll come.'

'With you? Anywhere,' he vowed and then slowly, with infinite tenderness he kissed her as if it was the first time, a gentle caress filled with more love than Maddie had ever thought possible. She leaned in to the kiss, holding him tight, never wanting to let him go. He had her heart, her soul and she knew that she had his. It was all she had ever wanted. She'd wanted adventure, to discover who she was. Maddie knew that her greatest adventures were about to start and that Dante Falcone would be by her side the entire time.

## EPILOGUE

SHE'D BEEN HERE BEFORE. A white dress. A bunch of flow-ers. An expectant groom. Last time she had been on the verge of being a Countess; this time she was planning on becoming a *contessa*. But the title didn't matter. The castle didn't matter. All that mattered was the man wait-ing for her and the small girl by her side.

'This is so romantic,' Arianna said, looking around at the other wedding groups in the foyer, all waiting for their number to be called, waiting for the moment they were finally married. 'When I grow up I want to do ex-actly the same.'

Maddie put an arm around her and held her close. 'When you grow up I think your father will hope you got married at the *castello*, but the truth is, Ari, it's not the wedding that's important, it's being married. It's not the setting. It's the vows you make and meaning them.'

Last time Maddie had planned a huge society wed-ding. The type that meant she had existed on no carbs and excessive exercise to make sure the slim-fitting de-signer dress had hung on her perfectly, the type where every family member, no matter how far removed, had been invited. A wedding that had required a team of wedding planners and had nearly induced a nervous breakdown in her mother when the napkins hadn't quite matched the tablecloths. She didn't want that again. Nor did she want any Runaway Bride headlines. She just wanted to marry Dante.

So here they were, still in New York, waiting in line at City Hall for a quick and simple wedding. They'd only had to give twenty-four hours' notice after registering for their licence and she and Arianna had spent the time shopping for a simple white dress for Maddie and a matching silver one for Arianna, before heading to a spa for facials and haircuts and mani-pedis. It was a far cry from her last hen weekend on the Côte d'Azur, but a lot more enjoyable, spending time with the serious girl who was going to be her new daughter. They had already decided that there would be no 'steps' in their family. And maybe riding roller coasters in Florida wasn't Maddie's first choice of honeymoon destination, but they had promised Arianna a week of fun before her au pair arrived to take her back to the *castello* and prepare her for school, while Dante and Maddie headed down to Costa Rica for a fortnight alone. Dante had drawn the line at hostels, but, as he had booked them a gorgeous villa right on the beach, Maddie decided she would allow him his way this time.

'Nervous?' Arianna whispered as the sweet couple in vintage dress who had been waiting next to them got up and walked into the chapel. Maddie's chest squeezed. They were next.

'Not at all. I'm just excited.'

'The only thing we need to be nervous about is telling Zia Luciana and Nonna that we got married at City Hall and they weren't invited,' Dante said, smiling at

Maddie with the sudden sweet smile she had fallen for just a few weeks ago.

'But as we will celebrate with them all in New Zealand at Christmas, and I will let my parents organise their own party for us, I think we'll be forgiven,' Maddie reassured her.

And then it was their turn. The three of them and a photographer who would act as a witness as well as recording the moment Maddie gave herself to Dante and he to her. The short ceremony passed in a blur. All Maddie knew was the intensity and love in Dante's eyes as he recited his vows, the feeling of rightness as she said hers, the sheer happiness when the clerk pronounced them married, the joy in Arianna's face as she hugged her new mother and the moment Dante took her hand and promised her huskily that he would never let her down.

It was all she needed to know. It wasn't the wedding… it was the marriage. And she was more than ready. The Runaway Bride had stopped running. She'd found her family at last.

* * * * *

# HOW TO
# ROMANCE A
# RUNAWAY BRIDE

TERI WILSON

For my friends and fellow writers in San Antonio
Romance Authors, my local RWA chapter.

You all inspire and uplift me every day.

"You dance secretly inside my heart,
where no one else can see."

Rumi

## Chapter One

Zander Wilde was seeing things. It was the only explanation. He was hallucinating. Or having a stroke. Anything. Because the woman in a frothy white wedding gown who'd just burst through the door of his birthday party at the Bennington Hotel couldn't possibly be real. Not when she looked so very much like Allegra had all those years ago.

"Let's make a deal. If neither of us is married by the time we turn thirty, we'll marry each other," Zander had said. "Agreed?"

"Agreed," Allegra had replied.

Zander's throat grew tight. He hadn't thought about that conversation in a long time. A very long time. Unless the past week or so counted. But it was normal to remember such things under the circumstances, wasn't it? He was turning thirty, and that impulsive little arrangement was a childhood memory. Nothing more. Nothing less. It didn't actually mean anything.

Except here she was, almost a decade and a half later, dressed from head to toe in bridal white.

No one else seemed to notice her sudden appearance, so maybe she was indeed a figment of his imagination. Either that, or the party guests had been distracted by the arrival of his enormous birthday cake. With any luck, it was the former.

He tore his gaze away from her and focused instead on the cake sitting on the table in front of him. The blaze from its thirty candles warmed his face. Someone started to sing the lyrics to "Happy Birthday to You"—maybe one of his sisters or another of the Wildes. He didn't even know. He couldn't seem to concentrate on the very real people and the very real celebration going on around him.

He glanced back up. She was still there—the woman in white—looking even more like Allegra. Same honey-colored hair tumbling about her shoulders in waves. Same petite frame. She pressed a hand to her abdomen and took a few deep breaths, nodding to herself the way she'd always done backstage before a dance competition when she was a teenager. Zander had witnessed this private ceremony of nerves on many occasions. He'd just never seen it performed when Allegra looked like she'd recently climbed down from atop a wedding cake.

Zander blinked. Hard. This was one realistic daydream.

He cleared his throat and fixed his attention on the candles melting all over the thick frosting of the chocolate-bourbon masterpiece the hotel's pastry chef had created. The pâtissier had really gone all out. It was just another perk that came with being CEO of one of New York's most legendary hotels, Zander supposed. He forced himself to smile—or tried, at least—and realized the singing had stopped.

"You going to blow those out?" Ryan Wilde asked.

Everyone around the table looked at Zander. His sister Tessa and her fiancé, Julian. His mother, Emily, along with about four dozen or so other party guests. All of Zander's staff and closest friends, including his date, whose name he couldn't quite recall at the moment.

Susan. Or Stacy. Something that began with an *S*. They weren't serious, obviously. Zander's dalliances never were.

*And now you're seeing imaginary brides.*

He was losing it.

No. No, he wasn't. He was perfectly competent. He was at the peak of his career. Two months ago, *GQ* had named him one of Manhattan's "Top Thirty Under Thirty." He was one of the most eligible bachelors in New York, and he had every intention of staying that way.

The ancient deal he'd made with Allegra was messing with his head, that's all. Which was more than a little irritating. Not to mention absurd on every level. Zander hadn't set eyes on Allegra Clark in over a decade, and he was certain it had been even longer than that since she'd given him a passing thought. She'd left Manhattan without even saying goodbye.

Enough reminiscing. Some things were best left

forgotten, and whatever had—or more accurately, *hadn't*—gone on between him and Allegra was definitely one of those things. He squeezed his eyes shut, took a deep breath and readied himself to blow out his candles. In the second before he exhaled, he heard something. A voice from his past, as breathy and velvety soft as he remembered.

"Oh, my," the voice said.

Zander looked up.

"It seems I'm interrupting something." The woman standing with her back pressed to the ballroom door offered a tentative smile. "I'm sorry."

Allegra Clark. Not a figment of his overactive imagination, but real. As real as her floor-length white gown and the bouquet of blush-pink roses in her hand.

Zander opened his mouth to say something, but he couldn't seem to form words. What in the hell was going on?

"It's nothing. Just a little birthday party," Zander's mother said. She shot a questioning glance at Zander and he stared back at her, paralyzed by shock.

Emily cleared her throat. "Join us. The more the merrier, and all that."

She jumped up from her chair, scurried toward Allegra and gathered her into a welcoming hug. His sister Chloe followed suit, and Zander began to wonder if anyone was going to mention Allegra's unusual attire or if they were going to keep pretending anything about this scenario was remotely normal.

"Thank you," Allegra said. She cast a panicked glance at the closed door behind her. Then her chin wobbled in a way that brought about a sudden, intense ache in Zander's chest.

He looked past Allegra, hoping with every fiber of his being that there was a groom standing somewhere nearby. Surely there was.

No such luck. There was no husband, apparently. A growing sense of panic welled in Zander's chest, which did nothing to improve his mood. He'd single-handedly restored the Bennington Hotel to its glory days. He was one of the most powerful CEOs in the city. He could snap his fingers and in an instant, a team of security officers would materialize and discreetly escort Allegra from the building. Under no circumstances should he be losing his cool over the sight of a woman in a wedding gown.

But this wasn't just any woman.

"Hey." Beside Zander, Tessa frowned. "Isn't that..."

"Yes. It is." Since Tessa was hearing impaired, Zander signed the words in addition to speaking them in a voice that sounded angrier than he intended.

He actually hadn't realized he was angry. Surprised? Yes. Confused? Absolutely. But angry? At Allegra? He wouldn't have admitted as much back in the day. But he supposed he was. In reality, he'd probably been angry at Allegra for a very long time.

"Allegra Clark. Wow," Tessa muttered. "After all this time."

"Yep," Zander said and drained his glass of Veuve Clicquot. He should probably do something. Or at least speak to her. But he was at a complete loss. He just sat there like an idiot, staring as his other sister and his mother made a big fuss over Allegra. They hurried her over to the bar, oohing and aahing all the way across the expanse of the ballroom.

"Let's get you something to drink. A brandy, perhaps. You seem rattled," his mother said.

Chloe beamed at Allegra. "Isn't that a lovely dress, though? You look beautiful."

She did, actually. Quite beautiful. Far prettier than Zander remembered, which was something of a shock. Even when they'd been at odds, Allegra had never failed to take his breath away.

He could remember with perfect clarity the first time it had happened—a simmering summer evening in early August. He and Allegra couldn't have been older than ten or eleven. They'd taken advantage of her father's place on the board of the Museum of Natural History and spent the day wandering among the dinosaurs in the building's cool air-conditioning. Allegra had been running ahead of him, like she always did, while he struggled to catch up. Then she'd stopped suddenly to turn and say something. For the life of him, he couldn't recall what she'd said. But he remembered everything else about that moment—the swirl of starlight in the windows overhead, the massive T. rex skeleton looming behind her in the darkness, strange and beautiful.

Most of all, he remembered the way his heart had stopped when she'd smiled. It was as if he'd seen her for the very first time, this girl he'd known for as long as he'd been alive.

*Allegra's pretty*, he'd thought. The realization had struck him like a physical force. He remembered clutching at the front of his T-shirt, not unlike the time a basketball had hit him hard in the back at recess and knocked the wind right out of him.

But they'd been kids back then, Allegra no more than a girl. The woman who'd just interrupted his birthday party was all grown-up, and to Zander's great dismay, she was very possibly the most stunning creature he'd ever set eyes on. She had impossibly full lips, eyes that glittered like sapphires and an arch in her left eyebrow that gave him the impression she'd accumulated more than her fair share of secrets over the course of the past decade.

"What do you suppose she's doing here?" Tessa turned to look at Zander.

Zander coughed and tore his gaze from the long row of tiny white buttons that ran the full length of Allegra's spine, stopping just above the curve of her lush bottom. "How should I know?"

Tessa's gaze narrowed. "Hey, didn't you ask her to marry you once?"

Zander clenched his jaw. "No."

Because he hadn't. Not technically. They'd had a deal. A stupid, childish deal. They'd been thick as thieves back then. Either one of them could have suggested it.

It had been Zander's idea, though.

That much he couldn't deny.

Allegra took the glass one of the women thrust at her and cleared her throat. "Thank you, um…"

Both of the women peering back at her looked familiar.

She took a swig of the amber liquid and nearly

choked. Allegra never drank alcohol straight up. Then again, she'd never run out on a wedding before. Today was a day of firsts, it seemed.

She stared into her glass. "What is this again?"

"Brandy," the older woman said. "Neat."

Allegra let out a snort. *Neat.* What a joke. There was nothing neat about her current situation. She couldn't have made a bigger mess if she'd tried.

She took another swallow, a smaller one this time. Her head spun a little. She was vaguely aware of her bridal bouquet slipping from her grasp and falling onto the ballroom floor with a thud.

The older of the two women bent to pick it up, and when Allegra took in her straight spine and the fluid grace of her movements, reality dawned. "Mrs. Wilde?"

"Yes, dear," she said, and Allegra blinked back tears.

Emily Wilde had been her childhood dance teacher. More than that, really. She'd been Zander's mother. Allegra had spent more time at the Wilde home than she had her own.

Her gaze flitted to the younger woman standing beside Emily. "Chloe, is that you?"

"It is." Chloe smiled. "It's so good to see you, Allegra."

What was happening? She hadn't seen any of the Wildes in years, not since she'd left Manhattan. Now here they were, at her wedding.

*No. You fled from your wedding, remember?*

*That's right.* Allegra probably shouldn't be drinking on an empty stomach. Emily and Chloe weren't at her wedding. Rather, they were in the room next door at some kind of fancy celebration. Allegra's gaze drifted from one end of the dazzling ballroom to the other. There were people everywhere. In her haste to escape her nuptials, she'd dashed into the first door she'd seen. It led to an adjoining ballroom apparently.

She'd crashed a party.

In a wedding dress.

*Wonderful.*

Allegra closed her eyes and took another fortifying gulp of her brandy. Somewhere close by, a throat cleared. A very masculine throat.

She opened her eyes and found a dashing man dressed in what could only be called a power suit parting the crowd and charging straight toward her with a few hotel staff members trailing behind him. Everything about the man exuded confidence, from his peaked lapels and slicked-back hair to the bold Windsor knot in his tie. But beneath his arrogant exterior, there was something undeniably familiar.

Allegra's knees went wobbly.

Zander. Zander Wilde. *Her* Zander.

Not that he'd ever actually been hers. They'd never dated or anything. He hadn't taken her to prom or the homecoming dance. They'd just been friends. Best friends. And for some reason, that had made Allegra feel even closer to him than if she'd been his girlfriend. Girlfriends came and went. Zander had *known* her.

But that was yesterday. Now she could only stand there and try to make sense of the fact that he was wearing a three-piece suit just like the one her father had always worn. She couldn't quite wrap her head around it. Not one bit. And he looked so…so…*serious*. Angry, even.

Allegra cast a glance over her shoulder in search of the object of his wrath, but there was no one there. She swiveled to face Zander again. Sure enough, his glare appeared to be aimed directly at her.

Her heart started pounding again. Her tummy did a little flip. But she didn't feel panicky. No, this was something different. Something not as frightening as a panic attack. In fact, it almost felt like attraction.

Odd.

And wrong. So very wrong. This was Zander. Her friend. Or at least he'd *been* her friend. Now he was just…nothing. And Allegra was still wearing the dress she'd chosen to wear to her wedding. *To another man.* So there was nothing remotely appropriate about the butterflies swarming in her belly.

She swallowed and decided they weren't butterflies at all. She was overwhelmed. Period. It had been quite a day. A lump formed in her throat, and she suddenly had to blink back tears.

Zander came to a stop directly in front of her. A furious knot tensed in his jaw. His very square, very manly jaw. Zander Wilde had done quite a bit of growing up since she'd seen him last.

"Allegra." He gave her a businesslike nod, as if she was a total stranger.

Why on earth was he acting so ridiculous?

"Zander." She threw her arms around him in a bear hug. Maybe it was a little presumptuous since they hadn't seen each other in so many years. But gosh, it was good to see him. Better than she would ever have imagined. The lump in her throat grew threefold.

Zander stiffened and promptly peeled her arms away

from him. "Could everyone let us have a word for a minute, please? In private."

Chloe smiled at Allegra over Zander's shoulder, then wandered to the far side of the ballroom along with the others. Emily, however, lingered.

Zander seemed to sense her presence. "You, too, Mom."

She shook her head. "Zander, maybe you should—"

"Mom, please. This is between Allegra and me." For a split second, his steely gaze grew soft. Allegra caught a brief glimpse of the boy she'd once known. Then before she could even smile at him, he was gone. "No one else."

"Fine." Emily glared at the back of her son's head, then aimed a parting smile at Allegra. "It's nice to see you again, dear. You look gorgeous. Such a beautiful bride."

Bride. Oh, goodness.

In her shock at seeing Zander again, she'd forgotten all about her dress. He clearly hadn't. The way he was staring, she might think Zander Wilde had never seen a woman in a wedding gown before.

"What was that all about? Clearing the room." She glanced at the hotel staff nervously hovering just a few yards away. "Are those your minions? Are you going to have them escort me off the property or something?"

Allegra laughed.

Zander didn't. Not even close. "Those are my employees. I'm the CEO of this hotel. No one is going to escort you off the property, but come on, Allegra. You can't be serious right now. What are you doing here? And why on earth are you wearing *that*?"

He waved a hand at her gown, but didn't seem to look directly at it. In fact, he appeared to avoid looking directly at her altogether and instead focused on a spot somewhere above her head.

This was getting more annoying by the minute. She'd just bailed on her wedding. She was mentally, emotionally and physically exhausted. She needed a nap and a good long cry. *Not* an argument. Especially an argument that had somehow started without her.

"I'll tell you why I'm wearing this as soon as you explain why you're being such a jerk. You used to be nice." She had no intention of confiding in him. Frankly, she couldn't think of a more humiliating idea. And she didn't want to cry in front of him, but bitter tears were already stinging her eyes. A sob caught in the back of her throat.

She should be married right now, but here she was. Alone. Just like always.

How had everything gone so horribly wrong?

She looked Zander up and down, from the top of his perfectly groomed head to the tips of his wing tip–clad toes. She wished he wasn't so good-looking. It made his new, smug attitude much more annoying. "What exactly is going on here?"

Zander's gaze narrowed. He crossed his arms over his chest, and Allegra pretended not to notice how much broader that chest had gotten since eleventh grade.

"What's going on is my birthday party. My *thirtieth* birthday," he said with a tone that implied she should have known.

Ten years ago, maybe even five, she would have. But Allegra had spent more than a decade trying so hard to eradicate bad memories that some of the good ones slipped through the cracks. The bad ones never did.

Her gaze strayed toward the birthday cake on the table in the center of the room. She'd run out on a wedding and crashed her oldest friend's birthday party all on the same day. And if the woman standing beside the cake looking slightly forlorn was any indication, she'd also interrupted Zander on a date.

"I'm sorry if I've ruined your party. Happy birthday." She swallowed. Something still didn't seem quite right. Why would Zander, who so clearly had grown into an adult man, be so upset about a birthday party?

She didn't care. This painful little reunion was over. Allegra had more important things to worry about—things like picking up the shattered pieces of her life. Again.

She gathered her billowing skirt in her hands and moved in the direction of the ballroom's grand double doors. With any luck, she could somehow make it to the hotel's registration desk without bumping into any of her wedding guests. Or, heaven forbid, the press. "I'll just get a room and—"

Zander cut her off. "Stop, Allegra. This isn't happening."

"What's not happening?" Ugh, was the hotel full? Couldn't Mr. Hotshot CEO pull some strings and get her a room?

She hated to ask him for a favor, especially when he was looking at her like he'd love nothing more than to turn her out on the street in her Vera Wang. But there were reporters outside. She needed a room. And she really, really needed to get out of her wedding dress and into something else. *Anything* else. Pronto.

"This. Us." Zander inhaled a deep, measured breath. Then he *finally* looked at her. Really looked. Allegra almost wished he hadn't, because these weren't the same eyes she remembered from her childhood, full of innocence and hope. She didn't know the man who belonged to these eyes. "I won't marry you, Allegra. Not now. Not ever."

## *Chapter Two*

Zander crossed his arms and told himself he'd done absolutely nothing wrong, despite the glare his mother was currently aiming at him from across the ballroom. He'd probably get an earful from her later on. Emily Wilde was no shrinking violet. She was a woman with strong opinions and a tendency to meddle, and now that Zander's younger sister was happily engaged as well as dancing with a major ballet company, Emily no longer felt the need to hover over Tessa. The family matriarch had moved on to Zander's personal life instead.

Oh, joy.

She wanted him married. She wanted grandchildren, preferably a boy, who could ensure that the Wilde family name and legacy would live on long after she was gone. Thus she made Zander curse his status as the only male offspring on a regular basis. He'd just as soon let some other guy get married and carry on the family name. Except there wasn't another guy. Just him, a fact that was all the more painfully obvious now that he had a bride standing in front of him.

*I won't marry you, Allegra. Not now. Not ever.*

Granted, it might have sounded a bit harsh, but he'd only said what needed to be said, plain and simple. Emily would no doubt accuse him of causing a scene, which was absurd. If anyone was causing a scene, it was Allegra.

She'd crashed his birthday party. *In a wedding gown.* Had she honestly expected him to just run off into the sunset and marry her? Had she gone insane since she'd left town?

She peered up at him, lush lips pressed together and a cute little wrinkle in her forehead. She didn't look crazy. She looked confused. Confused and undeniably gorgeous. Looking into her luminous blue eyes made Zander's chest hurt for some strange reason. He focused once again on the sparkling chandelier hanging over her head. That dress…those eyes—it was all too much.

"*Marry* me?" Her voice rang with incredulity. And if Zander wasn't mistaken, a fair amount of amusement.

He lifted an eyebrow. *You're the one in a wedding dress, sweetheart.*

"You can't be serious," she said, deadpan.

Zander didn't say a word, but simply held her gaze. He'd said his piece. There was no way he'd be held to a silly promise he'd made as a kid. Now she just needed to go back to wherever she'd come from before she embarrassed herself further.

Allegra's gaze narrowed, as if she was trying to peer

inside his head. Then her pretty pink lips curved into a grin. She was smiling? Now?

Maybe she really was unstable. The poor thing.

Zander reached for her hand. A mistake. A huge one. A long time ago, he'd read something in a magazine article that said a simple touch could possess memory, a notion he'd dismissed as sentimental nonsense. Memories lived in the realm of the mind. They were made up of thoughts, images and unflinching emotions. How could a person's flesh be capable of such complexities?

But the moment his fingertips connected with Allegra's, something strange happened. His limbs felt looser all of a sudden, and his spirit lifted. He remembered the soaring sensation of holding Allegra in his arms and twirling across the dance floor. He remembered ice-skating in Central Park, a lacy veil of snow in Allegra's hair and his heart pounding hard in a darkened museum. He felt like a kid again. It was like being knocked flat by a New York blizzard.

He dropped her hand and recrossed his arms. Revisiting the past had no place on his current agenda. She needed help. Obviously. He should call someone, but who? She no longer had any family in New York.

Did she have any family left at all? Anywhere?

"Look, Allegra—" he began.

She cut him off. "You seriously think I'm here because I want to marry you?"

She let out a giggle, then appeared to make a feeble attempt to keep her mouth shut. It was no use. Another giggle escaped, louder this time, until she was quite literally laughing in his face.

Allegra's laugh hadn't changed a bit. Once upon a time, it had been one of Zander's favorite sounds. Not anymore. "You find the idea of marrying me amusing, do you?"

"Actually…" She cleared her throat and managed to collect herself. For the most part. There was still far too much snickering going on for his taste. "I do."

"'I do.'" Zander lifted an eyebrow. "You even sound like a bride."

That managed to stop her snickering. "Oh, get over yourself. I haven't even seen you in thirteen years."

Actually, it was closer to fourteen. Not that Zander was counting. He clenched his jaw to keep himself from opening his mouth and saying it out loud.

Allegra's smile faded. "You're serious, aren't you? You actually think I came here after all this time to drag you to the altar. Tell me, Mr. Suit, what kind of evidence do you have to support this delusion?"

*Mr. Suit.*

Her voice dripped with disdain. Zander probably should have expected that. He hadn't. Then again, everything about this insane night was coming out of left field. *Happy birthday to me.*

"You mean other than your attire?" He ordered himself not to look at the dress again. But then he fixed his gaze on the delicate row of tiny shimmering crystals that ran along the curves of her shoulders.

"Circumstantial evidence," she said, sounding like the lawyer's daughter she'd been. Then she shrugged, and those glittering crystals dazzled beneath the soft light of the chandelier. "You're going to have to do better than that. Who says what I'm wearing has anything to do with you?"

"*We* did. You and me. Fourteen years ago."

He waited for her expression to betray her resistance, for a hint of what had transpired between them so long ago to show on her porcelain face. They'd loved one another once. Not romantic love, but something quite different. Something deeper.

Or so he'd thought.

She blinked but kept on looking at him like he was the one who was acting nuts. "I don't know what in the world you're talking about."

He had to give her credit. She was doing a good job of feigning innocence. A great job, actually.

Zander took a step closer. He didn't want to humiliate her in front of Manhattan's glittering elite. He just wanted to put a stop to things once and for all. If he was being honest, he also wanted her to leave. The sooner the better.

He'd grown accustomed to life without her. Things were simpler now. Rational. Predictable. Sure, it had been hard at first. There had been times when he'd closed his eyes and still seen her wild thicket of dark hair and those legs that seemed to go on forever as she struck a ballroom-dance pose. And maybe the warm vanilla scent of her perfume had lingered on his favorite sweatshirt for a time after she'd gone. But eventually it had faded away.

As had his questions.

Why had she left without saying goodbye? Why hadn't she ever come back, even for a visit?

Had she missed him the way he'd missed her?

He didn't want to ask those questions anymore, but if she stayed too long, he would. He knew he would. And he wasn't altogether sure he'd like the answers.

After the accident, she'd gone to live with her aunt in Cambridge. That much he knew. But Boston was just a train ride away. He'd never for a moment suspected she'd gone away for good.

Zander lowered his voice. "You can stop pretending, Allegra. We both know the truth. You're here because of our deal."

She frowned. "What deal?"

If Zander hadn't known better, he'd have thought she'd actually forgotten. But that wasn't possible. Was it?

Of course not.

Still, her acting skills had improved since her disastrous audition for the eighth-grade play. She'd cried in Zander's arms for hours after school that day.

He swallowed. "The deal we made to marry one another if we were still unattached by our thirtieth birthdays."

"Oh." She shook her head. "I'm afraid I don't remember that at all."

Zander stared. If Guy Lombardo's orchestra had appeared out of nowhere and begun to play "Happy Birthday to You," he'd have been less surprised. She wasn't here because of their deal. She didn't even remember it.

Unbelievable.

"Are you sure you didn't have that arrangement with somebody else? Gretchen Williams, maybe?" Allegra said.

*"Gretchen Williams?"* She couldn't be serious. He'd gone out with Gretchen exactly three times, and that had been three times too many. Besides, the last he'd heard, Gretchen had moved to Connecticut and had five kids. She hadn't needed a backup plan. "Absolutely not. It was you."

*It was always you.*

Zander's temples throbbed. He needed to get out of here.

But this was his place of business. He practically lived here. Disappearing wasn't an option. Besides, wasn't that Allegra's specialty?

"I see." Allegra's voice went soft, and she looked at him for a long silent moment. And somehow the silence between them seemed more truthful than anything they'd yet to say to one another.

Zander had the sudden urge to reach for her, to pull her into his arms and greet her the way he should have the moment she'd walked through the door. When she'd gone away all those years ago, her absence had just about killed him. He'd missed her, damn it. He still did, even after all this time.

Then Zander's cousin Ryan appeared at his side. The fact that Ryan was wearing his serious hotel-management face rather than his party-going-family-member face ensured that whatever sentimental moment Zander and Allegra might be on the verge of sharing was officially ruined.

Ryan cleared his throat. "Zander, I hate to interrupt. But we've got a problem. A big one."

"Right." Zander nodded. He couldn't decide if he should curse the interruption or be grateful for it. He gave Allegra a tight smile. "It was good to see you again. My apologies for the misunderstanding."

Then he turned his back on Allegra Clark without waiting for an explanation or even a goodbye. After all, parting words had never been their strong suit.

The sight of Zander's retreating pinstripes jarred something loose inside Allegra. Something that almost made her knees buckle. Something that made her feel dangerously close to coming apart at the seams.

She took a deep breath and counted to ten as she watched him walk away. He murmured something to the man beside him, strode past the untouched cake and disappeared through the ballroom's gilded double doors.

He'd walked right out of his own birthday party without so much as an apology. Or even an explanation.

*Typical suit.*

Allegra couldn't remember any of her own birthday parties that hadn't been interrupted in a similar fashion. Until she'd turned sixteen, obviously. On her sweet sixteen, she would have given anything to have her father there, kissing her cheek as he dashed off to some kind of work emergency.

Her throat grew tight. She squared her shoulders, slipped out of the ballroom and marched toward the registration desk. She'd managed to walk out on her own wedding today without shedding a tear. She would *not* let a brief encounter with Zander Wilde reduce her to a weepy mess.

Anyway, she was perfectly fine. She'd just been rattled to see him after so many years, which was totally normal. There was nothing to be emotional about at all as far as Zander was concerned.

*Except that he thought you'd come back to marry him, of all things.*

"Can I help you?" The young man behind the registration desk beamed at her. "Let me guess—you're checking into the honeymoon suite?"

"Um, no." She shuddered. "Definitely not."

"Oh." He glanced at her dress. Allegra couldn't wait

to take off the horrid thing. She just wanted to wrap herself up in one of the hotel's thick terry-cloth robes, climb into bed and sleep for a while. A century, maybe.

"Well, uh, how can I assist you, then?"

"I just need a room." Before he could ask, she added, "A single, not a double."

He frowned. "For just one person?"

Allegra sighed. Mightily. "Yes."

He nodded but still managed to look utterly perplexed. Too bad. "May I ask the name on the reservation?"

"I don't have one."

"No reservation?" His frown deepened. "I'm sorry, but we don't have any single rooms available without a reservation."

This day kept getting better and better. "Fine. I'll take a double."

But the desk clerk wasn't any more accommodating. "I'm afraid we don't have any double rooms available either."

Allegra's heart started beating hard again. This couldn't be happening.

"Fine. I'll take the honeymoon suite." Desperate times called for desperate measures, and these were indeed desperate times.

The hotel clerk shrugged. He was really beginning to get on Allegra's nerves. "That room is booked, as well. We're completely full. Without a reservation, I'm afraid I can't help you."

"Full? *Full?* As in there's not a room of any kind available?" It couldn't be true. Where on earth would she go? What was she supposed to do? Go marching back into her wedding to ask her erstwhile fiancé for a ride to the airport?

Even if the hotel clerk took pity on her and came up with a room, she had no way to pay for it. She'd walked out of the ceremony with nothing but her bridal bouquet. She wasn't even sure where her purse—and her wallet full of credit cards—was at the moment.

Why had she agreed to get married in Manhattan?

She should have insisted on a nice, simple ceremony in Cambridge, where she and Spencer actually lived. How had she let herself get talked into coming back here?

Because Spencer was a politician, that's why. He'd wanted a big, splashy wedding, one that would look good in all the newspapers. A grand show. Allegra just hadn't realized she was nothing but a prop.

How could she have been so monumentally stupid?

"We're completely booked." The clerk gave her a sympathetic smile, and something inside Allegra died just a little. "Can I do anything else for you? Call a car, perhaps?"

Behind her, someone chimed in. "That won't be necessary."

Allegra spun around and found herself face-to-face with Zander's mother. Emily Wilde wasn't exactly the first person she wanted to chat with after the oddly uncomfortable encounter she'd just had with Zander. But it was definitely preferable to talking to Zander himself. "Mrs. Wilde, hello."

"Since when do you call me Mrs. Wilde? I'm Emily, remember?" The older woman gave her a warm smile. "I didn't mean to eavesdrop. I was just on my way out since it seems the birthday party has ended, and I overheard."

"I was trying to get a room, but it seems the hotel is booked."

"Winter in New York is always a busy time of year. But, of course, you know that." Emily tilted her head. "Isn't your birthday right around the corner? I seem to remember it being during the snowy season."

Indeed it was. Just two weeks away. Allegra's thirtieth, which meant if she'd ever made that ancient deal with Zander, they still had fourteen days to make good on it. Not that they'd made any such arrangement. And not that she'd ever in a million years marry the man.

When had he turned into such a grump? And what was he doing running a hotel? The Zander she knew wanted to run the family business someday. The Wilde School of Dance. She'd have been less surprised to see him starring in a Broadway play than strutting around wearing a business suit, surrounded by minions.

*Zander Wilde's profession should be the least of your worries at the moment. You're homeless, and the only article of clothing you own is a wedding gown.*

"Allegra, you don't look well." Emily pressed a hand to Allegra's forehead. "You need to lie down, dear."

Allegra nodded. Emily was right. She'd never needed to rest so much in her life. She felt like she'd been running for the better part of fourteen years. In a way, she supposed she had. But it wasn't as if she could just curl up on the sofa in the hotel lobby.

Could she?

No, of course she couldn't. She'd probably get in

trouble. Or even arrested. She let out a hysterical laugh. Wouldn't that be the perfect ending to this horrible day? To have Zander call the cops on her.

Zander Wilde, who thought she'd been pining away for him since the day she'd left town.

"You'll stay with me," Emily said as matter-of-factly as if she'd just offered Allegra a stick of gum rather than a roof over her head.

"What?" Allegra shook her head. "Oh, no, I couldn't..."

But Emily had already removed her coat and was wrapping it around Allegra's shoulders as she led her toward the revolving door. "Of course you can. How many afternoons did you come home with us after dance class when you were a girl?"

More than Allegra could count. "But things are different now." She slowed to a stop two feet from the exit. "Emily, I can't. I'm afraid that might upset Zander. We had a disagreement a few minutes ago."

"I heard." Emily nodded. "Half of Manhattan heard, actually."

Fabulous. Just fabulous.

"It doesn't matter what Zander thinks. It's my house, not his." Emily gave Allegra's waist a gentle squeeze. "And if you don't mind my saying, it doesn't really look like you have a lot of options."

She didn't. Zero, in fact.

"Allegra, dear. I can't leave you here all alone. I owe it to your mom and dad to see that you're taken care of." Emily's voice dropped to a whisper. "Come on home."

At the mention of her parents, the last shreds of Allegra's resistance crumbled. She didn't have the strength to fight the past. Not tonight. Not now.

*Come on home.*

She wanted nothing more than to go home, if only she knew how to get there.

## Chapter Three

Zander stared at Ryan sitting in one of the wingback chairs opposite his desk and tried to wrap his mind around the bomb his cousin had just dropped. "A reporter called here to ask whether or not the hotel has been *cursed*?"

This was a first. Zander was no stranger to New York's tabloid press. He was fully aware of how brutal it could be. But a curse? That seemed beyond ridiculous, even for a rag like the *Post* or the *Daily News*.

"She wasn't asking exactly." Ryan frowned. "She's going to run with it."

Zander released a tense exhale. He didn't need this kind of complication. Today of all days. He was still a little rattled after his encounter with Allegra. *A lot* rattled, frankly. Mainly by her assertion that she didn't even remember their marriage pact.

*Then why the wedding gown?*

"Fine." He needed a drink. A *real* drink. No more birthday champagne. A martini, maybe. Something potent enough to eradicate the memory of the past half hour of his life, if such a drink existed. "A single negative tabloid article won't kill us, even one that says we're cursed. At least they get points for creativity."

He waited for the pained look on Ryan's face to relax a little.

It didn't. If anything, the crease between his cousin's brows deepened.

"It's not a tabloid," Ryan said. Then he uttered the only three words powerful enough to tear Zander's thoughts away from Allegra Clark dressed in bridal white tulle. "It's the *Times*."

This had to be a bad joke. The *New York Times* had won more Pulitzer Prizes than any other paper in the world. "Good one. You almost had me. But the Gray Lady is a New York institution. It's a serious publication. They'd never run a story about a hotel being cursed."

"Think again." Ryan lifted a sardonic eyebrow. "The Society section would."

Zander swallowed, longing once again for the smooth burn of vodka, vermouth and a little olive brine sliding down his throat. Things were apparently worse than he'd anticipated.

The *Times*, for God's sake. Only the society page, but still...

It wasn't *just* the society page, though, as Zander soon realized.

Ryan took a deep breath and lowered the boom. "Specifically, the Vows column."

Zander clenched his gut. "The Vows column? From the Sunday Wedding section?"

"The one and only." Ryan sighed.

Having the hotel lambasted on the front page would have been better than the Vows column announcing that the Bennington was cursed. People all over the damn world read the wedding announcements in the Sunday edition of the *Times*. Like every other luxury hotel in Manhattan, a sizable portion of the Bennington's business came from the wedding industry. Moonstruck brides and grooms.

He shook his head. This couldn't happen. Not after he'd worked so hard to restore the Bennington to its former glory. "I don't understand where this is coming from. Why would a columnist from Vows think we're cursed?"

Ryan frowned. "You seriously have to ask?"

"I do, actually."

*I do.*

The instant the words left his mouth, he remembered Allegra saying the same thing while she stood in front of him, looking like she'd just walked out of a fairy tale.

He'd taunted her. *You even sound like a bride.*

Now reality was finally coming together with horrific clarity.

*Damn.* He groaned. "We've had another runaway bride, haven't we?"

"Bingo." Ryan seemed to be fighting a smirk. "The bride who crashed your birthday party just now was the latest. You know, the one you assumed was here to strong-arm you into marrying her."

"Yeah, I get that." *Now* he did, anyway.

Zander sighed. No wonder Allegra had laughed in

his face. She hadn't turned up to make good on their deal. She'd been on the run from her own wedding to a completely different man.

Perhaps he shouldn't have jumped to conclusions. But the timing seemed awfully fortuitous. It wasn't as if he'd *wanted* to believe she'd come back for him.

*You sure about that?*

Beneath the surface of his desk, Zander's hands curled into fists. Of course he was sure.

Ryan's gaze narrowed. "What's the story there, if you don't mind my asking? The two of you were engaged once?"

"No," Zander said with a little too much force. Then, more evenly, he added, "It wasn't like that."

Ryan stared blankly at him, waiting for more.

Zander was in no mood to oblige. "Back to the matter at hand. We have two weddings on the schedule this weekend. Which one just went belly-up?"

Zander didn't personally handle the hotel's wedding-planning details, but as with everything else that went on beneath the roof of the fabled building, he supervised with a watchful eye. It was his job to know what was going on, and he definitely would have noticed if they'd had a wedding on the schedule with a bride named Allegra Clark.

Ryan took a beat too long to answer. "The big one. The Warren wedding."

The Warren wedding, as in Spencer Warren, city councilman and mayoral candidate for the city of Cambridge, Massachusetts. No wonder the *Times* had already taken notice.

The hotel roster had listed the bride's name as Ali Clark. So Allegra was going by Ali now?

Zander wasn't sure what he found more surprising—the fact that Allegra had changed her name or that she'd ever considered being a politician's wife.

It was time to face the facts. He no longer knew her. Allegra was a stranger now. She wasn't even Allegra anymore, and she didn't want to marry him any more than he wanted to marry her.

He also had far more pressing matters to deal with at the moment. "This is our third runaway bride in the span of a month."

Ryan nodded. "We also had one about twelve weeks ago."

No wonder the *Times* thought the Bennington was cursed. "Once the Vows column goes forward, no one will want to book a wedding here."

"We're screwed," Ryan said.

"No, we're not." Zander gave his head a slow, methodical shake. "We'll just have to prove them wrong."

He wasn't going down without a fight. He'd worked too long and too hard to let a runaway bride bring him to his knees.

Even a runaway bride he'd once been foolish enough to love.

Allegra woke the next morning when the first rays of soft pink sunlight peeked through the ruffled curtains of Emily Wilde's guest room. Her first conscious thought was how pretty the cozy attic space looked, with its white barrel-vaulted ceiling and antique pedestal sink in the corner. Her second conscious thought was that she couldn't remember the last time she'd had such a good night's sleep.

It defied logic. She was homeless, for all practical

purposes. Stuck in New York with no belongings, no job and no fiancé. No plan. Yet, she felt more at peace than she had in months. Maybe she'd actually done the right thing, for once. She'd made a good choice in coming back...coming home.

Except this wasn't home. This was Zander's mother's house. His mother's room. The pale gray flannel pajamas Allegra had slept in didn't belong to her either. They were at least three sizes too big. She could only guess they'd once belonged to Zander's father.

Still, it felt nice here. Peaceful. She peeled back the curtain and watched the snow float down from the sky. Slowly, softly, like feathers shaken loose from a pillow. A tiny black kitten tiptoed its way through the white fluff on the sidewalk down below. Everything was so picturesque that Allegra's heart gave a little lurch.

*Don't get used to it. You can't stay here. You* cannot.

Except where else could she go?

Somehow she'd thought she could figure it all out after she got some sleep. But nothing had changed. Not really. The hotel was booked. Even if they'd had a room and even if she'd managed to locate her purse, her debit card would have only been good for two or three nights. Four at the most. She'd spent every last dime on her dream wedding. There'd been the fancy caterer, the string quartet, the flowers...

An image of her extravagant bridal bouquet falling to the floor of the Bennington Hotel's ballroom flashed through Allegra's mind. She squeezed her eyes closed.

*Everything is going to be okay. It will.*

But when she opened her eyes, she found herself looking at a pouf of tulle at the foot of the bed. Her discarded wedding dress.

Everything was not okay.

She tossed aside the sheets, climbed out of bed and headed down the curved, Victorian-style staircase to Emily's kitchen. She needed coffee. A gallon of it, if possible.

"Good morning, dear. How did you sleep?" Emily sat at the kitchen table and looked up from the copy of the *New York Times* in her hands.

Allegra glanced at the front page. She spotted Spencer's name in a headline just below the fold and pointedly averted her gaze.

"I slept great, thank you." Allegra looked around the kitchen, with its blue-and-white-toile wallpaper and shelves crammed full of mismatched china teacups. It hadn't changed a bit since the last time she'd stood in this spot.

"Come sit down." Emily folded the newspaper closed. "I've got your breakfast warming in the oven."

"You didn't need to do that, Mrs. Wilde. Honestly, you've done enough."

"Nonsense." Emily planted her hands on Allegra's shoulders and steered her toward the table. "And stop calling me Mrs. Wilde. We're not in dance class. Besides, I've known you since you were so tiny that your head didn't even reach the top of the ballet barre."

Allegra sat and watched as the older woman removed a breakfast casserole from the oven that looked big enough to feed an army. Just how hungry did Emily think she looked?

"Here you go. Dig in while I get you some coffee." Emily slid a plate in front of her.

Allegra couldn't remember the last time someone had cooked her breakfast. Or any meal, for that matter. She could get used to this kind of royal treatment if she stayed here for any length of time.

Which she most definitely would not.

She shouldn't. She couldn't. "This is delicious. Thank you so much. For everything. I'm not sure what I would have done last night if you hadn't offered me your guest room."

"You were in a bit of a pickle," Emily said.

The understatement of the century. Allegra's stomach churned. She set down her fork and forced herself to meet Emily's penetrating gaze.

"Do you want to talk about it?" she asked.

*Maybe.*

No, actually. She didn't. Not yet, and not with Zander's mother. It was too soon and far too humiliating. "His name is Spencer Warren. But I'm guessing you know that by now."

Allegra glanced at the folded newspaper and her throat grew tight. Her hands started to shake, and she had to remind herself to take a breath.

Not another panic attack. Not now.

"I've made such a mess of things," she whispered.

"I'm sure you did the right thing," Emily said, and even though Allegra knew she was just saying it to be kind, it still made her feel a little better. "You can stay here as long as you wish."

"I can't." It was just too awkward. What would Zander say when he found out she was staying with his mother? A lot, probably. A whole lot.

"Of course you can. I'd love to have someone to dote on."

"But I need to get my life in order." Starting with a

job. And something to wear. And a place to live. "I'm a mess, Emily."

"Think of it as temporary, just until you get your feet under you. A month."

"A *month*?" How many times would she run into Zander if she was living at his mother's house for thirty days? Too many. "Absolutely not."

Emily shrugged. "A week, then. Allegra, I hate to break it to you, but you can't reinvent yourself in one day."

She had a point.

And a week might not be too terrible. How often could Zander come by in seven measly days? He was a CEO now. He probably spent all his waking hours at his fancy hotel. He couldn't even make it through a whole birthday party without working, which was a pretty good indication that he didn't have time to hang around his mother's brownstone. Plus seven days would give her time to come up with some sort of plan.

Still, something about this didn't feel right.

*You don't have a choice. Be grateful.*

She took a deep breath. "I'll stay a week, if you're sure it's no bother."

Emily waved a hand. "Why on earth would it be a bother?"

"Because I think I embarrassed your son last night. He seemed upset." Yet another understatement.

Emily shrugged and sipped her coffee. "He probably had it coming."

Actually he had. The misunderstanding was 100 percent his fault. He'd assumed she'd shown up in a wedding dress to marry him after all this time. What kind of person made such a nonsensical leap?

An egotistical one. One who was pathologically cocky.

One who'd just walked into the kitchen.

Allegra choked on a bite of eggs. "Zander."

He stood staring at her from the threshold while snowflakes swirled around his head. A shiver coursed through her, and he slammed the door behind him.

"Allegra? What are you doing here?" Zander's gaze dropped to her pajamas, then flitted back to her face. His eyes were red, his face wind chapped. He had a serious case of bed head, yet he was still dressed in his suit from the night before. He looked like he hadn't slept a wink since she'd watched him saunter out of his birthday party.

Allegra's head spun a little. Never in her life had she seen such a handsome exhausted man. His shoulders seemed even broader than they'd been just twelve hours ago. It was baffling. And infuriating. She looked down and stared pointedly at her plate.

"She lives here," Emily said.

Zander let out a bitter laugh. "Very funny."

"I'm not joking. Stop being rude to our guest."

Allegra blinked. *Our* guest? What did that mean? Then she remembered the enormity of the breakfast casserole. And the pajamas.

She lost her grip on her fork and it clattered to the table. She ignored it and fixed her gaze on Zander as the mortifying reality of the situation dawned. "Wait a minute. What are *you* doing here?"

"Zander lives here, too," Emily said far too sweetly. "Did I forget to mention that, dear?"

## Chapter Four

For the second time in less than twelve hours, Zander couldn't believe what he was seeing.

He blinked. Hard.

But it didn't do any good. When he opened his eyes, Allegra was still sitting at the kitchen table—in *his* chair—with her hair piled on top of her head, staring right back at him. The Princeton coffee mug in her hand—also his—had paused en route to her pillowy lips.

The longer she gawked at him, the looser her grip on the mug became. Zander sighed and reached for it before she spilled coffee all down the front of the pajamas she was wearing, because yes, those were his, too.

The brush of his fingertips against hers as he plucked the mug out of her hand seemed to pull her out of her trance. Wide-eyed, she swiveled her gaze to his mother. "Um, Emily. You did indeed forget to tell me that Zander lives here."

Zander wholeheartedly doubted it had been an innocent omission, mainly because his mother was avoiding looking him in the eye.

As if he didn't already have enough going on in his life without Emily Wilde playing matchmaker. Marvelous.

He took a gulp of coffee, forgetting it was actually Allegra's until her head snapped back in his direction. Her eyes widened, and he took another, more deliberate sip.

His house, his pajamas, his cup, *his* coffee.

Allegra arched a single eyebrow. "You still live with your mother?"

Technically, it was the other way around. He'd purchased the brownstone from his mother three years ago when the dance school first began to have financial troubles. But Allegra could believe whatever she wanted to believe. He didn't want to share personal family matters with her any more than he wanted to share his pajamas.

He shrugged. "It looks that way, doesn't it?"

Then he drained her coffee cup and set it down on the kitchen counter with a thud.

Allegra's gaze flitted to the mug, then back to him. Her cheeks flared pink. "So what's with last night's suit? Is this some of kind of CEO walk of shame?"

Quite the opposite. He'd been working all night, trying to figure out a way to get ahead of the Vows column. But again, Allegra could believe whatever she wanted. Especially since he could have sworn her deepening flush had a distinctly jealous edge.

He didn't want Allegra to be attracted to him. But he didn't particularly hate the idea either, especially since he'd made such an idiot out of himself the night before.

He crossed his arms, giving her a clear, unobstructed view of the unfastened French cuffs of his dress shirt. "I can't help but wonder why you find that idea so unpleasant."

She rolled her eyes, but Zander wasn't buying it. Not this time. "I'm just surprised, that's all. Especially since you seemed so preoccupied with marrying me the last time I saw you."

Emily stifled a laugh.

Zander loved his mother. He really did. But at the moment, she was trying his patience about as much as the reporter from the Vows column.

He narrowed his gaze at her.

Emily cleared her throat. "Allegra, dear. You've got things wrong. Actually—"

"*Actually*, I sleep at the hotel more often than I do here," Zander said. He didn't need his mother to be any more involved with this situation than she already was. He had bigger problems than whatever assumptions Allegra wanted to make about either his living situation or his sex life. And he certainly didn't want to discuss the latter in front of Emily. That would have been about the only way to make this conversation more awkward than it already was.

He cleared his throat. "The Bennington is full at the moment."

"So I heard," Allegra muttered.

"She had nowhere else to go, Zander." Emily looked up at him.

He knew better than to argue, and a part of him

didn't want to. He cared too much about Allegra to turn her out on the street.

But how had she ended up so alone?

*Not your problem. You have enough on your plate, remember?*

He cleared his throat and changed the subject. "Read anything interesting this morning?"

Emily followed his gaze until she, too, was staring at the folded copy of the *New York Times* on the kitchen table. "So you've seen it."

"Seen what?" Allegra asked.

Emily shook her head. "It's nothing, dear."

"That's not exactly true," Zander said, choosing not to examine why his mother seemed to have chosen sides in the matter.

He flipped through the newspaper until he landed on the Weddings page. His throat went dry as he looked at the headline. He'd already seen it, of course. He and Ryan had stayed up until the early-morning edition was released so they could get a full assessment of the damage.

It was extensive.

Familiar or not, looking at the words splashed below the Vows header still made his gut churn.

Is the Bennington Hotel Cursed?

He spread the paper open beside Allegra's place mat.

"Your hotel is cursed?" She blinked up at him, and for the first time since he'd stumbled upon her sitting at his kitchen table and making herself at home, Zander allowed himself to look at her. Really look.

She was gorgeous in ways that were both foreign

and familiar. How many times had she sat in that same spot? More than he could count. But never like this. Never with years of silence stretching between them. Even in his sleep-deprived state, there was a very real part of him that wanted to pull up a chair and just talk. Talk the way they used to.

He wasn't altogether sure why that wasn't possible. Maybe because her sudden appearance had just thrown a major wrench in his life, businesswise. Or maybe it had something to do with the way he couldn't quite keep his gaze from straying to the enticing swell of her curves beneath his pajamas. Either way, they couldn't just take up where they'd left off. They weren't kids anymore.

He clenched his jaw. "My hotel is not cursed."

"Of course it's not." Emily waved a dismissive hand. "We know that, dear. I don't understand how the *New York Times* could say such a thing."

"I suggest you read the first paragraph." Zander turned toward the coffee maker and refilled the mug in his hand. There wasn't enough coffee in the world for him to deal with the mess he had on his hands.

But when he turned back around and saw the color draining from Allegra's face as she read the article, guilt got the better of him. He set the full cup onto the table in front of her.

She glanced up at him, blue eyes shining bright.

*Don't read too much into it, sweetheart. It's just coffee, not an invitation to stay.*

Their gazes held until Emily broke the loaded silence. "I hadn't realized there'd been so many runaway brides at the Bennington lately. Zander, why haven't you said anything?"

"It seemed slightly odd, but calling it a curse never

crossed my mind. Probably because I'm a rational person."

Allegra cleared her throat.

Zander glared at her. "I'm very rational."

"I'm sure you are," she said, but he wasn't buying the innocent act. Not for a minute. "Tell me, did you assume all of the other runaway brides wanted to marry you, too? Or just me?"

He clenched his fists to keep himself from scooping her into his arms, carrying her out the door and depositing her into the nearest snowdrift.

"Four runaway brides in the span of a few months *does* seem strange," Emily said.

Great. If his own mom was buying into the Vows nonsense, what chance did he have?

"Until last night, no one seemed to care. Apparently, three runaway brides are acceptable. But not four." He looked pointedly at Allegra. "The fourth one means it's a curse."

Allegra's gaze narrowed, but Zander couldn't help but notice that she wasn't quite looking him in the eye anymore. "That's the dumbest thing I've ever heard. It's completely arbitrary."

"The fact that your groom is rather high-profile wasn't helpful. When a political candidate gets left at the altar, people tend to notice."

Too far.

He knew he'd crossed a line the moment the words left his mouth. The article wasn't Allegra's fault. Not entirely, anyway. He had no right to taunt her about her almost marriage. No right whatsoever, especially given how close he'd once come to tying the knot.

He didn't know why he was acting like such a jerk.

*You know exactly why.*

Allegra stared down at the newspaper.

*Look at me, damn it. Look at me and tell me again that you don't remember.*

"I'm sure each and every one of those brides had a perfectly legitimate reason for walking away," she said. Her voice had gone calm, but Zander could see the tremble in her fingertips as her hands twisted in her lap.

He hated himself just a little bit then. But he couldn't stop himself from asking. He wanted to know. He *needed* to know. "I'd love to hear what those reasons were. Seriously, I'm all ears."

It wasn't the time or a place for a heart-to-heart. He was exhausted, her wedding gown was probably still lying in a heap somewhere and they weren't even alone. But he couldn't think straight when she was sitting there looking like that.

So beautiful. So tempting.

So lost.

"Enough." His mother stood. "Zander, you need to get some sleep. You look like a train wreck. Besides, Allegra doesn't have time for the third degree right now. We have to get to work."

Allegra's head snapped up. "Work? Emily, I'm not sure what you mean."

His mother smiled. "The dance studio, dear. Surely you remember."

Zander turned to go. He'd heard enough. Allegra was back in New York. Back in his life. It made sense she'd end up back at the Wilde School of Dance, as well.

It was where she belonged, even after all this time. Once upon a time Zander had belonged there, too. But those days were over.

* * *

Walking into the Wilde School of Dance was as close to going home as Allegra would ever get. It looked exactly the same as it had all those years ago. Same smooth wood floors, same mirrored walls, same old blue record player sitting on the shelf inside the studio where she'd spent the majority of her childhood.

The wave of nostalgia that hit her when she walked through the door nearly knocked her off her feet.

She'd never imagined coming back here again. Ever. But given the choice of either accompanying Emily to the studio or staying back at the brownstone with Zander had been a no-brainer. Still, she purposefully turned her back to the collection of recital photos that lined the wall of the entryway and took a deep breath.

"Why don't you flip through the records and choose some barre music for the adult ballet class?" Emily slipped out of her coat and turned on the computer at the front desk. "You remember where they are, don't you?"

"Sure." Allegra couldn't quite believe Emily's dance school wasn't streaming music for class, but she was happy to have something productive to do. Anything to keep her mind off the last time she'd been in this building.

The record albums were lined up on the shelves beneath the turntable, right where they'd always been. As she flipped through them, she spotted several of her favorites—music that made up the soundtrack to less complicated days, when her biggest concern had been whether or not she'd remember the steps to her competition dance numbers.

She would have given anything to be able to go back to those days.

That was impossible, obviously. She hadn't realized just *how* impossible until she'd spotted Zander staring at her from across the Bennington ballroom.

Her throat grew tight. Why did she keep thinking about him?

*Maybe because you're wearing his coat.*

Indeed she was. And it smelled magnificent, like cedar and sandalwood. Wholly masculine.

She wiggled her way out of it and tossed it as far as she could throw it. It landed on the chair situated at the front of the room and was now draped over the seat as if Zander himself had just slid it off his broad shoulders.

Allegra's face grew hot. Again.

*Enough thinking about Zander Wilde.* She might have slept in his pajamas last night, but that didn't mean he had any place in her thoughts. No man did. She was starting over. Alone.

She slid one of the albums from its sleeve, placed it on the turntable and gingerly lowered the needle. The familiar sound of the needle scratching against the record's grooves filled the air. Without thinking about it, Allegra pointed her foot and began sliding it against the polished maple floor in a smooth *rond de jambe*.

"You always did have the best turnout," Emily said.

Allegra moved back into a normal standing position and crossed her arms. "I didn't hear you come in here. I was just messing around."

"Messing around quite beautifully. You've kept up with your technique." Emily winked. "It shows."

Allegra laughed. "You can tell that from one *rond de jambe*?"

"I could tell before you set foot in the studio. I knew the moment I saw you. You carry yourself like a ballerina, dear."

Busted.

Although calling herself a ballerina when she hadn't performed in nearly six months was a stretch. "I danced in the Boston Ballet for a few years. Just the corps de ballet. I wasn't exactly a prima."

Emily shook her head. "Don't do that. Don't undermine yourself. You're clearly talented. You always were. I just always thought you'd become a ballroom dancer."

Allegra's heart gave a little lurch. "Afraid not. I haven't danced ballroom in a long time. Not since…"

She couldn't finish. She didn't need to, though. Emily understood. She'd been the one to give Allegra the news on that rainy New York afternoon fourteen years ago.

*There's been an accident, dear. I'm sorry. So, so sorry.*

The words echoed in Allegra's consciousness. She remembered them as crisp and clear as if Emily had said them to her yesterday. She remembered the tremor in her voice, the raw devastation in her dance teacher's eyes. More than those things, though, she remembered being wrapped in the tightest embrace of her life. She remembered being held for hours as she'd cried.

Allegra's eyes filled with unshed tears. The voice she remembered so well from that day had been Emily's, but the arms that held her…

Those had been Zander's.

"He stopped dancing then, too, you know," Emily said softly.

Allegra hadn't known. Now that she did, his CEO demeanor made a bit more sense. "He didn't want to start over again with another partner?"

It took time for dance partners to grow accustomed to one another. Months. Sometimes years. Allegra and Zander had never danced with anyone but each other. Even after Allegra had moved to Cambridge to live with her aunt, she couldn't fathom dancing with another partner. So she'd packed away her ballroom shoes and thrown herself into ballet.

"Something like that." Emily's smile didn't quite reach her eyes.

Allegra's gaze strayed over her shoulder, toward the recital photos hanging in matching gold frames.

*Don't look. Do. Not.*

Her gaze flitted from one picture to the next until she landed on the one of her and Zander in their trademark tango pose—arms wrapped around each other, bodies pressed together tight. One of Allegra's legs was hooked over Zander's hip, and his hand gripped the back of her thigh. She gazed into the camera with a sultry stare, but Zander's attention was focused solely on her.

Something about that captured expression sent a shiver up her spine. The tense set of his jaw and the intensity in his gaze looked uncannily similar to the way he'd been glaring at her since last night.

They'd been pretending back then. They'd simply been teenagers playing dress-up. The seductive moves and the smoldering glances had been for show. Part of a performance.

At least that's what Allegra had told herself at the time.

She cleared her throat, averted her gaze and found Emily watching her intently.

"So it's settled. You'll teach class this morning," the older woman said.

Allegra blinked. "What? No…"

Emily shrugged. "Why not? Do you have other plans for the day?"

She didn't, other than the pressing task of getting her life in order. Which suddenly seemed far too exhausting to contemplate.

"Emily, I've never taught a dance class in my life." She didn't even have a pair of ballet shoes with her. Although the black wraparound dance sweater and leggings that Emily had loaned her for the day suddenly made sense.

"These students are total beginners. All you need to do is a half-hour barre, followed by a very simple adagio combination at center. Add a drawn-out reverence at the end, and boom. You're done. Come to think of it, you could probably handle the beginning children's classes, too."

Allegra shook her head. She was already living with the Wildes. She most definitely didn't need to be working for them, too. "This is a terrible idea."

"It would be a tremendous help. Tessa used to teach this class, but now that she's been promoted to prima at the Manhattan Ballet, she doesn't have time. We have six classes a day here, and I'm afraid I can no longer teach them all myself."

Emily was still teaching? Six classes a day?

Allegra had assumed Emily was retired from teaching. She'd even talked about winding down her teaching career back when Allegra had been a student. The plan had been for Zander's sisters, Tessa and Chloe, to take over the class instruction duties while Emily handled the business end of the school.

From the sound of things, neither one of them had time to teach. Tessa was busy dancing at the Manhattan Ballet, and Chloe was a Rockette. They simply didn't have the time to devote hours every day to the family school.

And Zander had clearly moved on.

Which meant he shouldn't be hanging around the place. That was certainly a plus. Maybe Allegra could help out. Just until she figured out a more permanent plan, obviously.

"This is only temporary. You realize that, right?" She'd committed to a week under Emily's roof. If she taught class for every one of those days maybe she could save up enough money for a new beginning.

It was a start, anyway. Right before the wedding, she'd moved all of her things out of the small apartment in Cambridge she shared with Talia Simms, one of her ballerina friends. Now she was stuck in limbo. Homeless as well as jobless.

She had to start somewhere.

"Just give it a try and see how it goes. Who knows? You might take to it."

She might. She'd always wanted to teach, but she couldn't make a career out of it. Not here. New York was one of the biggest cities in the world. *If* she decided to stay in Manhattan—and she was in no way certain she would—there were plenty of other places where she could teach ballet. She needed to be starting over, not running back to her past.

No matter how tempting the prospect might be.

Her gaze flitted back to the tango photo. Another shiver coursed through her, which she attributed to the whirl of snowflakes floating among the yellow taxicabs just beyond the studio's picture window.

Because it surely didn't have anything to do with Zander Wilde. Not anymore.

"My ballet shoes are back in Cambridge." Her voice sounded raw for some strange reason. Broken.

"No problem. We sell them. I have plenty on hand. I may even have your old dance bag around here somewhere."

Allegra swallowed around the lump that sprang to her throat. "The new ones, please."

She'd spent the past fourteen years refusing to look back, and she wasn't about to start now. Even if there might be more worth remembering than she was willing to admit.

# Chapter Five

Zander hadn't planned on returning to the office until he'd gotten at least a few hours of sleep, but that idea ultimately proved fruitless.

Every time he closed his eyes, he saw Allegra looking as comfortable as she could possibly be in his kitchen. In his clothes. In his life.

It was unsettling. More unsettling than seeing her in a wedding gown, if he was being honest with himself. Probably because a very real part of him had enjoyed coming home and finding her there. For a split second he'd even allowed himself to believe she'd been waiting for him.

Then reality had set in.

She hadn't been any more thrilled to see him than he'd been to see her. Perfectly understandable, given the way their little reunion had gone at his birthday party.

But any regrets he had at the way he'd behaved last night had vanished the moment he'd heard about the Vows column. Allegra's sudden reappearance had thrown his life into a tailspin on multiple levels.

And now they were roommates.

"Zander, have you got a minute?" Judging from the weary expression on Ryan's face as he appeared at the entrance to Zander's office, he hadn't gotten much rest either.

"Sure." Zander waved him inside, although he was fairly certain he didn't want to hear whatever news Ryan had come to deliver.

His doubts intensified when Ryan handed him a demitasse cup of espresso before taking a seat.

"Trust me, you're going to want that when I tell you the latest," Ryan said, gesturing toward the white china cup.

Zander took a swallow, relishing the taste of the rich, dark liquid. Bitter, like his mood. "What now?"

How much worse could things possibly get?

"The phone is ringing off the hook." Ryan sank into the chair opposite Zander's desk.

He'd been right. Zander did indeed need the espresso. A gallon of it might have sufficed. "Let me guess. Not one of those callers wanted to reserve the ballroom for a wedding."

Ryan shook his head. "Quite the opposite. We're getting cancellations."

*"Cancellations?"* Things could get much, much worse than he'd expected. Obviously.

He'd braced himself for a coming drought. Zander

wasn't an idiot. He knew it would be tougher to convince engaged couples to get married at the hotel since it was supposedly cursed, but he could tough it out for a few months. Once the Bennington actually managed to marry off a few couples, this whole debacle would blow over and everything would return to normal.

Of course that plan hinged on the fact that the weddings already on the books went as planned.

"You mean people believe in this curse so much that they want to move their weddings to a different location?" Unbelievable.

Ryan sighed. "So much so that they're willing to forgo the deposit. The Vows column carries some serious weight."

"We're not going to be able to dig our way out from under this until someone actually ties the knot here." Zander's head ached. What was he supposed to do? Drag people from the marriage-license line at city hall into his lobby with a priest and a wedding cake? "Tell me we've still got something coming up."

"I wish I could." Ryan crossed his arms. "As of right now, we don't have a single wedding scheduled in the ballroom until June."

Five months from now. He'd be bankrupt by then. "Unacceptable."

"It might be time to cut our rates."

Zander shook his throbbing head. "No."

The Bennington was one of the most luxurious hotels in the city. If word got around that they were lowering their rates, their lavish reputation would take a hit. It would also be a sure sign they were admitting defeat.

"There's only one desirable solution," Zander said.

Ryan's eyebrows lifted. "And that would be?"

"We get the Vows columnist to print a retraction." He'd tossed every possible solution around in his head, and it was the only surefire way to put an end to the curse rumors once and for all.

"That would be ideal. But how do we go about getting that done?"

"You chatted with the reporter. You two have a rapport. Why don't you wine and dine her a bit?" It was worth a shot.

Granted, Zander could wine and dine her himself. Page Six had named him one of the most eligible bachelors in Manhattan a year ago. He pretty much had the wining-and-dining routine down pat.

For some reason, he couldn't stomach the idea. He told himself it had nothing to do with Allegra's CEO-walk-of-shame comment. In fact, it would serve her right to see his picture in the society pages with his arm around another woman.

*Since when do you care about making Allegra Clark jealous?*

"You can't be serious," Ryan said flatly.

Zander cleared his throat. He needed to stop thinking about Allegra. She had nothing to do with this...

Except she sort of did. And not in a good way.

"You want me to date the reporter?" Ryan drew in a sharp breath, then released it. "Sorry, cousin, but that doesn't exactly fall under my job description as CFO."

"I didn't say you should date her. Just invite her to a nice dinner here at the hotel and politely ask her to reconsider the curse nonsense." Had the columnist ever actually been to the Bennington? Maybe a field trip was in order.

Ryan sighed. "I don't know. Do you really think it will work?"

"I think it's worth a shot." Mainly because it was their only option at the moment.

"Fine. I'll do it. Dinner, here at the hotel." He leaned back in his chair and lifted an eyebrow. "But first you answer one question."

Zander shrugged. "Shoot."

"Why me?"

Zander's gaze shifted to his empty espresso cup. "Who else would you suggest? The bellman?"

"You know that's not what I meant. I want to know why you don't want to take the reporter to dinner yourself." He gave Zander a wry grin. "You're deflecting."

"I'm not deflecting." He was *absolutely* deflecting.

And Ryan saw right through it. "This is about the Warren bride, isn't it?"

Zander's jaw tensed. "It's most definitely not."

After a brief pause, he added, "And don't call her that. Her name's Allegra. Allegra Clark."

"I know. That was a test, and you failed." Ryan snickered. "Big-time."

"Don't you have a phone call to make to the *Times*?" Zander picked up his Montblanc fountain pen, twirled it between his fingers and then set it back down again. He didn't seem to know what to do with his hands all of a sudden.

"What's the story there? You two were engaged a long time ago, right?"

"No, we weren't." Not exactly, especially since Allegra couldn't even remember their conversation.

Ryan frowned. "This wasn't the one who left you at the altar?"

Zander picked up the pen again and squeezed it. Hard. "That was Laura, and she didn't leave me at the altar. We agreed that getting married would have been a mistake. It was a mutual decision."

Would Zander have preferred that fateful conversation hadn't taken place in the church lobby just minutes before the ceremony was supposed to have begun? Hell, yes. But it had. He couldn't change history.

They'd hadn't been in love. Not really. And Laura had been right to wonder if Zander had been holding back. He had.

"If memory serves, Laura fled the church in her wedding gown." Ryan shook his head. "No wonder these runaway brides have you rattled."

"I'm not rattled." Zander tossed the pen onto his desk. It bounced a few times before clattering to a stop. Ryan shot him a meaningful glance. "My concern is for the hotel. Period."

"Yet you want me to 'wine and dine' the reporter instead of taking her to dinner yourself. And this decision has nothing whatsoever to do with the fact that Allegra Clark is staying at your brownstone?" Ryan lifted an accusatory eyebrow.

Zander hadn't shared that information, but naturally Ryan would have heard about it. Secrets weren't exactly a thing in the Wilde family.

"Forget it. I'll take the reporter to dinner myself." Zander shrugged.

"You sure about that?"

*No.* "I'm inviting her to dinner, not proposing marriage." Been there, done that, got the T-shirt. Never again. "I'll handle it. You're off the hook, cousin."

Ryan stood. "If you say so. You're the boss."

Yes, he was.

The boss. The one calling the shots. The one in charge. Why did it feel so much the opposite?

Allegra enjoyed teaching the adult ballet class so much that she ended up taking on the toddler creative-movement class right afterward, followed by preballet for five- and six-year-olds. By that time, she was ready for a break, so she ran out to get soup and a loaf of crusty French bread for her and Emily.

The deli around the corner looked exactly the same as it had back in high school, when she and Zander had spent hours studying after dance class. Even their corner booth looked the same, down to the small tear in the red vinyl seat. A lump formed in Allegra's throat when she spotted it, for reasons she didn't care to contemplate. So she faced the other direction as she waited for her to-go order and passed the time by calling Spencer's assistant.

She couldn't put it off any longer. She needed her things. At the very least, she needed her purse and her phone. Max, the deli owner, recognized Allegra and very kindly let her borrow the deli's landline. She dialed the number before she lost her nerve.

"Allegra, are you okay? No one's heard from you since, well…" The secretary cleared her throat.

*Since I ran out on my wedding and left your boss standing at the altar?*

"I'm fine. I'm staying with an old childhood friend here in Manhattan." She injected as much cheer into her voice as she could manage. *See how fine I sound?* "I left some things at the hotel, though, and I'm wondering if you could send them to me."

She braced herself for an icy response or, worse, a flat-out *no*.

"Of course. I have them right here. I was hoping you'd call before we checked out."

Her kindness hurt far more than a cold shoulder would have because it meant only one thing—she knew why Allegra had run.

"Thank you." Allegra rattled off the Wilde School of Dance's address as quickly as she could and slammed the phone down as her first tear fell.

*Did* everyone *know?*

"Here you go." Max handed Allegra a brown paper bag. "It's great to see you again. Are you back in New York for good?"

"Just visiting."

Right. As if this trip down memory lane was nothing but a fabulous vacation instead of what it really was.

What was it exactly?

"Where's your young man? Is he here, too?"

Allegra blinked. He was obviously talking about Zander, and she had no clue how to answer the question.

"Never mind me. I'm just a nosy old man." He waved a hand. "Come see us again while you're here if you get a chance."

"I will." Allegra swallowed around the lump in her throat.

She couldn't get out of the deli fast enough. She felt transparent, as if Max could see right through her. As if he knew that the last time she'd sat in his corner booth, she'd been whole and now she wasn't. Hadn't been for almost as long as she could remember.

She blinked against the snow flurries swirling

through the air as she made her way back to the studio. Tears pricked her eyes, and she wasn't altogether sure whether they were a product of the icy wind or the stinging humiliation of the conversation with Spencer's assistant.

*Did everyone know?*

The question ran through her mind like a song on constant repeat. She wasn't even sure why.

What difference did it make? Did it really matter if Spencer's secretary knew he'd been cheating on her all along? Or if his entire staff knew?

Those people weren't her friends. The bigger question—the one that really mattered—was far more troubling.

Had Allegra herself known?

The truth had slapped her in the face just minutes before she walked down the aisle. It was kind of hard to ignore the sight of her fiancé sticking his tongue down her wedding planner's throat. Even a smooth-talking politician couldn't spin his way out of that awkward encounter.

He'd tried, of course. And then he'd begged. He just needed her to go through with the wedding, and they'd figure out the pesky infidelity issue later. The election was in less than three months. He needed the positive press. The blushing bride. The happy-ever-after.

Even if none of it was real.

She'd nearly gone through with it. Then, halfway down the aisle, she couldn't catch her breath. She'd stopped dead in her tracks and stared down at the swath of ivory carpet scattered with pink rose petals, unable to move. Unable to think. She could feel her heartbeat in her throat, and she was certain she would die right there in her wedding gown, choking on dread.

She hadn't had a panic attack in years. Not since she'd joined the ballet. It had to mean something. When she'd dashed out of the ballroom at the Bennington, she'd been convinced it was a sign. Her subconscious had been telling her she couldn't go through with it. She couldn't marry a man who so obviously didn't love her.

But now, standing on the threshold of the Wilde School of Dance with her heartbeat once again clogging her throat, she realized she'd gotten it wrong. The thought of marrying Spencer wasn't what had nearly caused her to crumple to the ground in raw fear. It had been the realization that she'd suspected just what kind of man Spencer was all along.

She'd known.

She'd known, and it had never really mattered because she wasn't in love with him. Yet she'd been ready to marry him, anyway. Because so long as she was married to someone she didn't love with her whole heart, she'd never be broken again.

She'd lost everything the day her mother, father and little sister died on the way to her dance recital. Her world had bottomed out. She couldn't live through that kind of loss a second time. What better way to protect herself against that kind of grief than to go through life without really loving? Without really living?

*Oh, my God.*

The pieces were coming together now with shameful clarity. How long had she been lying to herself? Weeks. Months. Years.

The paper bag from the deli slipped through her

fingers and fell onto the snow-covered sidewalk with a splat. She tried to bend down and pick it up, but she couldn't. She was paralyzed again. Her breath came in terrifying gulps, but she still couldn't seem to get enough air. She clawed at her throat. Everything around her—the crawling traffic, the pedestrians pushing past her, the frost-covered streetlamps—began to blur around the edges.

*I'm losing my mind.*

She squeezed her eyes closed and tried to fight it. But it was no use. Fear was pressing down, suffocating her until she could no longer stand.

She sank to her hands and knees, barely conscious of the frigid pavement and the gritty rock salt digging into her palms. Soup was spilling out of the bag she'd dropped, leaking all over the sidewalk. She took another desperate inhale. The rich scent of tomato and basil caused bile to rise to the back of her throat.

*I'm going to be sick.*

It was all she could do not to curl into a fetal position right there in the middle of midtown Manhattan.

"Allegra?"

Somewhere beyond the fog in her head, she was vaguely aware of a person calling her name. A man.

"Allegra! My God, what's wrong?"

She forced her eyes open.

*Zander.*

He was there. How? When?

Allegra had never been so grateful to see a familiar face in all her life. She tried to say his name, but couldn't force it out.

He crouched down so they were on eye level, and

the worry in his gaze was too much to bear. Too real. Too familiar.

She grabbed onto the lapels of his suit jacket.

*Help me.*

"Listen to me, sweetheart. You're okay. You're having a panic attack, but everything is going to be fine." He gathered her into his arms and pulled her to her feet.

Her knees buckled and she leaned into him, burying her face against his shoulder.

"Can you hear me?" he murmured into her hair. "Nod if you can."

She nodded against his chest, barely conscious of the smooth silk of his tie against her cheek.

"I'm here. I'm here, and I've got you." His hands moved in soothing circles over her back. "Breathe, Allegra. Just breathe."

It seemed impossible, but with a little more coaxing, she managed a shuddering inhale.

"That's good," he whispered. "Again. Take another breath."

She did as he said.

Her heart was still beating so hard that her chest burned like she'd just run a marathon, but the fog in her head was beginning to clear.

"Come with me. Let's get you home."

*Home.*

Allegra's frantic heart skipped a beat. She knew better than to argue with him. Couldn't if she tried.

Tears were streaming down her face. She was sobbing, and she wasn't altogether sure whether it was a reaction to the panic still coursing through her or the smallest sliver of relief.

This was the Zander she remembered, the Zander

who'd once held her when everything fell apart. He was taking her home.

Such a place almost seemed possible.

*Almost.*

## Chapter Six

Only eleven minutes passed between the time Zander called for the Bennington's driver and the arrival of a sleek black limousine with the hotel's logo on the door. Eleven minutes in which he aged at least five years while Allegra clung to him like a wounded puppy.

He knew straightaway she was having a panic attack. Before his CEO days, Zander had been on duty as the hotel's general manager when a guest in one of the ballrooms experienced a similar incident. It had been years ago, but he'd never forgotten the raw fear in the young man's eyes. Zander had never felt quite so helpless in the face of suffering before.

Now he was seeing that same kind of fear shining back at him from the depths of Allegra's gaze, and it shook him to the core.

He'd held her while they waited for the car and spoke

as calmly as he could manage, whispering the same kind of assurances he'd given her on the day of her family's accident. Assurances that had turned out to be lies.

*Everything's going to be okay.*

*I'm here.*

*I'll always be here.*

He felt like the world's biggest impostor.

"Where to, Mr. Wilde?" the chauffeur asked, meeting Zander's gaze in the rearview mirror as the privacy divider began to rise. "The hotel?"

"No." Zander's voice was sharper than he intended, but Allegra didn't seem to notice. He cleared his throat. *Stay calm.* "To the brownstone, please."

That hadn't been the plan.

On the contrary, he'd spent the majority of his day figuring out a way to get Allegra out of his house. Once the housekeeping staff had completed their daily tasks and he'd gone over the reservations schedule with a fine-tooth comb, he'd located an available room on the eleventh floor.

It helped that Spencer Warren and his staff had cleared out, but he hadn't intended on sharing that information with Allegra. He'd simply planned on showing up at the dance school and handing her a key.

His throat grew thick just thinking about it. He'd felt so magnanimous. So damn charitable, when in reality, offering her a free seven-night stay in his hotel would have been purely self-serving.

He'd just wanted her as far out of his sight as possible. At minimum, out of his house. And now that room key sat nestled in his shirt pocket, directly beneath Allegra's tearstained cheek.

"We'll be home in just a minute." He bowed his head

to whisper into her hair, inhaling the lush scent of soft peonies in full bloom.

He closed his eyes. She smelled the same. Felt the same, nestled in his arms.

The same, but also different. Different in ways that were even more beguiling. More tempting. Just…*more*.

What the hell was he thinking, bringing her back to the brownstone?

*This is a bad idea.*

The worst. He was keenly aware of that fact, now that she was pressed against him. It felt too natural. Too much like she belonged there, next to his heartbeat.

But there was no way he was leaving her alone. Not when she was like this. Over his dead body.

"Your mother." Allegra looked up, wide-eyed, but remained tucked under his arm. "She's expecting me back in the studio. I told her I'd teach the afternoon classes. She's got to be wondering where I am."

"She's fine. I told her I was taking you home." He'd texted Emily as soon as he'd called for the limo and then set his phone to Vibrate. It had been buzzing away in his suit pocket ever since. He'd eventually switched it off completely.

The text messages and calls would have to wait.

"Thank you." Allegra voice was a hoarse whisper, and she gave him a wobbly smile. At the same time, a tear slid down her cheek.

Zander brushed it away with the pad of his thumb and then inexplicably let his fingertips linger on the delicate curve of her jaw.

*Stop touching her.*

The worst of the panic attack was over. She could breathe now, but she still looked dazed, with a faraway look in her eyes that was far too troubled for Zander's taste. He couldn't let her go. Not yet. "How long has this been going on, sweetheart?"

*Sweetheart.* Again.

In the back of his head, alarm bells rang.

"Awhile." Allegra's smile faded, drawing Zander's attention to her mouth. Every muscle in his body tensed. "It started after I moved away, after…"

He nodded. *After the accident.* He wasn't about to make her say it.

"But then the panic attacks stopped. For years." Her gaze shifted to her lap. "Until the other night."

*Interesting.* "The night of the wedding?"

She nodded.

Somehow that confession explained everything and nothing, all at once.

Then a horrific thought occurred to Zander, one he hadn't dared entertain before. "Did he hurt you? Because if he put his hands on you, if that's why…"

She blinked. "What? No! It wasn't like that."

He looked at her.

*What was it like, then?*

The question hovered between them, unspoken. But very much there.

Allegra inhaled a ragged breath. "He was cheating on me. I found out only minutes before the ceremony."

Zander's hands clenched into fists, and it was only then that he realized he was still touching her. Still stroking her cheek. "That bastard."

She rolled her eyes, but Zander couldn't help noticing a hint of a smile on her lips. At last, he let himself relax.

*She's fine.*

"I know you're in hero mode right now, but you can turn down the testosterone a notch or two. It's more complicated than it sounds." There she was—the impertinent runaway bride who'd crashed his birthday party.

Zander had missed that spunk more than he'd realized. Still, he didn't want to push. Not after he'd just found her on her hands and knees on a Manhattan sidewalk, unable to breathe. "We don't have to talk about this now."

"Good." She closed her eyes and let her head fall back onto his arm.

Zander's fingertips drifted lower until he was touching her neck. He moved his thumb up and down in the same tender circles he'd been tracing on her cheek. If it had been anyone else, it would have felt strange. Maybe even wrong. But they'd been dance partners.

Back when they were teenagers, they'd practiced for so many hours a day that sometimes Zander wasn't sure where his body ended and Allegra's began. Now that the icy wall between them had begun to thaw, it was all too easy to slip back into old patterns.

*Muscle memory. That's all it is.*

Just one body remembering another—remembering the dip of her lower back beneath his palm, the perfect fit of her hand in his. Once upon a time, those things had been familiar. Natural.

Innocent.

As right as it might feel now, the innocence that had once come with touching Allegra was notably absent. That was the difference, at least on his end. They weren't kids anymore. They were all grown-up.

He took a measured breath and focused his attention on the snow beating against the car window and the pale glow of the streetlights against the deepening winter sky instead of the woman in his arms.

Within minutes, she fell asleep, burrowing even closer. Zander did his best to keep his thoughts trained on practical matters. Mundane details, like how he'd need to get back to the dance school at some point to pick up his car, which he'd left parked at the curb, and the pile of paperwork that was no doubt piling up on his desk. He couldn't quite focus, though, and before long, he found himself watching Allegra sleep. The little furrow between her eyebrows vanished. Her whole body seemed to sigh, and for the first time since he'd found her cowering on the sidewalk, she looked almost peaceful. Content.

When the car turned onto Riverside Drive and the Hudson River came into view through a snowy haze, he gave her a gentle shake. "We're almost home."

Her eyelids fluttered open. Their eyes held for a second too long, and the awareness that Zander had been fighting for the duration of the ride settled over him with undeniable clarity. For the first time in years, he and Allegra were alone together. The chauffeur sat beyond the privacy divider, feet away. It might as well have been a mile.

He swept a lock of hair from her face and felt the full force of her glittering blue gaze deep in his chest. "Feeling better?"

She nodded. "Thank you again. I'm a bit embarrassed now…"

"Don't be. It was nothing." He swallowed. Hard.

He was lying, and they both knew it. Finding her like that—taking care of her, making sure she was safe—was definitely *something*. It had been for him, anyway.

"I mean it. I'm glad you were there." She licked her lips, and once again, Zander's gaze was drawn to her mouth. His heart stuttered to a near stop. "I'm glad you're here now."

Then her lips parted ever so slightly, and she pressed a gentle kiss to the corner of his mouth. Their faces were so close together that she only had to lift her head a fraction of an inch, but Zander still saw it coming. He could have changed what was about to happen.

A better man would have.

But Zander didn't want to be a better man. Not at that moment.

He'd waited a lifetime to kiss Allegra Clark.

She was dreaming.

Allegra had forgotten how exhausted she always felt after a panic attack, like she wanted to sleep for days.

Sometimes she had, especially in the weeks and months after she'd first moved to Cambridge. During the first six months she lived with her aunt, she'd missed twenty-seven days of school. Most of those days had been spent in bed. The others had been spent developing coping techniques—relearning how to breathe, relearning how to *live*.

Once she'd started dancing again, life had gotten easier. Not ballroom dancing, obviously. The thought of dancing with anyone other than Zander was out of the question.

Ballet, on the other hand, was perfect. She loved its classical roots, dating all the way back to the nineteenth century. Ballet was steeped in tradition. It was predictable. It was demanding, to be sure, but it would never surprise her. Never leave her reeling. She knew exactly what to expect when she showed up for class every day—a half hour at the barre, followed by a combination at center, a graceful adagio, a brisk allegro and, at the end, a reverence.

The predictability of it was a balm. Ballet helped her heal. Or so she'd thought.

The panic attack she'd had this afternoon was one of the worst she'd ever experienced. No wonder she could barely keep her eyes open.

But the dream felt so vivid. So real.

Zander was there and his mouth was on hers, kissing her. Tasting her.

Actually, *she'd* been the one to kiss *him*. Just a tender press of her lips. But then she'd let out a little groan for some insane reason, and now her tongue was sliding against his. The kiss became something else entirely, something wholly decadent. And it felt so good, so perfect. Fated somehow. As if this is what she'd been waiting for all along.

That's how she knew it was a dream. Real kisses didn't feel like this. Certainly not kisses between friends, and that's precisely what Zander was. A friend. That's what he'd always been, even in the past day, when they hadn't been on the friendliest terms.

Although the relief that had coursed through her when he'd scooped her up from the sidewalk had been shockingly intense. And when he'd called her *sweetheart*, something had come loose inside her. Something she'd been trying very hard to keep bound up tight.

Those things had been real. Could the kiss be just

a dream? A thoroughly wonderful, thoroughly *confusing* dream.

"Mr. Wilde, we've arrived."

The voice came from somewhere overhead and startled her into consciousness. She dragged her eyes open. Everything seemed to be moving in slow motion. Her body felt warm all over. Liquid and sweet, like melted honey.

But when Zander's face came into focus just inches from hers, she froze.

This was no dream.

*What have I done?*

They looked at one another for a long, loaded moment. He seemed just as stunned by the sudden turn of events as she felt. Maybe even more so, if the small shake of his head was any indication.

"I shouldn't have let that happen." His gaze darted to her mouth and then just as quickly flew back to meet hers. "You're upset, and I…"

Allegra swallowed. Nodded. Although she wasn't quite sure what she was agreeing with.

*What? I'm upset, and you're* what *exactly?* She wanted to interrogate him before they got out of the car and pretended none of this ever happened.

Because that was definitely Zander's intention. His jaw was clenched tight, and his eyes—dark and wild only seconds before—were now steely with determination.

"Mr. Wilde," the driver prompted.

Zander reached across Allegra to press a button on the car's ceiling. "Yes, Tony. Miss Clark and I are ready."

Allegra shook her head. She wasn't ready. If she

tried to stand right now, her legs probably wouldn't be capable of holding her up.

What was wrong with her? She didn't feel panicked anymore. Quite the opposite, actually.

She should definitely be capable of standing.

The phrase *weak in the knees* popped into her mind. She shook her head again.

*No.*

*Just...*

*No.*

She couldn't be attracted to Zander Wilde. She was working at his mother's dance studio. She was living *in his house*. The night before, she'd nearly married another man.

*But Zander thought that big white wedding gown had been for him. Remember?*

She blinked. Hard.

Zander had slid to the other end of the car, leaving an enormous expanse of smooth leather seat between them. As if that wasn't symbolic enough, he refused to make eye contact with her. He straightened the Windsor knot in his tie, cleared his throat and then straightened it again.

"Zander, I..."

The door closest to Allegra flew open. Beyond a swirl of snow, she could see a man in an overcoat and hat offering her his hand. Tony, presumably.

Somewhere in the periphery, Allegra caught a glimpse of a dash of black fur. It was the kitten she'd seen earlier from the window.

"Go on," Zander prompted.

She turned to face him again. "But..."

*But* what? She took a deep breath.

*But I just kissed you.*

"Don't worry. You won't be alone. I'll be inside in a few minutes. I need to make a call first." Zander pulled an iPhone from his pocket. He pressed the home button, but the screen remained dark. The phone wasn't even turned on.

"You should go on up and get some rest. I'm sure you're exhausted." He slipped the phone back out of sight. When he glanced at her again, he was wearing his CEO expression. Impassive and businesslike, to the point of looking utterly disinterested.

But his eyes betrayed him. Those familiar green irises of his were anything but neutral.

"Right." She nodded, and her face grew warm.

Zander was being a gentleman. He was offering her an out, a chance to pretend the kiss never happened.

He knew she'd been vulnerable. She'd been so disoriented that she'd almost believed the kiss had been a dream.

Hadn't she?

Of course. She never would have kissed him otherwise.

Maybe.

Probably.

But as she placed her hand in Tony's to climb out of the car and leave Zander behind, she didn't feel quite so confused anymore. The fog in her head had lifted. Her heartbeat was steady and strong. For the most part, she felt back to normal again. Like herself.

Yet somehow, undeniably, disappointed.

## Chapter Seven

Zander should have known something disastrous had happened the minute he walked through the Bennington's revolving door the following morning. To an outsider, everything probably seemed perfectly in order. Fresh flowers topped every available surface, the gold clock hanging from the lobby ceiling chimed right on time and the chandeliers shone in perfection.

But Zander was no outsider.

He knew the Bennington inside and out. He knew the bellmen were darting about not because they were busier than usual, but because they were studiously avoiding his gaze. He knew the manager's smile seemed just a bit strained around the edges. And he definitely knew that the selection of newspapers next to the coffee service seemed smaller than usual.

Something was missing.

Namely the *New York Times*.

He stopped at the coffee station long enough to pour himself a double espresso and then bypassed his darkened office to head straight for Ryan's.

"Good morning." He stood in Ryan's open doorway and sipped his coffee, hoping he was wrong. Maybe everything was perfectly in order. Maybe he was just imagining things. Maybe the *Times* delivery was simply running late. It wasn't unheard-of.

He didn't want to deal with another crisis this morning. Not after the day he'd had yesterday. Not after the kiss that he and Allegra were still pretending never happened.

Ryan looked up from his computer monitor and narrowed his gaze. "You're alive."

"The last time I checked, yes. Alive and well." Zander unbuttoned his suit jacket and took a seat.

*Alive and well.*

The last part was debatable, despite the fact that the day before had been his first afternoon off in as long as he could remember.

He'd kept his word to Allegra and stayed at the brownstone while she'd slept. He would have been useless at the office, anyway. Her panic attack had left him shaken.

The kiss that followed had just about killed him.

Ryan leaned forward and pinned Zander with a glare. "You left yesterday to run a mysterious errand and never returned. What the hell happened to you?"

A lot had happened. Too much. But he wasn't about to get into it with his cousin.

"Something came up," he said tersely.

"That's it? Something came up?" Ryan snorted. "I

hope it was important, because the *Times* skewered us this morning."

*What now?* Zander shook his head. "That doesn't make sense. The Vows column only runs on weekends. Don't tell me the actual News section has developed an interest in our alleged curse."

Impossible.

A trickle of dread snaked its way down Zander's spine. Ryan knew better than to joke about something this serious.

"The front page couldn't care less, but the New York City section sure has something to say about it." Ryan swiveled in his chair, grabbed a newspaper off his credenza and threw it down on the desk.

Zander scanned the page. If the hotel was getting more bad press, he'd have to take action. It couldn't go on. He wondered who was responsible, who he'd need to fire.

Then at last his gaze landed on a headline in the lower left-hand corner, revealing the identity of the offender.

Zander himself.

Bennington CEO a No-Show for Dinner Meeting, Leaving All of Manhattan Wondering: Is the Bridal Curse Real?

Zander clenched his gut. He'd completely forgotten about dinner with the reporter. No wonder Ryan had thought he'd been dead in a ditch somewhere.

*Damn it.*

Ryan cleared his throat. His hands were folded neatly in front of him on the surface of his desk. He seemed perfectly unruffled, rather like the polished veneer of the hotel lobby. He didn't have to spell things out for Zander, though.

They were well and truly screwed.

"Am I missing something here? I thought we agreed that you'd handle the reporter," Ryan said.

"We did." Zander nodded and somehow managed to tear his gaze away from the lurid headline.

"Then why didn't you show up?" A telltale angry vein throbbed to life in Ryan's temple.

As CEO, Zander was technically Ryan's boss. But CFO was pretty high up on the food chain. They'd always operated as more of a team, and Zander preferred it that way. Plus, they were both Wildes. They were family. Zander trusted Ryan with his life and vice versa.

But now, for the first time in his professional life, Zander had dropped the ball. Big-time.

He swallowed. "I forgot."

"You *forgot*?"

Zander nodded again. It was a piss-poor excuse, but it was the truth. "Why didn't any of the staff call me when she got here? I could have headed straight over. Being late would've been bad but infinitely preferable to standing her up."

He was grasping at straws, and they both knew it. The dinner had been Zander's responsibility. No one else's.

How could he have let this happen?

He closed his eyes. A headache was already blossoming at the base of his skull, no doubt because he knew precisely why he'd forgotten his date with the Vows reporter.

*Allegra.*

"The staff did call you. Multiple times. Then they called me, and I rang you for hours. When you never answered, I came here myself, but she'd already given up and gone home."

Where she'd obviously spent her evening writing another story about the supposed curse rather than being wined and dined. The City section had apparently been happy to put it in print for the world to see.

Perfect. Just perfect.

Zander reached into the pocket of his suit jacket for his phone. Sure enough, the screen was dark. He'd never turned it back on after he'd found Allegra kneeling on the sidewalk in a puddle of soup.

He turned on the phone and immediately got dinged with dozens of texts and voice mail notifications.

Too little, too late.

"Do you want to tell me what's going on? It's not like you to be this distracted. Although I have a feeling I already know the answer." Ryan lifted an eyebrow. "It's the runaway bride, isn't it?"

Zander stared at him and said nothing.

"Don't bother asking which bride I'm talking about, because we both know who I mean."

Zander clenched his jaw. "She has a name."

He couldn't stomach thinking of Allegra as *the runaway bride*. Not after hearing why she'd run. And definitely not after she'd kissed him.

"I'm going to take that comment as a *yes*," Ryan said.

Zander sighed. "Fine. I was with Allegra yesterday, but it's not what you think."

Not entirely, anyway.

"I rearranged some reservations yesterday and found her a room here. I thought it would be better for everyone involved if she stayed here instead of at the brownstone. She's teaching at my mother's dance school, so I went down there to give her a key." Zander paused.

He took a sip of his espresso and wished it was something stronger, possibly a manhattan. Then again, he'd already mucked things up enough. Now wasn't the time to start drinking during the day.

"And?" Ryan crossed his arms.

"And it wasn't the right time," Zander said quietly.

Ryan deserved an explanation. But as much as Zander owed him one, telling him about Allegra's panic attack seemed wrong.

He leveled his gaze at his cousin. "I realize that sounds vague, but you're just going to have to trust me. Can you do that?"

After a loaded silence, Ryan nodded. "Of course I can. I wouldn't be here if it wasn't for you."

"Thank you."

He didn't deserve such blind trust. Not after the massive mistake he'd just made. But he was grateful for it, all the same.

"We've got some major damage control to contend with, though." Ryan scrubbed a hand over his face. "I can't imagine how you're going to get in the Vows columnist's good graces now. Celestia Lane has you in her crosshairs."

"I think a direct approach is the best option." Zander scrolled through the contacts in his phone until he reached the listing for the *Times* switchboard.

Ryan's eyebrows lifted all the way to his hairline. "You think a phone call is going to take care of this?"

"It's worth a try." Zander shrugged, pressed Call and asked the receptionist to connect him to the Vows desk. Hold music blared in his ear while he did his best to ignore the smirk on his cousin's face.

"She's not going to take your call. You know that, right?"

Zander shrugged. "Sure she will. She's a journalist. Doesn't she have to take my call?"

"I'm beginning to believe you don't know anything about journalism." Ryan's smirk became larger and exponentially more annoying. "Or women, for that matter."

Zander arched an eyebrow. "I know plenty about women."

"I'm not talking about sex. I'm talking about *women*. Their emotions. What makes them tick, that sort of thing. Surely you know you have a tendency to come off a little cold?"

Zander's response was a disbelieving stare. His own cousin thought that highly of him?

He wasn't cold. And he knew more about women than simply how to get them into bed.

He knew that daisies had always been Allegra's favorite flower, which is why he'd been taken aback when they'd been notably absent from her bridal bouquet. He knew that *Jane Eyre* had been her favorite book since the day before her fourteenth birthday, when she'd read it from cover to cover in a single, uninterrupted sitting. And now, after yesterday, he also knew all about the delicious little sighing noise she made when she was being kissed.

So soft. So perfectly sweet. Like a kitten.

Perhaps those details only proved Ryan's point. Zander might not know everything about women, but he knew enough about one of them.

Allegra.

The only one who mattered.

*Used to matter*, he corrected himself.

They might have had a *moment* yesterday in the limo, but nothing about his relationship with Allegra had changed. After fourteen long years of silence, they were still virtual strangers. The kiss hadn't meant anything. She'd been disoriented. Disoriented and, most of all, grateful.

He'd taken care of her. Anyone else in his position would have done the same thing. It didn't make him a hero. It certainly didn't make him a love interest. It made him a friend.

Except friends didn't typically kiss one another the way Allegra had kissed him.

The receptionist returned to the line. "I'm sorry, Mr. Wilde, but Ms. Lane can't take your call at this time."

Zander cleared his throat. "I see."

The receptionist hung up on him before he could thank her.

Ryan leaned back in his chair. "I think now is when I get to say I told you so."

Zander chose to ignore that little barb. "It's not a problem. If the reporter won't take my calls, I'll just have to come up with another plan."

"Let me know when you get that figured out," Ryan said.

"Will do." Zander stood and made his way to the door. Call him crazy, but he preferred discussing business without being psychoanalyzed.

Particularly when it came to Allegra.

*Afraid of what you'll find out?*

Maybe.

Then again, maybe not. He was already painfully aware that the longer she'd been back, the more of a mess his life had become. He'd known he was in trouble the minute she crashed his birthday party.

He just hadn't realized quite how much until she'd kissed him.

It took the better part of the morning for Allegra to convince Emily that she was indeed well enough to make the trip to the dance school again and teach class. They hadn't left the house yet, so she still wasn't entirely sure she'd been successful.

She wanted to teach. She *needed* it. If she stayed at the brownstone all day, she'd have nothing to do but think about the events of the day before.

She'd kissed him.

*Zander.*

As if her life wasn't already so complicated that she'd ended up on a Manhattan sidewalk practically in the fetal position, she'd gone and kissed her best friend.

Correction: *former* best friend.

Although he'd certainly acted like a best friend the day before. More than a best friend, if she was being honest.

She might have been the one to initiate the kiss, but he'd certainly been an eager participant. Eager and *capable.*

Where on earth had he learned to kiss like that, anyway?

*Stop obsessing.*

"It was just a kiss. I'm probably making a huge deal

out of nothing, right?" Allegra set a warm bowl of milk down on the front steps of the brownstone in front of the tiny black kitten that she'd once again spotted tip-toeing through the snow.

The kitten let out a loud mew, which sounded too much like an argumentative commentary for Allegra's liking.

"Fine. I know I said it was the best kiss I'd ever had, but I was hardly in a condition to properly evaluate it. I was semiconscious at best."

That was a stretch, but what the kitten didn't know wouldn't hurt her.

Allegra wrapped her coat more tightly around her shivering frame while she watched the little cat lap up the milk. At least she'd gotten a few of her things back. Finally.

After she'd climbed out of Zander's limo, made her way upstairs and fallen into bed, she'd slept straight through until morning. When she'd finally gotten up, she'd found her handbag, cell phone and pale pink cash-mere coat lined up neatly on the downstairs sofa. The overnight bag she'd brought to the Bennington from Cambridge had been sitting right beside them. At long last, she was wearing her own clothes.

Her cell phone had needed charging, which was no big surprise. She'd plugged it in, wondering if Zander had laid everything out so neatly for her or whether it had been Emily. Then she wondered why on earth she cared. Zander wasn't even home. He'd left for work before she'd gotten out of bed, even though it had been early. She wasn't altogether sure what that meant either, although she suspected he was avoiding her.

It didn't matter. She had everything she needed for the time being. Clothes, the little bit of money in her purse, even a job. A temporary job, anyway. Just not a home.

"I guess we have that in common, don't we?" she muttered.

The kitten mewed and wound her way around Allegra's legs until the front door of the brownstone opened and the tiny cat dashed away.

"Did I hear you talking to someone out here?" Emily scanned the empty porch with her gaze.

*Oh, you know, I was just talking to a stray kitten about kissing your son yesterday. Totally normal conversation.*

"No." Allegra straightened, trying her best to look sane. "I mean, yes. But it was just a cat—the little black one I keep seeing out here."

Emily frowned. "In this weather? The poor thing could freeze."

"I brought her some warm milk and she seemed to enjoy it, but she bolted when the door opened just now."

Allegra squinted toward the horizon, but she couldn't spot the kitten. The animal had disappeared somewhere beyond the slow-moving taxicabs and the steam rising from the slick black streets.

Allegra turned back toward Emily. "You haven't seen her out here? Ever?"

"No, not at all." Emily shook her head and slid her key into the lock on the front door.

"That's so odd. She seems to be out here every time I look out the window." If it hadn't been for the empty saucer at Allegra's feet, she might have wondered if she'd been seeing things. Which would have been the icing on the cake of the tumultuous past week.

She swallowed and headed down the front steps of the brownstone. Today would be different. It had to be.

It wasn't until she reached the sidewalk that she realized Emily was still standing on the welcome mat, eyeing her with concern. "Are you sure you feel up to coming to the studio today? I can handle things if you need more rest."

"I'm fine." She pasted a smile on her face. "Honestly, Emily, I need to keep busy. I enjoyed teaching yesterday even more than I expected. I'd like to work at the studio for a while. Would that be all right?"

*A while.* Allegra wasn't even sure what that meant. Days? Weeks?

Fortunately, Emily didn't ask her to elaborate. "It's more than all right. It's perfect. The kids loved you yesterday."

"Good." Allegra nodded.

The day progressed with much less drama than the previous one. Emily insisted on running out to pick up lunch, which was perfectly understandable since Allegra had never returned from her ill-fated soup run.

She was alone in the studio for the first time. Just her and the memories.

Memories of learning how to waltz in Zander's arms. Memories of the way he'd held her—like she was something to be treasured. Revered.

If she was being honest with herself, yesterday hadn't been the first time she'd thought about kissing him. She'd thought about it once or twice when they were teenagers. More often than that, actually.

But he was *Zander*. Her dance partner. Her best friend. He probably would have laughed in her face if she'd just kissed him out of nowhere.

Allegra's fingertips grazed her lips as she let herself dwell on the memory of their kiss in the back of the limousine. The heat of it. The taste of it, rich with years of unspoken yearning.

Maybe he wouldn't have laughed if she'd kissed him all those years ago after all.

He certainly hadn't laughed yesterday. He'd kissed her right back, like a dying man in need of oxygen. Then he'd pushed her out of the car and steadfastly ignored her ever since.

She wouldn't make that mistake again. Not even while semiconscious.

Starting immediately, she also wouldn't keep dwelling on it. Being alone in the studio was sort of nice, if she ignored the weight of yesterday hanging in the air. It gave her a chance to slip into pointe shoes and try a few advanced ballet combinations.

She flipped through Emily's collection of record albums until she found music that was familiar from her tenure at the Boston Ballet. *Giselle.*

Allegra placed the needle of the record player down in the middle of the album, right at the start of the second act.

As a member of the corps de ballet, Allegra had never been a prima ballerina. She wasn't a star or even a soloist. Corps dancers performed together as a group. Their role in a ballet company was to move together as one. To blend in. In most productions, they served as little more than a beautiful backdrop to the principal dancers.

*Giselle* was different. Its second act was known as a *ballet blanc*. A white ballet. The corps dancers all wore sweeping white tulle. They were the real stars of *Giselle*'s Act II, portraying the spirits of doomed, heartbroken brides. They moved as one, hauntingly beautiful in their long, romantic tutus and gossamer wedding veils.

The irony wasn't lost on Allegra. It seemed oddly prophetic that *Giselle* had been one of the last ballets she'd performed. But like most dancers in the corps, she adored it. Dancing *Giselle* had been the highlight of her career. The moment the studio was filled with Adolphe Adam's familiar score, the steps came back to her as naturally as if she'd danced them just days ago, rather than two long years.

She closed her eyes and slid into a *glissade*. Once, twice. Three times. The next step was an excruciatingly slow, controlled *développé*. Allegra pointed her right foot and smoothly, slowly, slid it along her left calf. When it reached her knee, she unfolded her leg until was fully extended, stretched high above her head.

She held it there, relishing the tender ache in her muscles. It felt good to like this again. Right, somehow. Dancing had always made her feel strong. Whole. Invincible, even in her darkest days.

She opened her eyes, seeking her reflection in the classroom's mirrored walls. But the first thing her gaze landed on wasn't her own image. It was Zander's.

He was standing at the back at the room with his arms crossed, leaning languidly against the wall. Quietly watching her dance.

Allegra met his gaze in the mirror. She went breathless for a few beats until looking at him became too much and she stumbled out of her *développé*.

*What is* he *doing here?*

What reason could a hotel CEO possibly have for repeatedly dropping by his mother's dance school?

Allegra swept an errant strand of hair back into her ballerina bun as she marched toward the record player, the toe boxes of her pointe shoes tip-tapping on the hard floor. When she plucked the needle from the album, the silence that descended over the room felt stifling. Swollen with something she couldn't quite name.

"Zander." She cleared her throat and turned to face him.

"Allegra." He pushed off the wall and came closer, hands clenching briefly in his pockets.

His gaze traveled slowly down her body and finally landed on the pink ribbons crisscrossing her ankles. She felt like hiding for some silly reason.

He looked up again, and there was an unmistakable reverence in his dark eyes. "I assumed you were helping with the ballroom classes. You didn't tell me you were a ballerina now."

*You didn't ask.* "Used to be. I'm not a ballerina anymore."

"Not from where I'm standing. That was lovely." His voice went quiet. Rough. Allegra could feel its deep timbre in the pit of her belly. Then he cleared his throat and sounded like himself again. "I didn't expect to see you here. Emily swore up and down she'd make you stay home today."

Allegra hated the tug of disappointment she felt at the realization that he hadn't come to the dance school looking for her. For a minute she'd allowed herself to think that he wasn't actually avoiding her, but indeed he was.

Her face burned with embarrassment, followed very

quickly by irritation. She *worked* at the studio. She wasn't going to apologize for being there. "Do you always call your mother by her first name?"

He frowned. "Not always. Here, I do. Sometimes. Why do you ask?"

Allegra crossed her arms and steadfastly refused to look at his lips. "I don't know. It just seems a little…"

"Cold?" His left eyebrow arched.

"I was going to say strange." She cleared her throat.

Over Zander's shoulder, she could see their recital picture hanging on the lobby wall. She wanted to ask him why he'd stopped dancing after she left, but she was afraid of the answer.

"Your mom, I mean *Emily*, should be back any minute. I'm assuming you stopped by to see her?"

"I did, but I can't stay." Zander reached into the inside pocket of his suit jacket and pulled out an envelope. "Would you give this to her?"

"Sure, but like I said, she should be back soon." Allegra's fingertips brushed against his as she took the envelope. For a prolonged second, they both froze—hands touching, neither saying a word.

Zander's gaze dropped to her mouth, then he quickly looked away. Stepped back.

He shook his head. "I have to get back to the hotel."

"Right now?" God, she was pathetic. The way her voice cracked, it sounded like she was begging him to stay.

She didn't even *want* him to stay.

Did she?

"Yes." He gave her a tight smile. "It's cursed, remember?"

"Right." She nodded. "I'll see you later."

"Not tonight, I'm afraid. I'll be out late."

"Sometime, then." She turned to face the record player, because this weird goodbye was getting much too awkward all of a sudden.

*Just go away. Please go.*

He did.

She watched him walk away in the floor-to-ceiling mirror. Then she turned the music back on, and even though she knew it was just her mind playing tricks on her, she thought she caught a glimpse of herself in her costume from *Giselle*. The diaphanous tulle skirt, the long white veil.

So beautifully doomed.

Forever a bride.

Forever alone.

## Chapter Eight

Allegra was mildly curious about the contents of the envelope Zander left in her care.

Scratch that. She was aggressively curious. Curious to the point of almost giving in to her urge to hold it up to the light after he'd gone.

The Bennington Hotel's crest was embossed on the upper right-hand corner, but otherwise it was blank. Allegra couldn't see a thing through the thick cream-colored paper. The Bennington apparently didn't skimp in the stationery department.

This was for the best, obviously. Whatever was inside that envelope was none of her business. The odds of the contents having anything to do with her were slim to none.

She wasn't even sure *why* she was so curious, other than it might provide some insight into the mysterious

Zander Wilde, teen-ballroom-dancer-turned-buttoned-up-CEO and expert kisser. Which, again, was none of her business whatsoever.

What on earth was wrong with her? She'd never spied on anyone before. Not once. She'd never been one of those girlfriends who went through her partner's phone or scrolled through email messages. Maybe if she had, she wouldn't have been quite so surprised by Spencer's extracurricular activities.

Then again, maybe she just hadn't cared enough to pull a Nancy Drew where her ex-fiancé was concerned.

She swallowed. That wasn't exactly something to be proud of. Neither was poking her nose where it so clearly didn't belong. She placed the envelope on the chair in Emily's office, where she'd be sure to see it, and busied herself with selecting music for the afternoon classes.

But as it turned out, the contents of the envelope did indeed have something to do with her. Sort of.

At the end of the day, Emily presented Allegra with her first paycheck. She tried to give it back. After all, she'd only completed a day and a half of work, and she was also living in Emily's house.

But Emily had been adamant, and frankly, Allegra needed the money if she was ever going to move out of the brownstone.

And she was *definitely* moving out. She just had a few things to care of first. Like finding an affordable apartment. Emphasis on *affordable*.

*So you're actually moving back to New York? Permanently?*

She wasn't sure she was ready to think about that quite yet, which was probably the only benefit of not being in a position to rent her own place.

"Thank you." Allegra glanced down at the check in her hand, noticing right away that something was wrong.

For starters, it was made out for far too much money. She'd have to teach a month's worth of classes to earn that much. Possibly more. Then her eyes focused on the signature at the bottom of the check, and she saw Zander's name.

"Emily, I think there's been a mistake." She stared at the amount again. So many zeros.

Then her gaze flitted to the name of the payee. Sure enough, the check wasn't for her. It was made out to a real estate management company.

"What, dear?" Emily said absently.

"This is the wrong check." Allegra handed it to Emily as it dawned on her that she was holding the contents of Zander's mysterious envelope.

This had to be it. His signature was right there at the bottom of the check, and his name was printed in its upper left-hand corner.

Emily squinted at the rectangular slip of paper, then reached for her reading glasses. "Oh, goodness, you're right. I've been swamped all day setting up the online registration forms for next semester's classes. This is what I get for trying to do too many things at once."

She opened a folder on her desk and exchanged the check for another one inside. "Here you go."

"Thank you." Allegra glanced at the check. This one had her name written on it, along with a much more modest dollar amount.

"I'm sorry I can't pay you more. Things have been a little tight around here recently. It seems there's a dance school popping up on every street corner these days. I'm finding it hard to compete."

"Don't apologize. Please." Emily had already been kinder than Allegra had any right to expect. "I hate to hear that the school is struggling, though. Is there anything I can do to help?"

"Your just being here is helpful. We can certainly use your ballet expertise since Tessa doesn't have time to teach much anymore. I'm thrilled for her, of course. But the students and parents like to know their ballet teacher has professional experience. In a way, you're a godsend right now." Emily squeezed her hand. "Not just because you're family."

Allegra's lips curved into a stiff smile.

She wasn't family.

She hadn't been part of a family in a very long time.

Allegra folded the check into a tiny square to stop her hands from trembling. Before she realized what she was doing, she'd practically transformed it into an origami swan.

She unzipped her dance bag and shoved it inside. "I hope you don't mind my asking, but that other check looked like it might have been for the school's rent."

Emily sighed. "It is. Can you believe how much they're charging for this building these days?"

Allegra nodded, but she wasn't thinking about the dollar amount, although it was indeed astronomical. She was thinking about the masculine signature scrawled across the bottom. "*Zander* pays for this building?"

"He does." Emily's mouth tipped into a half grin. "I'm guessing he never filled you in on the situation at the brownstone."

Allegra shook her head. Had she actually asked that question out loud?

Where was her filter? Gone. Along with the rest of her self-control, apparently.

"Never mind. I'm sorry I said anything." Allegra's face suddenly felt impossibly hot. "It's none of my business."

But her subconscious was screaming.

*What situation at the brownstone?*

"He owns it now," Emily said.

Allegra went very still. Zander owned the Wilde family brownstone?

No. That wasn't possible. The house had been in the family for years, passed down from one generation to the next. Someday it would belong to Zander, along with Tessa and Chloe. But not now. Not yet.

Unless…

Emily nodded. "He bought it from me three years ago. I was going to close the school. The thought of it broke my heart, but financially, I couldn't keep it going anymore."

Allegra swallowed. She couldn't imagine the West Village without the Wilde School of Dance. It had become part of the landscape, as vital to the neighborhood as Magnolia Bakery and Pier 45.

"Zander wanted to help. I couldn't let him do it long-term. I just couldn't. So I offered him the brownstone instead. The generous down payment infused the school with a nice sum of cash, and he's paying out the rest by taking over the school's rent." Emily's smile was so sad that Allegra couldn't quite look the older woman in the eye any longer.

She sank into the chair on the opposite side of the desk and dropped her gaze to her lap. What Emily was saying didn't bode well for the future of the Wilde School of Dance. It also meant something even more unsettling.

Zander was her landlord. And possibly, sort of, her boss, too.

This changed things. Allegra wasn't altogether sure why or how, but it did.

"This place means a lot to him." Emily turned her gaze toward the classroom, with its shiny, mirrored walls and old wood floor, nicked with memories. "Probably more than you know."

Allegra returned to the brownstone at the end of the day with tender feet and a full heart. It had been months since she'd spent all day in ballet shoes. She hadn't realized how much she'd missed it.

Teaching wasn't at all like being part of a professional dance company, obviously. In many ways, it was better. All joy, no pressure. She could see herself getting used to it.

*Don't get ahead of yourself.*

She had no business contemplating staying on at the Wilde School of Dance, no matter how often her thoughts kept spinning in that direction, so the sight of the little black kitten tiptoeing along the kitchen window ledge was a welcome distraction.

Allegra paused in the middle of the room and let her dance bag fall to her feet. The kitten peered at her through the glass. The animal's ears were pricked forward, and one of them had a tiny nick near the tip.

"Hi there." Allegra took a tentative step toward the window.

The kitten stayed put. As Allegra drew closer, she

noticed the cat's slight frame was shivering. A thin layer of snow coated her ebony fur.

Allegra bit her lip. "Maybe I can bring you inside. Only for a minute."

Emily had gone straight to her book club after the school closed. But her earlier comments led Allegra to believe she wouldn't be opposed to letting the kitten into the house.

*This isn't her house anymore, remember?*

Allegra swallowed. She definitely remembered.

The kitten pranced back and forth the length of the ledge, pawing at the window.

Allegra sighed. "Fine. I'll let you in just long enough to get you warm and dry. But it's got to be our little secret, okay?"

She unlatched the window, and the cat leaped into her arms.

"You're trembling." She kissed the kitten's dainty little head and held her close. Her soft coat smelled like winter—frosty leaves with a hint of roasted chestnuts.

Allegra wrapped the kitten in the blanket slung over the back of the living-room sofa and checked her newly charged phone. According to the device's display screen, her voice mail was full. Not a surprise, considering she'd recently been the subject of a column in the *New York Times*.

Sure enough, the messages all seemed to have something to do with her canceled nuptials. A fair number of them were from reporters. Allegra deleted those straightaway. The ones from curious acquaintances claiming to be sympathetic friends went into the trash, as well. After the deleting spree, only two messages remained, both from Talia.

Talia's first message was cryptic—"Call me. It's important." Allegra assumed she must have left something behind at her old apartment or somehow still owed Talia for part of last month's rent, even though she was fairly certain the financial matters were all squared away. Or maybe she, too, was calling about the nonwedding. She'd witnessed the spectacle first-hand after all.

Allegra completely missed the mark. Talia's second message was more forthcoming, and she never would have guessed the reason for the calls.

"Allegra, it's me again. Talia. One of the corps members in the traveling production has a stress fracture in her foot. She's pulled out of the tour, and we need someone. Everyone at the company knows about your, um, predicament. I think the director might be willing to give you the job. It's a very small part, even for a corps dancer. But if you're looking to get back into dance, it would be perfect. I know you could handle it. Call me!"

Allegra stared at the phone until the kitten in her arms meowed, snapping her back to reality.

She wasn't seriously thinking about going on tour with the ballet company, was she? She hadn't danced professionally in months.

Even if her body could handle the physical challenges, she wasn't sure it was the sort of plan she had in mind. Spots on the touring company were temporary. They only lasted as long as the tour. What would happen after the tour ended?

She'd be right back in the same position she was in right now. Minus the part about living in Zander's house, which should have been a definite plus.

The kitten meowed again and began to knead her paws on Allegra's leotard.

*It's really not so terrible living here.*

It wasn't terrible at all, actually. It was nice. So nice that it scared her. Which was precisely why Allegra couldn't bring herself to delete Talia's messages.

Three days later, Zander wasn't having a bit of luck getting the Vows reporter to take his calls. Despite Ryan's words of warning, he was surprised by his lack of headway. Freezing him out seemed like an extreme reaction, especially given the fact that he'd already been subjected to a scathing mention in the City section of New York's most widely read newspaper.

The way Zander saw it, he and Celestia Lane were even.

He'd been forced to implement plan B. If the reporter wouldn't come to the phone, he'd simply have to get in touch with her another way. Unfortunately, the options were severely limited.

Zander couldn't very well camp out at the *Times* building. That had *stalker* written all over it. Plus, it reeked of desperation. Since the most recent *Times* piece, the Bennington reservations desk had once again been inundated with wedding cancellations. So Zander was, in fact, desperate. But the reporter didn't need to know that.

An accidental meeting was the only option. If he bumped into the Vows columnist in a social setting, then maybe they could have a normal, pleasant conversation and she could see that he was actually a decent human being. At the very least, he wasn't some kind of marriage-hating monster at the helm of a cursed hotel. Brides weren't actually running away from the Bennington in droves. Then maybe, just maybe, they could agree to some sort of truce. If he never heard the word *curse* again, it would be too soon.

The idea might not be foolproof, but it was the only thing he'd managed to come up with.

The most obvious flaw in his plan had been the fact that he didn't have the first clue where he could bump into Celestia Lane. Lurking around the Starbucks closest to the *Times* building had seemed like a sure bet. Again, that was out of the question for reasons having to do with desperation.

The solution was obvious. Where was the one place he'd be sure to find a reporter who spent all her time writing about couples tying the knot? A wedding.

Zander hadn't exactly relished the idea of spending what little free time he had attending the nuptials of complete and total strangers. But alas, that was his current situation. Oh, how the mighty have fallen.

He'd been to three weddings in as many days. That was a lot of wedded bliss for anyone to take.

The one upside to his strange new hobby was that he hadn't set eyes on Allegra since the day he'd walked in on her dancing at his mother's school. And that was a good thing. A *very* good thing.

She'd been so beautiful he'd forgotten how to breathe. From the moment he entered the studio, he'd been rendered speechless. Motionless. A rush of desire like nothing he'd ever experienced had hit him hard and fast. If not for the ballet barre digging into his back, holding him upright, he would have fallen to his knees.

She was so graceful. So damn ethereal. Like something out of a dream. Yet he knew those curves. His hands were intimately familiar with her wisp of a waist and the warm dip of her lower back. He knew Allegra's body almost as well as he knew his own.

Watching her dance had awakened an urge he'd managed to ignore for the better part of his adult life. He wanted to dance again. He wanted to move with her, slowly and sweetly. He'd had to shove his hands into his pockets and clench his fists to stop himself from claiming his place beside her and pulling her into a dance hold.

Any hope he'd had of forgetting about the kiss they'd shared in the back seat of the Bennington limo evaporated then and there.

He wanted Allegra.

He wanted to know what her womanly curves felt like beneath his hands as he moved her across a dance floor. He wanted to taste her again, this time while her lithe legs wrapped around his hips as he drove himself inside her. He wanted her to cry his name while he watched her come apart.

The desire had been there all along. Zander had been consciously aware of it humming beneath the surface of his skin during each and every one of their interactions. Even when she'd stumbled into the ballroom and he'd stared at her as the candles dripped onto his cake. He'd pretty much been a goner since he'd let his gaze follow the trail of her wedding gown's tiny white buttons down the length of her supple spine. Which was wrong on multiple levels, but at least he'd been able to set it aside.

There'd been far too much history between them to act on his attraction. Far too many unanswered questions.

Plus the obvious complication that she'd been dressed in miles upon miles of white tulle at the time.

The kiss changed things.

He couldn't ignore his craving for her. Not anymore. He couldn't look at her without remembering what her lips felt like touching his. Too lovely. Too intimate. Like getting a glimpse into a secret, forbidden paradise.

Zander had never had such a visceral reaction to a kiss before.

But this was Allegra.

She was the one who got away, even if Zander's sixteen-year-old self had been too much of an idiot to tell her how he'd felt. She was also the one who seemed to be on the verge of some kind of emotional breakdown at the moment, and he'd waited far too long to stop her the other day in the limo.

Maybe he *was* a monster after all.

Distance.

That's what he needed.

Thank God for the weddings. While they'd been a colossal waste of time thus far, since the Vows reporter hadn't turned up at any of the three, they'd at least been an effective diversion. Usually, by the time Zander returned to the brownstone after a night of bouquet tossing and drunken toasts, Allegra had already gone to bed. The house was dark and quiet.

The night before, however, he could have sworn he heard a *meow* sound coming from Allegra's room. He'd paused outside her door and waited. And then... nothing.

He was losing it. He'd never had a cat in his life. Neither had his mother. So now he could add auditory hallucinations to his list of current problems.

Zander expected to find things at the brownstone the same when the Bennington limo dropped him off after the third wedding. But as he unfastened his bow tie and climbed up the front steps, he nearly tripped on something. He crouched down and realized it was a small saucer of what looked like dry cat food.

Interesting, especially in light of the meow.

He straightened and spotted Allegra standing in the shadows, just to the right of the porch's large marble columns. She wore a bathrobe pulled tight around her slender frame. Zander's eyes narrowed, adjusting to the darkness. He'd never seen the robe before. It was bubble gum pink. Hers, obviously.

It must have been one of the items in the overnight bag she'd finally recovered. Finding her in pajamas that weren't his shouldn't have bothered Zander.

But it did.

He cleared his throat and refocused his gaze on her face, pale and lovely in the moonlight. "Allegra."

"Zander." Her gaze flitted briefly to the small bowl at his feet. "Um, hi."

He bit back a smile. "It's awfully cold for a late-night walk, don't you think?"

She shrugged. "I couldn't sleep. Some fresh air seemed like a nice idea."

Her breath was a visible puff of vapor, mingling with his. "How was your date?" She cast a pointed glance at his tuxedo, visible through the unbuttoned opening of his overcoat.

"I haven't been on a date."

*Would it bother you if I had?*

"Oh. Sorry, I didn't mean to pry." Her cheeks

flushed pink in the darkness, until they were practically the color of her bathrobe.

She was cute when she was jealous.

Which was exactly the sort of thought he shouldn't be having. "It's okay. I was working late."

He didn't feel like going into the whole wedding-crasher thing. It was borderline pathetic and, thus far, wholly ineffective.

Besides, he didn't want to talk about work at the moment. Or weddings.

"Right." Allegra nodded absently and pulled at the tie of her robe.

She didn't believe him. Fine. Let her think he'd been running around Manhattan with a different woman on his arm every night this week. Did it really matter?

*It matters. You know it does.*

"It's late. We should probably get to bed." *We.* As if they were a couple.

What was he saying?

He was beginning to regret drinking that second glass of champagne at the nuptials of the newly christened Mr. and Mrs. Robert C. Williams. Whoever they were.

He turned toward the door.

"Wait." Allegra reached for his forearm with one hand, while the other kept a firm grip on her robe. "Can I ask you something? Please?"

Zander paused, much too aware of the press of her fingertips just above his wrist, even through multiple layers of clothing. "You can ask me anything, Allegra. Always."

"Why didn't you tell me you own the brownstone now?"

The question caught him off guard. He wasn't sure what he'd expected her to ask him after midnight on a snowy evening, but that wasn't it.

"Does it matter?" His words felt like they were coming from deep inside his chest somewhere, and his voice dropped an octave or two.

"Yes, it does. It matters because you let me tease you about living with your mother when it's the other way around. She invited me to stay here without telling you about it, and I know you weren't exactly excited about the idea." She removed her hand from his arm and took a deep breath. "I also understand why."

The snowflakes seemed to swirl in slow motion all of a sudden, and Zander felt like he was back inside the limo again…back to the moment just before she'd kissed him. He could almost feel the weight of her head on his shoulder, feel the warmth of her body nestled against his.

"Allegra." He gave his head a small shake.

They didn't need to do this. Not anymore. This conversation was taking place years too late.

"I left, Zander. I left, and you never heard from me again." Her voice trembled with something he couldn't quite identify.

Whatever it was sliced through him, leaving him raw. Bruised.

So they were going there, whether he wanted to or not.

Finally.

"I'm aware of the facts," he said, gritting his teeth.

Was he supposed to pretend he hadn't missed her? Or that he hadn't called a dozen times before he finally got the hint and gave up?

"And you still let me stay. Why?"

He swallowed. "Because it was the right thing to do."

"I see." She smiled, but her bottom lip wobbled just a little bit. Just enough to make Zander wish he'd told her the truth.

*Because you belong here.*

*You always have, and you always will.*

He sighed.

How had it come to this? Once upon a time, he'd been able to say anything to Allegra.

Almost anything, anyway.

He took a tense inhale and reminded himself he'd handled things as best he could. They'd been kids back then. She'd just lost her family. It wasn't the right time to tell her he'd fallen in love with her. Not when she was so vulnerable, so lost.

Since she'd come back, though, he'd begun to wonder...

Maybe it had been the perfect time to tell her how he felt. Maybe it had been just what she needed to hear in her darkest hours.

"Allegra..." He took a step closer.

Then he heard it again—a plaintive meow. It was unmistakable this time. Loud. Clear. And strangely enough, it seemed to be coming from inside Allegra's robe.

His gaze dropped to her chest. It meowed again.

Zander's eyes moved back to her face, which was flushing furiously now. "Why do I get the feeling I've got another houseguest?"

She loosened her robe, and a tiny feline face peered

at Zander from behind thick pink terry cloth. "This isn't how it looks."

He arched an eyebrow. "You mean you don't actually have a kitten hidden in your bathrobe right now?"

"I do." Allegra bit her lip. Then she extricated the kitten from her clothes and let it burrow into the crook of her elbow, where it gave Zander the most pitiful look it could muster. "She's just a stray that I'm looking after. She's definitely not mine."

Zander's lips twitched into a grin. "Does the cat realize that?"

"I felt sorry for her, so I brought her inside. I heard her meowing out here a little while ago, so I came to get her again."

"What's her name?"

"I haven't given her one. I told you, she's just a stray." Allegra held the kitten tighter to her chest. "She was out here in the cold, all alone."

"We can't have that now, can we?" He ran a hand over the cat's soft head, and she purred, pushing her tiny cheek against his fingertips.

"No, we can't."

There it was again. *We.*

Their eyes met, and Zander could have sworn he was looking at the girl he'd danced with all those years ago, the girl she'd been before the day of their last recital.

Happy.

Whole.

"You can stay here as long as you like, Allegra." The night had gone soft and quiet, and his voice was a hoarse whisper in the dark. "Your nameless kitten, too."

*Just...*

*Stay.*

"Thank you." Allegra's bottom lip slid slowly between her teeth. "But she's really not mine. I'm only taking care of her. It's temporary."

Of course it was.

This wasn't a reunion. It was a respite. Allegra was only biding her time, trying to figure things out until she said goodbye.

Zander had nearly forgotten.

"Understood." He nodded. "Good night to you both, then."

And as he climbed the silent stairs of the old brownstone, he couldn't help but wonder—would there be a goodbye this time, or would she slip away again?

In the end, was there really a difference? He used to think so. Now he wasn't so sure.

## Chapter Nine

The idea came to Allegra right at the end of preballet class on Friday morning.

She'd just led the class of twelve or so four-year-olds through the reverence, somehow suppressing a grin at their adorably wobbly curtsies. Then Allegra concluded the class by giving each little girl a tight hug, a tradition she loved and dreaded in equal parts because it always left her with a lump in her throat.

Her students were so innocent, so untouched by the cruelty of the world in their pink tights and tiny ballet slippers. Sometimes she had to focus on the wall behind their heads when she wrapped her arms around their slender little shoulders instead of looking them in the eyes.

Today was one of those times.

Still, she hugged each and every tiny dancer and

whispered words of encouragement as they filed out of the studio door. *Great work today! See you Monday.*

"I love you, Miss Allegra," one of the girls mumbled into her shoulder.

Allegra's breath caught in her throat.

*Don't get attached.*

"Have a nice weekend, Lily," she said, shifting her gaze from the girl's springy red curls to the lobby wall.

The recital photos still hung there, of course. Allegra had gotten used to them now, though. She'd grown accustomed to the wave of nostalgia that washed over her when she studied them, even when she let her gaze linger a little too long on the photograph of her and Zander.

This time, her attention snagged on one of the older pictures. She walked closer and stared at it as her students threw themselves at the mothers, fathers and nannies in the waiting area—a ritual even more excruciating than the end-of-class hug.

The photograph was black-and-white, and unlike the other pictures, which were mostly posed recital keepsakes, this one looked like a candid shot. The couple in the foreground faced the camera in an open swing-dance hold, while dozens of other pairs spun dizzying circles behind them. All the dancers had numbers pinned to their backs, leading Allegra to believe the picture had been taken at a ballroom dance competition like the ones she and Zander had entered back in the day.

But up close she realized that didn't seem quite right. The couples in the photo weren't as slick and polished as competition dancers typically were, even the novices. Their wide smiles and sharp kicks had a joyful, almost manic feel.

Allegra angled her head, examined the photo for another second or two, then plucked it off the wall and carried it to Emily's office. "Is this photo what I think it is?"

Emily looked up from the costume catalog spread open on her desk and smiled. "That depends. If you're wondering if the couple up front and center are my parents, then yes. You're correct."

Allegra studied the smiling man and woman in the black-and-white image again. If they were Emily's parents, that made them Zander's grandparents. She could see it now. The man in the picture had the same broad shoulders, the same soulful eyes as Zander.

Her throat grew tight thinking about the way those eyes had looked at her the night before on the steps of the brownstone. Like he wasn't merely tolerating her presence but enjoying it. Like he wanted her to stay.

He'd been so sweet to the kitten, too. So gentle.

She couldn't keep the cat, no matter how very badly she wanted to. She might have a bed to sleep in and a roof over her head for the moment, but she couldn't stay at the brownstone forever. That would be crazy.

Allegra swallowed.

If staying in New York was crazy, why hadn't she returned Talia's call yet?

Living here permanently hadn't sounded crazy when Zander suggested it. He'd made it sound almost normal. Almost...*nice.*

*You can stay here as long as you like, Allegra. Your nameless kitten, too.*

Of course by the end of the conversation he'd looked

as if he wanted to take it back. His face had gone back to being as blank as a slate.

"I can't believe I never knew these were your parents. Zander never said anything." Allegra peered at the smiling man and woman in the black-and-white image. "But this wasn't taken at a dance competition, was it?"

Emily shook her head. "Good eye. No, it wasn't. Care to take a guess?"

"It's a dance marathon, isn't it?"

"Bingo." Emily beamed. "They were quite popular back in the day. I think that photo was taken in 1942. Maybe 1943. My mother and father were newly engaged and determined to be the last remaining couple on the dance floor so they could win the grand-prize money. My mom had her heart set on a society wedding at the Plaza, and the couple who danced the longest that night won three thousand dollars."

"That had to be a fortune back then. Did they win? Did your mother get her dream wedding?" Allegra hoped so.

Emily reached across her desk for the framed photograph and ran her fingertips lovingly over the picture. "They did. They danced for twenty-seven hours and fourteen minutes straight. Three months later, they said 'I do.'"

"At the Plaza?"

"No." Emily let out a laugh. "Believe it or not they got married at the Bennington."

"You're kidding." Zander's grandparents had exchanged vows at his hotel decades before he worked there? For some reason, that struck Allegra as outrageously romantic. Which was something of a shock, considering romance was the absolute last thing on her mind.

Along with weddings.

And Zander Wilde.

She took a deep breath. This conversation wasn't supposed to have anything to do with the past. Or romance. It was supposed to be about moving on. Plus one very important thing—money.

"Isn't there a college somewhere in the Midwest that holds a dance marathon once a year as a fund-raiser for their marching band?"

Allegra remembered reading about the event in a dance magazine a while back. The band members played old swing standards, songs from Glenn Miller and Benny Goodman, while students danced until they dropped. The annual event had become so popular that the most recent marathon had raised enough money for the band to buy all new instruments.

"I think you're right," Emily said, handing the picture back to Allegra. "Can you imagine how much fun something like that would be?"

"I can. And I'm glad you like the idea because I think we should have one." Allegra could already see it—streamers and retro bunting, a disco ball hanging from the ceiling. So perfectly retro. So perfectly *perfect*. "We could charge a modest entry fee, plus the couples could get supporters to pledge money for each hour they spend on the dance floor. We could give away a trophy to the winners, both the couple who lasts the longest and the dancers who raise the most money. All the funds could go to the school."

It could work.

If it did, maybe the school would get enough of

a bump to put it into the black. The money from the sale of the brownstone wouldn't last forever, and while Zander was obviously quite successful, he couldn't support the Wilde School of Dance indefinitely. Especially when brides were running away from his hotel in droves.

Allegra still felt a little responsible for the mess Zander was in. Okay, *a lot* responsible.

She kept telling herself the "curse" wasn't her fault. After all, she wasn't the *only* runaway bride.

Still. She'd been the most recent one. The most notorious one, apparently. And the *Times* wasn't backing down.

The damage was done. It was obviously too late for her to do anything about the curse, but maybe she could help Emily's school.

"It sounds wonderful. I love the idea, especially since it ties in with the Wilde family history. But I'm not sure I can pull off something like that on my own. I suppose Tessa and Chloe might be able to help."

"No need. I'll do it." It was the least Allegra could do after everything Emily had done for her. After everything she was *still* doing.

*It's Zander's house, remember? It's his bed you're sleeping in.*

She released a shaky breath. "If you like the idea, let me put together a dance marathon. I can get something planned quickly enough. We could probably get a lot of nice word of mouth just in time for class registration for the new semester."

The more Allegra thought about it, the better her idea seemed. They could raise some money and increase the size of their enrollment at the same time. It was win-win.

Of course if she committed to putting together a fund-raiser, she'd have to stick around long enough to see it through. Effectively, she'd be choosing to stay on as a teacher at the school. At least for another week or two.

But she could do that, couldn't she? She'd still have time to sign on for the ballet tour...

Maybe.

But that would require calling the ballet director or, at the very least, Talia. So far Allegra hadn't come close to contacting either of them.

"I'd hate to impose on you like that, dear," Emily said.

"It's the least I can do. I don't know where I would be right now if you hadn't helped me the night of the wedding. A dance marathon really wouldn't be too hard to put together." Allegra should know. She'd spent more time than she liked to admit helping organize campaign events for Spencer. Because that's what perfect political wives did instead of languishing on the bottom rung of a third-tier ballet company. Or so she'd been told.

She shuddered to think how close she'd come to making that her life, all for a man who'd been cheating on her. A man she wasn't sure she'd ever actually loved.

She was better off alone. Allegra was used to life on her own. It was better this way.

Predictable.

Safe.

Zander's image flitted briefly through her consciousness. His perfectly square jaw. His hands. His mouth.

A shiver coursed through her that felt anything but safe and predictable.

Something was wrong with her. Obviously. She had to get over this ridiculous infatuation she'd somehow developed with regard to her oldest friend.

*Concentrate. You've got a fund-raiser to plan.* "The most difficult part would be finding a location. After that, the rest should fall into place easily."

Emily shrugged. "We could always have it here at the school."

Allegra nodded. "We could. But I was thinking someplace bigger. Someplace special, so we could draw more people. I already have a few ideas in mind."

Technically, she only had one place in mind. But it was perfect, and she was almost certain she'd be able to pull it off.

"You really want to take this on?" Emily asked.

"I do." Allegra nodded.

This would be good. Not just for the school, but for her, as well. She clearly needed something to occupy her thoughts.

Something other than kissing Zander Wilde.

Another day, another wedding.

Zander still hadn't managed to get any face time with the Vows reporter, but he had high hopes for Friday night.

The midweek ceremonies had been long shots. He knew that. Most couples chose to get married on the weekend, particularly the kind of high-profile brides and grooms who were regularly featured on the wedding pages in the *Times*. Still, he had to try.

While his failure to cross paths with Celestia Lane

earlier in the week had been disappointing, Zander didn't consider it cause for alarm. Tonight was a different story.

Vows would run again in the Sunday edition. This was it. Tonight was his last chance to make a favorable impression on Ms. Lane before she once again offered up her thoughts on the Manhattan wedding scene for everyone in the city to read over weekend brunch. He needed the Bennington to be included in those thoughts. Favorably, if at all possible.

After a meticulous investigation that involved combing through the past three months' issues of *Vogue*, *Vanity Fair* and *Town & Country*, as well as a ridiculous number of hours poring over Page Six, Zander was certain he and Ryan had identified the wedding that would be splashed across the Vows headline this weekend.

The bride was a fashion stylist whose clients regularly appeared on the pages of the *Times*'s Lifestyle section, and the groom was a junior partner at one of the biggest law firms in the city's financial district. Both the ceremony and the reception were to take place at the Museum of Natural History, which—according to a rumor that had been repeated no less than four times in Page Six alone—was being lavishly decorated in a secret-garden theme. If the rumor was true, wedding guests would be treated to a three-course meal in the Milstein Hall of Ocean Life, in the shadow of the museum's iconic blue whale, surrounded by peonies and terrariums of succulents.

Zander couldn't have cared less about the plants. Or the meal. Or the whale. But he cared very much about the fact that the wedding was being hailed as the social event of the season.

Celestia Lane's appearance was a certainty.

So was Zander's.

He had the driver drop him off a block from the museum and walked the rest of the way down Central Park West. Best to forgo taking his car and using the valet in case they kept a guest list, because yes, he was still technically crashing.

Zander considered that a minor point, though, because he had no intention of going anywhere near the actual ceremony and reception. He knew better than to fake an invite to an event where every paparazzo in Manhattan would be in attendance. All he had to do was bump into the Vows reporter in the lobby. The museum was a big place, but it only had one main entrance. He'd imply he was there for a meeting of some sort, turn on the charm and, with any luck at all, get another dinner scheduled.

It was the best he could hope for.

The wedding was scheduled to begin at six o'clock, just fifteen minutes after the museum closed. Thank God. It was a small enough window to make his meeting excuse plausible.

The sun had just begun to dip below the New York skyline when Zander made his way toward the steps of the massive building. The stone figures atop the museum's Gothic columns were covered with a soft blanket of snow, and the sky darkened from blue to violet overhead.

Zander hesitated as he reached for the door. How long had it been since he'd set foot inside this iconic building?

A while.

Fourteen years, minimum.

He withdrew his hand, shoved it into the pocket of his overcoat and took a backward step.

This had been their place. His and Allegra's. They'd spent nearly as much time between the museum's hallowed walls as they had at dance practice.

As chairman of the museum's board, her father had retained an office right upstairs. It was in one of the Gothic building's turrets, which had delighted Allegra to no end. She'd once told Zander that when she'd been very small, she'd thought the museum was a castle. Her father's kingdom.

However, Zander could count the number of times he'd actually seen Preston Clark behind the desk of his exquisite turret office on one hand. Allegra's father spent most of his time in his law office on Park Avenue.

But that hadn't stopped Allegra from dragging Zander to the museum every spare moment they had. On the rare occasions when dance class ended early or was canceled altogether, they'd grab a burger at the diner around the corner from the studio and then head uptown. Zander hadn't needed to ask where they were going. It was a given.

Likewise, every one of Allegra's birthday parties took place at the museum. Long before Zander knew her well enough to complete nearly all her sentences, he'd labored under the misconception that she was just oddly passionate about dinosaurs. But it wasn't the bones that drew her there time and again. She'd been searching for something else.

Preston Clark rarely turned up to watch Allegra dance at the school's yearly recital. Zander couldn't recall the man spending more than five minutes at any of those birthday parties at the museum. If he couldn't be bothered to spend time in his daughter's world, she'd been determined to come into his.

Zander clenched his fists in the pockets of his overcoat. A lot of years had passed, but time hadn't erased the memory of the hurt in Allegra's eyes every time she'd peered past the red velvet curtain on recital evenings and seen empty seats in the audience where her parents should have been. Time hadn't made the bitter irony of the fact that their fatal accident had occurred on their way to watch her dance any easier to swallow.

They'd been on their way. Finally.

Allegra blamed herself, of course. "It's all my fault," she'd whispered, again and again, as Zander held her that night.

He knew it was wrong to hate a dead man, but Zander had never been so angry with anyone in his life as he'd been at Allegra's father in the agonizing hours that followed.

He still was, he realized, as he stared up at the museum's towering facade.

None of that mattered now, though. He hadn't come here to chase ghosts. He was here to save his business, and he couldn't do that while he was standing on the top step, gazing at his reflection in the glass double doors, imagining he was seeing a teenage kid instead of the man he'd become.

People were passing him now. Men in black tie and women in long beaded gowns were murmuring words like *pardon* and *sorry* while they stepped in front of him and entered the building. Wedding guests.

*Get ahold of yourself, for crying out loud. You have a job to do.*

Zander pulled the door open and stepped inside.

He glanced up at the violet light filtering through the rotunda, bathing the great room in winter's soft hues. Then he swallowed hard and forced himself to look past the two looming dinosaur skeletons, locked in eternal battle while New York's glittering elite sparkled at their feet. He swept the room with his gaze, searching for a glimpse of the Vows columnist. He'd studied the head shot beside her byline long enough to recognize her anywhere.

Just when he was on the verge of giving up, he saw her. She was walking straight toward him through the throng of people, her brow furrowed in confusion as she spotted him.

To say Zander was surprised as well would have been an understatement, although in a way it made sense. Perfect sense, because the woman walking toward him wasn't Celestia Lane.

It was Allegra.

## Chapter Ten

Allegra didn't question Zander's sudden appearance at the museum at first. On some level, she wasn't the least bit surprised to find him standing in the lobby after her meeting with the event planner. She felt like she'd been looking over her shoulder for a glimpse of him since the moment she'd stepped through the building's familiar columned entryway.

Which was silly, really. Why should Zander be at the Museum of Natural History on a random Friday night? This was the present, not the past. They weren't children anymore.

Yet there he was, dressed in one of his impeccably cut suits with his smoldering gaze fixed unwaveringly on hers as she crossed the room toward him.

Her breathing grew increasingly shallow with each

click of her stilettos on the mosaic tile floor. What *was* he doing here, anyway?

She gazed up at him. He was a good three or four inches taller than she was, even in her heels. The last time she'd been so close to him in this same spot, they'd stood eye to eye. So much had changed.

*Has it, though? Has it really?*

"Zander." She swallowed. "You're here."

"Indeed I am." He cast a glance at the crowd of elegantly dressed people spilling through the museum's doors.

When his gaze flitted back to Allegra, her stomach gave an annoying little flip. "I'm confused. What's going on?"

Had Emily told him where to find her?

No, that couldn't be it. Allegra had told her she had an appointment to talk to someone about a location for the dance marathon, but she very purposefully hadn't breathed a word about the museum. She didn't want to promise something until she was 100 percent sure she could deliver.

As it turned out, she couldn't.

Her father's name was engraved on a memorial plaque in the museum's turret offices, and an exhibition in one of the galleries had been named after him "in gratitude for over a decade of service." Almost everyone in the event-planning department remembered Allegra and had kind things to say about her father, but that was where the special treatment ended. The museum's schedule was packed for the next year and a half. The soonest they could accommodate the dance marathon would be the middle of next year, and even then, Allegra would be expected to pay the full going rate.

"You first," Zander said. "What are you doing here?"

"I had a meeting. It was disastrous." She tilted her head. "You?"

"I'm here for a wedding." Zander clenched his jaw. "Sort of."

"Sort of?" Allegra lifted an eyebrow.

How did a person *sort of* attend a wedding?

"Correct. Sort of." Again, his gaze darted toward the flow of guests moving from the glass double doors toward the Milstein Hall of Ocean Life.

"Oh, my God." Allegra let out a laugh and then dropped her voice to a conspiratorial whisper. "You're crashing, aren't you?"

"No." The corner of Zander's mouth quirked into a grin. "Okay, yes. But not the actual reception. I'm only lingering at the cocktail hour to see if I can find the reporter who keeps writing about the curse in the *Times*."

Again with the curse.

Things at Zander's hotel must be a lot worse than he'd been letting on.

"You're just going to pretend you're a guest and ambush her here in the lobby?"

Zander's eyes narrowed. "Do you have a better suggestion?"

Allegra looked him up and down. "It'll never work. You should have brought a date. She'll never buy the fact that Zander Wilde, bachelor at large, would go to something like this by himself."

Half the women in Manhattan would have probably leaped at the chance to crash a wedding with him.

She wondered why one of those women wasn't

standing beside him right now. Then she wondered why she cared. Or why his dateless status somehow took the edge off her disappointment over her unsuccessful meeting.

"I suppose you have a point." Zander glanced at the Cartier timepiece strapped around his wrist and frowned. "Any other advice? Perhaps something I can actually put into practice in the next five minutes or so?"

"You might have sent a gift for appearance purposes." She shrugged. "A toaster, maybe?"

"Again, not helpful. Unless you've got something from Sur La Table in that giant bag of yours?" He clenched his jaw again, and this time a rather fascinating knot formed in his chiseled jaw.

"Nope. Just pointe shoes."

Zander's eyes darkened a shade. Then his gaze dropped to her mouth and lingered for a moment or two. Just long enough for Allegra's knees to go a little wobbly. "Just pointe shoes. That's a shame, now, isn't it?"

There was an edge to his tone that sounded suspiciously flirtatious. Allegra wondered what it would be like to dance for him, to wind pink satin ribbons around her ankles and lose herself in a song. For real this time, not just for a few bars of music.

Just for Zander.

"I should go," she blurted.

"Right." The heat in Zander's fierce dark eyes cooled slightly. He nodded toward the Hall of Ocean Life, where music had begun to swell. "The cocktail hour has already started. I'm running out of time."

"Okay, then." Allegra's feet stubbornly refused to move. "I guess I'll see you later at home."

That word again. *Home.*

She rose up on tiptoe and pressed a chaste kiss to Zander's cheek. He smelled so good, so familiar, that her fingertips lingered on the smooth satin lapels of his tuxedo and her lips hovered near the corner of his mouth for just a moment too long.

Then Zander's hands were suddenly sliding from her waist to the center of her back, holding her in place.

Allegra squeezed her eyes shut. *Leave now. Leave while you still can.*

"You could stay, you know," Zander murmured. "You could pretend to be my date for this thing, since I apparently need one."

She pulled back slightly, searching his gaze. Was he serious?

He arched an eyebrow. "Unless you're in a hurry to get back to the brownstone to feed that sad little cat of yours."

Allegra's response was automatic. "She's not my cat."

Zander shrugged one shoulder. "Then I'm assuming you're free."

She was. But was it really a good idea to stay and crash a wedding with Zander?

*It's not an actual date. The whole evening is just pretend.*

Still, she wasn't staying.

Absolutely not.

She smiled up at him. "Lead the way."

Zander wasn't sure exactly when it happened, but at some point during the course of the evening, he stopped scanning the faces of the posh crowd, hoping to a catch a glimpse of Celestia Lane.

Maybe it was sometime around his second martini. Or was the chilled glass currently in his hand his third?

No telling.

The only thing he knew for certain was he'd needed something to take the edge off when Allegra slipped her hand in his as they'd entered the iconic gallery.

The bride and groom weren't messing around with their secret-garden theme. The room had been completely transformed. The great blue whale still loomed overhead, and the customary ocean-life exhibits flanked the immense space as always. But a mass of wisteria and wispy vines hung suspended from the ceiling, creating an enchanted forest. The glass display cases glowed bright blue in the dimly lit room, giving the atmosphere a mysterious, otherworldly feel.

It was like crossing a threshold and stepping into the Garden of Eden. His head spun, and certain other body parts took note, as well.

*Adam and Eve...*

*Zander and Allegra.*

So yes, a cocktail had been a very necessary diversion, because Zander could feel himself slipping away, falling under the spell of the lush surroundings.

Still, he was perfectly sober and he knew it. It wasn't the alcohol that made him forget that he and Allegra weren't on a real date—it was the way she tipped her head back when she laughed at something he said. It was the gentle weight of her fingertips resting on his forearm, even when no one seemed to be paying them any attention. It was the room itself—wild and heavy with the scent of orchids and memories.

He felt like they were on a real date, no matter how many times he reminded himself they weren't.

His gaze slid toward Allegra standing beside him, sipping from a slender champagne flute. She'd just finished a fifteen-minute conversation with the bride's sister and, due to Allegra's connection to the museum, managed to secure an actual invitation for them both to stay for the reception. Zander was fairly certain the two women had exchanged cell numbers. So much for flying under the radar. "Having fun?"

"Very much, actually." She searched his gaze and pulled a face. "Relax. You look far too serious. Going to a stranger's wedding isn't the sort of thing you can do halfway. In order to be believable, you need to go all in."

"Remind me again how many times you've done this."

"Zero." She shrugged. "But I've seen my fair share of Vince Vaughn movies. Face it. You know I'm right. Just like I was right when I said you needed a date. Otherwise I wouldn't be standing next to you right now."

She had a point.

She'd been onto something when she insisted he needed a date. He just wasn't 100 percent sure that was why he'd asked her to stay.

"So it's not uncomfortable for you, being around all this?" He gestured toward the cake table, where the bride and groom were currently engaged in the age-old tradition of smashing icing into each other's face.

*Ah, romance*, Zander thought wryly.

Allegra sipped her champagne, tilted her head and considered the couple. "Oddly enough, no. My own wedding feels like it was a million years ago. It was a mistake—one that I won't be repeating ever again."

"Never?" Zander's chest tightened. Just a bit.

She gave her head a definitive shake. "Never. I've realized I'm not the marrying type."

He narrowed his gaze but suppressed his nonsensical urge to argue. *Why do you care?* "So you're going to live happily ever after with your nameless cat?"

"Yes." She blinked. "I mean, no. Because she's not my cat."

He smiled into his martini. "Sure she's not."

Allegra cleared her throat. "Don't judge. You're practically allergic to this whole scene."

Zander lifted his gaze, but she was suddenly focusing intently on a dolphin diorama that he was certain she'd seen hundreds of times before. "What makes you say that?"

She glanced at him and gave him a thorough once-over. "For one, you look distinctly uncomfortable right now."

Probably because he'd only sort of been invited to this shindig. But also because the conversation had taken a somewhat dangerous turn.

"Second, you nearly had a heart attack at your birthday party when you thought I wanted to marry you." She smiled sweetly at him. Too sweetly. "You have *bachelor* written all over you."

He stared at her for a beat. The teasing smile on her lips began to look a little strained around the edges.

She set down her champagne glass on a nearby cocktail table. "Sorry, Zander. I…"

"I had a wedding, too, once, you know." The words

were out of his mouth before he could stop them. *Damn it.*

She grew very still. Her eyes were suddenly huge in her face. As big as saucers. "No, I didn't know. And now I feel even worse."

"Don't. It was a near miss, just like yours." He smiled, but it felt forced, and he knew better than to hope she didn't notice.

They couldn't hide from one another anymore. Not here. Too much had happened between these walls. And now here they were again, only this time it was different. *They* were different.

Zander was tired of trying to forget the heat simmering between them since they'd kissed. Tired of fighting his desire when he knew good and well she felt it, too.

"When was this?" she whispered.

He exhaled a tense breath. "Around two years ago." Had it been that recently? He supposed it had.

Zander had walked away from the church that day and never looked back, knowing with absolute certainty he'd done the right thing.

When he'd proposed, he'd fully intended to go through with the wedding. Obviously. He'd *wanted* to marry Laura. He thought he had, anyway.

But as the wedding date had drawn near, he'd been unable to shake the memory of his deal with Allegra.

*Let's make a deal. If neither of us is married by the time we turn thirty, we'll marry each other. Agreed?*

*Agreed.*

The idea that she might return to New York one day tormented him. What if she came home alone and found him married?

What if…

He ground his teeth together. Could he possibly have been more idiotic? He'd called off his wedding because of doubts—doubts based, in part, on a memory that Allegra had no recollection of whatsoever.

"It's in the past," he said.

*Like so much else.*

She nodded, but the look in her eyes just about killed him. As if she understood more than what he was willing to admit. As if she *knew*.

A waiter carrying a tray of fizzy champagne flutes stopped in front of them? "Another drink, sir?"

*God, yes.*

"Thank you." Zander exchanged his empty martini glass for one of the slender flutes. He took a sip but barely tasted it. Allegra was still watching him in a way that turned him inside out.

"Tell me about your disastrous meeting," he said, simply to change the subject. "Why are you at the museum on a Friday night, dressed to kill?"

His first guess had been a job interview, which he found intensely alarming for some strange reason. She seemed to like being back at the studio.

"I'm planning a fund-raiser for the dance school," she said.

Zander ignored the twinge of relief that this news prompted.

She wasn't going anywhere.

*Yet.*

"What kind of fund-raiser?"

Her smile brightened. "A retro dance marathon, like the one from the picture of your grandparents on the wall in the studio. Doesn't that sound perfect?"

"It does." Zander hadn't thought about that picture

in years, and now Allegra was apparently planning an entire fund-raiser around it.

It was indeed perfect. Fitting. Meaningful. And like everything else about Allegra, steeped in the past.

"I hoped we could have it here, but the calendar is full for the next year and a half. I can't wait that long."

"When did you have in mind?"

"Ten days from now, in time for next semester's registration." Her gaze shifted away from him.

As she focused on the bride, Zander couldn't quite shake the feeling there was more to her urgency than the new semester.

*She's already got one foot out the door.*

A muscle in his jaw tensed. "Have it at the Bennington."

Allegra's gaze flew back to his. "Seriously?"

"Why not? Our ballroom is just sitting there empty, remember?"

Which was precisely why he was attending this wedding reception in the first place. Why was he having so much trouble remembering that crucial fact?

"Thank you." Allegra beamed. "I'll handle everything. You won't need to be involved at all."

"Great," he said tersely.

He was just about to remind her that the school belonged to his mother, and he'd be more than willing to throw in some simple catering and a live band, but before he could, the bride's sister came swishing back in their direction in her billowy bridesmaid dress.

"Allegra!" She hugged her like she'd rediscovered a long-lost friend. "Come on. It's time for the bouquet toss."

"Um." Allegra shook her head. Vehemently. "I'm going to sit that out."

"Don't be silly. It'll be fun." The sister hooked her arm through Allegra's, apparently intent on dragging her along with her toward the crowd of women assembling on the dance floor.

"No, really. Zander and I were in the middle of discussing something, anyway. Weren't we?" Allegra cast a pleading glance at him as Beyoncé's "Single Ladies (Put a Ring on It)" blared from the loudspeakers.

He bit back a smile. "You just said I didn't need to be involved at all. Remember?"

She shot him a murderous glare.

"Best of luck, darling." He bent to kiss her cheek and whispered, "Weren't you just lecturing me about going all in?"

"I'm going to strangle you," she muttered under her breath.

"Don't worry. I'm sure you won't catch it since you're never getting married." He winked.

The sister gave her arm a final tug. Within seconds, Allegra was on the dance floor, pushing other women in front of her in a desperate attempt to wiggle her way to the back of the crowd of single ladies.

The bride started counting backward from ten.

"Ten, nine, eight..."

Allegra crossed her arms, glowered at Zander and mouthed, "You're dead."

"...seven, six, five..."

Zander waved at her. For possibly the first time since the night of his birthday, he had the upper hand. Every interaction with Allegra seemed to leave him feeling off balance and unsatisfied in ways he didn't care to think about. It felt good to be the one in control again.

"…four, three, two…"

He set down his drink and headed toward the spectacle. He'd never planned on forcing Allegra to really go through with it. He only wanted to rattle her a little bit. Tease her, just like old times. Then he'd swoop in at the last minute and escort her away from the fray where they could have a good laugh over it.

But as Zander crossed the room, a sense of unease knotted in his chest. What if she wasn't as fine with being at a wedding as she'd indicated? He didn't want to prompt another panic attack. What was he thinking?

"…one!"

Zander hastened his steps, but just as he reached the edge of the dance floor, the bridal bouquet went airborne. He lunged to wrap an arm around Allegra's waist and pull her close, but he was too late.

The bundle of white flowers sailed past his head and landed with a thud in the arms of a stunned Allegra.

## Chapter Eleven

Allegra's first instinct was to drop the bouquet.

So she did.

She simply let go of it and watched it fall to the floor as if she was playing a game of hot potato. Right away, someone let out a gasp. Allegra wasn't sure who.

A moment of shocked silence followed. Allegra could feel her heartbeat in her throat. She'd just thrown the bridal bouquet to the ground. How could she possibly explain this behavior? Never mind that. How would she explain her presence at this fancy party when the bride realized she wasn't an actual wedding guest, but only a very, very new friend of the bride's sister?

*Do something.*

Everyone was staring at her, which was only making things worse.

She bent to pick up the flowers and kept her gaze

glued to the elegant little pile of white peonies and garden roses at her feet. Somewhere in the periphery, she heard a voice call out, "Get it!"

And then all hell broke loose.

One of the bridesmaids dived toward the bouquet. Then another. And another. A few of the guests followed suit, until the scene looked more like something that should be going down on the five-yard line of a football field than at a wedding reception.

Allegra stood and stared, not quite believing what she was seeing.

"Let's get out of here," a low voice rumbled beside her.

She blinked, snapping out of her trance.

*Zander.*

His firm hand wrapped around her wrist, and she was consciously aware of her pulse booming against the pad of his thumb.

She nodded and stepped away from the chaos.

Zander cut a quick path through the cheering guests, and Allegra followed him. She wasn't entirely sure where they were going, but she didn't care. She just wanted to get away from the bouquet before she got stuck with it again...or worse. What if the wedding photographer wanted to take her picture? Blending in at a wedding reception was one thing. A total stranger appearing prominently in someone's wedding album was another.

Zander led her past the cake table and through the maze of white chairs and wild orchid centerpieces, back to the lobby, now quiet and empty since the party was in full swing.

Allegra took a deep breath. They were safe.

Her head spun a little. The sudden silence was disorienting after being at the noisy reception. Their footsteps on the mosaic floor seemed far too loud. Allegra's senses were on high alert. She could hear every little sound—the rustle of Zander's tuxedo jacket, the swish of her skirt, her breath coming hard and fast.

Zander paused, scrubbed a hand over his face and shook his head. "You caught the bouquet."

"No, I didn't." She shook her head. "Well, I did. But then it fell, so it didn't actually count."

The corner of his mouth tugged into a half grin. "That's not how it looked from where I was standing."

"Maybe you weren't paying attention."

"Oh, I was definitely paying attention. You threw those flowers at the ground like they were on fire." He lifted an accusatory brow.

Mr. Runaway Groom thought it was funny, did he?

"Maybe we should go back inside for the garter toss and see how you'd react if you ended up with it?" She spun on her heel and marched back toward the reception.

Zander caught her elbow. And then his hand slid slowly down her arm until their fingertips were intertwined. Their laughter grew quiet.

Allegra stood very still, almost afraid to turn around and face him. *Don't be ridiculous. It's only Zander.*

There was nothing to be afraid of. He was her friend.

But there was nothing friendly about the chill that coursed through her when he touched her this time. Nothing friendly at all. From the heavy thud of her heart to the delicious little flutter low in her belly, she felt alive in a way that both thrilled and frightened her.

She shouldn't be feeling this way around him.

Overwhelmed by his presence.

He filled up the room, every corner of the cavernous space. It defied logic, but she could sense him all around her. Not just beside her, but in the air itself.

She spun around, convinced she was only imagining the heat that seemed to flow from his fingertips to hers. She wasn't. It was in his gaze, too, in the way his eyes swept over her, almost as if he was seeing her for the very first time.

The wonder in his expression was so reverent—so new, yet at the same time so very much Zander—that it nearly made her cry.

Her gaze dropped to his mouth. God help her, she wanted to kiss him again. Only this time she couldn't blame her desire on feeling fuzzy and disoriented. She couldn't even blame it on nostalgia, because as much as she loved the comfort of his familiarity, she craved the newness of him more.

The square cut of his jaw intrigued her, as did the hard, broad expanse of his chest. He was so big. So solid. So very much a man now.

She'd spent quite some time wondering what it would feel like to slip her hands beneath his shirt and explore the taut muscles of his abdomen. To feel the masculine heat of his body and marvel at how very much it had changed over the years.

She swallowed.

Allegra didn't know where to look. She was convinced he could read her mind, and the thought mortified her to the core.

Her gaze shifted to the glass double doors. Beyond them, snowflakes danced against the darkened sky and the lights of Manhattan glittered like gemstones spilled onto black velvet. She'd forgotten how beautiful the city could be at this time of year. She'd forgotten so very much.

"We should probably get going now," she murmured in a voice that didn't sound at all like herself. She sounded hoarse and breathy. Desperate.

Zander's eyes narrowed. "Is that what you want?"

No. It wasn't at all what she wanted.

She couldn't bear to tell him that she wanted to feel him again—his lips, his tongue, his hands. The last time they'd kissed hadn't ended well. She had no desire to repeat that kind of embarrassment.

But she couldn't force the words out either. Zander knew her too well. She couldn't look him in the eye and tell him she wanted to go home.

*Is that what you want?* The question was still there, in his eyes. All she had to do was decide.

She took a deep breath and shook her head.

Zander leaned closer, his eyes hard on hers. Then he reached to cup her face with his free hand, drawing the pad of his thumb, slowly, deliberately, along the swell of her bottom lip. "Tell me what you want, Allegra."

*You.* She swallowed. *I want you.*

"This," she said, reaching up on tiptoe to close the space between them and touch her lips to his.

*What are you doing? Stop.*

But it was too late to change her mind. Too late to pretend she didn't want this. Because the moment her mouth grazed Zander's, he took ownership of the kiss.

His hands slid into her hair, holding her in place, while his tongue slid brazenly along the seam of her lips until they parted, opening for him.

Then there was nothing but heat and want and the

shocking reality that this was what she'd wanted all along. Zander.

Had she always felt this way? It seemed impossible. Yet beneath the newness of his mouth on hers and the crush of her breasts against the solid wall of his chest, there was something else. A feeling she couldn't quite put her finger on. A sense of belonging. Of destiny.

*Home.*

Allegra squeezed her eyes closed. She didn't want to imagine herself fitting into this life again. There was too much at stake. Too much to lose. But no matter how hard she railed against it, there it was, shimmering before like her a mirage.

She whimpered into Zander's mouth, and he groaned in return, gently guiding her backward until her spine was pressed against the cool marble wall. Before she could register what was happening, he gathered her wrists and pinned them above her head with a single capable hand. And the last remaining traces of resistance melted away. She couldn't fight it anymore. Not from this position of delicious surrender. Her arms went lax, and somewhere in the back of her mind, a wall came tumbling down.

The breath rushed from her body, and a memory came into focus with perfect, crystalline clarity.

*Let's make a deal. If neither of us is married by the time we turn thirty, we'll marry each other. Agreed?*

*Agreed?*

Her eyes flew open.

"Allegra?" Zander loosened his hold on her wrists, and she grabbed onto his shoulders to keep from slumping to the ground.

She gazed up at him, wide-eyed. *My God, he was right about the promise. He's been right all along.*

She wasn't sure what brought it back. Maybe this room, where they'd spent so much time together. Maybe the kiss. It had been no accident this time. This was a kiss steeped with intention, as was Zander's loaded stare. His hands were planted against the wall on either side of her head, and he was all but searing her with his gaze.

Willing her to remember.

"It was here, wasn't it?" she whispered, pressing her fingertips to her lips. She was coming apart at the seams. How could she have forgotten? How?

It had been late one afternoon in September. Indian summer. Outside, steam rose from the streets, shimmering over the city in a sultry haze. Allegra was still dressed for dance class in a plain black leotard that stuck to her dewy skin like glue as she and Zander moved uptown. They'd practiced for hours that day, preparing for an upcoming competition. Afterward, they'd shared a plate of cheese fries at the diner and walked to the subway with their hands linked together like they sometimes did.

Touching Zander was second nature to Allegra back then. They spent so many hours in a dance hold that she almost felt incomplete on her own. Untethered. She'd never examined what that out of sorts feeling meant, because again, it was *Zander*. Her partner. Why shouldn't she feel safe and natural in his arms? Why shouldn't his hand fit so perfectly into the small of her back?

Their intimacy had been so casual that she'd thought

it was meaningless. She'd gotten it wrong. It wasn't meaningless. Quite the opposite.

She could practically hear his voice again, just as it had been that September day.

*Let's make a deal. If neither of us is married by the time we turn thirty, we'll marry each other. Agreed?*

He'd pulled her close, rested his forehead against hers and whispered those words to her fourteen years ago in this very spot. And something wild and strange had wound its way through Allegra. Something that had made her feel more connected to him than she'd ever been before.

There'd been no hesitation in her response.

*Agreed.*

Six days later, her family had perished.

*Died on impact.* Those had been the words the policeman used. *They never saw it coming.* As if that was a comfort, a balm.

Allegra had never seen it coming either. She wished she had. If this was her destiny, if this was the twisted hand she'd been dealt, why couldn't there have been a sign? Some kind of a warning? Even a hint?

What would she have done differently if she'd known?

Everything. Mainly, she wouldn't have insisted her mom and dad come see her dance.

*This is my fault.* The thought had lodged itself in her head, pushing everything else out. Everything pure and true and good. All the new feelings she'd begun to have about Zander were replaced with the horrible reality that she'd become an orphan in the blink of an eye.

But how could she have forgotten the promise they'd made to one another that day?

*Because it hurt too much to remember.*

She'd chosen to forget so she wouldn't have to think about what she'd left behind.

"Is there something you want to tell me, Allegra?" Zander pressed his forehead against hers and slid his hands down her arms until they stood hand in hand. Just like before.

"I remember our promise," Allegra whispered. She shook her head, vaguely aware that her face was wet with tears. When had she started to cry? "I'd forgotten. But now…"

Now she knew.

He squeezed her hands so hard they went numb. "Oh, sweetheart."

He bent to kiss her again. Allegra tipped her face upward, toward his. Hungry. Eager. Ready to kiss him with eyes wide-open. At last.

But something stopped him—a noise, the clearing of a throat. Zander froze with his face just a fraction of an inch away from hers.

"Why, Mr. Wilde. Is that you?"

*Why now?*

Zander closed his eyes and cursed under his breath. He needed to get himself together before he turned around to face the woman behind him. He'd been waiting the entire week to talk to her, but suddenly she was the last person he wanted to see.

He opened his eyes, and by some miracle, Allegra was still standing there, looking at him with eyes brimming with tears and memories. He couldn't have conjured a better kiss in his dreams. She *remembered*.

But for some twisted reason, fate had chosen this very moment to toss the Vows reporter in his path.

"I'm sorry," he whispered and reached to brush a tear from Allegra's face. "Just give me a minute."

She nodded, but Zander could see hesitation slipping back into her sapphire eyes.

*Damn it. Why now?*

He turned, straightened the knot in his tie and extended his hand. "Zander Wilde. Apologies, you've caught me in a private moment. And you are?"

He knew exactly who she was, of course. She was the spitting image of the photo in her byline. Even before he'd seen her, he'd known who she was simply by the tone of her voice. Inquisitive with an edge.

"Celestia Lane, from the *New York Times*." She gave his hand a firm shake. "So sorry to interrupt. Although you seem to have chosen an awfully public place for a private moment."

Zander gave her a tight smile. If she'd been anyone else, he would have told her in no uncertain terms to mind her own damn business. But he was keenly aware that the fate of his hotel rested in her hands.

"My mistake." He pasted a smile on his face. "It's a pleasure to finally meet you in person."

Celestia Lane nodded. Her gaze flicked over Zander's shoulder, toward Allegra.

Zander felt like he was watching the beginning of a terrible accident playing out in slow motion with his hands tied. "I apologize for missing our dinner meeting a few nights ago. An emergency situation came up, and I was unable to get a call through to the hotel."

"I see," Celestia said absently.

The columnist was hardly paying attention to what

he was saying. She seemed much more interested in Allegra. "Aren't you going to introduce me to your friend, Mr. Wilde?"

Zander hesitated.

Behind him, Allegra blurted, "I was just leaving." *No.*

He turned and muttered, "Wait. *Please.*"

But she was already walking past him, headed for the door.

Celestia called after her. "Excuse me, do we know each other? You look familiar."

Zander cursed under his breath. The only way for this situation to get any worse would be if the reporter recognized Allegra as one of the Bennington's runaway brides. Specifically, Spencer Warren's runaway bride, the most notorious one of them all according to the Vows article.

The headlines would be devastating. The reporter would probably find a way to insinuate that Allegra's failed nuptials had something to do with her relationship with Zander. There was no doubt in his mind she'd exploit it. She'd turn whatever was going on between them into something ugly before the two of them even had a chance to figure it out for themselves.

It made Zander sick. Even so, he could understand it. Celestia Lane was a journalist, and he'd just been seen kissing one of the runaway brides a mere week after she'd fled her wedding ceremony at his cursed hotel.

It looked bad.

*Very* bad.

Allegra realized as much, too, obviously. She bowed her head and kept walking toward the exit. "Sorry, but you must be mistaking me for someone else. I don't live here. I'm just visiting."

She gave them both a quick wave, then pushed through the double doors, onto the snowy New York streets.

*Just visiting.* Zander told himself not to take those words to heart. Allegra hadn't necessarily meant them. She was trying to throw the reporter off the scent. But they seemed to lodge in his chest, choking him, all the same.

The reporter arched an eyebrow at Zander. "Your mystery woman forgot her coat."

He took a deep, pained breath. Things were getting worse by the minute. "I should go fetch it for her then. If you'll excuse me…"

"Of course." The reporter nodded. "It was a pleasure running into you, Mr. Wilde."

She turned to go, but not before shooting him an overly solicitous smile. A dreadful certainty settled over Zander.

He hadn't heard the last of Celestia Lane.

# Chapter Twelve

Allegra sat at the kitchen table in the brownstone the next morning, staring at her cell phone.

The little black kitten was curled into a cuddly ball in her lap, and a lacy veil of frost covered the kitchen windows. Steam rose from the coffee cup situated on the place mat in front of her. Everything was so serene. So *homey*. Allegra wasn't sure she could go through with what needed to be done.

*Just do it. Make the call.*

She picked up the phone and scrolled through her contacts, searching for Talia's number with a shaky hand.

*You're doing the right thing.*

She absolutely was. Last night had been a wake-up call.

If the reporter from the Vows column hadn't interrupted them, there was no telling what would have happened. Allegra had been on the verge of sleeping with Zander, all because of a dreamy memory.

She'd tried to tell herself that nothing really happened, that it was just a kiss. But deep down, she knew better. Remembering the promise they'd made to one another had rocked her to her core. It plunged her right back into her past, made it seem like she was experiencing that day in the museum for the very first time. For a bittersweet moment, she'd almost believed she was sixteen again.

Well, she wasn't.

She was a grown woman, not a naive teenager. She couldn't go around kissing Zander anymore, acting as if they could turn back the clock. Promises had consequences. Belonging to someone meant losing them one day. She knew that now. And the pain of those consequences was more than she could bear.

"Allegra!" Talia answered on the first ring. Her voice was so animated that she sounded as though she'd been sitting by the phone, waiting for Allegra's call. "It's so great to hear from you. I was beginning to think you'd decided to stay in New York forever."

"No." Allegra swallowed around the lump in her throat.

Why was this so difficult?

She couldn't stay here. She couldn't keep working at the Wilde School of Dance, and she couldn't keep playing house with Zander, or whatever it was they were doing.

What *were* they doing, anyway?

"So does this call mean what I think it means?" Talia asked.

"That depends." Allegra took a fortifying sip of her coffee. "Is the corps de ballet spot on the touring company still available?"

Talia let out an earsplitting squeal, which Allegra took as a definitive *yes*.

"I knew you'd change your mind," she said. "Traveling the world…dancing in another city every night. What could be better?"

She was right. It sounded perfect. It was everything Allegra wanted.

*Is it?*

Zander strolled into the kitchen and smiled at her as he headed toward the coffeepot.

Allegra's heart gave a little lurch. "Right. I have some things to finish up here before I go, though. What day does the tour start again?"

She couldn't leave until after the dance marathon. She'd given Emily her word. She had to see it through. She *wanted* to. Too much, if she was being honest with herself.

Which was precisely why she needed to leave. Now, while she still could. She was becoming too comfortable here.

Too happy.

"We leave in two weeks. If you're serious about this you need to give the ballet director a call. Do you still have his contact information?"

"I do." Allegra did her best to ignore the hard stare Zander was now aiming her way from the other side of the room.

"Good. You need to call him right now. I'm not joking. Hang up and call him before it's too late. Promise me," Talia said.

"I promise." Allegra's gaze was glued to the table, but it made no difference. She could *feel* Zander's eyes on her.

This wasn't the way she wanted him to find out about the tour. She'd planned on telling him later, once it was official. She'd purposely gotten up while it was still dark outside so she could make the call before he was up and about.

Maybe it was better this way, though, like ripping off a Band-Aid. There was no sense in postponing the inevitable.

"Okay, I'm hanging up now so you can do it. Make the call. See you soon!"

The line went dead.

Allegra quietly set her phone back down on her place mat.

"Going somewhere?" Zander's voice was so sharp it could have cut glass.

Allegra lifted her chin. "Maybe." *Seriously?* That wasn't the way to rip off a Band-Aid. She took a deep breath. "I mean, yes. One of the dancers on the Boston Ballet's touring company is injured. The ballet director wants me to take her place."

"Congratulations are in order, then." A vein throbbed in his temple. "Were you going to mention it this time? Or were you planning on letting me wake up one day to find you gone?"

He looked furious. He also looked insanely handsome, with his hair slicked neatly back, dressed in another of his immaculate suits. The way he was glaring at her made it seem more like a three-piece suit of armor.

Not that she could blame him for being angry.

But honestly, did he have to be such a jerk about it? He couldn't *pretend* to be happy for her? "That's not fair, Zander. I was absolutely going to tell you. And I'm not going anywhere until after the dance marathon. I was actually hoping I could come by the Bennington today after I teach class so we could get going on the plans."

"Ryan can help you with the arrangements. I'll speak to him about it this morning." He crossed his arms and leaned back against the counter, his languid posture wholly at odds with the serious glimmer in his dark eyes. "When were you going to tell me?"

She should have known he wouldn't let it go.

Allegra swallowed. "Once it was certain. I haven't spoken to the ballet director yet. He may not even cast me."

Could she do this? Could she really walk away?

The kitten hopped down from her lap and padded toward Zander. She let out a mournful meow, rubbed her face against his shin and wound through his legs in a figure eight.

Allegra averted her gaze. "I'm not running away. This isn't like last time, Zander. I promise it's not."

"Really?" He bent to scoop the kitten into his arms. "Tell me how it's different."

"I didn't have a choice. You know that. My aunt was my legal guardian, and she lived in Cambridge."

"I'm aware. That's not what I'm talking about. I'm asking you why I never heard from you again after you left." His voice lowered an octave, and the rawness of it made it impossible for Allegra to look at him.

She closed her eyes. "We were kids. I'd just lost everything…"

*I couldn't lose you, too.*

But she had. She'd pushed him away, and here she was doing it again.

She opened her eyes and lifted her gaze to his. He was stroking the cat and his expression had softened a bit, but his eyes remained blank and unreadable.

Last night, the tenderness in his gaze had nearly brought her to her knees. For a brief, shining moment, her life had felt like one unbroken story, instead of what it really was—two pieces, sliced right down the middle, both of them incomplete.

"We were in love," he said woodenly. "I was, anyway."

Allegra opened her mouth to argue but closed it again.

He'd been in love with her? He'd never told her. She'd never said anything to him about how she felt either, but that didn't mean those feelings hadn't been there. Allegra couldn't pretend otherwise anymore. The kiss had brought everything back.

She inhaled a ragged breath. *No air. There is no air in this room.* "Well, we're not in love anymore. That's how it's different."

A strained, suffocating silence fell over the kitchen.

When Zander finally spoke, his seemingly random question caught Allegra by surprise. "Have you given this cat a name yet?"

The kitten was purring louder than a freight train in his arms. Allegra could hear it from clear across the room.

She shifted in her chair. "No, I haven't."

He shook his head. "I didn't think so."

Seriously? He'd gone from blatantly stating that he used to be in love with her to complaining about her pet-parenting skills? The man was impossible. "Why does it bother you so much that I haven't named my kitten?"

"I thought she wasn't yours."

Allegra's face went hot. "She's not."

He shrugged. "I suppose that's a good thing since you can't drag a cat around on a ballet tour."

"Exactly." Allegra hadn't really thought about that yet, but it was fine. She truly had no intention of keeping the animal.

She glanced at the black kitten, looking tinier than ever slung over Zander's impressive forearm. Again, the room seemed devoid of air.

She pressed a hand to her stomach, but before she could invent a reason to excuse herself, her cell phone blared to life on the kitchen table.

Allegra picked it up and glanced at the screen. "It's the ballet director."

Talia must have been so excited that she'd made the call herself.

"What are you waiting for? Answer it." Zander pushed himself off the counter and deposited the kitten in Allegra's lap. The cat stretched her tiny little legs and kneaded her paws on Allegra's bathrobe.

Everything about this felt wrong. What was she doing? "Zander, I…"

But when Allegra looked up, the door was already clicking shut behind Zander's back.

The morning meeting at the Bennington finished in record time. Not, however, because the night manager and the reservations supervisor didn't have anything to report to Zander and Ryan. There was plenty to cover, including a rather sordid story about an award-winning actor who'd recently checked out after a full week in one of the penthouse suites. The meeting wrapped up early because Zander was operating like a machine.

A well-oiled one at that.

It felt good to throw himself back into his work. Work was logical. Sensible. The analytical nature of Zander's job was what attracted him to the business world over a decade ago. His acumen for facts and figures and his commanding presence were what kept him ensconced in the Bennington's corner office.

That commanding presence had been on full display since he'd taken a seat at the head of the conference room table at just after 8:00 a.m.

"I think we're finished here," he said, closing the leather portfolio embossed with the Bennington crest.

The people seated around the table glanced at one another and then filed quietly out of the room, with the exception of Ryan.

"Are you ready to go over the latest budget figures?" Zander motioned toward the spreadsheets fanned out in front of Ryan with his Montblanc fountain pen.

"Yes." Ryan gave him a slow nod, but made no move to reach for the documents. "Perhaps you want to talk about it first?"

Zander leaned back in his chair and crossed his arms. "Talk about what?"

"Whatever it is that's got you so wound up. You seem a little…"

Zander lifted an eyebrow. "Focused?"

Ryan nodded. "Staunchly so, yes."

"That's not a bad thing," Zander countered. "In fact, it's my job to stay focused on the Bennington."

Ryan held up his hands in a gesture of surrender. "No one's complaining. I just get the feeling there might be something you need to get off your chest."

"There isn't." Zander shook his head and dropped his gaze to the glossy surface of the conference room table.

What was there to talk about? Allegra was leaving. Discussing it with Ryan wouldn't erase the shock of walking into the kitchen earlier and overhearing her plans to go on an extended ballet tour. It wouldn't rid him of the heaviness he felt in his chest every time he thought about it.

It wouldn't make her stay.

"Okay, then." Ryan slid a copy of the hotel's latest profit-and-loss statement toward Zander.

"Wait, actually there's something I need to tell you." Zander leaned forward.

"Shoot."

He cleared his throat. "Allegra is putting together a fund-raiser for the Wilde School of Dance—a retro dance marathon. I told her she could have it here, in the ballroom. I'm assuming we still have availabilities next week?"

"We're wide-open." Ryan's gaze flitted to the column of red numbers on the financial statement. "Unfortunately."

"Good." Zander frowned. "Or not. You know what I mean. Anyway, I told Allegra you'd run point on this."

Ryan went silent for a beat. Then he said, "Really? I don't mind, but are you sure you don't want to handle it?"

"More than sure." Zander clenched his teeth.

He was as angry with himself as he was with Allegra. More so, actually.

Her news shouldn't have surprised him. He knew it was coming. Allegra ran. It's what she did.

When she was scared, she left and never looked back. If he'd thought for one moment the ballet tour was a career choice, he'd have been thrilled for her. Hell, he would have helped her pack her bags if it was what she really wanted.

But it wasn't. Her decision wasn't part of a career plan. She'd said herself that she wasn't a ballerina anymore. She was happy teaching at the studio. His mom couldn't stop talking about how much Allegra loved her students. She was a natural. He'd seen her teaching class, and she seemed happy. Happier than he'd seen her since before her family's accident.

He knew what was going on. Allegra was leaving because they'd shared a moment last night at the museum. She'd felt something for him. Something more than just desire.

And it scared the life out of her.

Ryan's gaze narrowed. He shrugged. "Fine. I just thought you might want to head this up since a dance marathon fits in with the retro-musical vibe you've been working so hard to establish here."

He was right. An event like the one Allegra had in mind perfectly matched the nostalgic ambience Zander aimed to achieve at the Bennington with the monthly Big Band Nights and the jazz bar he'd recently opened in the hotel lobby. To the staff they were known as Zander's passion projects.

"Plus you and Allegra have always made a good team," Ryan said quietly.

Zander let out a long exhale. "Years ago. Things change."

Then again, some things never did. History was repeating itself. Only this time, he and Allegra weren't kids. She had a choice this time. She could stay.

*Stay.*

Just four letters. One little word. Yet he'd been unable to make himself utter it earlier. He'd talked circles around it, but he'd never come out and asked her to stay.

What was the point? She'd been planning her escape since she'd moved into the brownstone. Who was he kidding, anyway? The only reason she was even in New York was because she'd nearly gotten married. It wasn't fate. It was just a big, messy mistake.

"So." He sighed. "You'll work with her on the dance marathon?"

"Sure." Ryan nodded, but he still looked doubtful.

Too bad. Zander wasn't changing his mind. "Great. Give her whatever she needs—catering, music. I'll leave it to your discretion. It's for the dance school, which could use the help, especially since the ballroom is sitting there empty, anyway."

Zander's executive assistant suddenly appeared in the doorway of the conference room. "Excuse me, gentlemen. There's someone here to see Mr. Wilde—a Ms. Celestia Lane from the *New York Times*."

Zander and Ryan exchanged a glance.

"Show her in," Zander said.

"Very well."

With the assistant out of earshot, Ryan muttered, "This should be interesting. I'm guessing there's something else you should probably fill me in on?"

"I ran into her last night."

What was she doing here? Zander had allowed himself to breathe a sigh of relief when there'd been no mention of the curse in the paper this morning. The Bennington had even managed to book a wedding. Just one…a month from now. But it was better than nothing.

Somehow, though, Zander had a feeling this impromptu visit from the Vows columnist wasn't good news.

"And?" Ryan asked under his breath.

Zander stood to button his suit jacket. "And I have no idea what she's doing here."

Ryan rolled his eyes. "Well, that explains everything."

Zander's assistant escorted the reporter into the room. Celestia declined her offer of sparkling water or a cappuccino and then smiled brightly at Zander. "Good morning, Mr. Wilde."

He knew right away something was off. She looked far too pleased with herself. "Good morning. This is a surprise."

He introduced her to Ryan and all three took a seat.

"What can I do for you, Ms. Lane?"

"You can give me a quote for my column tomorrow, for starters. It's all about how I saw the CEO of the Bennington in a 'private moment' with one of his hotel's runaway brides." She smirked. "At a wedding, no less."

Zander said nothing. Beside him, Ryan sighed and pinched the bridge of his nose.

"I knew your companion looked familiar. Imagine my surprise when I did a little digging and discovered she was none other than Allegra Clark, Spencer Warren's former fiancée." Celestia reached into her massive designer handbag and pulled out a notebook.

Zander looked pointedly at the notebook and rolled his eyes. "Save it. You didn't come here for a quote. If you were going to run with this story, you would have already done so."

Ryan cleared his throat. "Zander, maybe we should hear her out."

He lifted his eyebrows and waited for her to elaborate.

"The story will run in Vows tomorrow morning, with or without your input." She tapped her pen on her notepad and waited.

Zander still wasn't buying it. She wanted something, and that something wasn't a quote. She was holding out. He just wished he knew what for.

"You write for the *New York Times*, Ms. Lane. This kind of story is beneath both you and your publication. It's a gossip piece." He gave her a tight smile. "As is your curse theory."

"I agree." She shrugged. "Unfortunately, the curse story got a lot of traction. It's been very popular."

"I gathered." His empty ballroom spoke volumes.

"The readers want a follow-up story, and my editor is demanding that I give them one. Believe me, I'd rather write about a wedding here at the Bennington. But there don't seem to be many of those taking place." She sighed. "So why don't you tell me what I'm supposed to write about, Mr. Wilde?"

Zander should have been relieved. The ball was in his court.

But he couldn't come up with a single thing she'd be interested in.

*Concentrate.* There had to be something.

"I have an idea," Ryan said.

"Yes?" Celestia held her pen at the ready.

"Let's hear it," Zander said.

"Leave Zander and Allegra out of the paper, and in exchange we give you exclusive coverage of the next wedding to take place at the Bennington." Ryan smoothed down his tie. "You said you'd rather cover a wedding, so let's do it. The next time someone ties the knot here, we'll give you a front-row seat. If the bride runs, you'll have a story. If everything goes off without a hitch, you'll have one, too. It will be the end of the supposed curse. Either way, it's win-win."

Ryan's gaze flicked briefly toward Zander. Zander gave him a barely perceptible nod.

It was great idea. Fantastic, in fact.

Celestia smiled. "I like it."

"I thought you might," Ryan said.

"But I'd need a guaranteed invitation for both myself and my photographer."

Zander's answer was swift and unequivocal. "Done."

"Assuming we can get the bride and groom to agree, of course," Ryan added.

"They will." Celestia flipped her notepad closed. "Trust me, there isn't a bride on earth who doesn't want her wedding in the *Times*."

"So we have an agreement?" Zander stood and extended a hand.

"It looks like we do, Mr. Wilde." The reporter slipped her hand into his and gave it a shake.

Zander's mouth curved into a tight smile. "I look forward to not seeing my name in the paper tomorrow." *Or ever.*

"I'll be waiting for your call. Get in touch the minute you've got a date for me. I'll be here with bells on."

Celestia gave them both a flippy little wave on her way out. "Good day, gentlemen."

Once she was gone, Zander's smile faded. He shoved his hands into his trouser pockets and turned toward Ryan. "Why do I feel like we just made a deal with the devil?"

"Because we sort of did."

Zander clenched his gut. "Not helping."

"Don't worry, cousin. We can use this to our advantage. Think about it—the guaranteed *Times* coverage is perfect. She's right. Every couple in the city wants their wedding photo in her column. Give it a week. We'll have more weddings booked here than we can handle." Ryan cut him a triumphant grin.

He was right. The plan was brilliant. Unless...

"There's just one hitch," Zander said.

"I know." Ryan nodded. "You don't even have to say it."

*What if the bride runs?*

## Chapter Thirteen

Allegra stood beneath the glittering disco ball suspended from the ceiling of the Bennington Hotel's ballroom, not quite believing her eyes. "Ryan, how did you do this in less than ten days?"

The space had been transformed from top to bottom. If Allegra hadn't known better, she would have thought she'd stepped back in time. Red, white and blue bunting lined the walls, and streamers crisscrossed overhead. There were so many of them that she could barely see the deep blue ceiling, painted to look like a starry midnight sky. A bandstand was set up at the far end of the ballroom, and the parquet dance floor had been extended so it took up nearly the entire room. Allegra's favorite part of the entire setup, the pièce de résistance, was a wooden flip board with a vintage school clock for counting down the hours danced and the number of couples remaining in the marathon.

Everything was exactly as she'd envisioned it. Perfect. She felt as if she was standing inside a 1940s dance hall...

Or in the photograph of Zander's grandparents.

"Are you kidding? I didn't do all of this," Ryan said as he unfolded a white wooden folding chair to add to the section set up for spectators. "The staff helped. It's for a great cause. Everyone around here loves Emily and supports the school. They've all pitched in. It's been a group effort."

His gaze shot upward. "And as I recall, you were the one on a ladder at two in the morning hanging those streamers."

"Oh." She grinned. "I guess I was, wasn't I?"

"Yes, you were. If you forgot, it's probably because you've devoted so much time and energy to this dance marathon that you're delirious." Ryan plunked another chair into position. "I think we're ready, though. You should probably head to the brownstone and get some rest or you'll never manage to dance for twelve straight hours tonight."

Allegra's smile faded. "Oh, um, I'm headed out to change clothes and get ready, but I'm not dancing tonight."

Ryan planted his hands on his hips and frowned. "Is that a joke? You're not participating in this shindig? I figured you'd be the first one out on the dance floor cutting a rug."

Allegra rolled her eyes. "Cutting a rug? I think you're taking this whole retro thing a bit too seriously."

Ryan narrowed his gaze. "I see what's going on here. You're just like him, you know."

"Just like who?" Allegra busied herself securing

the corner of bunting so she wouldn't have to look him in the eye.

She had a good idea who he meant.

"Zander," Ryan said.

Bingo.

"I don't know what you're talking about. Zander and I—"

"Are both experts at deflection." He shook his head. "I've never seen two people so adept at changing the subject the minute the conversation becomes uncomfortable."

"I'm not uncomfortable." But the room suddenly felt very warm. "I'm just not planning on dancing tonight. I'll be far too busy."

"Which is exactly what Zander said earlier. Word for word." Ryan winked. "I rest my case."

*Don't say anything. Do. Not.*

"So Zander isn't planning on coming tonight?" Allegra said, because apparently no amount of self-lecturing could keep her mouth shut.

She couldn't help it. She had to ask.

Zander had clearly been avoiding her, and she'd been doing the same as far as he was concerned. They hadn't exchanged a word since the morning he'd walked in on her conversation with Talia. She'd barely set eyes on him, save for a glimpse of him every so often at the Bennington. Every time she spied him striding across the hotel's opulent lobby in one of his power suits, looking like he'd walked right off the cover of *GQ*, she turned and headed in the opposite direction.

But he was everywhere. The bridal curse no longer seemed to be hurting business. Zander had been parading brides-to-be around the hotel on a regular basis.

She wasn't sure how many weddings were actually on the books—if there were any—and she hadn't asked.

She didn't know what to say to Zander. He thought she was running away, and she wasn't sure how to convince him otherwise. Probably because a very small part of herself wondered if he might be right.

Ryan shrugged. "He hasn't said whether or not he'll show tonight, but he made it very clear he wouldn't dance."

"Well, that makes two of us." She couldn't. No way.

Dancing with Zander again would feel like ripping open an old wound. Or walking headlong into a memory—a memory that would leave her raw and vulnerable.

She couldn't be that close to him. She couldn't look him in the eyes while he held her, knowing he could feel the pounding of her heartbeat against his chest. Maintaining any sort of distance was hard enough when they were living under the same roof. It was impossible when he touched her.

The last time he'd been within a foot of her, she'd kissed him. Who knew what would happen if they danced together again?

At the same time, she couldn't fathom dancing with anyone else.

Zander was her first dance partner.

Her *only* dance partner.

There'd been a tenderness to their partnership that Allegra had never felt with another man. As ridiculous as it seemed, dancing with someone else would have felt like a betrayal.

Ryan shot her a weary glance. "Please tell me there are couples who've signed up for this event—couples who are planning on actually dancing instead of standing around pretending not to have feelings for each other."

"Plenty of people have registered for the marathon. Over one hundred couples, in fact." Allegra had uploaded notices on every dance-related group on social media that she could find. Plus the Bennington and the Wilde School of Dance both sent out email blasts. The event had already raised thousands, just in registration fees.

"That's fantastic," Ryan said. "I'm impressed."

"But you're wrong about Zander and me. We don't have feelings for each other." Allegra crossed her arms and then promptly uncrossed them. She couldn't seem to figure out what to do with them. Or where to look, because Ryan's gaze had quickly become too probing. Too *knowing*.

"Are you sure about that?"

"Absolutely," she said.

*Liar.*

She bit the inside of her mouth.

Her bags were packed. Her plane ticket was booked. There was no reason to stick around after the dance marathon. She was flying to Boston in the morning, just in time to join the company tour. This time next week, she'd be onstage. A different city every day.

"As long as you're sure," Ryan said.

He didn't finish the thought. He didn't have to.

*As long as you're sure, because after tomorrow it will be too late.*

"Everything is in order for your wedding next weekend." Zander turned to face the couple he was escorting from his office to the Bennington entrance. He smiled.

"You have my personal assurance that the ceremony will proceed perfectly according to plan."

*Unless you dash out of the building in a puff of lace and tulle.* He glanced at the bride and somehow managed to bite his tongue.

"Excellent." The groom-to-be shook Zander's hand.

He held the door open for them, and the happy couple exchanged a giddy glance before heading out into the bitter New York air.

Zander had witnessed a lot of those giddy glances over the past week. He'd been working overtime to get a wedding booked as soon as possible. Fortunately, Ryan's outrageous idea seemed to be working.

Curse or no curse, guaranteed coverage in the Vows column was too tempting for most Manhattan brides to resist. The phones at the Bennington were ringing again. Zander was neck-deep in lovey-dovey couples. He should have been used to the wistful glances by now, but somehow witnessing them always felt like getting punched in the gut.

He took a seat on one of the plush velvet sofas in the hotel lobby, scrolled through the contacts on his cell phone and stopped when he reached the entry for the Vows desk.

Celestia answered on the first ring. "Hello, Mr. Wilde."

"Ms. Lane." Zander did his best to sound polite. It was a stretch after everything the reporter had put him through. "I'm calling to let you know we've got a wedding confirmed for later this week."

He gave her the necessary details.

"Perfect. My photographer and I will both be there." She sounded positively elated, which only exacerbated Zander's dark mood.

*You'd better be there.* "Good. And nothing new in the paper before then, correct?"

"That was our deal, and I'm standing by it," she said.

How had he managed to let the fate of his hotel rest in this horrible woman's hands?

"But you've got to hold up your end, as well. If another wedding takes place before then, I expect a call."

"Understood," Zander said.

He ended the call as quickly as possible.

It was almost over—the curse business, Allegra, all of it.

Everything was falling into place nicely. At last. He should have been happy. Hell, he should have been doing cartwheels down one of the Bennington's hallways.

A man and woman stumbled past him from the direction of the ballroom. They were both flushed and slightly disheveled, hanging on to one another for support. But their wide smiles radiated joy, and one of them was humming a tune—"Walkin' My Baby Back Home."

Zander looked away.

He'd managed to avoid the dance marathon thus far. It had started hours ago, and the air in the Bennington had been thick with music all evening. Big-band standards like "In the Mood" and "Sing, Sing, Sing (With a Swing)."

Zander was determined to stay away. Doing so had been relatively easy—or possible, at least—while he'd been busy with bridal appointments. But now his foot was tapping along to the faint strains of an old Frank Sinatra tune.

He stood, fully intent on summoning his driver and

heading back to the brownstone. But instead of walking toward the valet, he found himself drawn to the ball-room. He told himself he was simply doing the right thing, fulfilling his obligation as a Wilde. The event was a fund-raiser for his mother's school after all. How would it look if he didn't even make an appearance when the big dance was taking place right under his roof? The entire family would be there—Emily, Ryan, Tessa and Julian. Even Chloe had promised to show up, dragging one of the Rockettes' stagehands along as her dance partner.

Zander's absence would have been notable.

*Five minutes.*

That's it. He'd stay for one song—two max—and then get the hell out.

The music grew louder as he approached. Zander paused at the ballroom entrance, bracing himself, but he was swept into the jubilant crowd almost at once. The room was full to bursting. Couples spun past him, dancing the Charleston and the Lindy Hop and a few other dance variations he remembered from his brief tenure as a competitive dancer.

He backed out of the way as the couple right in front of him stopped in place to do a crocodile roll. The male dancer's legs parted, and his partner shot between them, flipped over, then popped back up into a dance hold.

The space was a hive of activity. He'd never seen anything like it, even on the occasions the Benning-ton had hosted Big Band Night. This was Big Band Night on steroids.

Despite the crowd and the noise and the wall-to-wall revelry, Zander's gaze immediately found Allegra, as though drawn to her by some invisible force. A feeling passed through him that felt too much like relief when he saw her walking toward the bandstand with her full skirt and red crinolines swishing around her slender legs. She was breathtaking, wearing a white halter-style dress decorated with bright red cherries and her hair swept away from her face in double victory rolls.

More important, she was alone.

The tension that had gathered between Zander's shoulder blades loosened a little. He wasn't sure what he would have done if he'd walked into the ballroom and seen Allegra dancing with someone else. He just knew that a part of him would have died inside.

He realized it wasn't rational. It definitely wasn't fair. This was a dance marathon, and he and Allegra weren't even technically speaking to one another at the moment. He had absolutely no right to expect her to stay off the dance floor.

He didn't care, though. He was past the point of pretending anything he felt for Allegra made sense. And he definitely felt…something.

He couldn't identify what those feelings were, other than they were mired in history and laced with a vague sense of regret.

He shoved his hands into his pockets and leaned against the wall as he watched her climb the steps of the bandstand and position herself behind the microphone. He had no reason to regret anything. She'd made her choice, and there was nothing he could do about it.

"Impressed?"

Zander turned. His mother stood beside him, dressed in khaki with a military hat propped on top of her head at a jaunty angle.

"Love the outfit," he said. "It's very 'Boogie Woogie Bugle Boy.'"

"Thanks." She aimed a questioning glance at his tie. "Honestly, couldn't you have dressed for the occasion? You look like a corporate raider who wandered in here by mistake."

Zander's jaw clenched. "I look like a CEO, because that's what I am."

"Message received. You're not dancing tonight." She sighed and leaned closer so she wouldn't have to yell over the music. "But that doesn't mean I'm letting you off the hook. You still haven't answered my question. Impressed?"

He nodded. "Quite. This is really something. I'm guessing the school will be in a much better financial position after tonight."

"It will." His mother cleared her throat. "But that's not what I meant."

Her gaze cut to the bandstand, where Allegra was about to address the crowd. "She's remarkable, isn't she?"

"Yes." Zander sighed. "She's also leaving tomorrow."

"Right. But she's not gone yet, is she?" Emily winked at him.

"I think it's time for me to go." Zander pushed off the wall, but his mom snagged him by the elbow as Allegra's voice rang out over the loudspeaker.

"Congratulations, dancers! You've made it past the three-hour mark!" Her eyes met his across the crowded room. There was an unmistakable hitch in her voice, but she continued. "Don't forget to dance past the water station. In about half an hour, we'll have volunteers passing out sandwiches. In the meantime, dance on!"

The dancers all cheered, and the opening bars of Glenn Miller's "A String of Pearls" rang out as she stepped away from the podium.

Zander lost track of her in the crowd, but he knew she was making her way toward him. He could feel it.

Which was definitely his cue to leave, but he couldn't seem to make his feet budge.

"Zander! We've been wondering when you'd show up, right, Mom?" Tessa threw her arms around his neck and kissed his cheek. "Isn't this fantastic? I can't believe Allegra put this together so quickly." She waved an arm toward the dance floor.

Zander waited for Tessa to face him again before he responded so she could read his lips. "It's remarkable. But where's your dance partner?"

He signed the words in addition to speaking them. Tessa was almost completely deaf as a result of a head injury she'd suffered in dance class a few years ago. She hadn't let her physical challenges stand in her way, though. She'd since become one of the Manhattan Ballet's most popular principal dancers.

"Julian's playing piano with the band." She smiled at her fiancé, pounding away on a white baby grand in the center of the stage. "But that means I'm free if you want to take me for a spin. How about it? Do you want to dance?"

The moment the words left Tessa's mouth, Allegra reached the edge of their grouping. The timing couldn't have been more awkward, unless, of course, Allegra hadn't overheard anything.

But the stiff smile on her face told Zander she was fully aware what Tessa had just said. Their eyes met and held for a second, until she dropped her gaze to the floor.

Tessa turned to face her. "Allegra, look who finally decided to show up."

Allegra glanced at him again and swallowed. "Hello, Zander."

Tessa sighed. "I was just trying to persuade him to dance with me, but as you can see, he looks less than thrilled at the prospect."

"Tessa." Zander shot his sister a warning glance, but she was facing the opposite direction, still chattering away, oblivious.

Emily released her hold on Zander's elbow and touched Tessa gently on the shoulder, capturing her attention. "Can you come help me with something, dear?"

Tessa shrugged. "Sure." She extended her hands, palms facing up, and moved them back and forth in the ASL motion for *what?*

"Dance-school business," Emily said. She wrapped her arm around Tessa's waist and pulled her away.

Tessa shot a confused glance over her shoulder, then looked back and forth between Zander and Allegra. "Oh." Her eyes grew wide. "Of course. Happy to help."

Zander let his eyes drift shut and took a deep breath. He knew he should have stayed away.

When he opened his eyes, Allegra was still there. She'd moved to stand beside him, so they were facing the dance floor, side by side.

"You could have danced with your sister, you know. It wouldn't have bothered me," she said, refusing to meet his gaze. Her attention remained firmly fixed on the couples twirling across the room.

"Note taken." He suppressed a smile.

He didn't believe her for a minute, even though the potential dance partner in question was his sister. The situation couldn't have been more innocent.

That didn't matter, though. Zander understood. He would've felt jealous beyond all reason if he'd just seen someone else ask Allegra to dance, be it George Clooney or her great-grandfather.

He sneaked a glance at her profile. God, she was gorgeous. The surroundings, steeped in nostalgia, emphasized her timeless beauty. She never failed to take his breath away—yesterday, today, tomorrow.

A bottomless sense of loss settled in the pit of his stomach.

*What if there is no tomorrow?*

Every instinct he possessed told him to look away. Not just *look* away, but *walk* away, too. Walk away without a backward glance.

Instead he let his attention linger on the graceful curve of her neck and then drift to the lush swell of her lower lip, as red and tempting as ripe fruit.

A pair of dancers bumped into Zander from behind, waving an apology as they danced past. Zander's knuckles brushed against Allegra's. She still didn't look at him, but instead of pulling her arm away, her fingertips laced gently with his.

Zander grew very still as they stood hand in hand. Connected, yet at the same time, miles apart. The fact that he couldn't bring himself to let go, even though he knew what sadness dawn would bring, made him realize that this night, this sliver of a moment, was their second chance.

Their *last* chance.

He gave her hand a tender squeeze, and at last she turned her gaze on him. Her sapphire eyes were red rimmed, shiny and wet with a bittersweet combination of pain and hope. Shattered bits of sparkle.

He didn't want to remember her this way. If this was the image of Allegra he was left with, he'd never forgive himself.

He ran the pad of his thumb along the palm of her hand. "Shall we dance?"

She bit her lip, and for a prolonged moment, Zander forgot how to breathe. Then she smiled a smile that reached all the way to her eyes. "I thought you'd never ask."

## Chapter Fourteen

Allegra allowed Zander to lead her onto the dance floor and pretended not to notice the stares of his family members.

But they were all watching from the other side of the room, making the moment seem even more significant than it already was. She even thought she saw Ryan do a double take when he looked up from his glass of champagne and spied them together beneath the glittering disco ball.

"Ignore them," Zander whispered, pulling her into his arms. "Pretend it's just you and me out here. Just like old times."

She let out a nervous laugh and forced herself to relax against his body. "Pretend. Got it."

She could do that. She'd been pretending for such a long time that she was practically an expert.

*You wanted this, remember?*

She did. She'd wanted to dance with Zander since the second he'd walked into the ballroom. Not doing so felt wrong on every possible level. In some corner of her mind, she still knew it was a very bad idea, but her body didn't seem to care. She belonged in his arms with her legs and feet moving in time with his.

But now that it was actually happening, she wondered if she could actually go through with it.

Had dancing with him always felt so…

Intimate?

There was no other word for it, really. His face was only a breath away. She could feel the steady pounding of his heart against her chest. And the skillful way he took the lead, guiding her movements, made her weak in the knees.

If this was what it felt like to dance with Zander Wilde, what would it feel like to go to bed with him?

Her gaze slid toward him, and she tried to imagine it, grateful that he couldn't read her mind.

"Is everything in order for your trip tomorrow?" he murmured.

She blinked. Were they really going to talk about her departure while they were dancing?

"Well?" He raised a single dark eyebrow.

Apparently so.

Maybe it was for the best. Maybe, just *maybe*, if they had this conversation now, she could convince herself that the dance was simply a dance. Nothing more. Just two people swaying to the music. Maybe she could even manage to ignore the shiver that coursed through her every time her hip brushed against Zander's groin. Maybe she could forget the gentle pressure of his hand on the small of her back, and the way the heat of his touch seemed to burn right through her dress.

"Yes." She swallowed. Who was she kidding? She wouldn't have been any less aware of Zander's touch if she'd been forced to solve a complex math equation. As it was, she could barely speak in anything but monosyllables. "Train."

The corner of his mouth hitched into a knowing smirk.

She took a deep breath. "I mean, the train. I'm taking it from Grand Central to Boston in the morning."

Barely coherent, but at least she'd managed to form a full sentence.

"I see." His fingertips dipped lower, grazing her bottom.

He seemed cool as a cucumber, wholly unaffected by the slide of her thigh between his legs as they crossed the dance floor. It was beyond irritating.

She lifted her chin and did her best to mirror his detachment. "Look, I know you're angry that I'm leaving. You may as well admit it."

"I'm not angry, Allegra," he said evenly.

Her heart gave a little hitch. Her stupid, stupid heart.

So he wasn't angry. He was just indifferent.

"Good." She stiffened a little, and he seemed to sense it.

He pulled her closer. "You seem disappointed. And here I thought the kind thing to do would be to let you go without any histrionics."

He was right. What was wrong with her? She didn't want to leave on bad terms. She just wanted to know that he felt *something*. It didn't have to be anything close to the deeply rooted feelings she had for him.

*So now you have feelings for Zander Wilde?*

She cleared her throat. Of course she didn't have feelings for him. She just couldn't think straight while her body was pressed so firmly against the solid wall of his chest and while his lips brushed against her ear every time he dipped his head to speak to her. It was utterly confusing. She'd never felt so irritated, sad and aroused all at the same time.

"I'm not disappointed," she countered.

"You really think I don't know you well enough to sense when you're upset? Think again." A telltale knot of muscle flashed in his jaw. Maybe he wasn't quite as disinterested as she'd thought.

"Aha. You *are* mad. I knew it." She grinned triumphantly.

"You're ridiculous." He shook his head, but the corner of his mouth hitched into a half grin.

"Is it really so ridiculous to want to get everything out in the open before I leave again?"

He paused, and his gaze darkened. "Everything?"

Now was the time to change the subject, to say something frivolous and go back to ignoring the swirl of maddening emotion that simmered just below the surface whenever they were in a room together.

But she couldn't. Not while they were dancing.

"Sure. All of it." Dread mingled with the delicious heat that had settled low in her belly. "What would you like to know?"

"Tell me why you never came back, why I never heard from you again." His eyes shifted away from her, and his grip on her hand seemed to involuntarily tighten. "I missed you like hell."

The breath rushed from her body, and she glanced toward the exit.

"Don't even think about running away from me, Allegra. You're the one who started this. Now we're going to finish it. Tell me." His fingertips pressed more firmly into her back until she was flush against him.

She could feel everything, every part of him. There was nothing between them but an unsettling intimacy that squeezed the air from her lungs. Even though it frightened her to death, she couldn't tell him anything other than the truth. "Because it hurt too much to be here, Zander."

His gaze shifted back to her, his expression unreadable. "Does it still?"

"Sometimes." She swallowed hard. "It's just easier to be away."

"Away?" He shook his head and his footsteps slowed, until they were almost standing still in the center of the dance floor while dozens of other couples twirled and spun around them. As if they were stuck, suspended in a moment, while time kept whirling on in dizzying *pirouettes*. "You mean it's easier to be *alone*."

Such raw, honest words. Words she couldn't bring herself to say. She couldn't even form a response.

"You can't even commit to a stray cat. That's no way to live, Allegra." He stared her down, daring her to argue. As if she was his opponent instead of his dance partner.

She looked at him standing there with his self-righteous expression, and she was suddenly enraged. Enraged for reasons too numerous to count, but mainly at his ability to see straight through her, even after all this time.

"You have a lot of nerve, you know." She glared at his broad shoulders and realized she was mad at them, too, for being so strong, so damn tempting. Solid and muscular, as if they could carry a world of burdens. "You're angry at me for leaving and never coming back. But you knew where I was the whole time. If I was so important to you, why didn't you ever come to Boston? It's just a train ride away."

Their feet slowed to a complete stop. Zander let go of her hand in order to cup her face and force her to meet his gaze. His eyes were darker than ever. Dark and serious. He was quiet for a long moment, and the silence between them was so thick it seemed to drown out the music coming from the bandstand.

Finally, he spoke. "Who says I didn't?"

Her heart slammed against her rib cage. "What?"

He couldn't have come to Boston. She would have known. It couldn't be true.

But the look on his face told her it was. His lips inched upward into a smile so weighed down by sadness that she could barely stand to look at it. Nor could she bring herself to look away.

"When?" she breathed.

"Opening night of *Giselle*. I went to see you dance. It was about a month after I called off my wedding."

None of the words coming out of his mouth were making sense. He'd been in the audience at the Boston Opera House?

Now that she thought about it, she realized that's how Emily must have known to invite her to teach at the Wilde School of Dance. But that didn't explain why Zander had come all the way to Boston and never said anything.

He'd come to find her right after calling off his *wedding*.

That had to mean something.

"I don't understand. Why didn't you tell me? Why didn't you let me know you were there?" She shook her head.

This was the moment of truth, and it never would have happened if they hadn't danced together. She'd known all along that dancing was the one thing that would break down the wall between them, and she'd been right. The wall hadn't just fallen. Zander had smashed it into a pile of rubble at their feet.

"I went to bring you roses backstage, but somebody beat me to it." His smile hardened into place.

Heat rushed to Allegra's face. "Spencer."

He nodded. "I saw him knock on your dressing-room door. When you opened it, I noticed the diamond solitaire on your finger and put two and two together."

She felt like crying all of a sudden. She'd spent so much of her life grieving, and now this loss felt like one too many. A missed chance.

"Why?" she said hoarsely.

"Because above all, I wanted you to be happy. You deserve that, Allegra. You deserve all the happiness in the world. At the time it looked like you'd found that with Spencer, so I came back to New York."

"No." She shook her head. "I mean why did you go to Boston in the first place? Why did you go there to find me after such a long time?"

He reached up, brushing his fingertips lightly against her cheek. Her throat tightened. Desperation clawed at her like an animal. This wasn't the same as hearing he'd loved her when they were teenagers.

He'd come to find her. She almost wanted to clamp her hands over her ears because she knew whatever he was about to say wouldn't be something she could push away and pretend didn't matter.

She wasn't ready to hear it.

But if not now, when?

"It's you, Allegra. It's always been you."

Air.

She needed air.

"Allegra?" Zander's brow creased, changing his tender expression to one of concern.

She nodded. "I'm..." *Fine. Totally fine.*

Except she wasn't. How could she possibly be, after what Zander had just said to her?

She swallowed. "Actually, can we go?"

"You want to leave?" He searched her gaze.

"I do." Heat rushed through her face. She glanced around at the other dancers, spinning like tops, then back up at Zander.

Bits of light reflected off the disco ball, showering him in radiant prisms. He looked as though stars had fallen from the sky and landed on his shoulders. She suddenly wanted to be alone with him. She wanted that very much, more than she could possibly articulate.

"Take me home? Please?" she asked, sliding her hands down his arms and weaving her fingers through his. Then she directed her gaze very purposefully at his mouth.

"Absolutely." His voice dropped deliciously low, and it scraped her insides, leaving her even more raw and vulnerable than she'd felt after his startling admission.

Their remaining moments at the Bennington passed

in a blur of cheery goodbyes and assurances from Ryan and Emily that she'd done more than enough. Of course they'd stay and see the marathon through until the end. The music seemed to be moving at double speed, and her head spun. She almost felt as if she was hovering above the scene, watching the girl with the cherries on her dress being escorted from the ballroom by the dashing Zander Wilde.

Then they were on the sidewalk, beneath the golden glow of the Bennington's marquee, where he kissed her. And she was right back in the moment, where everything was sharp and real. A shiver coursed through her, and Zander slung his coat over her shoulders while they waited for the car, but she wasn't cold at all. She was hot. Her veins were on fire, and she felt too much. Wanted too much.

She wanted *him*. Now.

They barely made it through the door of the brownstone before he pinned her against the kitchen counter and kissed her gently before catching her bottom lip in a tantalizing bite. She gasped, and his mouth dropped to her neck while his hands slid to her wrists, ringing them like bracelets as he held her in place.

Then he angled his head and kissed a trail from her jaw to her shoulder, and she thought she might die right then and there.

"I need to see you," he groaned against her sensitive skin.

She could feel the length of his erection pressing against her through their clothes like an erotic promise as she reached behind her neck to unfasten the closure of her halter dress. She held her breath as her dress fell away.

"So beautiful," he whispered, and she could feel his eyes on her as real as a caress.

He didn't touch her until she was completely exposed, with her dress and panties pooled at her feet. She was burning, desperate for his hands, his tongue, his manhood.

And there was no awkwardness, no hesitation whatsoever. It seemed like the most natural thing in the world to be bared to him, to sigh into him as he cupped her breasts and his mouth found her nipple.

"Zander." Her voice was a breathy plea.

The ache inside in her was nearly intolerable. Bottomless and deep, and somehow tied specifically to Zander. To the bond they shared. It was agonizing and exquisite, all at once.

He sucked hard at her nipple, then released it and blew gently on her puckered flesh.

"Zander, please…" she begged.

"Tell me." He sounded every bit as tortured as she felt. "Tell me what you want, darling."

"This." She reached to take hold of his hard length through his trousers, earning a low, masculine growl.

Her heart felt like it was going to pound right out of her chest as he scooped her into his arms and carried her through the darkened house, toward his bedroom.

What were they doing?

Was this a mistake?

It no longer mattered. There was no turning back. She'd made up her mind. Long ago, if she was really being honest. It felt like they'd been spiraling toward this moment since the second she'd burst in on his birthday party. She closed her eyes, and she could still see his stunned face, lit by his birthday candles.

*Make a wish.*

Maybe he had. She definitely wished for this at some point along the way. Now here they were, and as much as she wanted it, the reality of what they were about to do frightened the life out of her.

"This doesn't change anything," she whispered into the warm crook of his neck.

She was still leaving. This wasn't a promise. It was a goodbye. The only *proper* goodbye, the only way she'd ever be able to walk away.

She'd never be able to tell Zander what he meant to her. Her bruised and battered heart wouldn't let her. Even if she'd been capable of that kind of vulnerability, she'd never have been able to find the words.

How did you tell someone they were the family you always wanted, the home you'd never really had? What ceremony of words could impart that kind of bond? Did such words even exist?

If they did, Allegra didn't know them. Words would never be enough. Her body would tell him. When he touched her, there were no lies, no holding back. The truth was in the shiver that coursed through her when his mouth closed around her nipple again. It was in the heat gathering in her center as he set her gently on the bed and his fingers slipped inside her while his thumb circled her with a finesse that she'd never known.

A sob rose to the back of her throat, even as her hips strained upward, seeking relief. Seeking *him*.

She refused to cry. She didn't want tears. She wanted to know what it felt like to have Zander inside her. She tugged at his clothes, fisting her hands in the sleek silk of his suit jacket until he paused long enough to undress. Then he was on the bed beside her, all lean muscle and taut bronze skin. So big. So warm. So very, very, hard.

*It's you, Allegra. It's always been you.*

The tears were coming, whether she wanted them or not. She squeezed her eyes closed tight, fighting them as best she could.

"Open your eyes, baby." His lips touched hers, gently this time. Tender and sweet. But his mouth was hot and ripe with delicious promises. He was taking her somewhere she'd never been—to a place where there was no turning back. "Look at me."

He was poised at her entrance, waiting. Wanting.

She did as he said and opened her eyes.

*This doesn't change anything.*

But as he pushed inside her, filling her at last, she knew it was a lie. Change was inevitable. It was already happening. She was opening to him. Not just her body, but her heart. Her soul. Her everything.

They wouldn't be the same after tonight—neither of them. *Everything* would change. It already had.

"You're so beautiful." He cradled her face in his hands as he began to move, sliding in and out of her.

Somewhere beneath the swirl of heat and pleasure, Allegra realized it was like dancing. The connection was so similar, but far more intense. Two bodies moving together in perfect sync—the hypnotic push and pull, the fire in Zander's eyes as he guided her through the rhythm, setting a pace that kept her right on the edge of coming apart.

Dancing had always been what they'd done best together. No fumbling words, no fear of letting go—just the music and the fluidity of their footsteps and absolute trust in one another. It was like that now, too, only instead of music, they moved in time to the sound of their shuddering breaths, the sweetest of sounds.

It had never been like this for Allegra with anyone else. She knew it never would again. This was it. This was the way it was supposed to be, the way it was when two people were in love.

Her breath caught in her throat.

*Love?*

No. She wasn't in love. She couldn't be. She didn't *want* to be. Love led to pain—the kind of pain that dragged you to your knees. She'd been through that before, and it had taken her years to learn to stand upright again.

*No.* She swallowed hard and shook her head, but then Zander's hips began to roll in an excruciatingly slow, seductive circle and his hands slid to cup her bottom, holding her still as he ground into her. She gasped and arched against him, alive with sensation. "Yes, Zander. Yes."

A deep shuddering moan slipped from her lips as her hands traveled down the length of Zander's back. She wanted to touch him everywhere. She wanted her fingertips to memorize every square inch of his hard, muscled body—every dip and plane.

He made a growling sound she'd never heard from him before. It was the sound of infinite satisfaction. Purely male. Purely sublime. It was so raw, so intense, that it nearly did her in.

Was this the same man she'd known nearly all her life? This fierce, powerful lover?

He was. And on some level she'd known it would be like this. Deep down in her marrow, she'd known.

Because she knew Zander. She knew the real him, and he knew her like no one else ever had. Ever would.

That's why this giving herself to him mattered. She knew it did, even as she pretended to believe otherwise.

"Come with me, darling," he murmured into her hair.

She could feel his pleasure building in time with hers. Every muscle in his body was tense, and his signature control was slipping away with each thrust. He was right on the brink with her, dancing on the edge. Then his teeth scraped her collarbone, and she couldn't hold back any longer.

She shattered around him, climaxing hard. But she never broke her gaze. She watched him through it all, wanting, *needing*, to remember everything about this moment—the tremble that racked through him as he found his release, the tender way he held her through the aftershocks and, most of all, the look in his eyes.

She could see a world in those deep brown irises she knew so well. A shimmering, beautiful future. Her and Zander. A real family. A life—hers for the taking.

If only she could be brave enough to grab hold of it.

Within minutes of spilling himself inside Allegra, Zander was hard again. When he touched her, when he kissed her, everything seemed to come alive. He'd known it would be like this when they finally dropped all pretenses and gave themselves to one another.

Yet the intensity of their connection also took him by surprise. How could he have been prepared for the reality of Allegra's beautiful body? For the satisfaction he found in every little whimper she made when he pushed her thighs apart and licked her until she cried his name? If a lifetime of knowing her hadn't prepared him, nothing could have. She was a sensual surprise and the most constant object of his desire, both at once.

She arched against his mouth as he pushed a finger inside her. So warm. So wet. He paused to watch her, glorious in the darkness.

*Slow down.* His thoughts were screaming. *Make it last.*

But he couldn't. He could barely keep himself from coming again and she wasn't even touching him. He was scarcely in control of his desire, scarcely in control of anything. Time was slipping away...seconds were passing with each kiss, each undulation of her perfect hips.

One night wasn't enough. How was he supposed to discover all her secret wants, her most hidden yearnings, when he couldn't hold back his hunger for her? He'd been waiting so long, *wanting* so long, that he was like a man who suddenly found himself drowning after a decade without water.

*Breathe. Just take a breath and savor.*

But her hands were in his hair, tugging hard. And before he could stop himself, he was sliding up the length of her body and entering her again, shuddering at the feel of her velvet heat.

His mind went blank then. Her hands slid to his backside, forcing him deeper, and he gave himself up to pleasure. He pumped harder, faster, until, in a staggering moment of restraint, he stopped just long enough to flip their position so she sat astride him.

She'd never looked as beautiful as when she rode him, breasts swaying in the silver moonlight, her hair spilling down her back. *This*, he thought, *this right here*. This was the way he'd remember her after she left. With fire in her eyes, not tears. Fire and light. Light so bright it seemed to reach straight into his chest and set him aflame.

He felt it hours later, smoldering deep inside. His need for her was constant...there, always there...even as she fell asleep with her limbs draped languidly over his and her waves of hair fanned out on his pillow. Even as he closed his eyes and the night finally claimed him.

Even when he woke up to the soft rays of morning and found her gone.

## Chapter Fifteen

Zander went through the motions of searching the brownstone for any sign of Allegra on the off chance that she'd simply sneaked out of bed for a glass of water or something.

But it wasn't necessary.

He knew.

She wasn't there. He knew because she'd somehow taken the air out of the brownstone with her. He walked from room to room with a knot in his chest, struggling to take a breath.

There wasn't a sign of her anywhere—not in the upstairs guest room where she'd slept for the past several weeks, not at the big farm table where she liked to dawdle over her morning coffee and most notably, not in his bed. If the pillow beside his hadn't been warm to the touch, he might've been afraid he'd imagined their fateful reunion and that she'd never actually come back to New York at all.

He lowered himself into one of the chairs at the kitchen table and dropped his head into his hands. How could he have been such a fool? He'd actually allowed himself to believe that making love to Allegra had meant something. Because that's what it had been—love. Not just sex.

He was in love with Allegra Clark.

And just like last time, she'd left without saying goodbye.

But not everything was the same as it was last time, was it? He'd been blindsided when she'd gone to live with her aunt in Cambridge without giving him a chance to tell her how he felt. This time, he'd known it was coming. He'd hated it, but he'd known.

She'd even reminded him of the truth of the matter last night. She'd been naked in his arms, bared and beautiful, but still she'd made her intentions clear.

*This doesn't change anything.*

He'd heard it, but he refused to believe it.

He lifted his head and stared at the empty chair across from him. Her presence was somehow still there, as if she'd left part of herself behind. A ghost, haunting him with reminders of what should have been.

He closed his eyes and saw himself going through the motions of everyday life—meetings at the hotel, family events, meaningless dates with women whose names he wouldn't bother committing to memory.

He could do these things.

He'd done them before.

After the trip he'd made to Boston to see Allegra dance *Giselle*, he'd reset the clock. He'd finally let go.

Had it hurt? Of course. Back then, he'd let himself believe that despite the fact that they hadn't set eyes on one another in over a decade, he could bring her back. Or he could stay there with her, if necessary. He'd have given up the Bennington. He'd have given up everything to repair the damage done all those years ago.

But the ring on her finger had been a wake-up call. The time had come to move on. For good.

And he had.

If he could do it once, he could do it again.

He stood and headed for the French press. This was how people started over—by doing one thing at a time. First, coffee. Then…

He didn't have a clue, but he'd figure it out.

On the way to the cabinet, his foot made contact with something hard and sent whatever it was skidding across the kitchen floor. He let out a string of curse words, but when he bent to inspect his throbbing toe, his gaze landed on the offending object.

It was the china saucer that Allegra had been using to feed her kitten. Correction: the kitten she adored but insisted didn't actually belong to her.

Zander picked it up and ran his thumb along the saucer's rim. It had a tiny nick on the edge, much like the mysterious notch he'd noticed on one of the little black cat's ears.

Something about that tiny chip caused him to come undone. He wasn't entirely sure why. Maybe because he'd stumbled upon a physical reminder that Allegra had actually been there. Or maybe it was because Allegra and the little cat had a few things in common.

Both wild. Both fragile. Both deserving of far more than the lousy hand life had dealt them.

As if on cue, the cat materialized. She leaped from a shadowy corner of the room and landed on Zander's shoulder. He reached up and gathered her in his arms, and a purr rumbled deep in her tiny chest.

"You're home," he murmured, running his thumb between the kitty's ears. "I think it's time to go find her and bring her home, too. What do you say?"

The cat blinked up at him and let out a quiet meow. Somewhere in the back of Zander's mind, Allegra's voice resonated with a bittersweet lie.

*This doesn't change anything.*

The hell it didn't.

Grand Central Station was a tomb at five thirty in the morning.

Allegra's footsteps echoed on the smooth marble floor as she crossed the length of the quiet main concourse. The Tiffany-blue celestial ceiling loomed overhead, an infinite sky.

But it wasn't infinite. It wasn't even a sky. It was an illusion, much like her early-morning escape from Zander's bed. She'd thought if she left while he was still asleep it would lessen the pain of parting. For both of them.

Oh, how wrong she'd been. Her heart was in her throat, and there was an emptiness inside her like she'd never known. Worse than grief. Worse than having her world ripped out from under her. Because fate hadn't caused this terrible chasm, not this time. This time she'd plunged the knife into her own heart.

She'd done it again. She'd run away. Not because she wanted to, but because she had to. It was becoming something of a habit.

Her gaze snagged on the four-faced opal clock in the center of the terminal—5:35 a.m. Was Zander awake yet? Had he realized she'd gone?

He would be furious, and he had every right to feel that way. It had been the only way, though. If she'd had to look him in the eye and tell him goodbye just hours after he'd been inside her, she never would have gone. And then what?

*Then you could have stayed.*

No.

She bit down hard on the inside of her cheek and hauled her dance bag farther up on her shoulder. If she stayed, she'd live in constant fear of losing everything she held dear. The panic attacks would come back. She'd lose every last shred of control over her life.

No attachment, no fear. She'd go on tour with the dance company. She'd sleep in a different city every night, without strings and without the kind of emotional entanglements that threatened to pull her back into a place of unfathomable vulnerability. She'd be fine. She'd be safe.

She'd be alone.

Zander's voice rose, unbidden, to the forefront of her consciousness.

*You can't even commit to a stray cat. That's no way to live, Allegra.*

She swallowed, gulped a lungful of air and then swallowed again. Her stomach churned. Bile rose to the back of her throat. It tasted bitter and black, like the worst fear possible. Like panic.

*Not now. Please not now.*

She glanced around, as her heart raged inside her chest and a deep, sudden chill knifed through her body.

Her hands shook. Her feet began to tingle, and she had trouble taking a step.

Her surroundings blurred around the edges and tipped sideways, until the Tiffany-blue ceiling became the floor. She collided with a few commuters, before stumbling toward a wall and slumping against it as she slid to the ground.

She pressed her face to the wall's cool marble surface and closed her eyes.

Another panic attack.

Why?

This wasn't supposed to be happening. There was nothing to be afraid of anymore. She'd beaten fate to the punch. She'd willingly given up the opportunity to be gutted by loss.

*But it found me, anyway.*

She wasn't sure how long she sat there, paralyzed by fear. By regret. By the sinking realization that she'd just made the biggest mistake of her life. A half hour? An hour? Maybe longer.

She thought she might die, surrounded by strangers in a place where people came and went, running toward life while she'd been trying too hard to run away. Eventually her heartbeat slowed to normal, and she was able to take a breath and release it without choking. She dragged herself to her feet and staggered to the closest bathroom.

Inside the stall, she pulled her cell phone out of her dance bag to check the time. Had she missed her train?

But her phone was dead. She'd been so busy with the dance marathon she hadn't charged it in days. Perfect. Just perfect.

She tucked it back in her bag, splashed water on her

face and headed back to the concourse. She turned toward the legendary clock, its four opal faces glowing pale gold, awash in snowy morning light streaming through the grand arched windows.

Then she froze.

She blinked, convinced she was seeing things. Perhaps her panic attack had been more severe than she realized, because her imagination had taken over. Her wildest dream was somehow standing in front of her.

Zander was right there, next to the clock. Waiting. Waiting as patiently as if they'd agreed to meet there and embark on a long journey together. He held the little black kitten tucked into the crook of his elbow, and a white bakery bag dangled from his other hand—the kind they'd once used to collect Valentine's Day cards when they were children.

Was this real?

"Going somewhere?" he asked, arching an eyebrow.

"Um, yes." What was she saying? This was a miracle. He'd come for her. She'd done everything she could to push him away. She'd left him in the cruelest way possible, and here he was. She couldn't run anymore.

She didn't *want* to run.

She cleared her throat and gave him a wobbly smile. "I mean, no. It seems I've had a change of heart."

His lips curved in to a satisfied smile. "I hope that's true, because you disappeared this morning before I had a chance to wish you a happy birthday."

Her birthday.

She'd completely forgotten.

"You remembered." She shook her head. "With everything that's happened lately, it slipped my mind."

"Not mine. This day has been marked on my calendar

for more than a decade. We had a deal, remember? And that deal ends today." He offered her the bakery bag.

She took it with a shaky hand, afraid to look inside. Afraid that none of this was real and in a minute she'd wake up to find she'd been dreaming.

"Open it." There was a rough tenderness to his voice all of a sudden, as if he, too, feared it might be nothing but a perfect, wistful daydream.

It wasn't. It was real—as real as the platinum engagement ring that circled the candle atop the pink cupcake nestled inside the bag.

"Zander?" She stared down at the diamond nestled on a perfect swirl of frosting. She took a few deep breaths, until she finally trusted herself to reach inside the bag and retrieve the tiny cake without dropping it.

She did, and when she looked back up, Zander was down on one knee, gazing up at her as if she'd never run, as if he'd known all along she'd eventually find her way back to him.

"I've been waiting for this day since we were sixteen years old, Allegra. And I never stopped loving you. I can't promise you that you'll never lose anyone again. But I can promise you that as long as I live, I'll be your home." The kitten mewed, as if putting an exclamation point on the most beautiful proposal she could have imagined. Zander smiled and finished with the question she couldn't wait to answer. "Will you marry me?"

"Yes," she whispered.

Then, in the shadow of a clock that had welcomed soldiers returning from war and travelers who'd finally reached the end of long weary road, Allegra Clark threw her arms around Zander Wilde.

At long last, she'd come home.

* * *

Zander slid his arms into his tuxedo jacket and checked the time on his Cartier—11:00 p.m.

In an hour, Allegra's birthday would be over. Time was running out if they wanted to marry before the expiration of their childhood deal. And they most definitely did.

They'd toyed with the idea of heading straight from Grand Central Station to city hall. But they'd waited a lifetime to marry each other, and they wanted to do it right.

It just so happened the Bennington ballroom was available. Ryan and Emily had insisted on the ceremony's late hour in order to put together something special. *A proper wedding*, his mother had said. Allegra deserved to feel like a bride, and Zander couldn't argue.

But he was more than ready to make things official. He wanted Allegra in his life, and in his bed, permanently.

"Everything's all set." Ryan strode into Zander's office and looked him up and down. "It appears you're ready, as well."

Probably because he'd been waiting for this day since he was barely old enough to get his driver's license. "I am."

"Excellent. Celestia just arrived, and everyone else is seated. Let's do this." Ryan headed back out the door and down the Bennington's long hallway.

For a moment, Zander was stunned into inactivity. When he recovered, he caught up with Ryan in just a handful of large purposeful strides. "Hold up. What did you just say?"

"I said let's do this."

"Not that part." Zander raked a hand through his hair. "The part about Celestia Lane."

"Oh. What about it?" Ryan crossed his arms. His expression was perfectly neutral, as if this was the most mundane conversation in the world.

"What's she doing here?" Zander hissed.

"I called and invited her. I *had* to. We promised her a scoop on the next wedding to take place at the Bennington, and this is it."

Seriously?

It took every ounce of restraint Zander could muster not to wring his cousin's neck. Or better yet, fire him. Celestia Lane was the last person he wanted at his wedding. The very last.

*He has a point, though.*

As much as Zander hated to admit it, Ryan was right. If the reporter heard about this wedding after the fact, she'd accuse him of hiding something. She'd probably call an end to their truce and renew her negative reporting on the hotel and the absurd curse.

He'd given her his word. He'd even reiterated his promise as recently as last night.

He was stuck.

At the moment, he couldn't have cared less about the hotel. He was about to exchange vows with Allegra. But Celestia Lane was already there, and as promised, she had a photographer in tow.

Ryan looked up from fastening one of his cuff links and frowned. "You don't look well. Actually, that's an understatement. You look downright sick. Don't tell me you're getting cold feet. The last thing we need right now is *another* curse."

Zander glared at him.

Ryan shrugged one shoulder. Was that an actual *smirk* on his face? "Although *runaway groom* has a rather unique twist to it. It sounds classic, but unexpected. Don't you think?"

"I think I'm going to pummel you. That's what I think," Zander said.

Ryan clamped a hand on his shoulder and pulled him into a one-armed hug. His expression turned earnest. "You don't need to worry, cousin. She's not going to run."

Zander swallowed. "Am I that easy to read?"

"Not typically, but in this instance, yes."

"It's not the hotel I'm concerned about. You know that, right?" The Bennington would survive, no matter what happened tonight in the ballroom. It had been around since 1924. If the hotel could withstand the Great Depression, it could handle a few runaway brides.

That's what he'd been telling himself since the curse rumors had started, anyway.

If Allegra changed her mind about marrying him, the hotel would be fine.

His heart wouldn't.

"I know," Ryan said quietly.

"I'm in love with her." Zander shook his head. "I'm not sure I can remember a time when I wasn't."

"I know that, too." Ryan eyed a passing waiter carrying a tray of champagne. "Shall I get you a drink?"

"No, I'll be fine. The curse is messing with my head all of a sudden. That's all."

He and Allegra belonged together. For all practical purposes, he was betting his hotel on that fact. He would have bet his life on it, too, in a heartbeat.

What was about to take place beneath the ballroom's glittering indigo sky had been set in motion over a decade ago. He'd been a teenager back then, barely more than a kid. But when he'd turned his gaze on Allegra that day at the museum and suggested they marry when they were older, he hadn't been offering her a backup plan. It might have sounded like that's what he meant, but it wasn't. He knew neither of them would marry anyone else. The idea was inconceivable.

He might have stumbled over the words, but his intention had been clear. He wanted to marry Allegra. She was his dance partner, his confidante, his friend. He wanted them to be more. So much more.

Forever.

"I don't think the curse is messing with your head." Ryan buttoned his tux jacket and gave his bow tie a final tweak. "You know why?"

"Don't keep me in suspense," Zander said.

Ryan grinned. "Because you're forgetting something very important. There *is* no curse."

Zander laughed. "Touché."

"Now, let's go get you married." Ryan jerked his head in the direction of the ballroom.

Zander had seen the Bennington ballroom more times than he could count. He'd seen countless couples get married beneath its massive shimmering chandelier, from royalty to movie stars to heads of state. But he'd never seen the space look as breathtaking as it did right then.

Pale pink roses and orchids cascaded from the ceiling. The floor was covered with a blanket of flower petals. The lights were turned down low, and hundreds of white candles flanked the aisle leading up to the spot where he took his place and waited for the bridal march to begin.

But the surroundings paled in comparison to the beautiful sight of Allegra entering the room, bathed in candlelight, with a crown of flowers in her hair and stars in her eyes. Her dress was simple, elegant, with a bodice that looked almost like a dancer's leotard and a frothy skirt of layer upon layer of delicate tulle. She'd never looked more balletic, more lovely.

Deep in Zander's soul, a single word took root.

*Mine.*

In the end, he paid no attention whatsoever to Celestia Lane and her photographer. He barely even noticed his family members, although they were all there. His mother. Chloe. Tessa and Julian. Ryan, too, of course. He escorted Allegra down the aisle in place of her father.

But Zander only had eyes for his bride. She was exquisite. She was his. And for what felt like the first time since the day she'd lost everything, she was walking straight toward him instead of away.

She never looked back.

Not once.

She put one foot in front of the other and walked headlong into her future, *their* future, leaving the past behind.

# *Epilogue*

*The New York Times*
*Vows Exclusive Report*

Bennington Hotel CEO Marries Childhood
Sweetheart in Intimate Ceremony, Putting Curse
Rumors to Rest

The Bennington Hotel's runaway bride curse is
no longer.

Manhattan hotel king Zander Wilde wedded
ballerina Allegra Clark late last night in the Bennington's famous starlight ballroom, surrounded
by misty-eyed family members.

The bride and groom met when they were just
nine years old, paired together as ballroom dance
partners. After more than a decade apart, they re-

cently reconnected on Mr. Wilde's thirtieth birthday in the very same ballroom where they tied the knot.

Yesterday wasn't just their wedding day, but also the bride's birthday. Wedding guests were treated to both a wedding cake and birthday cupcakes from Magnolia Bakery after the private ceremony.

The newlyweds plan to make their home in Manhattan, where the groom will continue at the helm of the Bennington and the bride will serve as codirector of the Wilde School of Dance.

When asked about the city's fascination with the hotel's curse, the groom declined to comment and instead referred us to the Bennington's Chief Financial Officer, Ryan Wilde. The dashing CFO assured Vows that romance is alive and well at the legendary hotel. To which we respond...

Might Ryan be the next Wilde to take a trip down the aisle?

\* \* \* \* \*

# COMING SOON!

We really hope you enjoyed reading this book. If you're looking for more romance, be sure to head to the shops when new books are available on

# Thursday
# 12th July

# MILLS & BOON

## Coming next month

### CARRYING THE BILLIONAIRE'S BABY
Susan Meier

'Go ahead. Just lay your hands on either side.'

He gingerly laid one hand on her T-shirt-covered baby bump.

She reached down and took his other hand and brought it to her stomach too. 'We may have to wait a few seconds…oops. No. There he is.' She laughed. 'Or she.'

Jake laughed nervously. 'Oh, my goodness.'

'Feeling that makes it real, doesn't it?'

'Yes.'

His voice was hoarse, so soft that she barely heard him. They had a mere three weeks of dating, but she knew that tone. His voice had gotten that way only one other time—the first time he'd seen her naked.

Something inside her cracked just a little bit. Her pride. He might be a stuffy aristocrat, but there was a part of him that was a normal man. And she had to play fair.

The baby kicked again, and she stayed right where she was. 'Ask me anything. I can see you're dying to know.'

He smoothed his hands along her T-shirt as if memorising the shape of her belly. 'I'm not even sure what to ask.'

'There's not a lot to tell. You already know I had

morning sickness. At the end of a long day, I'm usually exhausted. But as far as the baby is concerned, this—' she motioned to her tummy '—feeling him move—is as good as it gets.'

'I care about all of it, you know.'

'All of what?'

'Not just the baby. You. I know you want to stay sharp in your profession, so you don't want to quit your job, but…really… Avery. If you'd let me, you'd never have to work another day in your life.'

She studied him. This time the offer of money wasn't condescending or out of place. It was his reaction to touching his child, albeit through her skin.


Continue reading
**CARRYING THE BILLIONAIRE'S BABY**
Susan Meier

*Available next month*
www.millsandboon.co.uk

# LET'S TALK

# *Romance*

For exclusive extracts, competitions
and special offers, find us online:

**f** facebook.com/millsandboon

🄾 @millsandboonuk

🐦 @millsandboon

Or get in touch on 0844 844 1351*

For all the latest titles coming soon, visit
millsandboon.co.uk/nextmonth